Mile High with a Vampire

"Do you?"

Quinn blinked her thoughts away at that question and peered up at Jet blankly, wondering when he'd moved in front of her. She could feel the heat of his body, he was so close.

"Do I what?" she asked with confusion.

"Like me?" he asked with amusement, and when she flushed and started to lower her head, Jet caught her chin with one finger and raised it back up, not letting her escape. "Come now. Be fair. You can read my mind so you know that I think you're incredibly beautiful and have been crazy stupid attracted to you ever since I flew you, Marguerite, and Julius to Toronto from Albany four years ago."

Quinn's eyes widened at that news, because she hadn't read his mind and hadn't known that. She hadn't even known he'd been her pilot before this flight.

"Surely you can at least tell me if you find me even a little attractive and might like me the teensiest bit?"

By Lynsay Sands

Mile High with a Vampire
Meant to Be Immortal • Immortal Angel
Immortal Born • The Trouble with Vampires
Vampires Like It Hot • Twice Bitten
Immortally Yours • Immortal Unchained
Immortal Nights • Runaway Vampire
About a Vampire • The Immortal Who Loved Me
Vampire Most Wanted • One Lucky Vampire
Immortal Ever After • The Lady Is a Vamp
Under a Vampire Moon • The Reluctant Vampire
Hungry for You • Born to Bite
The Renegade Hunter • The Immortal Hunter
The Rogue Hunter • Vampire, Interrupted
Vampires Are Forever • The Accidental Vampire
Bite Me If You Can • A Bite to Remember
Tall, Dark & Hungry • Single White Vampire
Love Bites • A Quick Bite

Highland Treasure
Love is Blind • Hunting for a Highlander
My Favorite Things • A Lady in Disguise
The Wrong Highlander • The Highlander's Promise
Surrender to the Highlander
Falling for the Highlander
The Highlander Takes a Bride
To Marry a Scottish Laird
An English Bride in Scotland
The Husband Hunt • The Heiress • The Countess
The Hellion and the Highlander
Taming the Highland Bride • Devil of the Highlands

The Loving Daylights

LYNSAY SANDS

MILE HIGH WITH A VAMPIRE

AN ARGENEAU NOVEL

AVONBOOKS

An Imprint of Harper Collins*Publishers*

This is a work of fiction. Names, characters, places, and incidents are products of the author's imagination or are used fictitiously and are not to be construed as real. Any resemblance to actual events, locales, organizations, or persons, living or dead, is entirely coincidental.

First Avon Books mass market printing: October 2021
First Avon Books hardcover printing: September 2021

Print Edition ISBN: 978-0-06-295640-8
Digital Edition ISBN: 978-0-06-295636-1

Cover design by Nadine Badalaty
Cover art by Tony Mauro
Cover images © Dreamstime.com

FIRST EDITION

21 22 23 24 25 CWM 10 9 8 7 6 5 4 3 2 1

MILE HIGH
WITH A
VAMPIRE

One

Quinn was torn from a deep sleep to find herself in a world of noise and chaos. Shivering, she peered around with confusion, trying to understand how it could be so cold in the middle of summer, and what was happening to cause the shrieking and screaming going on around her. It wasn't easy to sort out at first. A bitter wind was slapping at her, taking her breath away and making her hair thrash and whip around her face, intermittently obscuring her vision. Between that and the lights blinking on and off, she caught brief images of seats and small tables around her, as well as smaller, loose items flying every which way . . . and then in a brief moment of light and no hair in her eyes, she spotted a coffee cup flying toward her head.

Quinn instinctively leaned sideways in her seat, and turned her face away to avoid the item. That's when she spotted the women in the seats across the aisle from her own. Amazonian in size, both were screaming and clutching frantically at their armrests, their wide eyes focused on something ahead and a bit below them. The sight was enough to nudge her memory, and Quinn recalled that she was on a plane, traveling from Italy to Canada. She swiveled her head to see what the women were looking at with such horror, and her own eyes immediately widened with dismay. They were looking at a hole about a square foot in size in the side of the plane. Their altitude and that opening were the source of the cold, brutal wind swirling inside the cabin, some part of her mind realized, but it was the position of the hole that caused most of her alarm. It was above the seats along the wall, probably a smashed window, but it was below the women. Because the plane was in a near nosedive, plummeting toward the earth.

How had she missed that? The question had barely shot through her thoughts when something slammed into the side of her head. A surprised grunt of pain slid from Quinn's lips and her hand started toward the now sore spot on her scalp, but a second blow from an unknown object made her give that up to simply bend forward, below the cover provided by the seat backs. She bent until her chest rested on her knees and she was staring at the carpeted floor, and then covered the back of her head with her hands. It was what the flight attendants always said to do during those safety run-throughs at the start of every flight, and seemed the smartest thing to do now.

Quinn had barely finished taking the position when she heard what sounded like an engine starting. It was only then that she realized the sound had been missing when she first woke up. The plane began to level off as if the pilots were fighting to get it out of its dive. She found herself holding her breath and listening to the engine with concern. It didn't sound like it had when they'd taken off. The steady hum it had been now sounded more like a stuttering cough, she thought, and then her breath left her on a cross between a moan and a gasp when a violent shudder went through the plane. It was accompanied by a roar of ripping metal that seemed to come from all around as she was jolted painfully against her seat belt.

Gasping for breath now, Quinn looked toward the women in the seats across the aisle and blinked with confusion, followed by horror. A gaping hole had opened up along the side of the plane, and the women who had been seated across from her were gone, along with their seats and part of the floor. All that was left was a view of the world outside the plane, dark night with the darker shapes of trees whizzing past as the plane started to spin. They'd managed to level out too late and were now careening through what appeared to be a forest.

Sure they were all about to die, Quinn bowed her head and closed her eyes to pray. It was a simple prayer. "Oh God, oh God, oh God" slipped from her lips in an almost silent litany of despair and pleading, and then the plane jolted again with another accompaniment of tortured metal before coming to a shuddering halt.

Amazed to still be alive, Quinn sat up to peer around. Her gaze slid over the long rend in the side of the plane. It started where the broken window had been, went past where the two now missing women had sat, and stretched all the way to just before the back seats where the last two of her five companions on this flight were even now sitting up to look around as well. It was like some giant had reached out and peeled the wall of the plane away to look inside, she thought as she unsnapped her seat belt.

"Trees rip wing off. Take wall with it."

Quinn blinked at that grim explanation spoken with a heavy Russian accent, and turned to the woman who had given it. Kira Sarka. The tall blonde and her much smaller bodyguard, Liliya, were already out of their seats and at her side.

"You are good, *da*?" Kira asked, her gaze skimming Quinn where she sat.

"Da," Quinn murmured, and then cleared her throat and said, "Yes. Thank you. Are either of you hurt?"

They looked fine, but there had been a lot of things flying around inside the plane: the cups and glasses they'd used and other items from the little galley between the cockpit and the passenger area. She thought she'd even seen a laptop whiz past at one point.

"*Nyet.* We go find Nika, Marta, and Annika. You check pilots."

Quinn frowned at the mention of the three women. Marta and Nika had been the women in the seats across the aisle from her own. Annika had been farther back in one of the two seats that had faced Kira and Liliya. Those seats were now missing too, she saw, as was the table that had been between the quartet of seats. She'd forgotten all about the third woman.

"Wait, I'll come with you. They might be hurt and need me," Quinn said, standing up. But she paused to grab the back of her seat to steady herself as she became aware of how shaky her legs were. It was to be expected after an incident like this, but annoying just the same.

"*Nyet.* Immortals need no doctors. Mortals do. See

to pilots," Kira ordered, and then was gone before she could protest further.

Not that Quinn would have protested. Kira was right. As immortals, the Russian women who had been torn out of the plane wouldn't need assistance beyond blood if injured. But their pilots were mortal and would need her help. If they were alive, she thought with concern as she slid into what remained of the aisle and started forward through the destroyed cabin of the plane. That last shuddering jolt that had brought them to a halt must have been the plane crashing into something, and the front of the plane where the pilots sat would have taken the brunt of the impact. Quinn wasn't at all sure of what she would find in the cockpit. While she and the other two immortals hadn't been hurt, the air was heavy with the scent of blood. But that didn't mean anything. The galley was awash with the thick liquid, a result of the refrigerator flying open at some point during their crash and vomiting its contents everywhere. The blood bags it had held had burst against the walls and counters as they flew around.

Grimacing as her feet squelched on the blood-soaked carpet, Quinn tried to mentally prepare herself for what was coming as she approached the door.

Pain pulled Jet from unconsciousness. Moaning at the brutal pounding in his head, he blinked his eyes open with irritation and frowned in confusion at the scene around him. He was seated upright in semidarkness with just the lit screens and a bunch of lighted buttons on the instrument panel and center console to see by.

It was enough for him to recognize that he was in the cockpit of a plane.

Right, he thought a little fuzzily. Working. Flying a bunch of she-pires from Europe back to Canada.

They weren't flying now, though, he noted. At least the hum of the engine was missing. Had they landed? Why did his head hurt? Christ, he must have fallen asleep on Miller and—

Jet's thoughts died as he instinctively turned to look at the older man he'd agreed to copilot for on this flight. Jeff Miller was a good twenty years older than him, a damned fine man, and an excellent pilot. He had mentored Jet when he'd first started with Argeneau Enterprises more than four years ago. Jeff Miller was someone Jet respected and looked up to. He was also presently being attacked by one of the she-pires.

"Get away from him! Leave him alone!" Jet barked, grabbing the creature's arm to jerk her away from where she was bent over his friend and coworker.

The woman straightened and swung toward him at once, and Jet gaped when he recognized her. He'd been told that they were shuttling some Russian princess type and her four bodyguards, as well as one American immortal, to Toronto, but had been doing the preflight checks when the women had boarded. Miller had been the one to greet them. Jet hadn't realized that Quinn Peters was the American. Now his gaze slid over her pale face and petite figure.

Jet had first met the immortal on one of his first flights when he was called out to collect her, Marguerite Argeneau Notte, and Julius Notte from Albany, New York, and fly them back to Toronto. Six months later he'd flown Quinn to Italy to live with her sister and son. He hadn't encountered her since, and looked her over now, taking in the changes time had wrought in her. They weren't physical. The beautiful Asian woman looked much as she had the first time he'd seen her. She was still small . . . everywhere. Small nose, small pouty lips, small face with wide cheekbones. She didn't stand more than five-foot-two, though he suspected she was closer to five feet, and she was still so slender he had the urge to take her out somewhere and feed her. Everything about her was small, except her eyes. Those were huge and a deep dark brown that was almost black, speckled with the silver flecks that gave away her status as an immortal.

The only thing that had changed about her in the four years since he'd first seen her was that her straight dark hair had grown out and now reached past her shoulders. Otherwise, she appeared much the same. At least physically. But the woman he'd met the first time had been in a bad way, her eyes bruised and caught between grief and horror as Marguerite had urged her onto the plane and seen her seated. Quinn hadn't even seemed to be aware of where she was or who was with her. She'd appeared locked in some kind of semicatatonic state. Six months later she'd been more aware, but nearly as quiet, responding to his welcoming her aboard with haunted eyes and a polite smile that had seemed sad to him.

She was much more alert and sharp now as she turned from Miller to scowl at him for grabbing her so roughly. That expression passed quickly, though, superseded by an almost professional expression as she took him in.

"How do you feel?" she asked in a mild tone, removing his hand from her elbow and clasping his wrist as she looked into first one of his eyes and then the other.

"You were unconscious when I entered. Was it hypoxia or did you hit your head when we crashed?"

Jet's eyes widened at her use of the medical term for oxygen deficiency, but then he recalled that she was a surgeon, or had been in her previous life. Before she'd been attacked and turned into an immortal by her crazed husband after the same thing had happened to him. Jet had learned that from the other immortal passengers he'd flown around. Enforcers, the vampire version of cops, were surprisingly chatty on his flights. Part of it was because many of them considered him a friend, but he suspected another part was a natural need to unwind and work through what they'd experienced on their missions. A lot of them did that by rehashing what happened, and he was considered a trustworthy person to talk to despite being mortal himself. You didn't fly for Argeneau Enterprises if you weren't deemed trustworthy.

Pretty much everyone Jet flew around for Argeneau Enterprises was an immortal, which, according to the special training he'd been given when he first started flying for the company, was a more scientific breed of what was basically a vampire to his mind, although they disliked being called that. He supposed he couldn't blame them. Vampires were dead and soulless. These people were not. They were humans who had been infected with bioengineered nanos that had been created to fight disease and repair injuries from inside the body. Unfortunately, those nanos used blood to propel themselves as well as to do their work. More blood than the human body could produce, which caused a need for taking in blood from an outside source. The nanos had altered their hosts to ensure they could get that blood, giving them increased strength, speed, and even night vision, as well as fangs to make them the perfect predator. And then, just to give them an edge in that category, the nanos had given them the ability to read and control their prey too. So . . . vampires. Just not dead ones. And fortunately, they retained whatever conscience they'd had before the turn. That being the case, most stuck to bagged blood from blood banks, rather than feeding "off the hoof" as their kind liked to call it. Those immortals who didn't were considered rogue, and hunted by the others.

"Did you pass out from lack of oxygen or from a blow to the head?" Quinn asked, apparently assuming he hadn't understood what hypoxia was. She was taking his pulse, and checking his eyes for signs of whatever doctors looked for in cases like this, he realized. And she'd had her fingers, not her fangs, pressed to Miller's throat when he'd jerked her around. He'd seen that before he'd recognized her.

Jet was just about to explain that he understood what hypoxia was, and tell her that it, along with altitude awareness, were standard training for pilots when she spoke again.

"Mr."—her gaze dropped to his name plate—"Lassiter?" she said, reading his last name. "Do you recall what happened?"

"Something hit me in the back of the head," he muttered, his voice surprisingly raspy. "Knocked me out. I missed the landing."

Jet glanced around as he admitted that, his gaze sliding over the darkness beyond the front windshield. It was full night outside the cabin, so there wasn't much he could see. The dim glow cast by the instrument panel didn't reach beyond the cockpit's windscreen, but what it revealed inside was enough to alarm him. The windshield had shattered but remained intact on his side, leaving a spider's web of cracks. But the glass on Miller's side was mostly gone and the windshield frame itself had been pushed inward, as had the instrument panel and the metal around it.

Jet's gaze followed the crushed and compressed metal to where it seemed almost to have swallowed a good portion of Jeff Miller. His legs and lower body appeared to disappear into the metal, which looked to be cutting into his chest. Jet lifted his gaze to the man's face and then closed his eyes when he saw the gray cast to it. Miller was mortal like him, or had been. "He's dead."

"Yes," Quinn said quietly, and then added, "He probably died instantly."

Jet's mouth tightened. He knew she was trying to comfort him, but nothing was going to do that. Miller had been a good friend. Ten minutes ago, they'd been chatting and laughing as Miller told him of his teenage daughter's latest antics. Now he was dead and that daughter was fatherless.

"You've got a bump, but there's no abrasion."

Jet blinked at that announcement, realizing only then that she'd released his wrist and was now examining his head, her fingers moving gently through his short hair.

"I'm fine," he growled, quickly undoing his seat belt and standing up to avoid her touch. A curse slid from his lips when the world immediately seemed to swing around him and he was forced to grab for his seat back to steady himself. Instead of his seat, he ended up latching on to Quinn's arm.

While she stiffened, she didn't shrug him off, but covered his hand with her own and cautioned, "Just take it slow. You've had a shock. You'll be cold, clammy, light-headed, and shaky. Just take deep breaths . . . and put this on. You're shivering."

Jet blinked open eyes he hadn't realized he'd closed to see that she was holding out his aviator jacket, though he wasn't sure where she'd got it. He'd removed it earlier and set it over the back of his seat before buckling in for the flight, but he doubted it had still been there after the crash. Muttering a "Thank you," he took the leather coat and tugged it on as he sucked in deep drafts of air. Those deep breaths caused a twinge of pain in his chest, but he continued anyway.

Jet knew all about shock. This wasn't the first time he'd experienced it. Life had got hairy on more than one occasion while flying fighter jets for the navy. A completely different experience than his position with Argeneau Enterprises, a large umbrella corporation with several companies under it. The company was large enough that it had its own collection of planes and pilots to fly its executives and other individuals around the globe. It was a job every civilian pilot in the business dreamed of getting: well-paid and cushy with all sorts of extra perks to make up for the fact you were flying vampires around. Not that the pilots applying so eagerly for a job with Argeneau Enterprises knew that was part of the job. To the rest of the world there was no such thing as vampires, but any pilot who flew them around found out otherwise. It was information the pilots needed for their own safety, as well as that of their clients'. In case of situations like the one they were presently in, he acknowledged, and started to consider what had to be done now. He needed to call in an SOS and distribute the blood they carried to any injured immortals on board.

The thought made his mouth tighten with distaste. The whole bloodsucking business was the one part of the job Jet occasionally still struggled with. The only reason he'd been able to accept it at all was because Abigail, his best friend since childhood and more like a sister than anything else, had become one five years before. She'd been turned to save her life, but she was now a life mate for, and happily married to, an immortal who was more than a century old. Despite that, she was still the same old Abs he'd always known and loved. That had to mean something, didn't it? So while his instinctual reaction to this business of "immortals" had been fear and repulsion based on the old horror movies about vampires that he'd grown up on—which is pretty much what immortals were no matter what they liked to call themselves—Abigail had made him decide to give them a chance. She couldn't be a monster and be the same caring, loving woman he'd always known. At least that's what he told himself, and while he'd mostly come to the conclusion that this was true, some small part of his brain still struggled with it a little.

"How are the rest of the passengers?" he asked after a couple more breaths, but the question was more out of politeness than any real concern. Quinn looked completely unharmed and he had no doubt the others were fine too. It seemed obvious that the cockpit had taken the worst of the damage. Besides, like herself, the other passengers were all immortal and therefore hard to kill, so he wasn't really listening when she answered.

"We lost three of the women. Ms. Sarka and her bodyguard, Liliya, went out to look for them."

"Good, good," Jet muttered, and then blinked as her

words sank in. Turning on her sharply, he rasped, "What do you mean we *lost* three of the women?"

"The side of the plane opened up and they, their seats, and part of the floor were suddenly gone," she explained solemnly.

"What?" he gasped with disbelief, and then stumbled past her to the open door of the cockpit. He had to pass through the small galley to get to the passenger section, but could see the great gaping hole before he had. The whole right side of the plane was gone, from a couple feet into the passenger section, to just before the last pair of seats on that side. So was the wing, he saw, looking through the opening to the dark woods outside. Jet had never seen anything like it and shook his head with horror and dismay.

"Miller was just coming back from using the restroom when there was some kind of popping sound outside," he murmured more to himself than Quinn. "We lost both engines and then the air pressure went, and with the cockpit door open all sorts of shit started flying around. I remember Jeff shouting and rushing to his seat, and then something hit me in the back of the head and . . ." He shook his head helplessly. The blow had knocked him out. Miller had been left to handle the crisis on his own.

Jet's mouth tightened unhappily. Miller had a rep as a flying ace. It was how he'd got the job at Argeneau Enterprises. This landing proved he deserved the rep and the position. He'd got them down relatively intact. That being the case, it was damned unfair that he hadn't survived the landing himself.

"They're coming," Quinn said suddenly, slipping past

him and moving to the gaping darkness where the wall used to be.

Jet peered from her to the opening with confusion. He hadn't heard anything, but wasn't terribly surprised when two blondes, one petite like Quinn and one who could have passed for an Amazon, appeared out of the darkness and leapt up into the plane. Kira Sarka and her bodyguard, Liliya. Jet had been their pilot many times.

Kira, the larger woman, glanced from Quinn to Jet and then arched an eyebrow. "Where is Captain Miller?"

"He didn't make it," Quinn said quietly.

Regret and resignation crossed the woman's face. "Is shame. He was good man. Fly me often," she said somberly, and then shook her head and turned toward the yawning night outside the cabin. "We go."

Quinn seemed as surprised at the announcement as Jet was, but started to follow the woman without comment. Jet was less easily led.

"Just a damned minute," he protested, grabbing Quinn's arm to stop her. "We need to call this in so they'll send help."

"We tried," the smaller blonde, Liliya, told him. "Our cells get no signal out here."

Jet frowned at that, but said, "Then the smartest move is to wait here where the ELT is, and there's at least some protection from the animals and elements."

"ELT?" Kira asked with interest.

"Emergency locator transmitter," he explained, and then realized that probably meant nothing to her and added, "It's an emergency alert installed in most planes. The signal will lead rescuers to us."

"When?"

"When what?" Jet asked with uncertainty.

"When will rescuers get here?"

"I don't know," he said with irritation. "Maybe a couple of hours, maybe tomorrow."

"You do not have hours," Kira assured him solemnly.

He scowled, but then suddenly narrowed his eyes and asked, "Where are the other three women? Didn't you find them?"

"*Da.* We find," Kira said, her mouth flattening grimly.

"They aren't dead?" he asked with amazement, because that seemed the only reason the women might return without their comrades. Had they somehow been beheaded when they were ripped from the plane? Or had the engine attached to the wing of the plane that had ripped away, exploded, and burst into flame, burning them up? From what he understood, those were the only two ways to kill an immortal.

"Not dead."

"Well, we should go get them and bring them back here," Jet said, moving to the edge of what remained of the floor.

"Nyet," Kira said sharply, stepping into his path.

"They are all three injured and unconscious," Liliya said quietly. "Marta and Nika are in a tree, still strapped to their seats. Annika is on ground, but her seat is mangled, the armrests crushed around her."

Jet winced, thinking that had to hurt, but said, "All the more reason to bring them back here and—"

"Let them tear you to pieces?" Kira interrupted with that dry suggestion.

Jet's eyes widened incredulously. "What?"

"Their wounds are bad," Liliya explained. "They are unconscious all of them right now, but when they wake up it will not take them long to free themselves from their seats. We need to get you far away before that to keep you safe." When he stared at her blankly, she added, "When they wake up they will be desperate for blood."

"We carry blood," Jet said, turning to hurry back to the galley, but his footsteps slowed as he neared that area and he noted the open refrigerator door and the blood covering the floor and walls. It must have burst open during the crash, spilling its contents. The blood bags hadn't survived the turbulent landing.

"It would not have been enough anyway if their injuries are as bad as I suspect."

Jet stiffened at that calm voice from behind him and turned to find Quinn directly at his back with the Russians on her heels. None of them appeared surprised at the state of the galley. But then they'd probably noticed the problem earlier while he'd been too stunned at the missing side wall and wing to notice the thick crimson liquid he'd traipsed through to get to the passenger section of the plane.

"We go," Kira repeated firmly. "The smell of blood will draw them here, and the only blood they will find is yours."

"Where are we going to go?" Jet asked with concern. "We were somewhere over the Great Clay Belt in Ontario when we lost the engines. There are bears, moose, lynx, and fox out there. We—"

His words died as a long, agonized shriek cut through the night air. Jet had never heard anything like it; it was a mix of agony and madness. He actually felt goose bumps rise up on his arms and the back of his neck as the sound was echoed by another.

"They are waking," Liliya pointed out with concern.

"*Da.* We go now," Kira announced, and in the next moment Jet found himself hefted over the Amazon's shoulder and carried off the plane.

Two

Quinn wasn't sure how long they'd been running, but while that first long shriek had been joined by others that had seemed to follow them through the woods, the screams had fallen off since then. They'd either run far and fast enough to leave the three women behind, or the injured women had stopped at the plane and were searching for blood in the wreckage.

Quinn glanced around at the woods. Dark as it was, she had no trouble seeing. One of the perks of having been turned was night vision, and that came in handy now. They wouldn't have been able to move away from the plane at all without their night vision, and certainly couldn't have run through the woods. The forest was old, the ground uneven and strewn with branches and fallen trees here and there. Quinn had kept her gaze on the ground to avoid a tumble up to this point. Now she watched the trees blur as they flew by and felt a moment's wonder at the speed they were achieving.

Unlike her twin sister, Petronella, Quinn had never been very athletic. As a mortal she'd been too busy studying to become a doctor and then a surgeon to bother with physical activities. And while she'd been an immortal for four years, she hadn't got any more physical, so being able to move like this was new to her. It was also amazing, as was the fact that she wasn't tiring yet, despite having been running full out for what she was sure must be at least forty-five minutes to an hour.

Her gaze slid to the pilot hanging over Kira's shoulder, and Quinn frowned as she took in his pallor and noted that he seemed to be unconscious. It reminded her that he'd suffered a head injury and that hanging upside down might not be that good for him. Concern sliding through her, Quinn picked up speed and began to close the distance between herself and Kira Sarka, intending to get her attention and insist she stop. In the end, she didn't have to, though. Quinn was still a good thirty feet behind when the Russian began to slow and then stopped on her own. By the time Quinn reached her, Kira was easing the pilot off of her shoulder to lay him on the ground.

"You check him," Kira said as she straightened. "I must climb tree. See where we are."

"I will climb," Liliya said at once, a frown in her voice.

"*Nyet.* Stay here in case they are close and attack. Protect the mortal," Kira said firmly, and was gone before the smaller woman could protest.

Clucking with irritation, Liliya moved to Quinn's

side and then frowned as she glanced down at the pilot. "He's pale."

"Yes," Quinn murmured, and knelt to examine him.

"What is wrong with him?" Liliya asked, kneeling next to her to get a better look at the man.

"He was knocked out during the accident," Quinn answered as she clasped his wrist and took his pulse. "He probably shouldn't have been hanging with his head down like that."

"Is better than torn apart by Nika, Marta, and Annika," Liliya said solemnly.

Quinn frowned at the words. She hadn't spoken to any of the Russian women prior to the plane's crashing, but Liliya and Kira seemed perfectly normal-type women. Surely, the other three were too?

"They wouldn't really harm him, would they?" she asked now. "I mean, we're all civilized people, and civilized people don't just go about attacking—"

"They were badly injured," Liliya pointed out. "Very badly."

"Yes, but we heal quickly. Their bodies will have been making repairs since they were injured and by now they are probably almost back to normal, or on their way to it."

"Da," Liliya agreed solemnly. "But it will take a lot of blood to make repairs. More blood than their bodies hold. They will be in agony and desperate for more."

"Still—" Quinn began, but Liliya cut her off.

"They will be suffering the blood lust. There is nothing civilized about an immortal in the throes of blood lust. They are mindless with agony and thirst, and would drain their own mother dry in search of the life-giving elixir that can end their pain." Her gaze shifted to the unconscious pilot. "Any one of them would have to drain him to get the blood they presently need. But there are three of them. Even though we all know and like him, they will fight like three starving dogs over one carcass," she predicted, and then assured her, "If they catch up to us, they will tear him apart."

Quinn was silent for a moment, Liliya's words repeating in her head on a loop and bringing images to mind that could have been straight out of a slasher movie, and then a rustling from the woods to their left made her glance sharply around. There was nothing to see. It had probably been some kind of woodland creature, but Quinn wasn't willing to take the chance and stood abruptly. "We should keep moving."

"Da," Liliya agreed, and bent to grasp the pilot by one upper arm. "Take his other arm. If we carry him like that between us, his head will be up."

Quinn automatically bent to grab the man's other arm. She'd been told that as an immortal she would be faster, stronger, and have better night vision, but had never cared enough to ask how much faster and stronger, or even to test it out for herself. She cared now, though, and was learning as well. Their brief run through the woods had proven the faster and better night vision part of that assurance. She assumed that meant she was stronger now too, but was still somewhat surprised when she could hold half the pilot's weight with one hand as Liliya was doing, and without any difficulty at all. The man, who was a good six and a half feet tall, and looked healthy—probably weighing between two hundred and two hundred and thirty—felt lighter to her now than the five-pound weights she used to use in exercise class as a mortal.

His height forced them both to extend their arms over their heads to hold him high enough to keep his feet from dragging, though.

"We wait for Kira, then go." Liliya had barely made the announcement when Kira suddenly slammed to the ground in front of them. While the woman had climbed up the tree, she'd jumped from the top rather than climb back down. The impact of her landing was like a boulder being dropped from the tops of the trees. Quinn actually felt the ground tremble under her feet, but Kira didn't seem at all jarred by the landing.

"They come. We go," Kira said abruptly, and turned to lead the way through the woods.

"Did you see the lights of a town or anything while you were up there?" Quinn asked as she and Liliya followed in the larger woman's wake with the pilot dangling between them.

"*Da*. Lights from small town or settlement far to south," Kira announced. "We head that way."

Quinn wanted to ask how far to the south, and how far away the other women were, but Kira burst into a run before she could and Quinn left off asking any more questions for now. Instead, she joined Liliya in putting on speed to keep the woman in their sights. Despite their speed and strength, it was hard to do. Carrying the pilot between them slowed them down considerably. Not because of his weight, but because they couldn't always travel three abreast. There was no path through the trees, and they grew close together in some spots, forcing one or the other of the women to drop back so that they traveled almost sideways through the narrower areas. Each time they were forced to do that, it slowed them down a little. They were doing just that at one point when Kira apparently glanced back to notice and barked, "We must move more swiftly. Liliya, put him over your shoulder."

Quinn was at the back of the trio and didn't see what Liliya saw, so was completely taken by surprise when, rather than listen to that order, the other woman suddenly cursed, shouted what sounded like a warning in Russian, and dropped her hold on the pilot altogether.

Coming to an abrupt halt as the pilot sagged in her hold, Quinn stared past him to Liliya, her expression probably as shocked as Kira's was as the larger woman—still looking over her shoulder—began to slow.

"What—?" Kira began in confusion, but it was as far as she got before she ran into the huge dark shape Liliya had apparently spotted. At least Quinn suspected that was why the petite blonde had dropped the pilot's other arm to rush forward. She must have spotted the large creature beyond Kira, recognized that the woman was rushing blindly into trouble, her attention turned backward as it was, and shouted a warning even as she rushed forward to try to help.

The large shape was a bear, Quinn realized with dismay as the beast reared up on his hind legs with a roar. The animal had been moving away, probably warned of their approach by Kira's shout, but they were moving too fast for a collision to be avoided. Perhaps if Kira had stopped abruptly at Liliya's warning, what followed could have been prevented. But she hadn't, and the bear, a creature that had to be nearly four hundred pounds and a good seven feet tall now that it was on its hind legs, turned and swung one huge paw out at Kira. The beast's claws caught the Russian in the face and neck, raking the tender flesh there as it dashed her into the tree next to them.

Whether it would have stopped to maul her as well, Quinn would never know. Liliya reached the pair then and attacked the bear. It was the most ridiculous thing Quinn had ever seen. Liliya was her own height of five-foot-nothing, and probably didn't weigh more than her own hundred and five pounds, yet she raced right up to this four-hundred-pound, fur-covered giant, punched it in the stomach, and then when her first punch made the black bear drop to all fours on a huff of sound, she punched it several more times in quick succession, striking it in the face and nose.

Apparently, that was too much for the bear. Squealing in pain, the beast didn't even try to strike back at Liliya, but wheeled around and raced off into the trees, leaving the petite blonde scowling after it.

"God in heaven."

Quinn blinked at those murmured words and glanced to the man in front and to the side of her, noticing only then that he hadn't sagged in her hold when Liliya had released her grip on him, but was simply standing. He'd apparently regained consciousness during the brief run while he was upright. Quinn was about to ask him how his head was doing when Liliya's horrified gasp caught her attention.

The stench of blood reached her at the same time as the sound, and Quinn forgot all about the pilot and rushed forward to join Liliya where she knelt next to Kira. The Amazon lay crumpled against the base of the tree she'd hit, her neck at an odd angle.

"Her neck's broken," Quinn muttered with a concern

that only grew when Liliya shifted the Russian to lie flat on the ground and Kira's head fell to the side, revealing the bloody pulp the side of her face and neck were. The bear's claws had sliced through her skin like knives through butter, starting at her nose and digging deeper as it reached her ear and neck.

Every single one of the five claws must have sliced through her jugular, Quinn thought grimly as she noted the amount of blood on Kira, the ground, and still pulsing from her neck.

The surgeon in her coming to the fore, Quinn placed a hand over the injured woman's throat to staunch the flow of blood. "We should—"

"You must take Jet and go," Liliya interrupted grimly, removing Quinn's hand from the wound and using her hold to push her back. "Now."

Quinn blinked in surprise at the harsh order. "Who is Jet?"

Liliya's eyes widened with amazement even as she said, "The pilot."

"You mean Lassiter?" she asked uncertainly.

"Lassiter is his last name. He goes by Jet," Liliya explained.

"Oh," she mumbled, but thought it was a stupid name. A nickname because he was a pilot, she supposed, and then shook the matter from her head and said, "But Kira—"

"Kira is wounded and has lost a lot of blood," Liliya interrupted impatiently. "She is now almost as much of a threat to Jet as Nika, Marta, and Annika. You must get him away from here and to safety. Find the town or camp Kira saw from the tree and call for help for Kira and the others. They will need blood and lots of it."

Releasing the grip she had on her wrist, Liliya turned to peer down at Kira, muttering. "And tell them they must be quick if they wish to save Jet and whatever settlement it is you call from."

"What?" Quinn asked with amazement. "Surely you don't think they'd attack a town?"

"They are hungry and mindless," Liliya said grimly. "Mad with blood lust. They will attack anyone they encounter that can satisfy that need. Now go before she wakes up. Get Jet as far from here as you can."

"Alone?" Quinn gasped with dismay. "Can't you at least come with us?"

Liliya shook her head at once. "I cannot leave Kira. I am her guard, always to be at her side. You will have to continue without me. Now go."

Quinn hesitated, a frown curving her lips as she peered down at Kira. She didn't want to go on alone. She felt safer with the Russian women. She didn't know the first damned thing about the woods, or bears, or . . . even about immortals, really. Why the hell hadn't she let Marguerite teach her as she'd tried to do?

"Go!"

Startled into movement by that bellow, Quinn scrambled to her feet, and then glanced around sharply when someone took her arm. It was the pilot. He'd followed her to Kira and Liliya and heard everything. Now he was urging her away from the women.

"We'd better get moving," he said, steering her in the general direction they'd been traveling in before their encounter with the bear.

Still, Quinn dragged her feet. She'd never been in a situation like this and felt completely out of her depth. "I'm not sure—"

"I am," Jet said grimly. "Can't you hear them? They're getting closer again and now Kira might be in as bad a shape when she wakes up. I'd rather not die in the woods torn apart by she-pires."

"They aren't she-pires," Quinn snapped, and then fell silent for a minute and listened, her eyes widening as she heard the shrieks in the distance. They *were* closer than they had been when Kira had stopped to climb the tree. They were gaining ground. Hunting them, she thought, and swallowed anxiously, her gaze sliding to Liliya. She almost begged the woman to come with them, but Jet started dragging her away before she could.

"We have to move," he insisted, urging her through the trees.

"You do, not we," she said, yanking her arm away. She was more than a little irritated at being manhandled. Her husband used to do that, pushing her around, steering her here and there like she was a child who needed to be directed.

"You're right," Jet said grimly, taking a step back from her. His expression was suddenly grim and cold. "I don't know why I thought a she-pire would bother to help a mere mortal like me get away from other she-pires. Stay with them, then. But I'm getting the hell out of here."

He hurried away, bursting into a run, and Quinn stared after him, scowling, her conscience pricked.

"He doesn't have a chance without you," Liliya said quietly, drawing her gaze around to see that the petite blonde had straightened and joined her. "They'll run him to ground and drain him dry."

Quinn shifted unhappily at the suggestion, but said, "I'm not likely to be much help. I don't know the woods, and I—" She shook her head helplessly. "I don't know what I'm doing. I'm not strong enough to carry him, or—"

"You are," Liliya interrupted firmly. "You're immortal. You're as strong as I am. You can throw him over your shoulder just like Kira did. And you aren't injured or lacking in blood so can outrun Kira and the others. His life depends on you, Quinn. So do the lives of the people in the camp or town Kira saw from the tree. Every mortal close enough for them to get to is in danger until Mortimer, the head of the Enforcers, sends rescuers with blood," she said solemnly. "And that won't happen until you get somewhere with a phone and call them in."

"Oh God," Quinn breathed, feeling sick to her stomach at the idea of so many lives depending on her strength and speed. Those had never been her long suit. She was a surgeon. Her mind had always been her best tool.

"Then use your mind," Liliya said now, obviously having read her thoughts. "Use your mind and your new strength and save these people, Quinn. You are their only hope."

"Right," Quinn breathed.

"I'll try to run interference and slow them down, but you have to go now," Liliya said, giving her a gentle push. "Jet is as helpless as a toddler against immortals. He won't survive without you."

Liliya didn't have to push her again; Quinn had started to move as soon as the last word left the small blonde's mouth. It was the bit about his being as helpless as a toddler. It made her think of her son, Parker. He'd been eight when her husband had attacked them both. Quinn hadn't been able to save him from his own father, something that had tortured her these last four years. Her confusion and dismay at finding her life altered so drastically after her husband had turned her into a vampire was bad, but it was nothing next to the guilt she suffered over not being able to protect her son.

Well, Jet—she still thought it was a stupid nickname—Lassiter was someone's son, and Quinn didn't need more guilt. She didn't really believe she could save him against four crazed immortals. But if she didn't try, she'd never forgive herself.

Jet was having some pretty unpleasant thoughts about immortals in general and one beautiful she-pire in particular when he heard someone coming up on him quickly. He'd been running flat out since leaving Quinn and the Russian women behind, but terror had him digging deep and finding an extra burst of speed. It didn't make any difference, of course. He simply couldn't outrun an immortal.

Not wanting to be run to ground like an impala taken down by a lion, he waited until he knew his pursuer was close enough that he was about to be overtaken, and then swung to confront his attacker. Jet recognized Quinn one heartbeat before she bent slightly and tackled him like a football player out to kill him.

At least that's what it felt like when her shoulder slammed into his stomach and stole the breath from him. But when he was able to breathe again an agonized moment later, Jet found himself upended over her shoulder, his head hanging just below her ass and his hands dragging over the forest floor as it moved by below him at incredible speed.

Grimacing, he drew his arms up and clasped his

hands to keep them from dragging as Quinn continued racing in the direction he'd been headed. The woman didn't even slow to explain; she just charged on, her arms wrapped around his upper legs, holding him in place over her shoulder as she jumped over fallen logs, and swerved to avoid trees in their path as they sped through the forest.

Relief swept through Jet then. He at least had half a chance with her help. Of course, his pride was a little bent out of shape that he needed the help of the petite creature carrying him, but Jet was a realistic-type guy. She wasn't human and while she might be small, so were bullets, but they could save a guy's life in certain situations. The thought made him wish he had one of those special dart guns the Enforcers used. It might have given him a fighting chance against the she-pires howling for his blood. In fact, in future he decided he'd insist one be present on board any plane he piloted. If he survived to fly again . . . and if he continued to pilot for Argeneau Enterprises, Jet thought grimly, scowling half at the thought and half at the fact that his head was starting to pound again as it had when Kira Sarka had carried him around like this. He supposed it had something to do with his head wound and the blood rushing to it.

Trying to distract himself from the growing pain, he considered whether or not he really wanted to continue to fly for Argeneau Enterprises, ferrying immortals around.

Jet recalled his excitement at being offered the job for the company, and sighed to himself as he admitted that taking this job may have been a huge mistake. At least with other companies you only had to worry about terrorists blowing you up, or hijackers shooting you.

Or dying in a crash, he thought suddenly as Jeff

Miller's face slid through his mind. While he was glad the man hadn't survived only to be torn apart by she-pires, Miller was dead, while Jet at least had a chance at survival, if only a slim one.

It would have been worse if Miller had survived but had been pinned in his seat, he acknowledged now, and Jet's mind strolled down that pathway for a moment, playing out like a horror movie. He could imagine himself refusing to leave the other pilot behind, and either standing his ground and dying with the man, or being tossed over Kira's shoulder and taken against his will. And then having to listen to Miller's screams of horror and pain as he was fed on by three crazed she-pires while the Amazon carried him off into the woods.

Grimacing at his own wayward thoughts, Jet tried to clear his mind and turn it to more constructive things. Like how to escape the injured she-pires so desperate for blood, and find civilization and a phone. As far as he could tell, Quinn was just running blindly through the woods, trying to put space between them and their pursuers. But she'd have to stop eventually. He suspected she was using up energy at an accelerated rate with her efforts, and she couldn't do that indefinitely without fuel. Food would be the preferred fuel, of course. But he wasn't sure she might not need blood. Was he willing to let her feed on him, if necessary, to ensure they both survived?

His immortal friend, Abs, said her kind could make the person they bit feel pleasure when they fed from them. She'd told him that when Tomasso had bit her the first time he'd distracted her with kisses and caresses and all she'd felt was an incredible ecstasy before she'd fainted.

He imagined that now. In his mind Jet was seated in a beautiful bower with Quinn kneeling before him. She took his head gently in her hands and kissed him, her body leaning into his, her small breasts brushing against his chest, her hands in his hair. He had no trouble imagining his excitement as he kissed her back, his hands clasping her hips and then moving around and down to cup her behind, squeezing, and urging her tighter against him, before sliding away and up to find her breasts. In his mind he kneaded and caressed those breasts, finding her nipples through the cloth of the white silk blouse she was wearing and pinching and tweaking them as she broke their kiss to moan softly in pleasure before her lips slid across his cheek.

Her smell filled his nostrils, exotic and exciting, as her warm breath moved over his throat, and then her lips brushed across the sensitive skin of his neck . . .

It wasn't the first time Jet had imagined a scenario like this. Immortals were incredibly attractive creatures. He suspected it was some sort of trick, that the nanos that made them what they were also sent out pheromones or something that made them seem extra attractive to mortals, because he had yet to meet one he didn't think was hot as hell. But Quinn had affected him differently than the others. He'd thought her hot, but he'd also felt an odd protective instinct with her every time their paths had crossed, and she'd stuck in his mind long after each flight. He'd thought of her often over the last four years, wondering how she was, what she was doing and had often sought those answers from other passengers on his flights who might know her . . . But she'd also wandered into his thoughts at the most inopportune times. While having sex with the various women he'd dated over the last four years, he'd found himself closing his eyes and imagining it was her.

Her large silver-tinged dark eyes looking up at him, her sweet pouty mouth gasping his name as he drove into her . . . And then he'd open his eyes to the woman he was really with and give his head a shake, trying to remove Quinn from his thoughts.

Seeing her standing there in the cockpit after the crash had been something of a shock. For a moment he'd thought he was imagining her, but then she'd spoken, her tone so cool and impersonal, as professional as the doctor she used to be, and he'd felt nothing but disappointment. While he'd been fantasizing about her for years, she didn't even seem to recognize him as someone she'd met before.

Jet knew he shouldn't be disappointed. She hadn't been in a good place on the first flight, or even the second, and they hadn't even been introduced. He doubted she'd really seen him either time. Still, it was hard to acknowledge that a woman who'd taken up so much room in his mind these last four years hadn't spared one thought for him during that time.

Pushing these thoughts away, Jet returned to the possibility of her needing to feed off of him and what that might entail. Thinking about that had helped him ignore the pounding in his head. It had also made him forget, if only briefly, that he was fleeing for his life at the moment. Although, really, Quinn was the one doing the fleeing. He was just being carried along, but he pushed that firmly from his mind and returned to his earlier fantasy of the bower. Only this time rather than kneeling in front of him, Quinn was straddling his lap, her silk blouse gone and her perfect little breasts encased in only a lacy white bra. In his mind, he now removed it with more dexterity and skill than he'd ever shown in reality, and her breasts were suddenly free between them. As Jet began to kiss and caress her excited nipples, Quinn began to shift on his lap, her body riding over his erection through their clothes and increasing their excitement so that he began to suck almost violently on the nipple in his mouth in response . . .

Three

It was very strange for Quinn to be carrying the large man as she was. As a mortal, she'd had to give up carrying her son, Parker, around the time he turned four. He'd got too heavy for her to manage after that, and yet now she was carting a much larger male around like he weighed nothing. It got stranger still when his arms suddenly snaked around her hips and he began to nuzzle the back of her leg just below her ass. At least she thought he was nuzzling her . . . or was he kissing her leg? Sucking on the oddly sensitive skin and sending little shock waves of pleasure through her body?

Good Lord! Stumbling to a halt, she started to look over her shoulder to see what the hell the man thought he was doing and then paused and went still, her head lifting and nose and ears straining.

"What is it? Why are you stopping?" Jet asked, his arms dropping away and voice oddly raspy.

"Do you smell water?" Quinn asked, her original reason for stopping forgotten as she sniffed the air.

"Smell water?" Jet sounded bewildered by the question, but then said, "No."

"I do," she murmured, turning in a slow circle. "I hear it too."

"You *hear* it?" he echoed with bewilderment. "How can you *hear* water?"

"Rapids," Quinn said with certainty, and then started moving again, setting out in the direction she was sure the sound and smell were coming from.

Liliya had said to use her mind and new strength to save Jet and anyone else who might be in the path of the injured immortal women. While at first Quinn had just been running willy-nilly in the direction Kira had indicated there was some sort of town or camp, the moment she'd smelled water on the air, her brain had kicked in.

Moving through water was supposed to make it harder to track a person in the woods, wasn't it? At least she'd read a story once where it had worked to avoid dogs tracking the heroine. Surely it would work for immortals too. At least that's what Quinn was hoping. She also hoped they were lucky enough that if the women lost their trail they would just wander around the woods until help could get to them, rather than pick up their trail farther along and track them to where other mortals might be.

Quinn was moving a little more slowly than she had before. She was still running, but not full out as she sought the river she believed lay ahead of them. She didn't want to charge through a bush and right off a cliff into rapids or something, so felt a little caution was necessary. But in the end she needn't have worried. The trees did fall away rather abruptly, but then she found herself on a rocky cliff or outcropping that extended a good ten feet before dropping off to the rushing river below.

With trees no longer blocking out the moon and stars, it was much brighter along the river. Almost as good as daylight to her eyes. Even Jet should be able to see pretty well here, she thought as she moved to the edge of the outcropping and peered down at the white water rushing by six or seven feet below. Rapids, as she'd thought. They ran for a quite a distance before following the curving river to a calmer section ahead.

"Are you going to put me down?"

Quinn glanced toward the butt next to her face as if it had spoken, and then stepped back from the cliff edge, turned, and bent at the waist to set the big man on the ground. She wasn't surprised when he immediately swayed on his feet, his face slowly paling as the blood rushed from where it had no doubt been pooling in his hanging head. Expecting that reaction, she'd grasped his arms to help steady him and waited patiently for him to regain his footing, her gaze moving over him as she did.

"Jet" Lassiter was a big man. She'd put him at six and a half feet or so, which made him about a foot and a half taller than her. Quinn and her twin sister, Pet, were both five-foot-two, but that was only when wearing shoes. They both refused to measure their height barefoot. Five-foot-two sounded better than the five-foot-flat she suspected they really were, and both of them loathed being so small.

Smiling faintly at her own thoughts, Quinn took in the man's short, dark brown hair and then stopped with surprise on his eyes. She'd never seen eyes the shade his were except in medical texts. They were a bright green-blue that was rather stunning, and made more so by the long lashes framing them.

Oh, yeah, those eyes were killer, Quinn thought, and had no doubt women fell at this man's feet in droves. Realizing she was staring, she forced her gaze to lower, following his straight nose down to a wide mouth with a thinner upper lip, before dropping farther to take in his wide shoulders and what she could see of his muscular chest beneath the dress shirt, tie, and leather aviator jacket he wore. Her gaze had just continued down to his long, long legs encased in black dress pants when Jet sighed and turned to move to the edge of the rocky outcropping and peered down at the water racing past below.

"There is no way in hell we can cross the river here."

Quinn dragged her gaze away from the man's tightly rounded ass and up to the back of his head at those grim words, then moved to his side to peer down at the violent water below.

"No," she agreed, and then pointed out, "But it calms down some farther along."

Jet followed her gesture when she pointed downstream, but his expression was troubled as he took it in. Finally, he said, "The water's moving pretty fast here. It might look calm ahead, but there could be undercurrents."

Quinn frowned at the suggestion, but then heaved a resigned sigh. "I think we have to take the chance. We need to lose Kira and the others. I can't run forever without becoming a possible threat to you myself."

Quinn regretted those words almost at once. She didn't want the man seeing her as a crazed blood-lusting creature like Annika, Marta, Nika, and possibly even Kira now had become, but it was something she was starting to worry about as she began to experience the mild cramps that warned of a need for blood. Hoping to keep him from thinking too hard on what she'd said, she added, "And I don't want to lead them straight to other mortals. We need to put some distance between them and us. Enough that help can get here before anyone is hurt."

Quinn left a whole lot out that time, like her fear that she would fail at this. That they either wouldn't get away at all, or that she'd get Jet to civilization only to find she'd led the others straight to a bunch of unsuspecting mortals who would be sheep to the slaughter.

"The idea is to escape the she-pires, not drown trying to escape them," Jet said solemnly.

Quinn's mouth flattened at the term *she-pires*. It wasn't the first time he'd used it, and it didn't suggest he thought much of immortals, which included her now. But Quinn could hardly blame him. She was struggling with accepting what she was herself. They called themselves, and now her, immortals, but that felt like little more than a nicety to her. To her way of thinking, if it walked like a duck and quacked like a duck, it was probably a duck, and much to her distress she now had fangs and needed to take in blood to survive—a vampire.

Blowing out a slow, depressed breath, Quinn turned away from the water to scan the tree line behind them, hope rising within her when she spotted a downed tree just inside the woods some twenty feet farther along. She hurried over to examine the tree. It was big, the trunk so large she couldn't wrap her arms around it. But it also had its branches still attached. There were none for the lower twelve feet or so, though, and really, they didn't need more than ten feet to hold their weight, she was sure. The problem was going to be breaking off the rest of the tree from what she needed. It wasn't like she had an ax.

Grimacing, Quinn moved along the tree trunk. It hadn't fallen flat when it toppled; the upper end had landed on a rocky outcropping that jutted about four feet out of the ground. The rock's base was about three feet in diameter, but narrowed to a finer point at the top where it disappeared into the tree trunk.

"What on earth are you doing?" Jet asked with alarm, rushing to stand at the base of the outcropping when she started to climb it to get on the tree trunk.

"Logs float," Quinn pointed out as she pulled herself up on top of the tree now.

"Yeah. So?" Jet asked, eyeing her with concern as she straightened on the tree trunk and then sidestepped until she was standing on the upper half of the tree that stuck out past the outcropping.

"So," she said, and then paused to smile at him brilliantly before leaping into the air and coming down hard on the tree. Quinn had never jumped before. Not since she'd been turned at least. It was something else she hadn't tested yet: how high she could jump, or how hard she would come down. Much to her alarm, it was very high and very hard. She sailed up into the air a good twelve feet, and then plummeted down at an alarming rate.

Judging by Jet's expression as she descended, Quinn was not the only one dismayed by what was happening. That wasn't very encouraging, but Quinn had little time to worry over it before she slammed into the top of the tree, heard a loud crack and screech, and then found herself plummeting to the ground with the end of the tree she'd snapped off. Fortunately, it was only four feet off the ground. Unfortunately, she didn't manage to keep her feet under her and fell to the side into the shattered end of the tree trunk.

"Are you all right?" Jet was at her side at once, helping her up.

"I'm fine," Quinn said, wincing when straightening sent pain through her stomach. "Let's get this log down to the water. We can hang on to it and use it to go downriver a ways and then—"

"You're hurt," Jet interrupted, his voice grim.

Sighing, Quinn stopped trying to distract him and glanced down to see the blood spreading out around a tear in her blouse. Or had been spreading out, she thought. The bleeding had apparently already stopped because the stain was larger than a hand but wasn't getting any bigger. Turning away from him, she tugged her top out of her dress pants and pulled it up so she could look at what she'd done to herself. It was a nasty scrape, a good six inches wide and deep enough to be painful, but it was already healing . . . and using blood to do it, she thought unhappily.

"How bad is it?"

Quinn let her top drop back into place, but it was too late. Jet had walked around in front of her even as he'd asked the question and got a look before the cloth covered it. Sighing at the concern on his face, she moved around him to the end of the log without branches, saying, "I'm fine. Let's just get this log in the water and get moving."

Much to her relief, after the briefest of hesitations, he let the subject go and joined her to examine the log. It had dropped off the outcropping when the trunk had snapped. Quinn walked around it and then gave it a push with one foot. Fortunately, huge as it was, it moved easily enough.

"We'll have to carry it downstream," Jet muttered, glancing toward the water and probably judging how far they'd have to carry it to get it to where the water was calmer.

By her guess, it was a good eighty feet and she didn't think they could manage it. She might be stronger than she had been as a mortal, but Hulk-type strength was needed here, and she was quite sure she wasn't *that* strong. "I think we should just roll it to the edge of the cliff and then I'll run downstream to the calm water and you can roll it in, then I'll catch it when it reaches me."

Jet considered the option, but after a moment, he shook his head. "We don't know how strong the current is. It could hurtle into you at speed and hurt you, or you might miss it and it'll just sail past you and we'll be back where we started."

Quinn scowled, her gaze moving over the tree with concern. She might have hurt herself for nothing if they couldn't get it to the river.

"My friend Abs can lift the back end of a car," Jet announced suddenly.

Quinn peered at him blankly.

"We grew up together. She was mortal but is an immortal now," he explained solemnly. "And she can lift the back of a car a good two feet off the ground. Cars weigh a couple of tons. This log can't weigh more than seven or eight hundred pounds. Surely we could manage it together."

Quinn stared at him silently, a dozen questions suddenly rolling through her head, like how close a friend was this Abs, and what kind? And why on earth had she even tried to lift the back end of a car? But when Jet bent to grasp one end of the log and strained to lift it, she let her questions go and moved to the opposite end to help.

Much to her amazement, with the two of them working they managed to get it off the ground. Actually, it wasn't even all that heavy to Quinn. In fact, she suspected she might have been able to carry it by herself, but she didn't want to hurt the man's self-esteem. She knew from her marriage that men had fragile egos that needed constant cosseting, so once they had the log aloft and were moving, with Jet at the front, she shifted closer to the center of the log to take more of the weight, but didn't suggest he let go.

"This looks like a good spot," Jet gasped once they'd gone several feet past the last of the rapids. "How do you want to do this?"

Quinn glanced to the water and then toward what she could see of the river ahead. It curved out of sight another sixty feet up shore. Finally, she suggested, "I guess we just set it in the water and hold on to it to ride down the river as far as we can, then steer it to the opposite bank and get out there if we see rapids ahead."

She supposed Jet agreed with that plan when he grunted and started to wade into the water.

He hadn't taken more than a handful of steps away from shore before muttering, "This is far enough," and pushing the log off of his shoulder, forcing her to release her hold as well. Their height difference had forced Quinn to walk with her arms fully extended over her head to hold on to the log, but she hadn't minded, and almost felt guilty that she hadn't tried to carry it on her own when Jet released a groan of relief once the weight was off his shoulder.

The log hit the surface of the river with a *thwap* that sent warmish water splashing over them both. It also sank briefly under the surface before popping right back up. The moment it did, Quinn grabbed the end next to her and began to walk it out to deeper water. Jet followed, rubbing his shoulder as he went, then slung that arm over the front of the log once the water had reached his chest. By that time, the water was up to Quinn's chin.

"Get a good hold on the log and I'll push us off," Jet suggested after glancing back to see her just clasping it with her hand. Once Quinn had put her arm over the log as he was doing and nodded, he pushed off, sending them moving downstream at a desultory pace that made Quinn anxious rather than relieved. They needed to put as much distance between themselves and their pursuers as possible, and their stop to get the log and carry it to the water had already slowed them down.

Glancing back the way they'd come, she eyed the spot where they'd left the woods with concern, but didn't see anyone. Even so, when her feet brushed over a boulder in the water, she planted them on the rock and pushed off, increasing their speed considerably.

Jet immediately shifted his position so that he was almost in a dead man's float on the river's surface, but with his arm holding on to the log he kept his face and a good portion of his chest out of the water. It wasn't until her knee banged against another boulder under the surface that she realized why. This wasn't a nice flat-bottomed river. There were obstacles looming under the surface and they were likely to get banged up at this speed if they weren't careful.

Copying Jet, Quinn let her feet rise behind her and adjusted her hold on the log to keep as much of her upper body out of the river as she could. Fortunately, that seemed to do the trick, or they were just lucky and their log's path avoided the worst of the underwater obstacles.

The water slowed as the river widened and Quinn alternately kicked her feet at times, or pushed off of passing boulders to keep their speed up as they floated along. At first, Quinn tried to figure out their next move once they were out of the water, but that was relatively simple. They would ride the river as far as they could to save energy, and then make their way to the inhabited area Kira had spotted ahead as quickly as they could. Once there, she'd call for help and hope that rescuers reached them quicker than the Russians could catch up to them. Unfortunately, since she had no idea how long they'd be able to float downriver or where they would get out of the water, that's the best she could do when it came to planning, and her mind soon drifted to thoughts of her son, Parker, her sister, Pet, and to her life now and what she should do with it if she survived this escapade. Returning to her old life pre-turn was impossible. Everyone thought she'd died in a car crash with her husband, son, and sister. She couldn't even really return to her old profession for fear of being recognized, which meant she had to start over. Even after four years, Quinn wasn't sure how to go about that. Which was why she'd been on this flight to Toronto, Canada. She was hoping that a few therapy sessions with Gregory Hewitt, a psychologist there, could help her figure that out.

"Stop kicking."

Torn from her thoughts by those words, Quinn glanced with surprise to where Jet hung on to the log ahead of her. "I'm not kicking you."

"No. Stop kicking your feet in the water to propel us forward," he explained. "We're picking up too much speed and we don't know what's around this next bend."

His words made her frown. In truth, Quinn had slid so far into her thoughts that she'd forgotten to work at keeping them moving quickly. She hadn't kicked for—well, judging by how far the moon had moved in the sky overhead, she'd guess it may have been a good hour, maybe a little less. Yet they were moving rather swiftly, extremely quickly, really, she thought, and then realizing that Jet was looking back at her expectantly, she said, "I'm not kicking."

His eyes widened slightly, and then he cursed and shifted so that his body was perpendicular to the log. "Kick," he growled now, beginning to kick his legs in the water. "The water's picked up speed. We must be approaching rapids. We need to get to the opposite bank and get out."

Quinn shifted around until she was perpendicular to the log like Jet, but she'd barely managed one kick before another curse from Jet made her glance around. They'd reached the bend, and there *were* rapids ahead. They were too close now to move the log to shore before getting sucked into the rapids.

"Get away from the log! Swim for shore!" Jet yelled, releasing his hold on the tree trunk and striking out for land.

Quinn stared after him with alarm, but couldn't make herself release her death grip on the log. She wasn't much of a swimmer. Dog-paddling was the extent of her skills in the water and dog-paddling wasn't going to get her to shore, so she clung to the log, watching silently as Jet swam. He looked to be a powerful swimmer, but the currents and speeding water were slowing him down. Still, from what Quinn could see in the last glimpse she had of him, it looked like he was going to make it to shore, and then the log shot into the rapids, and her concern turned to herself.

What followed was terrifying chaos. The rush of the water was a roar in her ears as it slammed into and over her, filling her eyes, nose, and mouth and leaving her unsure which way was up or down. Quinn had been told immortals could only die from fire or beheading if the head was kept away from the body too long, but it felt to her like she was drowning as she unintentionally swallowed mouthful after mouthful of water in a desperate bid to get air. And then pain crashed through her panic, radiating from her hand when it was crushed between the log and a boulder.

Quinn instinctively screamed in pain, or tried to. Water immediately filled her mouth, cutting off the scream as she tumbled away from the log and was swept off by the rapids. Still, she struggled to keep her head above water and regain some control of her whirligig ride . . . until her head slammed into a boulder and she lost consciousness.

With her immortal strength and speed, Jet expected Quinn to reach shore first and be waiting there to help him from the water. But when his feet touched bottom and he began to wade wearily to safety, a glance along the shoreline didn't reveal Quinn there, and he thought she must have swum behind him to be sure he made it. He didn't look around right away to see if that was the case. Fighting the fast-flowing water to swim to shore had left him exhausted both physically and mentally and he merely stumbled the last several feet out of the water and onto shore before thinking to turn and look at the madly coursing water he'd just left.

Confusion covered his face when he didn't see Quinn swimming toward him, or at all, really. The log was bobbing wildly in the rapids, the back end rising as the front end dropped into an eddy, and then slamming back down and the front rising as it rode out of the eddy. It was then he saw the small figure flailing in the white water. She hadn't made it out and was off the log, being tossed about and beaten by the rushing water.

His exhaustion forgotten, Jet cursed and straightened to run along the shore, his attention half on the rocky shoreline he was traversing and half on Quinn's travails in the water. It was immediately obvious she had no idea what she should be doing. She made no effort to keep her toes out of the water and her feet headed downstream first. She wasn't even managing to keep her face above water, and if she were mortal, he knew she wouldn't have survived her wild trip down the rapids. But she wasn't mortal, so he followed grimly and then ran out ahead when he saw that the rapids ended in a calmer section there.

Jet didn't stop the moment he reached the calm water, but ran a good twenty feet beyond it, and then cut into the water and dove in to swim out a third of the way across this wider section of river, managing to position himself in front of Quinn when she came out of the rapids. He was just far enough out and just in time to snag her foot as she floated past. Dragging her to him in the water, he took one look at her bruised and battered face and then began to drag her toward shore.

Once he reached shallow water, he scooped Quinn into his arms and carried her the rest of the way. She was a little thing, and shouldn't have been heavy, but her clothes were waterlogged and Jet's muscles were spent after his own battle with the swiftly running water. He only managed to carry her a couple of feet up the rocky shore before his legs collapsed.

Dropping to his knees, he eased Quinn to the ground and then sat on his haunches to look her over. Her one hand looked like someone had dropped a boulder on it and there was a huge bump and bruise on the side of her forehead, but the other bruises he'd noted on her face were already fading away like water drying under the sun. The head wound and her hand would take longer to heal, he knew, and all of it would use up blood she could ill afford losing just now.

Jet didn't think she'd be loco like the women who had been torn from the plane during the crash, but he wasn't sure, and briefly considered leaving her and continuing on his own, but he just couldn't do it. Jet didn't question why; he just knew he couldn't leave her alone here in the woods. He'd let her feed off of him if necessary, but they were walking out of those woods together or not at all.

Sighing, he glanced around. The log had made it out of the rapids and was now floating placidly downstream, looking none the worse for wear. Other than that, everything looked quiet and peaceful. He didn't see anyone in the water or on either shore of the river. That didn't mean they weren't nearby, though, and he knew he needed to get Quinn out of the open. Or, at least, *he* needed to get out of the open. He was the walking blood bag to the women hunting them.

Straightening his shoulders, Jet scooped up Quinn and staggered to his feet to stumble into the trees until he found a pine or spruce tree—he couldn't tell in the dark—with branches low enough to provide cover. He then set Quinn down and crawled under the low-lying branches, pulling her behind him. Once he had her close to the trunk, he released her and flopped down on his side. The night was cooler than the water had been—he'd guess around seventy degrees—and their both being soaking wet made the night air feel cooler still. The last thing Jet did before exhaustion claimed him was spoon her and wrap his arms around her when Quinn began to shiver in her wet clothes.

Four

Quinn was standing in the hospital where she used to work, watching with bewilderment as people rushed this way and that, each one hurrying to handle some medical emergency or other and not one of them seeming to notice her presence. She glanced down at herself and saw she was wearing a bloodstained, white silk blouse and black pants. They were the clothes she'd worn on the plane, the ones she'd been wearing in the river, which was the last thing she remembered—spinning and tumbling through the rapids, swept along by the water like a cork caught by the currents.

She'd thought she was drowning, Quinn recalled, and now wondered if she had. Perhaps Marguerite had been wrong and immortals could die in other ways besides fire and decapitation. Perhaps she'd drowned in that river and was now a lost soul wandering the halls of the hospital where she used to be a surgeon before her old life had been ripped away from her.

"Is this where you used to work?"

Quinn turned sharply at that question and blinked as she found herself watching Jet approach. Unlike her, his clothes were pristine, his black slacks, white dress shirt, and black leather aviator jacket were as sharp as they had probably been when he'd put them on. Even his black, white and red striped tie hung perfectly.

"Did you die too?" she asked, finding the idea terribly sad for some reason.

"What?" Jet asked with surprise.

"I asked if you died too, Mr. Lassiter," Quinn said gently, wondering if he didn't realize that he had. It seemed the only explanation for both of them being in a hospital. Maybe this wasn't the one she'd worked in. Maybe this was the hospital their bodies had been brought to in Ontario.

"Please, call me Jet," the pilot said.

Quinn couldn't prevent the grimace that twisted her lips at the suggestion, and said bluntly, "I'd rather not. No offense, but if we're dead, don't you think we should use our real names rather than silly pretentious nicknames?"

"Jet *is* my name," he told her with gentle amusement. "It's short for Jethro. But I've been called Jet since I was a kid."

Quinn blinked at this news and then closed her eyes on a groan. "Oh God," she muttered, and then forced her eyes open again almost at once. "I'm sorry. I just assumed it was a nickname and thought . . ."

"It was silly and pretentious?" he suggested when her voice trailed off with embarrassment.

"I'm sorry," Quinn repeated on a sigh, her shoulders

slumping. It seemed her afterlife was going to be peppered with as many embarrassing mistakes as her real life had been.

"Don't be," Jet said good-naturedly. "Jet *would* be a pretty silly and pretentious nickname for a pilot. I understand totally. In fact, that's exactly how I felt about one of the guys I went through training with who insisted we call him Ace."

"Short for Acheron?" she guessed.

"Nope. His real name was Eugene, and unlike the flying aces he decided to name himself after, he hadn't shot down a single enemy aircraft, let alone the number that would have earned him such a title. That's why going by Ace was so pretentious and silly."

"Oh." Quinn smiled crookedly, her shoulders relaxing. "Jethro, huh?"

"Yes, ma'am," he answered, stepping back out of the way as several figures in blue gowns and masks wheeled a gurney with a patient on it between them, obviously hurrying for surgery. Once it had disappeared around the corner, he considered Quinn solemnly. "So, you think we're dead?"

Quinn's shoulders drooped again, and she shrugged unhappily. "It's the only explanation I can come up with for being here. Besides, no one appears to be able to see us," she pointed out.

He glanced around, seeming to consider that, and then said, "I don't know. Immortals aren't supposed to be able to die from drowning. Maybe this is a dream."

Quinn snorted at the suggestion. "A nightmare I'd believe. Dream? No."

"Why would a hospital be a nightmare?" he asked with interest. "You used to be a surgeon, didn't you?"

"*Used to* being the key words in that statement," Quinn said bitterly, stepping back herself now as a man in surgical scrubs rushed by with a nurse next to him briefing him on the patient he was about to operate on. Turning her attention back to Jet, she added, "I used to be a cardiothoracic surgeon. This just reminds me of everything I lost."

"Being immortal means you can't be a cardiothoracic surgeon?" he asked.

"Basically, yes," she said wearily.

"Why? Can't you just change your name and move to a different state and—" He paused when she started to shake her head.

"Unfortunately, no," she told him solemnly. "I'm afraid it's a very small community. There are only something like thirty-five hundred certified cardiothoracic surgeons, and our numbers are dropping. Only thirteen hundred were certified in the last ten years. That makes it a very small pool to swim in and raises the risk of someone—another doctor or nurse in the field—recognizing me." Quinn cast a miserable look around the hospital and added, "And it doesn't help that I have published articles, given interviews, and been a keynote speaker at conventions that almost all thirty-five hundred cardiothoracic surgeons attended. I'm too recognizable in the field to risk it."

"I see," Jet said quietly, and then glanced around briefly before saying, "In that case this *would* be depressing. I think a change of venue is in order, then."

"A change of venue?" she asked uncertainly.

"Yeah. This place is too busy and noisy and apparently just depresses you. We should go somewhere else," he decided.

"I don't know if we can," Quinn said uncertainly. "Our souls probably can't stray too far from our bodies, and if they're here in this hosp—" Her words died abruptly as the hospital setting was suddenly gone and they were standing in a restaurant with old-fashioned tile on the floor and actual booths. There was a counter one could sit at running the length of the back of the restaurant in front of an open window to a kitchen, and it reminded her of a place she'd once eaten in, in a small town she, Pet, and Parker had stopped in on one of their daycation drives as mortals.

"This is better," Jet said with satisfaction, and Quinn turned to him with amazement.

"Did you do this?"

Jet hesitated, and then shrugged and admitted, "I'm not sure. I was thinking we should go somewhere else. Maybe find a restaurant or coffee shop since I'm hungry, but definitely somewhere happier, and—poof, we were here."

Quinn gazed around the warm and cheery restaurant. It was definitely nicer than the hospital had been, she thought, and then her stomach growled, voicing its opinion on the new location.

"Booth or stools at the counter?"

Jet's question drew her attention away from her examination of the restaurant to his pleasant face. But she didn't answer him right away. She was too busy trying to sort out what was happening. If she was dead, surely she couldn't just zone in and out of places? *Was* it a dream?

"My choice would be a booth," Jet said when she remained silent. "And chocolate shakes and fries."

Quinn swallowed the sudden saliva in her mouth at

the mention of shakes and fries, and nodded. When Jet immediately moved to the nearest booth, she followed and slid in on one side while he took the other.

"Chocolate shake and fries?" he asked.

"Strawberry shake and fries," Quinn decided, and there were suddenly shakes and fries on the table between them, strawberry for her, chocolate for him.

Quinn eyed the fare with curiosity. She'd never had a dream like this, where she just thought of something she wanted and it appeared. Wouldn't it be wonderful if life was like that? If she could just think that she wanted to be a mortal gal on a date in a restaurant and it was so? No more immortal business, no fangs or need for blood, no being chased through a boreal forest by crazed immortals in the midst of blood lust.

Unfortunately, life wasn't like that. So, she'd best just enjoy the dream, Quinn decided, pushing all thoughts and worries about her real life away and leaning forward to take a sip of the strawberry shake. Her eyes widened and she moaned as thick, cold strawberry creaminess filled her mouth.

"Good?" Jet asked, watching her with fascination.

Nodding, Quinn swallowed the icy mouthful, and admitted, "I haven't had one of these since med school."

"Why?" Jet asked at once.

"They're bad for you," she said promptly. "Sugar and fat. Heart attack city." Her gaze slid to the fries next to her shake and she unconsciously licked her lips.

"I'm guessing you haven't had fries for a while either, then?" Jet said with amusement as she salivated over the golden goodness, almost afraid to try them. When she shook her head to indicate she hadn't, he said, "Go on. Try one."

His voice was deep and silky and incredibly sexy, and it made Quinn narrow her eyes on him suspiciously. "Let me guess. I really am dead, and you're the devil sent to tempt me."

Jet nodded solemnly. "I'm the devil, come to tempt you to eat a fry, which everyone knows is a sin punishable by an eternity in hell."

Quinn wrinkled her nose at his teasing and reached for the vinegar among the various condiments placed in a neat little collection against the wall at the end of the table. As she splashed the clear liquid over her fries, she said, "Laugh if you wish, but every journey starts with one step. First, it's a shake and fries, and then it's a gluttonous orgy of food on the table."

"Ooooh, you said orgy," Jet pointed out with glee, and then chuckled at her blush. "What if I promise I won't suggest another item of food?" he asked, his tone turning distracted as he watched her switch out the clear bottle of tangy liquid for ketchup and begin pouring that liberally over the vinegar-soaked fries.

Quinn shrugged, her attention absorbed in what she was doing as she now switched the ketchup for salt and began to shake that over the ketchup and vinegar topping. She was nearly drooling at the prospect of finishing dressing the fries and actually being able to eat them.

"Dear God, you aren't really going to eat those like that, are you?" Jet asked with disgust when she continued to shake the salt on until crystals were actually visible as a thick layer on the top.

"Have you ever had fries like this?" Quinn asked as she set the saltshaker back.

"Hell, no," Jet assured her.

"Then you have no right to comment. Try one and then you can speak your mind," she challenged, eyeing him across the table.

Jet peered from her face to the fries with distaste and started to shake his head in refusal.

"Funny, I had no idea you flyboys were such cowards," Quinn said lightly, picking up her fork and stabbing several goop-covered fries.

Muttering something under his breath, Jet picked up his own fork and stabbed one of her fries, then quickly shoved it into his already grimacing mouth. That grimace faded as he chewed, however, and Quinn began to grin when he reached for the vinegar before he'd even finished chewing and swallowing.

"That was exactly my reaction when I first saw Cynthia Vance eating her fries like this," she told him.

"Cynthia Vance?" he queried as he finished pouring the vinegar over his own fries and reached for the ketchup.

"A girlfriend in high school," Quinn explained. "We had third period lunch together in grade twelve and used to go to a restaurant next to the school. The first time I saw her eat them like this I was disgusted. She said, 'Don't knock it till you try it,' or something to that effect and goaded me into trying one." Smiling wryly, she shrugged. "The next thing I knew I couldn't eat fries any other way. At least I used to," she added, her tone turning wry. "I haven't had fries since around the time I graduated med school either."

"Good God. For that long?" Jet asked with dismay. "That's practically a crime. Fries are awesome."

"Yeah, they are," she agreed on a little sigh as she

gathered more fries on her fork. "But I'm in health care. I have to live by example and eat healthily. Someone guzzling down grease, sugar, and salt is hardly in a position to lecture their patients on a healthy diet, are they?" she asked, but then her lips flattened out as she recognized her husband's words coming out of her own mouth. Patrick was the one who had nagged her into a fat-free, taste-free vegetarian diet, and the words she'd just regurgitated were the exact argument he'd used.

"Please don't tell me you're one of those rabbit-food-eating people."

Jet's question, spoken with mounting horror, drew her from her thoughts and Quinn opened her mouth to say yes, she was, but then paused to reconsider. Was she? Was she really? The truth was she hadn't enjoyed living off salads and seeds. She'd missed French fries, pizza, and burgers. And—oh my God—cakes, Quinn thought suddenly. Fudge brownies, strawberry shakes, potato chips, and cookies . . . The list of things she'd missed over the years was endless.

"No," she said finally. "I don't think I am."

"You don't think?" Jet asked, one eyebrow raised.

Quinn grimaced and shrugged. "I'm afraid I have eaten mostly rabbit food since I was pregnant with Parker, so nearly"—she did the math quickly in her head; Parker was twelve now and she'd started eating vegetarian six months before he was born—"nearly thirteen years now. But I didn't really enjoy it, so don't think I'm a dedicated rabbit-food eater."

Jet considered that, his gaze moving over her, but simply said, "That seems a shame. Why eat vegetarian if you didn't enjoy it?"

"Sometimes in life you have to do things that you might not enjoy . . . for your own good," she added when he frowned.

"Maybe that's true when it comes to blood tests and colonoscopies and stuff like that, but not eating. Good Lord, a person has to eat three times a day. What kind of life is it if you don't enjoy at least some of those meals?"

"Pretty unappetizing," Quinn muttered under her breath, and didn't tell him that wine had helped wash down most of her meals over at least ten of those years while she was mortal. Looking back on it now, she recognized that she'd been well on the way to becoming an alcoholic. Wine hadn't just helped wash down her meals, it had taken the edge off her irritation with her husband's late hours and arrogant bossiness.

"Well, that's really sad."

Quinn glanced at Jet with a frown, half-afraid she'd spoken about her wine drinking aloud. "What is?"

"That you spent thirteen years eating that way if you didn't enjoy it," he explained. "I'm not saying you shouldn't eat healthily for the most part, but life is too short to avoid such pleasures altogether." He frowned as he finished saying that, and then added dryly, "Well, it's short for most of us anyway."

"Maybe," she said with a shrug. "But as Patrick used to say, food is fuel, and like an expensive car given only premium gas, we should feed our bodies only premium food." She scowled and then added, "Mind you, while he said that a lot, I found a cache of M&Ms and chocolate bars in his desk after he died, and when I was going through his paperwork after everything settled down, I noticed he had charges on his credit card bills for McDonald's and other fast-food restaurants. So, I suspect he just didn't want me to get fat. I mean, he did start on this kick about our eating healthy when I began gaining weight while pregnant."

Jet's eyebrows rose at this. "I kinda thought it was normal for a woman to put on weight while pregnant."

"Yeah," Quinn said on a sigh, and then told him, "Pet thought he was just being a controlling ass, but then she didn't like him from the start. She didn't think he respected me or how hard I worked and . . ." She sighed and shook her head. "I'm afraid in the end I agreed with her. Patrick didn't see me as an equal. Or maybe it would be closer to the truth to say he didn't want me to be an equal. I think he wanted me to continue to be the cheerleader to his star quarterback like in high school."

"Instead, you both ended up being quarterbacks," Jet suggested. "Your husband was a doctor like you, right?"

Quinn hesitated and then explained, "Actually, he was an oncologist to my cardiothoracic surgeon."

Jet's eyebrows rose at this. "So, you were the quarterback and he was the cheerleader."

Quinn blinked in surprise at the suggestion. "No. You were right—we were both quarterbacks."

Jet looked dubious at this claim. "I think a heart surgeon beats out an oncologist for position of quarterback." When she opened her mouth to protest, he asked, "Who needed more schooling and training?"

"Well, I did," she admitted reluctantly.

"Uh-huh," he said, not seeming surprised. "And who made more money?"

"Me," she said almost apologetically. "But oncologists—Cancer is . . ."

Jet arched his eyebrows, waiting patiently for her to finish her thoughts aloud, but every time Quinn opened her mouth she heard her husband's words leaving her lips and stopped. Mostly because she was now questioning her husband's words. She had been since he'd attacked and turned her. Maybe even before that. According to Patrick, oncology was the most important area of medicine. Cancer killed in huge numbers, and didn't discriminate, taking both the old and the young. Everyone trembled when a cancer diagnosis was spoken. Not so much with heart problems. Hell, half of her patients wouldn't follow diets or even take their pills regularly.

Even so, Quinn hadn't really agreed with Patrick's assessment but, suspecting his self-esteem was a little bruised by her success, she'd kept her mouth shut and let him spout off about how much more important he was than everyone else. Now she said what she really believed. "Everyone working in the medical profession is a quarterback, from nurses to brain surgeons. Every one of them is necessary and important. Doctors, whether general practitioners or specialists in oncology or cardiothoracic surgery, couldn't get along without the nurses, the phlebotomists who take the blood to be tested, lab technicians, X-ray technicians, and so on."

"I like that view," Jet said solemnly.

"It's the truth," Quinn said with a shrug, and then wanting to be fair, she added, "As for my husband, I think I might be giving the wrong impression here. Patrick was a good man, and a very good oncologist. He cared about his patients and did his best by them."

"What about you and Parker?" Jet asked, and when she stared at him blankly, not sure what he meant, he asked, "Was he a good husband and father?"

Quinn sighed and peered down at her plate, surprised

to note that it was empty. She'd eaten every last fry while they'd talked. Now she set her fork down and took a sip of her shake while she considered the question. Finally, she sat back and said carefully, "Well, he wasn't an alcoholic, or drug abuser, and he never hit or was verbally abusive to either of us."

"That's kind of the basics expected by most women. Like tires on a car," Jet pointed out, eyeing her closely now as if trying to read her mind.

"Yes. You're right, of course," Quinn murmured. Toying with her fork on the plate, she said slowly, "He was a good husband at first, very affectionate and supportive. He encouraged me to pursue cardiothoracic surgery." Pausing, she licked her lips and then admitted, "But in the end I think he regretted it. I think he struggled with my success. I was gaining quite a rep in my field. I was starting to draw attention and garner job offers from the big-name hospitals across the country. I was even asked to be the keynote speaker at a convention the week he died, and the more success I had, the more he seemed to withdraw emotionally, and the more he seemed to need to control things around us." She paused briefly before acknowledging, "And I let him."

"Why?" Jet asked at once.

"Because it was easier." She was so ashamed to admit it, the words were almost a whisper, but then Quinn cleared her throat and went on. "Because my job was so high stress, and I had to always be in control and on top of things there, it was actually something of a relief just to let him helm the ship at home, even if I didn't always like the outcome." She didn't add that even his emotional withdrawal had been easier for her, because it had allowed her to withdraw as well. Dealing with another's emotions and needs could be exhausting, and between Parker and her work, Quinn's life had already been exhausting and demanding enough. Not that she'd found Parker's needs exhausting or overly demanding. That had been different. She loved her son and had always made time and found the energy for him. Quinn simply hadn't been able to find either when it came to dealing with her husband's insecurities and the need for control they caused.

Jet was silent for a moment, but rather than comment on what she'd said, he asked, "And how was he as a father?"

"He loved Parker," she said firmly.

"I hear a but," Jet said quietly.

Quinn glanced down sadly at her ketchup-stained plate as she thought about her son and the lack of relationship he'd had with his father. Finally, she said, "Well, like most men, Patrick was completely useless when Parker was a baby. He wanted nothing to do with diapers and burping, and forget him getting up in the night with him," she said, rolling her eyes, and then realizing how bad she was making Patrick sound, she tried to be fair and added in his defense, "But he was an oncologist and needed his rest."

"And you were a cardiothora-thingie," Jet pointed out.

Quinn smiled at his mangling of her profession's name, but didn't correct it for him and said, "I wasn't yet. I was in the middle of my five-year surgery internship when we had Parker."

"Oh. Well, still. You'd have needed your sleep too," he argued.

"Yeah," she agreed. "Fortunately, Patrick agreed to get a nanny so that my surgery internship wouldn't be interrupted." Quinn didn't mention that it had taken nagging and threats to get him to do that. She simply hadn't been able to manage her internship and being a full-time mother both, especially not when—after insisting they start a family at that point—Patrick hadn't lifted a finger to help her with Parker. In fact, if it weren't for her sister, Quinn probably would have dropped her internship and become a general practitioner. But Pet hadn't allowed that to happen. She'd stepped in to help with Parker, and was the one to suggest hiring a nanny, and then had encouraged her to harass and nag Patrick until he gave in.

"What was he like as a father once Parker was out of diapers?" Jet asked.

Quinn grimaced before she could stop herself, but then cleared her expression. She was determined to be fair here. "He was proud of him. Parker's exceptionally smart," she explained. "He's a freaking little genius, really, and Patrick was proud of him for that."

"That's it? He was proud of him?" Jet asked, tilting his head. "Did he take him to ball games, or to movies? Or take him fishing? Anything?"

Quinn actually felt tears sting her eyes at the question. Those were the things she'd wanted for her son, a father who spent time with him and took him out to do guy things together. It was what she'd expected and hoped for, but . . . "Patrick was very busy with his practice. He didn't have a lot of spare time."

Jet nodded silently, but there was a deep understanding in his eyes that made her uncomfortable. She felt like she'd blabbed that her husband had basically ignored their child for the most part, and that she'd often felt like a single parent, and by the time of the attack and his death, she'd been considering divorce for several years but was just too busy to pursue it. That was the truth, though. She had been considering divorce. She hadn't been happy, and Patrick certainly hadn't seemed happy in their marriage anymore either. He hadn't been happy since a year after Parker's birth. That was when Patrick suggested they start trying for another child. His plan was one every two years until they had three, he'd said. But Quinn had been horrified at the prospect. With his lack of help and interest in the child they already had . . . well, she'd refused to have a second one at that point, saying they'd wait and have another child once she was done with her internships. It was the first time she'd said no to him and not let him have his way. She didn't think he'd ever forgiven her for it. By the time she was done with her internships, she and Patrick were hardly sleeping together anymore and the marriage was already on shaky ground. Having a second child when she was considering divorce hadn't seemed a smart idea.

And all of this was something Quinn had been avoiding thinking about these last four years. It had felt unfair and unfaithful to think of her husband's flaws when he was dead. So did her anger at his attacking and turning her and her son, and she still had a lot of that anger, but couldn't even think about it without feeling guilty for being angry at her dead husband.

Pushing these thoughts away as too depressing to consider, Quinn picked up her shake and sat back to consider the man across from her rather than the man who had betrayed her.

Jethro Lassiter was a good-looking man. He was also tall, and well-built, with dark hair. He looked the physical, outdoorsy type. Her husband had been tall and dark haired too, but his body had been more lean and . . . well, he'd looked like a doctor, someone who spent more time with books than doing physical things. He hadn't been broad-shouldered and muscular like Jet.

"So, your father used to take you fishing and to movies and ball games?" she asked to change the subject.

Much to her surprise, Jet shook his head. "My dad was a navy pilot too. He died in the Gulf War when I was two. But I always imagined that's what it would have been like if he'd survived and been around to help raise me." He smiled crookedly and added, "And now I imagine doing all those things with my own child someday. Giving them the childhood I missed out on. So I can enjoy it vicariously, I suppose," he confessed with a grin.

Quinn smiled, charmed by the idea that he was already imagining the child he hoped to someday have and was actually planning to spend time with his offspring. She suspected he'd be a good dad, the kind she'd hoped for her own son to have, she thought, but tilted her head slightly and asked, "You were a navy pilot before working for Argeneau Enterprises?"

Jet nodded.

"Oh," she breathed, imagining him flying fighter jets into dangerous missions. "Your mother must have been horrified when you joined the navy after your father died that way."

Jet shrugged. "I'm afraid my mom didn't take losing my dad and being a single parent too well. Although, mostly, I think it was guilt."

"Guilt?" she asked with confusion.

Jet nodded. "It seems Dad had been unemployed for

a while when she found out she was pregnant. They had a big fight about it, her demanding he get a job or she'd leave him. He stormed out and joined the navy that night." Jet shrugged. "Two and a half years later he was dead and she kind of crawled into a bottle and still hasn't crawled out." He pushed his own plate away and sat back before smiling faintly and adding, "Fortunately, our neighbor, Marge Forsythe, was a wonderful caring woman who was more than happy to take care of me when my mom wasn't able to. Marge basically raised me along with her daughter. We were the same age, so Abs and I have always been best friends."

"Abs?" Quinn echoed with confusion.

"Abigail Forsythe, now Notte," he explained. "Her mom is the neighbor who helped raise me. Well, she raised us together, really. We're more like brother and sister than anything."

"Abigail Notte?" Quinn's eyes widened incredulously and she sat forward. "Any relation to Santo Notte?"

"Yeah. Abigail's husband and life mate, Tomasso, is Santo's cousin," he explained.

"Oh my God!" Quinn breathed, her eyes going wide. "Then you and I are related by marriage."

Jet blinked in surprise at the claim. He'd never really thought of it that way, and wasn't that comfortable thinking that way now. Good Lord, he'd been lusting after her for four years. He didn't want any sort of familial tie, even if only through marriage. So he pointed out, "Well, Abs and I aren't legally related."

Quinn waved that away. "You just said you're like siblings. Which makes you my sister's husband's cousin's wife's brother."

"Well, that fits the old six degrees of separation rule," Jet muttered.

"Yes, it does," she agreed, and then said, "I think Parker must have met you at one of the Notte family dinners. I remember him chattering away about some pilot he'd talked to," she said thoughtfully, and then shrugged and offered him a warm smile as she held out her hand across the table. "Well, nice to meet you, Jet."

His eyebrows rose and he hesitated, but then did reach out one large hand to enclose hers. It was a really big hand. Hers disappeared inside of it and Quinn felt a small tingle slide from her fingers and palm, up her arm, from the contact as they stared at each other. But neither of them actually shook; they just held hands across the table for a moment and then both broke the hold at the same time and sat back to eye each other with speculation.

Quinn had no idea what he was thinking, but she was wondering how old he was and if he was married. He was probably married, she decided. He was too damned good-looking to escape the hordes of females that would have chased him. Besides, she was pretty sure he was more than a couple years younger than her own forty years and she was no cougar. Not that it mattered. She was in no position to be interested in anyone right now anyway. She needed to get her head on straight before she even considered dating, and Quinn knew it. She had a son she had to consider. A son whom she'd left in Italy with his aunt Pet and uncle Santo earlier that day, where he was waiting for her to get her shit together.

Quinn's mouth tightened at that thought. She'd flown to Italy three and a half years ago, determined to bring her son back with her. Instead, she'd stayed to visit her sister, who had been caring for him while she recovered from the turn. In the end, she'd just not returned to America. She'd rented a cottage and lived in Italy for three and a half years, moping around in misery when she wasn't homeschooling her son. Finally, Pet hadn't been able to take it anymore. She'd tried gentle talks and encouragements the first couple of years, but finally this last year she'd gone the hard-ass route, telling her that she was wasting her life and moping around being miserable, and didn't her son deserve better than a mother who wasn't even wholly present mentally and emotionally most of the time?

Her sister knew she was struggling with this whole immortal business and her feelings about Patrick. She'd started badgering her to go back to North America, but Toronto rather than Albany, and she'd given her the name of an immortal psychologist who might be able to help her. Gregory Hewitt. Quinn had almost laughed when Pet had mentioned the name. Marguerite had suggested she see the man before Quinn had flown off to Italy, but she'd refused, assuring her that some time with her sister would mend what ailed her.

She should have listened to Marguerite, Quinn acknowledged to herself now. She'd gotten to know the woman pretty well during the time she'd stayed with Marguerite and her husband, Julius, after waking up to the nightmare her life had become, and had realized rather quickly that Marguerite was a very wise woman.

Ah, well, Quinn thought now, better late than never. She'd go back to Toronto, and go see this psychologist, who happened to be Marguerite's son-in-law, and get her head on straight. Then she'd get on with her life and be a proper mother to her son. She didn't have time for men before that was all done, and probably wouldn't afterward for a while.

"Do you want anything else or would you like to go for a walk?"

"A walk?" Quinn asked, glancing around with confusion when Jet gestured out the window next to them. Her eyes widened when she saw that there was a beach across the street from the restaurant they were in, and the sun was setting. It was quite lovely. Nodding, she slid out of her side of the booth and allowed him to take her arm to walk her out of the restaurant.

Five

"I wonder where we are." Quinn looked around with curiosity as they crossed the empty avenue to the equally empty beach. The street was lined with businesses, but for some reason she couldn't read the signs on the buildings. They were kind of out of focus to her. There were no cars and the beach just started suddenly on the other side of the road.

"I don't know," Jet said with unconcern. "Everything is kind of familiar but not. Like that restaurant reminded me of a diner Abs and I used to go to after school when we were teenagers, but it wasn't exactly the same. And this beach reminds me of a spot I visited in Europe once." He shrugged, not seeming bothered. "Since it's all a dream, I'm not going to worry about it. It makes a nice break from reality."

"Yes," Quinn agreed, her mind shying away from thoughts of reality and shifting to the man beside her.

She was much more comfortable with Jet now that she knew his adopted sister was married to a cousin of her sister's husband. Not that she'd really been uncomfortable with Jet from the start, but now she felt more connected somehow.

"So, what made you want to be a surgeon?" he asked as they approached the water's edge.

Quinn considered the question solemnly as they walked, and then smiled wryly and said, "As embarrassed as I am to admit it, I think I originally wanted to be a doctor to show up my sister."

"What?" Jet glanced at her with disbelieving amusement. "How? Why? I don't understand."

Quinn grimaced and nodded. "It's hard to explain."

"Try," Jet encouraged.

She hesitated, but then started by giving him a quick rundown on her history. "Okay. Well, Pet and I were born in China."

"Okay," Jet said quietly, not seeming surprised.

"But our father died when we were very young and our mother remarried," Quinn continued. "And then she and our stepfather died and we were adopted by our godmother and her husband from America when we were six. We moved to Albany, New York, and took their last name: Stone."

"Were your first names changed as well or were you always Quinn?" he asked.

"Our first names were always Pet and Quinn. Although Pet's name is really Petronella. We just call her Pet because it's easier."

"Like they call me Jet," he said with a nod.

She murmured agreement and then continued. "Anyway, Pet had some trouble adjusting. She . . ." Quinn sighed and shook her head. "She seemed always at loggerheads with our parents."

"Your new adopted parents," Jet said, wanting to make sure he was understanding.

Quinn nodded. "Yes. The Stones."

"But you didn't have trouble adjusting?" Jet asked.

"I . . . I don't know," Quinn said with a frown, and then shrugged unhappily. "I—Pet was always causing trouble, and I always felt like I had to smooth things over and behave to make up for it, so I never really considered how I felt."

"Ah," Jet said with understanding.

"Ah, what?" Quinn asked, narrowing her eyes on him. She found it hard to believe he understood. She certainly didn't.

"You just said it," Jet said with a shrug. "She was the troublemaker, so you had to smooth things over no matter how you really felt. You picked your roles."

"Roles?" she asked uncertainly.

"Sure. Pet was the troublemaking black sheep, and you were the good girl, doing what was expected," he said easily, and then asked, "So was it your parents who thought you should be a surgeon?"

"They were both doctors," Quinn admitted. "They had a family practice, and because my marks were good, they were always going on about my growing up to be a doctor too, and joining the family practice someday."

"But you rebelled," he murmured with a nod.

"Rebelled?" she squawked with amazement. Quinn had never done a rebellious thing in her life. As he'd said, she was the good daughter to Pet's troublemaker. *And hadn't that been one hell of a burden?* her inner voice asked suddenly, making Quinn frown. Had she resented always having to be good?

"Sure, it was a form of rebellion," Jet said, distracting her from the question, and then pointed out, "You went into surgery. Obviously, you're never going to join the family practice when you're a cardiothoracic surgeon."

"You remembered the word that time," Quinn pointed out with amusement, but was considering what he'd said. Had her choosing surgery been her own form of rebelling? A good girl's rebellion? It was certainly true that her parents had no longer expected her to take over the family practice. But they were proud of her. It wasn't like she'd forsaken medicine altogether and become a university professor like Pet.

"So, was your sister upset that you became a surgeon?"

"What?" Quinn asked with surprise, and then shook her head. "No, of course not. She was proud of me."

"So, she didn't feel shown up by your becoming one?"

Quinn stopped walking as she considered that. No, despite what she'd told herself and everyone else for years about why she'd become a surgeon, Pet hadn't been shown up by it. As far as she knew, Pet had never begrudged Quinn for her choices, whether it was for always being the dutiful daughter, or following in their adopted parents' footsteps and joining the medical profession. In fact, the only decision of Quinn's that Pet hadn't backed up one hundred percent was her marriage to Patrick. Even then, though, Pet had only asked a couple of pertinent questions, mentioned the few things that made her wonder if marrying him was smart, like his calling her his little china doll. But in the end, her sister had accepted her decision and never let her feelings on

Patrick show again. For Quinn's sake, Pet had always been welcoming and open to Patrick.

Which was doubly impressive since he'd been more than sarcastic and often unwelcoming to her "loser sister" as he'd called her on occasion. Patrick had been a snob about medicine. If you weren't a doctor of some sort, you were somehow beneath him, and he'd considered Pet a slacker for going into history rather than medicine when she was obviously smart enough to be a doctor. But Patrick had only been rude about Pet when he was looking for a fight with Quinn, which is what he got when he insulted her sister to her. If he'd ever dared insult Pet to her face . . . Well, frankly, Quinn suspected it might have ended their marriage rather abruptly.

"Pet's a history professor, isn't she?"

"Yes," Quinn said, glancing at him with surprise. "How did you know that?"

"She told me."

Quinn nearly goggled at the man. "You've met my sister?"

"Sure. I've piloted dozens of flights she, Santo, and Parker have been on over the last four years," he informed her. "Although Parker didn't fly with them as often after you moved to Italy."

Quinn eyed him with curiosity, wondering how he knew when she'd moved to Italy.

Before she could ask, Jet said, "Santo and Pet are great. They're perfect for each other. And Parker's a good kid. Smart as a whip too."

"Yes. He is," Quinn said softly, thinking of her son.

"He came up to the cockpit to ride with me on most of the flights he was on, and each time asked tons of questions. I wouldn't be surprised if he couldn't fly the damned plane himself by now."

"I wouldn't be surprised either," Quinn said with a grin. Her son was brilliant and inquisitive and had probably researched flying after getting off the plane the very first time. By now he probably *could* fly one.

"Pet or Santo would always come up after a while to make sure Parker wasn't troubling me. Sometimes both of them would," Jet added. "They'd often stay to talk for a bit too."

"I can see that," Quinn said with a faint smile. Her sister had always been a chatty Cathy compared to her more reserved self.

"And then too, Abs has invited me to a Notte family shindig or thirty over the last four years and they're usually at those, and talk to me then as well. I like all three."

"I'm sure they like you too," Quinn assured him, but was thinking of all the times Pet had tried to convince her to come to one of those Notte family shindigs while she was in Italy these last three and a half years. Quinn had refused each time, insisting they go on without her. She might have met Jet at any one of them. How would she have reacted to meeting him in such a social situation?

"Do you?"

Quinn blinked her thoughts away at that question and peered up at Jet blankly, wondering when he'd moved in front of her. She could feel the heat of his body, he was so close.

"Do I what?" she asked with confusion.

"Like me?" he asked with amusement, and when she

flushed and started to lower her head, Jet caught her chin with one finger and raised it back up, not letting her escape. "Come now. Be fair. You can read my mind so you know that I think you're incredibly beautiful and have been crazy stupid attracted to you ever since I flew you, Marguerite, and Julius to Toronto from Albany four years ago."

Quinn's eyes widened at that news, because she hadn't read his mind and hadn't known that. She hadn't even known he'd been her pilot before this flight.

"Surely you can at least tell me if you find me even a little attractive and might like me the teensiest bit?"

"I—" Quinn hesitated, swallowing thickly. It was hard to think with him so close. The finger he'd used to raise her chin had moved along her jaw where it was running lightly back and forth in a surprisingly affecting caress. And he smelled so good. Yummy even, she thought, unconsciously moving closer and inhaling deeply. Damn, he really did smell delightful! She just wanted to bury her face in his neck and surround herself with his smell.

"Quinn?" he asked gently.

"Yes," she murmured, one hand rising to touch his stomach and then glide up toward his pecs.

Jet's eyebrows rose and he asked uncertainly, "Yes? You find me a little attractive too?"

"Very attractive," she assured him. "And I think I need you to kiss me." She had no idea where the words came from, but it was how she felt so didn't call them back. She'd obviously shocked Jet, though, if she were to judge by his expression.

"Really?" he asked as if afraid she would snatch back the offer.

"Oh, yes, please," Quinn breathed, moving closer still until her body glided against his.

She didn't have to ask again. Jet bent at once to cover her mouth with his and *damn* . . . Quinn had experienced passion before in her life. Her relationship with Patrick had started out very passionate, but it had been nothing like this. The moment Jet's mouth touched hers it was like someone flipped a switch in her body. Every nerve from her lips down to her toes was suddenly tingling and vibrating in her body.

Quinn found herself stretching, her back arching and toes curling as her hands crept around his neck, and her fingers slid into his hair tangling in the soft dark strands. Liquid heat was already pooling between her legs at the gentle caress of his lips against hers and it made her want more. She opened her mouth under his, and he accepted the invitation at once, his tongue gliding in to wrestle with hers. They both groaned at the explosions that set off. Quinn's whole body was suddenly trembling, her legs weak with need so that she was clutching at him now to stay on her feet. But then she wasn't having to stay on her feet anymore. She was on the ground, and the sand was cool beneath her back in contrast to his heat as he pressed her down into it, and then his hands were moving, gliding over her body, caressing here, squeezing there.

One of his hands found a breast, and Quinn gasped into his mouth, her back bowing to thrust herself more fully into the caress as he fondled her through her blouse. She found herself wishing she wasn't wearing it, that she was naked. But this time the dream didn't accommodate her and present her naked for his pleasure; instead, Jet had to stop caressing her to tug at her top.

Quinn wasn't surprised when the buttons gave way, but couldn't find it in herself to care. She was even grateful for it because it allowed him to tug the silk out of the way. The lacy white bra was tugged aside next and then Jet broke their kiss and slid down to claim the nipple he'd revealed, drawing it into his hot mouth.

Quinn opened her eyes on a cry and stared up through the branches of a pine tree, little mewls and moans of pleasure slipping from her mouth as his tongue swirled over and around her nipple as his lips suckled.

God, it felt so damned good, she thought faintly. She felt alive for the first time in four years. And then his hand moved down between her legs and she bucked, thrusting into the heel of his hand as he pressed it against her.

"Yes. Jet. Please," she begged, and used her hold on his hair to drag his lips away from her breast and back up to her mouth to kiss him feverishly as he caressed her through her slacks. But she wanted to touch him too. So, keeping the fingers of one hand tangled in his hair to ensure he didn't break their kiss, she let the other slide down his body, feeling her way down his chest and then his stomach before finding the bulge between his legs. Pausing there, she covered and then squeezed his erection through his dress pants and this time it was Jet who broke their kiss.

Turning his head away on a grunt, he gasped her name almost in protest, but he was thrusting against her hand even as he did, and she smiled and then kissed and licked his neck as her fingers slid over him. He felt and smelled so damned good, so delicious, so . . .

Without realizing how it happened, Quinn was suddenly sinking her teeth into his neck. Jet moaned in pleasure, but Quinn's eyes opened and she froze in sudden horror as she realized what she was doing, and then she was pushing him off of her and scrambling to get away from him.

"Quinn?" Jet murmured with confusion, and started to sit up, cursing when he hit his head on one of the low-hanging branches of the pine tree he'd dragged Quinn under after fetching her from the river. Rubbing his head, he glanced around with confusion. Bright morning sunlight was filtering through the branches, dappling the area with dark and light, and he supposed one of those bits of light had landed on his eyes and woken him up from the best damned dream he'd had in ages. He'd been with Quinn, and they'd—

The memory died in his mind as he realized that she wasn't there under the tree anymore. Where had she gone?

Concern snaking through him, Jet crawled out from under the low-lying branches and then dragged himself to his feet and looked around, frowning when he noted the position of the sun in the sky. It wasn't early morning—more like midafternoon, he realized, seeing the position of the sun in the sky. They'd slept a good portion of the day away. It made him wonder if the crazed Russian immortals had run right past where they were sleeping, or if they too had slept somewhere. He spent a moment hoping for the first option until he recalled the unsuspecting mortals at the settlement Kira had spotted when she'd climbed that tree.

They would have been helpless against them, he

thought unhappily, and then noticed Quinn down by the river. She was kneeling at the shoreline, splashing water in her face.

Running one hand over his own face to try to wake himself up fully from the crazy passionate dream he'd just been enjoying, Jet started forward, grimacing when his erection protested at the movement.

"Down, fella," he muttered, dropping his gaze to the burgeoning hard-on trying to poke its way out of his slacks. Christ, that had been a hot dream. Real sex had never been half as exciting as just kissing and caressing Quinn in a dream was. Somehow, he didn't think that was good for him. If the woman had intruded on his thoughts when he was with other women before this, it could only be worse after that experience, he worried.

Shaking his head, he continued forward, his gaze taking in the petite woman by the water. She wasn't just splashing water on her face; she was splashing it all over her chest too, he noted with a small frown, but before he could ask if she was all right, she apparently heard him approaching.

Quinn leapt to her feet and swung around to face him, then began to back away, putting space between them.

"I'm sorry," she blurted miserably. "I don't know what happened. One minute I was having a dream that we had fries and then walked on a beach, and the next thing I knew I was biting you for real and I'm so sorry."

Jet stopped, his hand going to his neck and his eyes widening, though it wasn't at the two small wounds he felt on his throat. It was a combination of her words and the fact that her blouse was hanging wide open, the buttons missing, and one of her breasts was out of the cup of her bra, and on display. Just as it would have been if the dream he'd had was real. Had it been a dream? He was pretty sure it had been. At least at the start, but they'd been lying close together when he'd fallen asleep. He'd been spooning her. Perhaps the dream had slipped over into reality when they'd begun to kiss and caress and—

"I won't come near you, I promise," Quinn said now. "You'll have to go on alone. You're obviously not safe with me anymore."

That snapped Jet out of his thoughts and he frowned, letting his hand slide from his neck and back to his side. But he didn't immediately address what she'd said; instead, he said in the calmest voice he could manage, "I think we had best move away from the water to somewhere with a little more cover to discuss this, Quinn. Kira or the others could come upon us at any moment here."

Quinn shook her head. "I think you should just go. I'm as much of a threat now as they are."

"No. You're not," Jet assured her. Still using his calm voice, he took a step toward her, holding his hand out. "Please, let's just move a little way into the trees and talk."

When Quinn shook her head wildly and backed farther away, Jet stopped at once, and peered along the opposite shoreline as he debated what to do. Finally, he just looked at her and asked, "Were you dreaming we were in a hospital and then an old-fashioned-style restaurant with booths?"

Quinn froze at the question, her mouth dropping open.

That was answer enough for Jet to know that it had definitely been a shared dream, but he continued. "We had shakes, and fries with enough vinegar, ketchup, and salt on them to kill anyone with a mortal ticker, and then we walked on the beach. We talked about family and I admitted I was attracted to you and have been for over four years and then we . . . er . . ." Rather than put words to what they'd done, he gestured to her open top.

Quinn looked down with confusion, and then gasped and tucked her breast back in her bra even as she pulled her blouse closed. She then tried to do up the buttons, but there weren't any to do up. He'd popped them off trying to get to her breast in the dream . . . and apparently in real life too. In the end, she tied the tails of the blouse together under her bra. It left her stomach on display, but her bra and what it protected were covered now.

Once that was done, she raised her head and asked with some dignity, "How do you know what I was dreaming?" Then she frowned. "And how the hell did my clothes get ruined in real life from a dream?"

"Well, I'm thinking we shared the dream," Jet said quietly, knowing exactly what that meant.

Apparently, Quinn didn't, he realized with amazement when she frowned and asked, "Is that possible? How could we share a dream?"

Jet could hardly believe the question. She was the damned immortal, supposed to know this business, not him. He only knew because Abs had explained about life mates and their symptoms to him to reassure him that she wasn't moving too quickly and making a mistake when it came to her and Tomasso. Which was something he'd worried about. At least until he'd got to know the guy and watched him with Abs for a bit. The two really were perfect for each other.

"It's not possible," Quinn muttered.

Jet scowled at her announcement and shifted his feet.

"Then how do I know what we were dreaming? How do I know that your father died when you were tiny and then your mother and her new husband when you were six and you were shipped off to Albany, New York, to be raised by your godmother and her husband who are both physicians with a family practice they wanted you to join?"

When she stared at him silently, apparently at a loss as to how to explain it, he assured her, "It is possible. We had a shared dream. It happens all the time . . . Between possible life mates."

"What?" she squawked with dismay.

"It's one of the ways life mates recognize each other. Shared dreams are one of the symptoms," he explained, and then scowled. "And Marguerite should have taught you that while she was explaining everything else about immortals four years ago. Why the hell didn't she?"

"She might have," Quinn admitted unhappily. "But I'm afraid I wasn't a very good pupil. I didn't listen half the time and . . . I was having trouble accepting what I was. It's why they let me go to Italy. They were hoping Pet could help me adjust and finish my training." She grimaced and then confessed, "But I let her think my training was done. I just wanted peace and quiet and to be left alone to deal."

Jet was silent for a minute, but then rustling from the woods made him shift nervously and glance around. "Well, I'm not staying out here in the open to discuss this. If you want to talk I'll be in the woods . . . all alone, waiting for either you or one of the blood-lusting locos to find me."

Turning on his heel on that note, Jet walked into the woods. It wasn't like he had a choice. He couldn't force the woman to come talk to him, but he was hoping she'd follow if only to try to convince him to go on without her. Really, though, he was hoping she'd want to discuss this life mate business. He certainly did. Jet had never imagined that he'd be a possible life mate for an immortal. But it explained a lot. His obsession with the woman these last four years after just seeing her board the plane a couple of times had more than once made him feel loco. Like one of those creepy stalker-type guys. He felt a little better knowing there might be a good reason for it. Christ! He was a possible life mate to her. Now what?

While he asked the question, his brain didn't have a ready answer. Never having imagined that he might be a life mate to someone, Jet had never contemplated such an issue and wasn't at all sure if he even wanted to be one. Being a life mate meant turning like Abs had done, and that meant becoming a blood drinker, which just sounded disgusting to him.

That passion, though, part of his mind argued. Damn . . . A man could live off that alone for several lifetimes. Hell, just thinking about it was reawakening Mr. Happy in his pants.

Grimacing, Jet adjusted himself and glanced around until he spotted a handy log to sit on. It was long dead, gray from the elements leaching any last remains of life from it. But it seemed solid enough and didn't crumple under his weight, so he relaxed on the log and waited, not at all sure Quinn would come to him. He was mightily relieved when she slid out of the woods a moment later and then hesitated, eyeing him uncertainly.

When Jet patted the log next to him, she moved forward, but she didn't sit where he'd indicated. Instead, she picked the opposite end of the log, as far from him as she could get.

They were both silent for a minute. Jet because she was so damned beautiful. The woman was lovely in her professional garb and persona, but with her shirt tied like that, leaving a deep neckline that revealed the curves of her breasts and left her stomach on display, not to mention her hair all poofy and wild around her head from their make-out session, she was fucking breathtaking. He just wanted to tug her shirt open again, but remove her bra as well this time and—

"Do you really think we're life mates?"

Jet blinked his lusty thoughts away, wiped away the drool at the corner of his mouth with the back of one hand, and cleared his throat. "Yes."

That was it. Yes. It was all he could manage just then. Mr. Happy wasn't very happy being restricted to his dress slacks all swollen and hot as he was, and Jet was quite sure the blood now engorging Mr. Happy had come straight from his brain, because it seemed pretty empty of all but what he'd like to do with Quinn at the moment.

Quinn sighed heavily and peered down at her hands sadly. "I don't think I'm ready for a life mate, Jet. I need counseling or something first. Actually, I need to get my shit together, figure out what I'm going to do with my life, and get to it so I can look after my son, and I need to figure all that out before I even consider getting involved with someone in a romantic way."

How about just no-strings-attached crazy monkey sex, then? some part of Jet's mind screamed, but he abruptly shook the thought from his head as inappropriate and considered the fact that while he wasn't at all sure he wanted to be a life mate either, her saying she wasn't ready for one still hurt. Weird, he thought, but then cleared his throat and said, "Perhaps we can worry about that later. Right now, I think we should concentrate on getting to civilization and finding some help for the other ladies from the plane."

"Right." Quinn stood abruptly, but turned apologetically to him. "You need to go on without me. I'll try to locate the others and hold them off long enough for you to—"

"That's not going to happen," Jet interrupted firmly, and when she opened her mouth to protest, he held up a hand to silence her, before saying solemnly, "Quinn, I won't make it out of these woods without you. I would if I didn't have crazy blood-hungry vamps on my ass, but I do, and I'm only mortal. You can't hold back four of them on your own, and I can't outrun them on my own. I need you."

"But I bit you," she cried as if he might have forgotten that fact. He hadn't. In fact, he was recalling the increased pleasure and excitement he'd experienced when she did it and was thinking he wouldn't mind experiencing it again. Besides, she needed the blood, so really, he was being selfless.

"You got pretty banged up in the rapids," he said. "And you're really pale. You obviously need blood. And I need you to be strong and healthy to help me survive," he added solemnly. "I think you should bite me and take some blood. Just enough for you to be able to get us to help," he rushed on quickly when she began to protest. When she hesitated, looking uncertain, he pointed out, "It's not just for me, Quinn. Whatever people there are in the town or camp Kira saw are under threat too. We need to call in help or they could be killed as well."

When her shoulders drooped in defeat, he almost sagged with relief. He really did need her help to get away from the Russian immortals, and he wasn't too proud to say so. Jet knew his strengths. He'd been trained in self-defense both before and while in the navy and could carry his own against most men, and even a lot of animals, although he wouldn't have willingly taken on a bear. But he was mortal, with a mortal man's strength. He could not go up against immortals and win. Not without a damned weapon or something.

"How do you want me to do this?"

Jet glanced at Quinn at that question and then hesitated briefly, before holding out his wrist. He'd really rather return to what they'd been doing earlier, and go from there, but speed was somewhat important here, so the wrist seemed the fastest vein for her to tap.

Quinn eyed his wrist anxiously, but then moved closer. She didn't sit down. She didn't have to. She was short enough that she could take his hand and raise it to her mouth with him sitting. Jet closed his eyes, expecting the same pleasure and bliss he'd experienced when she'd bit his neck earlier, but after a moment during which she hesitated, what he felt was sharp pain and a drawing sensation that hurt like a son of a bitch and made him whimper like a girl.

Quinn froze at the sound, her eyes shooting to his face. She'd been worried that she'd have trouble bringing her fangs on and doing this, but the moment she'd raised his wrist to her face and his smell had enveloped her, her fangs had slid down and drool had formed in her mouth. Still, she'd hesitated a moment before biting, not at all comfortable with doing this. But she had, and now she frowned and withdrew her fangs as she saw the pain on his face.

"I'm sorry," she said sincerely as she released her hold on his arm.

"Fuck," Jet muttered, rubbing his wrist as he stood to pace away. "That freaking hurt. Why the hell did it hurt? It didn't hurt when we were—" Stopping abruptly, he swung back to her. "Abs said she didn't feel it the first time Tomasso bit her. That he distracted her with kisses and caresses."

Quinn eyed him uncertainly. "Okay."

"And that's what was happening when you bit me the first time and I didn't feel pain then," he pointed out, moving back to her. "So, if we kiss and do stuff again, you should be able to bite me without hurting me."

Quinn's eyes widened. "You want me to—?"

That was as far as she got before he bent and kissed her. There was no buildup this time, no brushing of lips against lips. This time his tongue was out, seeking entrance the moment their mouths met.

Quinn opened to Jet without hesitation when his mouth covered hers. Her arms crept up around his neck and then she gasped and wrapped her legs around his waist when he suddenly straightened, taking her with him. She was vaguely aware of his moving, but was too distracted by his thrusting tongue tangling with hers to pay it much attention until she felt the tree press into her back. Pinning her against the tree with his lower body, Jet broke their kiss and leaned his upper body back to see what he was doing as he went to work at undoing the knot she'd put in her blouse to keep it closed.

Quinn had barely glanced down to see that that was

what he was doing when he managed to undo her blouse and tug it open to reveal her lacy bra to his view. She watched him run one finger along the edge of the lace, and then that finger slid under the delicate cloth and tugged it down under first one breast and then the other.

His hands were immediately claiming the bounty he'd revealed and Quinn leaned her head back against the tree and moaned as he caressed her.

"Beautiful," he murmured, and then claimed her open mouth and kissed her again.

Quinn kissed him back eagerly, her hands clutching at his shoulders as she arched into his caress, and then he broke their kiss and offered her his neck. Her fangs immediately slid out and down, but she hesitated, afraid to hurt him, and then she ran her lips lightly over his throat, but didn't bite, instead, she slid her hand down between them to find the bulge of his groin. Quinn had to urge him back a bit and let herself slide down his length an inch or two to reach it, but then they both groaned as she covered his hardness and began to rub and caress him.

"Oh God, Quinn," Jet groaned, nipping at her ear with excitement, and Quinn finally let her teeth glide into his neck.

She felt him stiffen against her, and almost withdrew her fangs, afraid she was hurting him, but then he began to thrust into her caressing hand, moaning, "Oh, yes, Quinn, yes. God, baby. Oh my God."

Relieved, she left her fangs in and continued to caress him, her own body responding as if she was caressing herself, the sensation building on top of the excitement of his hands moving over her breasts, kneading and squeezing and then tweaking her nipples. It was all blurring together and building inside of her, wave after wave of mounting excitement and need, and then a distant shriek caught her ear just as Jet suddenly moaned and staggered.

Quinn was already removing her fangs from his neck when he then dropped to his knees, taking her with him. Pulling back, she peered at him with concern as he opened his eyes.

"Don't stop," he moaned, but he was swaying slightly and she knew she'd taken more blood than she probably should have. Reaching for his wrist, she took his pulse, relieved to feel it only a little elevated, and then another shriek sounded in the distance. She couldn't tell how far away they were, but if they could hear them, they were too close as far as she was concerned, and Quinn hugged Jet briefly, and whispered, "We have to go."

"Yeah." He sighed the word into her hair, stirring it with his breath.

"Can you get up?" she asked, standing up now, and offering him her hand.

Jet took it, but only used it to steady himself as he stood.

"How are you?" he asked with a small frown. He was swaying on his feet, his expression a bit disoriented, and she brushed a strand of hair back from his face and smiled.

"I'm good. Better. You will be too, once I get you to safety. Now wait here for a minute." Urging him closer to the tree, she leaned him against it so he wouldn't fall over, and then quickly scrambled up the tree. Quinn didn't think about it, she just did it, which was pretty impressive, really. She had never climbed a tree before, not even as a kid. But her strength made it a breeze and she climbed up as far as the tree would hold her and then moved the branches blocking her view to peer out at the surroundings.

She spotted the encampment first, and it was definitely looking like some kind of camp or hotel, not a town, and then she followed the sound of another shriek and looked back the way they'd come the night before. At first, she couldn't see anything, but then she thought she spotted movement in a distant tree and immediately began to scramble back down the one she was in. The encampment was closer than the movement Quinn had seen in the trees behind them, but as fast as immortals moved she wouldn't have long to get Jet and the people in the camp away to safety before the Russian women would be on them.

Jet was still leaning against the tree when she landed on the ground next to it. Quinn didn't take the time to explain; she simply hefted him over her shoulder and broke into a run in the direction of the camp . . . and started to pray.

Six

"What the hell do you mean you don't have a phone? Everyone has a damned cell phone nowadays. Why don't any of you?"

Jet blinked his eyes open at that roar, wincing even as he did. His head was pounding like a bass drum. He'd think he was suffering from one hell of a hangover if his memories weren't intact. Unfortunately, his memory was just fine and the last thing he recalled was hanging down Quinn's back, nausea roiling up in him and pain beginning to thump in his head as she ran through the woods, leaping over logs and swerving around trees in her path as she raced desperately to save him, and presumably the six—no, seven—people now facing her across the room with a combination of concern for her bloody and disheveled state, and apparent irritation at her bellowing.

"Ma'am, you need to calm down and tell us what

happened," the darker haired of the two men among the seven people said soothingly. "Obviously you've been through something horrible, but you're safe now and—"

"I'm not safe!" Quinn snapped, and then shifted impatiently and added, "Well, I am, but you people and Jet aren't and—" Her voice broke off as she glanced his way and saw that he was awake. "Oh, Jet," she breathed, rushing to where he was pushing himself up to a sitting position on the large leather couch he'd been lying on. "You're awake. How do you feel? You fainted."

"I didn't faint," he growled, reaching up to rub the knot on the back of his head where most of the drumming seemed to be going on. Noting her expression, he grimaced and admitted, "All right, so I fainted. It was the blood rushing to my head and all the swaying and banging around I was doing against your butt as you carried me through the woods. Damn, woman, you have a bony ass," he complained. "We really need to feed you something besides alfalfa sprouts and kale. For real," he added, since she'd eaten fries in their shared dream.

A choked sound from Quinn drew his gaze to her face to see that she'd flushed bright red and looked like she'd swallowed her tongue, and then Jet realized what he'd said and closed his eyes on a sigh. "I'm sorry. I didn't mean that. Well, I sort of did. Your behind is all bone and it hurt hitting my head against it over and over again, but I'd never say that if my head didn't hurt so much. I appreciate—" His attempt to thank her for saving his life died in his throat when a glass of water appeared before his eyes.

"This might help," a husky voice said as he blinked at the glass.

Jet followed the hand holding the glass up an arm to a beautiful face with long red hair around it, and two huge breasts under it. There was no neck, he noted with alarm and then realized that was because the woman was bent over, offering him the glass. Jet couldn't help shifting his gaze from her face to her breasts and back as he thought with dismay, Dear God, the poor girl probably got terrible backaches carrying those monsters around.

A small sound rather like a growl made him glance to Quinn then. Much to his amazement—and, all right, a little pleasure—Quinn was staring at the redhead like she wanted to rip off her head. She was jealous, he thought, and smiled at the idea until Quinn turned her furious gaze on him. Hiding his smile behind a frown, he took the glass from the redhead and stood up abruptly.

"Where are we n—oh," he finished weakly as the room did a little dance around him.

Quinn caught the glass as it slipped from his hand, and took his arm to steady him. She urged him to sit back down as she answered the question he hadn't finished. "We're at a private fly-in fishing lodge. One hundred and sixty miles from civilization and apparently without a phone or a car to make our way out of here."

"I told you," a tall, blond male who looked to be Jet's own age said testily. "A car wouldn't do any good. There are no roads out here. People and goods have to be flown in and out."

Quinn scowled at the man and then told Jet, "I heard the plane fly out while I was still about fifteen minutes away. It had just dropped these guys off to open the lodge. Apparently, this place is only open eight weeks of the year and has been closed since the end of last August. The plane won't come back for two days when the first guests are scheduled to fly in."

"Well, that's not good," Jet said grimly, and then frowned. "If they didn't get here until today, then what were the lights Kira saw last night?"

"Brittany and I got in yesterday," the blond male admitted reluctantly. "The plane your friend heard was leaving after dropping off the rest of our crew today."

Jet nodded, and then took the glass of water Quinn was holding out and quickly gulped the cool liquid down. Surprisingly enough, it actually helped a bit. At least the pounding in his head seemed to be easing a little by the time he finished.

Murmuring a polite, "Thank you," Jet handed the glass to the redhead who had given it to him and then turned back to Quinn as she addressed the guy who was apparently in charge. "You must have some way to contact the outside world in case of an emergency. A CB radio or something?"

"A CB wouldn't do us any good out here," the man said, rolling his eyes as if her suggesting it was ridiculous. "We're too far from anywhere for that. We have a satellite phone in the office that—"

"Take me to it," Jet interrupted.

When the man hesitated, looking like he was going to refuse, Jet turned to Quinn and said, "Control him and make him."

Quinn looked surprised at the suggestion and then bit her lip and admitted, "I don't know how to do that."

Jet's eyes widened in shock. "What? But you were

turned four years ago. Didn't Marguerite . . ." His voice trailed away as he recalled their earlier conversation. Shared dreams obviously weren't the only thing she hadn't learned about.

Cursing, he turned to survey the group of seven around them. Two of them were around his age, the redheaded woman and the blond man. They seemed to be the ones in charge if he were to guess by the fact that they were wearing name tags that read Jason (Manager) and Brittany (Asst. Manager) on their dark blue polo shirts. The rest of the group around them merely had names on the nametags on their baby-blue polo shirts. The people in baby blue were made up of four young women and one young man who all looked to be between eighteen and twenty. The men in this group were attractive and well-built, and the females were all pretty and well-endowed.

Either the lodge catered to rich old perverts who liked having large-breasted women around, or the guy in charge of hiring did, Jet thought. He'd always preferred smaller, well-shaped ones himself. Like Quinn's, he acknowledged as his gaze slid around the expensive trappings of the room they were in. It looked like a large living room with log walls, cathedral ceilings, and big leather furniture everywhere. Everything was layered with a coat of dust that supported the story that it had been closed for ten months.

"The satellite phone is only for business calls or emergencies."

That announcement from Jason, the manager, drew Jet's gaze and attention back to the matter at hand and he scowled at the guy. "This *is* an emergency, or did you miss the fact that I was unconscious when she carried me in, and she has blood all over her shirt?"

A lot of the starch went out of the guy at once and he glanced from Jet to Quinn, concern beginning to pluck at the corners of his mouth as he muttered, "No, of course I didn't miss that, but she won't tell us what's happening."

"Our plane crashed, three of my passengers were injured, and a fourth was attacked by a bear as we were trying to make our way to help," Jet spat out, but hesitated briefly, before adding, "And the bear chased us here. It's a big crazy bastard. Rabid, I think, and if it gets here before we get help it'll probably kill us all."

Bad choice, he decided when the guy's concern gave way to suspicion and he asked, "You want me to believe that this little girl outran a bear to get here? No one can outrun a bear," he said with disgust. "And she was carrying you, for heaven's sake."

"Jet, we don't have time for this," Quinn said grimly, her gaze moving to the door and back. "They weren't that far behind us when I checked from the tree."

"How far?" Jet asked with concern.

She shook her head. "I'm not sure. Maybe fifteen minutes if we're lucky."

"Who weren't far behind you?" Jason the manager asked, his eyes narrowed.

This time it was Quinn who answered, coming up with a brilliant lie. At least it seemed pretty brilliant to him when she held out her hand and said, "I'm Dr. Quinn Peters from Albany, New York."

The man took her hand automatically, a little respect entering his expression at the word *doctor*. Quinn's suddenly take-charge, professional voice probably helped too.

"Of course you're right, and it isn't a bear we're worried about," she admitted, and then her gaze flickered briefly to Jet, before returning to Jason as she explained, "We were flying back from Europe and our plane did crash. Mr. Lassiter was the copilot. We lost the pilot in the crash, but who we were running from are the patients we were transporting. They got out of the plane, and they're dangerous." She glanced at Jet again and then announced, "They were mental patients."

"Mental patients?" the redheaded Brittany destined for back issues gasped with dismay. "Oh, the poor dears."

Quinn grimaced at the words, but said, "No, you don't understand. They aren't—They—"

"Look," Jet said, picking up the tale when Quinn faltered in the face of the young girl's sympathy. "These aren't your garden variety mental patients. There are four of them," he added, and hoped that was true, but knew it was possible that Liliya had got hurt trying to slow the others down and might now be suffering blood lust as well. Pushing that worry away for now, he continued, "And they're some of the most dangerous individuals you'll ever encounter. Think Hannibal Lecter, Leatherface, Michael Myers, and Norman Bates," he suggested, listing the first four horror-movie psychos that came to mind. "They're dangerous and out for blood, and we're directly in their path."

"Oh God. I knew I should have taken that job at the Krispy Chicken in town," one of the girls moaned unhappily. "The pay might not have been as good, but at least in town you don't get old men hitting on you, and psychos trying to kill you."

"Shut up, Jeanette," Jason snapped, but he was looking from Quinn to Jet, obviously trying to decide if they were telling the truth.

Fortunately, in the brief silence that followed, a high shriek sounded from somewhere outside. The chilling sound drifted to them through an open window next to the entrance, and sounded as mad and terrifying as the last time Jet had heard it. The Russians were unhinged with need and they were coming. They didn't sound like they were fifteen minutes away.

"What was that?" Jeanette gasped as she and the other younger females cowered together.

"I'm sure it was just a loon or something," Jason muttered, but he moved over to reach through the bars over the open window and slammed it closed. He then quickly barred the door. "Jeanette, you and the others go around and make sure the bars on all the windows and doors are locked in place. I'll take Mr. Lassiter to the satellite phone."

"Oh my God, we're gonna die," one of the girls moaned as Jet followed the manager from the room and down a long hall to an office.

Quinn watched the men go, and then glanced around at the staff rushing away. Most of them fled the room, presumably to check windows and doors in other rooms, but the busty Brittany, who had been fawning over Jet, remained to double-check the bars on the other windows in this room. Quinn watched her and then asked, "Are there bars on the windows upstairs?"

The structure was a large two-story building with lots of windows on both floors. She'd noticed that as she'd hurried across the manicured lawn with Jet over her shoulder. Fortunately, not expecting anyone, none of the staff members had been looking out the windows to see her whiz across the yard from the woods at immortal speed. In fact, she was pretty sure she'd interrupted a staff meeting and startled a good ten years off of every one of the young people's lives when she'd rushed inside with Jet over her shoulder and slammed the door behind her.

"Yes. Every window has bars. We hadn't started removing them yet, but we did open a couple of windows before the others got here. It's good the girls are checking. They'll close them," Brittany assured her, and then babbled a bit nervously, "The bars are to make sure no one breaks in while the lodge is closed. Ten months is a long time, and there are some old crazies wandering the wilds up here. And, of course, everything in the lodge is top of the line and expensive. The owners wanted to be sure no one broke in during off-season and set the place on fire or something, so had the bars installed."

Quinn didn't comment. She suspected the woman was just speaking out of anxiety anyway.

"It'll be fine, right?" Brittany asked. "They can't get through the bars. I mean, of course they can't." She tittered nervously and then added, "It's not like they have chain saws and stuff like Leatherface or something . . . Right?"

Quinn stepped up to the nearest window, grasped two of the bars and pulled each to a side. Her breath left her on a sigh of disappointment when the bars began to bend away from each other. She'd been hoping they were strong enough to help keep the immortals out, but if she could bend them—

"Oh my God!" Brittany gasped with dismay. "The bars are broken."

"I didn't break them," Quinn said quickly. "I just bent them a little. See. I'm bending them back."

"Yeah, but you shouldn't be able to," Brittany squawked. "They're supposed to be steel. They're obviously defective."

"Oh." Quinn stepped back from the window and then asked with a frown. "Do you have a safe room or something here?"

"No." Brittany bit her lip unhappily, and then offered, "The best we have is the booze box."

"Booze box?" Quinn echoed with bewilderment.

"A steel cage down in the basement where the expensive alcohol and stuff are kept," Brittany explained. "We call it the booze box."

"How big is it?" Quinn asked at once. "Can you all fit into it?"

"Maybe," Brittany said slowly.

"Show me," Quinn said, moving toward her and following when Brittany turned and hurried from the room.

The redhead led her along the hall Jet and Jason had disappeared down moments ago, and Quinn listened as she followed the woman. She came to an abrupt halt outside a door marked Manager and reached for the doorknob when she heard Jet's voice from inside.

"Are you coming?"

Brittany had stopped next to another door farther

down and Quinn let her hand drop from the knob to follow the woman. She could find out what Jet had learned after she checked out the cage. It probably wouldn't be much stronger than the bars over the windows, but they only had to slow the women down long enough for help to get to them. The problem was she wasn't at all sure they could manage that.

"They reached the plane half an hour ago. They've already retrieved Jeff Miller's body and are tending to Annika."

Jet lowered his head at Bastien Argeneau's words. He hadn't been sure who to call once he'd got his hands on the satellite phone. Lucian Argeneau had hired Jet, but the man's nephew, Bastien, was the president of Argeneau Enterprises and the guy who signed his checks, so he'd called him. But Bastien had linked the call into Lucian even as he'd told him that his uncle was leading the rescue effort that had headed out to search for the plane when it hadn't arrived in Toronto and it had become apparent that the plane had gone down.

Unfortunately, it had taken some time to locate the plane. There was a lot of cloud coverage north of the lodge where Jet and Quinn now were. The ceiling around the plane had ranged from five hundred feet and a one-mile visibility to a zero-foot ceiling and one-eighth-of-a-mile visibility, he was told, and the helicopters had had to circle, cross, and circle the area over and over again to pinpoint where the ELT was coming from. But they'd finally located the plane.

"I'm sorry about Miller, Jet," Bastien said now. "I know he was a good friend."

"Yeah," Jet murmured, swallowing thickly, and then his hand tightened on the phone and his head came up slightly. "Did you say they're tending to Annika? She hadn't escaped her seat and got away from the area?"

"No." Lucian was the one to answer, his voice grim. "She was too badly hurt to get out of her seat. Her neck and back—hell, every bone in her body—looks to have been broken, and the armrests of her chair were crushed around her body. She didn't have enough blood in her to heal half of her injuries and couldn't get out of her chair."

Jet thought that was the longest speech he'd ever heard Lucian Argeneau give. He suspected that meant the man had been horrified by the state Annika had been in when they'd found her. Jet understood that, but found himself grateful for it. It meant one less loco immortal in the throes of blood lust to fight off if their rescuers didn't get here in time.

"How long until we can expect you here?" Jet asked now.

"Where are you?" Lucian asked abruptly.

"A fly-in wildlife lodge called—"

"I know the *name* of the lodge," Lucian said dryly. "You mentioned it earlier. But where the hell is it? I need coordinates."

"Oh." Jet turned to Jason, who was hovering next to him. "They need—Here, just tell him how to find us," he said, and passed the phone to the man. It seemed more expedient than Jason giving Jet instructions and his passing them on. He suspected every second would count here. The shrieks from outside were growing nearer and becoming more fevered. It was like the women knew they were closing in on their quarry.

With that thought in mind, while Jason spoke on the phone Jet moved to the window and peered out. There were no crazed immortals rushing toward the building. They were still in the woods, making their way here. Thank God, he thought, and then held his breath as he listened to the mournful sounds from outside, trying to sort out if the shrieks were coming from just one woman or three or four. Had Liliya joined the pack, or was she okay? Maybe she was fine and had managed to keep at least Kira away and they'd only have two immortals to deal with.

"He wants to talk to you."

Jet gave up his position by the window and moved back to take the phone.

"Fifteen minutes."

"That long?" Jet squawked with alarm.

"We are in a helicopter not a fighter jet," Lucian snapped. "And you are a good fifty miles from where the plane crashed. Speaking of which, how did you manage that in fourteen hours over rough terrain?" he asked.

Had it really only been fourteen hours? Jet wondered with amazement even as he answered, "Quinn carried me."

"Then what the hell took so long?" Lucian barked now. "She should have been able to cover that in—"

"She got hurt in the rapids and we had to stop for a while," Jet interrupted, not willing to listen to criticism of the woman who had saved his life.

A long silence rang in his ears and then Lucian asked, "And she is there with you? Is she safe to be around?"

"Yes. I gave her . . ." Jet paused to glance at Jason and then muttered, "Medicine."

Lucian understood and grunted at that news. "Tell her we are on our way, but to do her best to hold them off until we arrive."

"I will," Jet muttered, but he was speaking to dead air. Sighing, he dropped the phone on the desk and stood up.

"How long did he say it would take for them to get here?" Jason asked anxiously, following him to the door.

"Fifteen minutes," Jet said grimly.

"But that's how far away your friend thought those mental patients were, and that was five minutes ago," Jason pointed out worriedly.

"Yeah," Jet sighed. "I guess we'd better look for weapons."

"Weapons?" Jason echoed with amazement, either shocked that Jet was bringing it up, or shocked that he hadn't thought of it himself.

"Yeah, weapons," Jet said grimly. "I'd ask for garlic and crosses but those won't work unfortunately."

Jason looked confused by his comment, but said, "We have a shotgun."

Jet pursed his lips. "A flamethrower would be more useful, but beggars can't be choosers."

"Here it is."

Quinn halted beside Brittany, her eyes moving with interest over the steel cage in the very back room of the lodge basement. She'd expected one of those human-sized gerbil cages with thin lines of steel making up one-inch squares from top to bottom, but this cage looked more like a jail cell. It had steel bars an inch in diameter running up and down and side to side about every eight inches in both directions. But it was also little more than six feet wide and about the same deep. Not ideal to hold nine people.

"It might be tight, but I think we can all fit in," Brittany said, and Quinn looked at her with disbelief. Seeing her expression, Brittany pulled briefly on her lower lip and then muttered, "Well, I said it would be tight."

Sighing, Quinn turned a grim expression to the cage, wondering who would be dragged through one of those eight-inch squares first . . . and if they'd survive it. Because they might all manage to squeeze in there—if they moved everything presently in the cage out of it—but they wouldn't be able to get away from the sides. They'd be like fish in a barrel, waiting to be snatched and dragged out by one of the immortal women.

"Brittany?"

Both women turned toward the dark-haired young man entering the room. His name tag read Shawn, Quinn noted as he joined them.

"Jason and that other guy are done with the call and looking for the two of you."

"Thanks, Shawn," Brittany said, patting his shoulder as she moved past him, and then she paused and swung back to hand him a set of keys. "Can you move all the boxes out of the booze box?"

"All of them?" he asked, turning to stare at the cache of stacked boxes in the cage.

"Yes," Brittany said, and then frowned at Quinn sharply when she said, "No."

Ignoring her, Quinn said, "Stack a layer of boxes

along the cage walls inside, top to bottom, and remove the rest."

"There is no way nine of us are going to fit in there with a layer of boxes making it even smaller," Brittany protested.

"You'll have to manage it," Quinn said firmly. "You really need those boxes between you and the . . . mental patients," she finished grimly, and then turned to lead the way to the door, adding, "Besides, there will only be eight of you."

"Even eight won't fit with the boxes lining the inside."

"You'll just have to hold your breaths and get really friendly," Quinn said firmly, noting that the woman hadn't asked who wasn't going to be inside the cage.

Brittany started to follow her out of the room, but then paused to say, "Work fast, Shawn. I'll send the girls down to help you."

"Thanks, Britt," the young man said with relief. He was already inside the cage, beginning to shift the crates around.

"There you are."

Quinn stopped just inside the door to the front room, her gaze moving to the shotgun Jet was carrying as he turned from watching out the window and rushed toward her.

"A last resort. It might slow them down a little," he said, his gaze following her to the gun he carried. But then he raised his head and announced, "Lucian Argeneau is on his way here with help. They already found the plane."

"How long until they can get here?" Quinn asked at once.

"He said fifteen minutes," Jet admitted with a grimace. "But they had good news too."

"What's that?" Quinn asked, not sure what news could be good news at this point.

"They have Annika. She never made it out of her seat. She was too badly injured to manage to free herself."

"Oh," Quinn murmured. It actually was good news of a sort. At least it would be one less blood-crazed immortal to deal with, she supposed, and then asked, "Did they mention seeing Kira and Liliya?"

Jet shook his head solemnly and Quinn sighed. So, they would either have two or four immortals to contend with. Or maybe three if Liliya hadn't been too badly hurt while trying to slow down the others. Good Lord, she wished she knew which it would be.

Another shriek came from outside and Quinn frowned at how close it sounded. They'd be here soon if they weren't already.

"Jet?" Jason said suddenly.

He glanced around in question. "Yeah?"

"A woman just came out of the woods and—Jesus, how is she running so fast?" Jason gasped.

Quinn was moving before the man finished speaking. She'd barely reached him when the window shattered, fingers—bent clawlike—bursting through on long bony arms, reaching for him and missing by a hair's breadth as Quinn just managed to tug Jason out of reach.

"My God, what is that?" Brittany gasped with horror.

Quinn was asking herself the same question. She'd never seen such an emaciated figure in her life. It was like the nanos had eaten away more than just blood.

Or perhaps there was just so much blood in a body that once it was all taken away—really removed from veins, organs, and tissue—there was little left. The fingers, hands, and arms looked like bones with dried-out gray skin stretched over them, she noted, and then the arms withdrew and an equally emaciated and badly scarred face pressed against the bars. At first Quinn thought it might be Kira. Her face had been clawed by the bear, after all. But then she realized that this woman's hair was darker and she decided it must be Nika. Apparently, like Annika, Nika had taken a lot of damage too. Aside from the crisscross scars on her face, her neck was twisted slightly at an odd angle, as was one of her arms. Her body hadn't been able to fully repair itself.

The sound of another window breaking somewhere in the house made Quinn glance worriedly around, and then Nika said, "Jee-ot. Cooome, Jee-ot."

It sounded like the woman was trying to talk around broken glass, Quinn thought, and then noticed movement out of the corner of her eye. She turned just in time to see with some shock that Jet was moving toward the woman in the window, his face blank.

"No!" she screamed, leaping forward and catching his arm to pull him back before he could reach the window. Cursing then, she shoved him toward the hallway, barking, "Out of the room! Now! All of you!"

The other women had returned from their tasks and joined them in the room, she saw as they all stampeded for the hall, the staff members nearly mowing each other down in their desperation to get out of the front room. Quinn couldn't blame them. She was an immortal herself, but she'd never seen or expected to see something like this. Nika looked like a monster.

A cross between a zombie and the vampire of myth. That was bad enough, but the immortal had also made Quinn aware of a problem she hadn't considered. She might not have been sensible enough to learn how to read and control mortals, but every one of the women about to try to claw their way into the building had. She didn't just have to protect Jet and the others from the women; she had to protect them from themselves too, or at least their inability to keep from being controlled by the women laying siege to the place.

"Block the door," she barked as she pushed Jet into the hall. Leaving the others to tend to it, she urged Jet to a chair outside the manager's office, and then eyed him worriedly. When she saw the blankness lifting now that he was no longer in Nika's view, so no longer in her control, Quinn sighed and released him. She then turned to see how the others were doing at blocking the door to the hall. Quinn shook her head with dismay when she saw that all they'd done was jam a chair under it.

"That won't do," Jet said suddenly, standing up beside her.

"I know," she said wearily. "We need something heavy. Or several somethings heavy."

"Why don't we just go down to the cage?" Brittany said anxiously, already sidling toward the basement door.

"Because we need to slow them down long enough for help to get here," Quinn said quietly. "If we just head down to the cage without putting obstacles in their way, help might not reach us in time."

"There were filing cabinets in the manager's office," Jet said suddenly.

"You'll never move those," Jason said with dismay. "They're chock-full of paper and weigh a ton."

"Perfect," Quinn said grimly.

Moments later she and Jet had moved all three filing cabinets from the manager's office to stack them in front of the door. Quinn could have moved them herself, but as Jet had pointed out, a display of strength like that might have freaked out their hosts and they were already freaked out enough from seeing Nika in the shape she was presently in.

Quinn didn't want them scared of her too, so he took one end and she the other and they shifted them. She wasn't foolish enough to think the filing cabinets would stop Nika and the others from getting through the door, but it might slow them down a little. Hopefully, enough to allow Lucian Argeneau and the others enough time to get here. It was their only chance.

"I don't hear anything out there anymore," Jet muttered.

Quinn glanced across the filing cabinet they'd just set down, and then straightened and listened. She didn't hear Nika out front anymore either, she realized, and shared a concerned glance with him. "Maybe she's trying another way in."

The words had barely left her mouth when the sound of breaking glass brought small yelps from a couple of the women cowering farther up the hall.

"That came from my office," Jason said anxiously.

"There's a cell made up of steel bars downstairs," Quinn told Jet solemnly. "They call it the booze box because it's where they keep the booze and other expensive items. I think the cross bars might make it strong enough to keep Nika and the others out, or at least slow them down. How much time is left on the fifteen minutes until help gets here?"

Jet glanced at his wristwatch, and then frowned and tapped the watch face before letting his wrist drop with a sigh. "The dip in the river must have killed it. That or it got banged around at some point since the crash. It's reading the same time as it did when I finished the call. But I'd guess we probably have at least another five to ten minutes."

"Jee-ot. Hee-elp mee, Jee-ot."

Quinn shuddered as Nika's garbled cry reached them muffled from the manager's office, but then turned with concern to the young women cowering together up the hall when a couple of them burst into tears.

"Downstairs," Jet said firmly. Picking up the shotgun he'd set aside while they'd moved the filing cabinets, he took Quinn's arm to urge her away from the door they'd just blockaded. They had to pass the office door to get to the others, and Quinn eyed it warily as they hurried by, quite sure the door would crash open any moment and they'd be under attack.

"Move, people," Jet growled once they'd made it past the door to the manager's office and were approaching the group. "Downstairs now."

"But we'll be trapped down there!" That tearful protest came from the girl Jason had called Jeanette earlier, but several of the others nodded and seemed reluctant to move.

"We're getting in the booze box," Brittany announced reassuringly, giving a couple of the girls a push to get them moving. "We'll be safe in there."

"We won't all fit," another girl worried even as she stumbled toward the door to the basement.

"Yes, we will. Shawn is moving the booze crates out," Brittany said, and then glanced back to Quinn with dismay. "I was supposed to send some girls down to help." She didn't wait for a response from her, but then began hustling the girls under her charge along more swiftly, saying, "Come on. Hurry. He might need help. We have to get the crates out to make room. We'll be safe in there."

Much to Quinn's relief, that seemed to calm the other girls and get them moving more quickly. Even Jason abandoned Quinn and Jet and ran to catch up to them as they hustled to the door to the basement and rushed down.

"Go make sure they leave a line of crates around the walls of the cell," Quinn suggested, slowing to a stop at the door to the basement. "It'll mean you guys will most likely be standing on top of each other, but you'll need them in place to keep Nika and the others from being able to grab you and try to pull you out through the bars."

Jet nodded, but then arched an eyebrow. "What are you going to do?"

"I'll try to slow them down up here if they get inside," she said quietly.

"Oh, hell, no," Jet said grimly, urging her forward again.

"We won't all fit in the cell, Jet. And if I can slow them down—"

"Then you can slow them down outside the cell," he countered grimly. "I want you where I can see you. I don't want to be downstairs worrying that they've ripped your head off or something."

Quinn didn't protest again. She supposed she could

stand guard outside the cell as well as upstairs. Besides, she wasn't that eager to do it at all. It was just that someone had to, and as the only immortal present she had the best chance of surviving an attack by the women.

"No, no. Leave the crates Shawn has stacked against the bars," Brittany was saying when Quinn led Jet into the very back room in the basement where the booze box was. It seemed the assistant manager had changed her mind on their being necessary now that she'd seen what they were contending with. Quinn supposed she was imagining Nika's gray, snakelike arms and clawed fingers reaching through the bars to grab and tear at them.

"Don't be ridiculous, Brittany. There won't be enough room for all of us with the crates," Jason said impatiently.

"There will have to be," Brittany said sharply. "We can sit on each other's laps if necessary, but those crates need to stay . . . Or do you want to be the one on the outside of the group with nothing stopping that . . . *thing* upstairs from reaching through the bars and clawing at you?"

It was all she had to say. Mouth thinning, Jason and the others set down the crates they'd started to remove and turned their attention to the ones in the center instead. With all of them working, it took less than a moment to remove the remaining crates, and then the small group began to crowd into the center of the cage.

"You too," Quinn said when Jet remained by the door where he'd taken up position to watch the basement hall for their pursuers' approach.

"We need to blockade this door first," Jet muttered, pushing it closed.

Wondering why she hadn't thought of that herself, Quinn nodded and glanced around. The only things in the room with any weight to them were the crates of alcohol that had been removed from the cell. She and Jet worked quickly, carting the crates over and stacking them in front of the door. She suspected it was a waste of energy and the crates wouldn't slow them down for more than the second or two it would take to push the door open with the added weight, but it was better than nothing.

Worried about the Russians reaching them at any moment, Quinn didn't bother hiding her strength, carting crates stacked four and more high compared to the two or three Jet could manage. She heard the murmurings that caused among the people crowded inside the cell who could see, but ignored it.

"That's the last crate," Jet said grimly as he set it down.

Quinn nodded. "You need to get in the cell with the others now."

Jet frowned and hesitated, his gaze sliding from the door, to her, to the cell, and then he shook his head and hefted the shotgun he held. "I'll stay out and help you."

"You can't help me, Jet," she said solemnly. "They can control you."

"But—"

"Look," she interrupted, fear making her lose her temper. "I'm not some black belt fighter like my sister. I've never even been near a fight before this. It's going to be tricky enough without my having to worry about keeping you from shooting me in the back or going to one of them while I'm fighting another. Just get in the damned cell and let me do what I can."

Concern creasing the corners of his eyes, Jet nodded, handed her the shotgun, and started to turn toward the cell, but then paused and swung back. Much to her amazement he grabbed her by the upper arms, dragged her up against his chest, and bent to kiss her.

Quinn suspected he had meant it to be a very swift kiss, a peck, really. Meant to convey his gratitude, his worry, and every other emotion they were all experiencing. But they were life mates. Or at least they were something, Quinn acknowledged, because despite the situation and the terror of the moment, the second his lips touched hers, the world melted away and they were clinging and trying to devour each other right there between the frightened people in the cell and the blockaded door.

It was a crash from the floor above that finally had them breaking the kiss.

"They're inside," Quinn panted, her fingers tightening on the shotgun she held between them. Then she stepped back out of his hold. "You better get in the cell."

Jet's mouth thinned, but he didn't argue this time and allowed her to urge him to the cell. The people inside were pretty much on top of each other already, but managed to make enough room for him to squeeze in. Quinn closed the door behind him and then frowned and glanced up at the people inside. "How do I lock this?"

"There's a padlock on the shelf against the wall," Shawn told her.

Quinn found it and quickly locked the cell door closed, trying to ignore the fact that the door was the only part of the cell not protected with a stack of crates . . . and Jet was pressed up against it.

"There's nothing we can do about it now," he said quietly when she raised her distressed gaze to his. "Go on. I have faith in you."

Quinn managed a crooked smile and turned to face the barricaded door to the room. She raised the shotgun to aim at the door, and then bit her lip. The door was a good fifteen feet away and she'd never used a shotgun before. She'd probably miss anyone coming through the door at this range, she thought unhappily, and moved closer, stopping ten feet from the door for a moment before moving another couple of feet toward it.

Deciding that was close enough, Quinn raised the gun again and aimed for the center of the door. She then held her breath and listened for any sound that could tell her where the Russians were. She heard movement upstairs. It sounded like running feet and then another mournful shriek reached them. It was followed by a loud scraping sound overhead.

"That's the filing cabinets," Jason said, his voice unnaturally high.

She heard Jet curse and someone else praying, and they listened to the thundering footsteps overhead move toward the back of the building more slowly than she expected. They were searching each room was her guess as she listened. It seemed like a decade had passed when she noticed that the noises were coming from somewhere outside the door of the room they were in, and then the crates began to shake and tremble as the door opened, pushing them across the floor. Quinn closed her eyes and pulled the trigger on the shotgun. The weapon jumped in her arms, jerking back sharply into her shoulder. Wincing at the pain, she opened her eyes and blinked when she found herself staring at Lucian Argeneau. The man wasn't looking at her, though;

he was staring down at the huge hole in his shoulder where she'd shot him.

Raising his head, he arched one eyebrow at her. "Somehow I expected you to be happier to see us."

"Oh, shit," Quinn breathed, and dropped the gun.

Seven

"I'm so sorry. Oh my God, I can't believe I did that," Quinn babbled, whipping off her shirt and balling it up as she rushed across the room to Lucian Argeneau. Going up on her tiptoes, she pressed the cloth against the man's wounded shoulder to stop the bleeding, as she assured him, "I never would have pulled the trigger if I'd realized it was you."

"Which you surely would have known if you'd bothered to open your eyes before pulling the trigger," Lucian Argeneau growled through clenched teeth as she put pressure on his wound.

"Or if you'd bothered to call out or knock or something," Quinn pointed out a bit sharply with annoyance. "Why the hell didn't you? Now I'm going to have to live with shooting the great Lucian Argeneau. Dear God, like I don't have enough on my conscience," she muttered, lifting the cloth to see that the bleeding was slowing incredibly quickly. Of course it was. He was immortal, she reminded herself. Still, she pressed the cloth tightly back in place, rather pleased when Lucian sucked in a sharp breath.

Glowering down at her, he snapped, "I was being quiet because I didn't want to warn anyone that we were here until we found Kira and Liliya."

"Quiet my ass," Quinn snorted with disgust. "We could hear you pounding around—Wait! You haven't found the women?" she asked with alarm.

"We have Nika and Marta, but not Kira and Liliya," he growled, pulling her hand and the balled-up cloth away from his shoulder. "Where are they?"

"How the hell am I supposed to know?" Quinn asked with agitation, and slapped the cloth determinedly back to his shoulder. "The only one I saw was Nika. Though we did hear another window break around the side while she was at the front."

"So, is it safe to come out, or not?" Jet asked from behind them. "'Cause it's kind of hard to breathe in here with us all squished together like this. I think one of the girls has already fainted and I'm feeling a little lightheaded myself."

Quinn glanced around with concern at that, her eyes widening with dismay when she saw that Jet was being crushed against the bars by the crowd behind him as they struggled for room to breathe.

"Anders!" Lucian suddenly bellowed right in her ear. "Get in here. I found the mortals."

"Did he say mortals?" Brittany asked as Quinn turned back to Lucian Argeneau and slapped at his hand to keep him from pulling away the cloth she had pressed to his shoulder.

"Stop that. We have to stop the bleeding," she told him sharply.

"I am immortal," he reminded her. "The nanos will stop the bleeding. I need blood, not a doctor."

"No blood," a beautiful mocha-skinned man announced, entering the room. "We just gave the last of it to Kira and Liliya."

"You found them?" Quinn asked, relief soaking through her the moment the man nodded.

The fellow—Anders, she presumed—ran wide eyes over her in her bra and slacks as she again slapped Lucian's hand away from the cloth she was holding to his chest. His lips twitched with amusement, but he said, "Yes. Kira was hurt pretty badly, but was still in control of herself. However, her injury weakened her. Liliya was just helping her across the yard to the lodge when they were spotted."

"I'm so glad," Quinn breathed, relieved to know Liliya hadn't been hurt.

"Uh, Quinn?"

Frowning, she glanced back to the cage, her concern deepening as she took in Jet's coloring.

"Here," she said, grabbing Anders's hand and pressing it over the cloth on Lucian's shoulder before sliding her own out. "Hold that for a minute," she ordered, and then rushed over to the cage to grab the padlock. Quinn stared at it blankly for a minute and then lifted her head and asked, "Does Shawn still have the keys? Shawn?"

There was murmuring from behind Jet, and then he groaned as he was pressed even more tightly against the bars as the people behind him tried to move to look for Shawn.

"Oh my God, he's on the floor. I don't think he's breathing," someone cried.

Cursing, Quinn snapped the padlock off the cell and caught Jet when the door swung open and he started to fall out.

"Breathe, Jet," she muttered, dragging him away from the door so the others could escape. Quinn set him down against the wall, checked to be sure that he was still breathing, and then straightened and hurried into the now nearly empty cell. Jason and Brittany were the only ones still inside with the unconscious man. Jason was watching as Brittany performed mouth-to-mouth on the unconscious man.

Quinn urged him out of the way, and knelt to take Shawn's pulse. Much to her relief there was one. The young man was still alive.

"He's waking up," Brittany said with relief.

Quinn peered at Shawn's face, smiling when he opened his eyes and stared at her.

"Are you an angel?" he asked faintly.

Quinn's eyebrows rose slightly, but she merely shook her head and scooped him up to carry him out of the cell. Even with most of the people who had been crammed in there gone, the inside of the cell was still hot and airless. She set him down next to Jet, who was awake now and looking much better, then she straightened and peered around, scowling when she saw that Anders was not holding her shirt over Lucian's wound as she'd instructed.

She was about to head over to rectify that situation when something warm and heavy was draped over her shoulders. Glancing down she saw that it was Jet's aviator jacket. He was on his feet now, looking a little flush as he tried to tug it closed in front.

"Oh, thank you," she murmured, shrugging first one arm and then the other into the jacket.

"My pleasure," Jet growled, zipping up the front for her. "Young Shawn's eyes were about to fall out of his head he was goggling at you so hard."

Quinn's eyebrows rose at the jealousy she heard in his voice, and then she leaned up and kissed his cheek quickly, before taking his hand and drawing him with her as she went to where Lucian, Anders, and a third man were now talking. The newcomer was a dark-haired behemoth of a man who made her think of her brother-in-law for some reason. While Santo was bald and this man had long, dark hair, he was of a similar size to her brother-in-law. He also had a similar mouth and the same black eyes with silver in their depths, she noted. Her eyes widened slightly when Jet said, "Dante. Good to see you."

The large, dark-haired man turned a relieved smile on Jet, his gaze moving over him with concern as he stepped forward to shake his hand and say, "I am glad you are well, Jet. Abigail and Mary have been having fits."

Realizing then that he was Dante Notte, the brother-in-law of Jet's best friend/adopted sister, Abigail, Quinn left them to talk and moved over to Lucian.

"Stop poking at me, woman!" Lucian barked, swatting at her hand when she began tugging the ragged edges of his shirt away from the wound to get a look at it.

"I'm not poking. I'm a doctor, I'm examining," Quinn snapped.

"You're annoying," he countered with irritation.

"Well, that's gratitude for you," she muttered with disgust.

"Gratitude?" Lucian choked out with disbelief. "You shot me!"

"Only because you didn't warn me that it was you and not one of those crazed, blood-lusting loco Russians running around," Quinn responded, flushing with embarrassment, and then she bit her lip and asked, "How are you feeling? You lost a lot of blood. You aren't going to go all loco blood-lusty on us too, are you?"

Lucian scowled at her darkly and then growled, "Anders, take this creature and her mortal upstairs, please. I want them on the helicopter the minute it returns."

"Of course," Anders said mildly, and then arched an eyebrow. "Which one is her mortal?"

"The one presently attached to her hip, trying to look down his own jacket at her breasts," Lucian said dryly.

Quinn glanced around with a start to find that Jet and Dante had joined them. She was just quick enough to see him jerk his head up and scowl at Lucian. "I was just trying to make sure the jacket was done up enough to cover everything. It's a bit large on Quinn and the zipper doesn't come up as high on her as it does on me."

"Of course," Lucian said dryly, and raised an eyebrow at Anders. "Why are they still here?"

"Because I'm finding this amusing?" Anders suggested.

Dante burst out laughing at that, and then shook his head and offered, "I will see them out. I have to go back to the others and help with the cleanup anyway. Besides, I am sure you can use Anders's help down here."

Lucian grunted at that, which Quinn guessed was

agreement when Dante began to usher them from the room.

Quinn dragged her feet, though, and glanced over her shoulder toward the lodge workers, asking, "But what about Brittany and the others?"

"They will be taken care of," Dante assured her. "Everything will be taken care of. You are no longer on your own in this, Quinn. We will handle everything and you and Jet can rest now until the helicopter comes back."

"When will that be?" Jet asked as they made their way along the basement hall to the stairs.

"The helicopter was leaving to take Kira and her girls to Cochrane as I came below. The pilot said it would take close to an hour and fifteen minutes to get there. Figure fifteen minutes to half an hour for him to get Kira and her women off the helicopter and load it back up with blood and whatever else the pilot is bringing back, and then another hour and fifteen minutes to fly back," Dante calculated aloud. "So, probably about three hours," he announced apologetically.

"Three hours." Jet almost moaned the words as they started up the stairs. Quinn wasn't surprised. She was sure he must be as exhausted as she was. Besides which, she just wanted to get back to civilization and some form of normalcy.

"There are bedrooms upstairs," Dante pointed out. "If the two of you wish to lie down and rest for a while, I can come wake you up when the helicopter returns."

"That sounds good," Jet said, and then asked, "Do you have any food on you?"

"No," Dante said apologetically.

"No?" Jet nearly goggled at that news. "What the hell, man? You and Tomasso always have food on you. I've never seen you without it."

"I had Snickers bars, but I ate them all while we were searching," Dante admitted, and then said, "But surely they have food here?"

"They should," Quinn said, joining the conversation. "Brittany said the provisions were delivered with her and Jason yesterday," she told them, remembering that was one of the things the girl had babbled to her as she'd led the way back upstairs after the girl had shown her the booze box. Frowning, she added, "I don't know where the kitchen is, though."

"I do," Dante announced as they reached the upper hall. Slipping around them, he said, "Follow me." And led them up the hall, through the front room where Nika had thrust her arms through the window, and then down another hall on the other side of the building.

"Eat what you wish—Lucian will have it replaced before we finish here," Dante said as they entered a large kitchen. "But if you nap after, use the rooms nearer the stairs so I do not have to search half the place when the helicopter arrives."

"We will," Quinn and Jet said at the same time, and then smiled tiredly at each other as the other immortal left the room.

"Well, let's see what we have," Jet breathed, moving to the refrigerator and pulling the door open. "Wow. A lot of choice here."

"Oh?" Quinn moved beside him and pushed up onto her tiptoes to look over his arm at the contents on offer. Her eyes widened when she saw the fully stocked fridge. "Wow. Look at all those veggies and—"

"Oh, no," Jet said at once, nudging her away from the refrigerator. "Don't even look at the green stuff. You're eating real food, not salad and seeds."

"Nice idea, but your so-called 'real' food needs cooking, and I'm not much of a cook," Quinn admitted unhappily.

"Lucky for you, then, that I am," he said lightly, urging her toward the table in the center of the room. "Go sit down and I'll make us something."

Quinn smiled faintly as he hurried back to the refrigerator. He seemed a lot more chipper, his exhaustion falling away with the prospect of food before him. Dropping to sit on one of the chairs at the table, she asked, "So, how come you know how to cook?"

"Alcoholic mother, remember?" he said with amusement as he retrieved an onion, pepper, cheese, and milk from the fridge. "It was learn to cook or starve. I couldn't eat at Abs and her mom's house *every* night of the week."

"Oh," Quinn murmured, recalling that conversation about his mom from the dream. It seemed they'd definitely shared it, she thought as she watched him set the items he'd collected on the table and return to the refrigerator for eggs and a couple more items.

"Fortunately, Mom-Marge was happy to teach me to cook when I hung around at their house," Jet said, transferring the new items he'd gathered to the table and then moving off to start opening cupboards and drawers.

"You called her Mom-Marge?" Quinn asked with interest, following him with her eyes.

"Yeah." He smiled fondly as he returned to the table with a large bowl, a cutting board, and a paring knife. Setting them on the table with the rest of the stuff, he shrugged and added, "It's what she was." His smile faded now and he added grimly, "Unfortunately, the navy didn't see it that way when she died and I tried to get leave to attend the funeral. As far as they were concerned, if she wasn't a blood relation, I didn't need to attend." He shook his head grimly and sat down to start peeling an onion. "Actually, that's part of the reason I refused to sign on for another tour. I was so pissed at them for not letting me go to her funeral . . ." Expression turning sad, he shook his head unhappily. "I should have been there for Abs. And I never got to say goodbye to Mom-Marge."

Quinn reached out to touch his arm in sympathy and Jet looked up with surprise and then smiled at her crookedly, before turning his attention back to the onion and murmuring, "You're good with sharp things. Why don't you grab a knife and help me by slicing up the pepper?"

"That I can do," Quinn said with forced cheer, and stood to go find a knife. It took opening a couple drawers, but she finally found one and returned to the table to set to work on the green pepper, cutting it in half and removing the seeds. She started to slice the pepper into long strips and then slice those into pieces, and then paused to ask, "Like this?"

Jet checked out what she'd cut so far and nodded. "Perfect."

"Great," she said wryly, returning to slicing. "I may have had to give up surgery, but at least I have veggie slicing to fall back on."

Jet chuckled at her comment and said, "I don't know. Seems to me you have lots of skills besides wielding a scalpel."

"Like what?" she asked with disbelief. Wielding a

scalpel was pretty much all she knew. Quinn was very aware that she was a one-trick pony.

"You handle a gun pretty well," he pointed out, and teased, "You blasted a nice big hole in Lucian downstairs."

"Ha, ha," Quinn said dryly.

Voice more serious, and concentration on the onion he was dicing, Jet added, "And you saved the lives of eight mortals today. That's pretty impressive."

"*We* saved them," Quinn said firmly.

Jet snorted at the claim and said cheerfully, "Well, that's bullshit."

"It's true," she insisted. "I couldn't have done it without you."

"All I did was slow you down. You could have reached the lodge quicker if you hadn't had to drag me around," he pointed out, and then he raised his head and met her gaze solemnly, and said, "You don't have to worry about my ego, Quinn. I know what I'm good at and what I'm not. It doesn't bother me that I needed you to survive today, and last night. Someday there may be a situation where I can save our asses. This was not one of those days." He shrugged. "It's not a big deal."

Quinn watched silently as he worked. He really didn't seem bothered by the fact that she'd had to save him and the others. Not that she really had. The arrival of Lucian and his men is what really saved them, but she *had* carried Jet here, and then she'd dragged Jason away from the window before Nika could grab him. She'd also kept Jet from going to Nika when the Russian had taken control of him, and then she'd placed herself in front of them all, ready to fight for them down in the basement . . . And Jet didn't mind.

That was rather surprising to her. Patrick would have had fits at the idea of her saving him. Actually, he would have made it impossible for her to do so. He wouldn't have let her carry him unless he was unconscious, and once here he would have tried to take charge rather than share decisions with her as Jet had. And when it came to getting into the cage, he wouldn't have. He would have insisted on taking the shotgun and staying out of the cage, whether it meant risking being controlled and made to shoot her or not. His ego wouldn't have allowed anything else.

She wondered why the two men would have reacted so differently. Why would Patrick have needed to try to control everything and try to be the hero when he couldn't, while Jet was okay with stepping back and letting her handle things when the situation called for it? She didn't see him as any less manly because of it. Actually, it was the opposite. Jet seemed stronger to her than Patrick ever had. He was more dependable somehow, more self-assured, maybe. He knew his strengths, but he also knew his comparative weaknesses as a mortal and didn't try to pretend they didn't exist or were something to be ashamed of. He treated them like they were just a part of him rather than something to cover up.

"Here we go."

Quinn glanced up, surprised to see that while she'd been distracted with her thoughts, Jet had finished dicing the onions, found a grater and grated the cheese, and even mixed the eggs and milk and whisked them to a frothy state.

"What can I do?" Quinn asked as he found a frying pan and set it on the stove.

"There's juice in the fridge. Why don't you pour us

both a glass? Or maybe make coffee. Or both," he added wryly.

Quinn went for the third option and made coffee as well as pouring them both a glass of juice. She then found plates and silverware to set the table and finally found bread and started to make toast. That, she could manage. By the time she'd made four slices of toast and buttered them, Jet was cutting the omelet in half and sliding a portion onto each of the plates she'd set on the table.

"Wow," Quinn murmured as she set the toast on the table and sat down. "That smells good. I guess you really can cook."

"Maybe you should try it before you make such statements," Jet said with amusement as he set the frying pan in the sink and quickly ran water into it. Joining her a moment later, he noted that she hadn't even tried it yet, and said, "Dig in."

Quinn picked up her fork and knife and a moment later slid a piece of the omelet into her mouth. She then groaned appreciatively.

"Yeah?" Jet asked with a grin, cutting into his own portion.

"Oh, yeah," she sighed with pleasure once she'd swallowed, and then, arching an eyebrow at him, she added, "Too much of your cooking and I won't have a bony ass anymore."

Jet stilled and then raised an apologetic face to hers. "I didn't mean that. My head was just pounding and I was cranky. Besides, you know nanos ensure you're at your peak condition. Peak to them isn't skeletal and bony. And it was actually the backs of your legs I was hitting. You were running, your muscles extended and hard when my head slammed into them. But your bum is actually really nice and soft and curvy. It fit perfectly into my hands when we were—" He cut himself off abruptly there and turned his attention back to the omelet almost desperately.

They were both silent for a moment, both eating and avoiding looking at each other, but then Quinn couldn't stand it anymore and said, "I know it was a shared dream, but I don't understand . . ." Frowning, she shook her head, but when Jet lifted his head to meet her gaze, she struggled on. "I don't know what was real and what wasn't. We were on the beach and I asked you to kiss me. That part was the dream, wasn't it?"

Jet nodded. "Yes."

"Right. And you did. Kiss me, I mean, and then . . ." She hesitated, recalling his hands moving over her body, the excitement and passion of it, the heated need, and blurted, "And then we were on the sand and you ripped my blouse open, and moved my bra aside and—" She broke off, her hand rising to cover one breast rather than say he'd been suckling at it, and she was surprised to feel her nipple tingle under the leather jacket as her hand moved over it. Quinn was positive her nipples were erect. Just the memory of what they'd done in the dream was affecting her.

Shaking her head, she hurried on, saying, "I opened my eyes and I was looking up through the branches of the pine we were under in reality," she admitted. "And afterward my blouse had been ripped open. The buttons were all missing. When did the dream stop and how did it become reality?"

She saw Jet swallow, and shift in his seat, and then he cleared his throat and said, "I don't know. The last thing

I recall before the dream is dragging you under the pine tree for cover. It was cold, and you were wet and shivering, and I spooned you. Maybe you rolled over in your sleep while we were dreaming and . . ." He shrugged helplessly. "Maybe we started to kiss in reality, while still asleep?"

"And you ripped my shirt open while we were asleep?" she asked uncertainly, and then pointed out, "But I was looking up through pine branches when I opened my eyes."

Jet licked his lips, his gaze dropping to her mouth and down lower to her hidden breasts, then he suddenly stood to carry his plate to the sink, mumbling, "As far as I know I didn't wake up until the dream ended when you suddenly pushed me away in it."

Standing, Quinn followed him with her plate and said, "I must have been awake before you, then. But if I woke up before you, why didn't the dream end sooner for you? You must have been awake too without realizing it."

"Maybe," Jet allowed, and stiffened when her arm brushed his as she set her plate in the sink.

"Quinn, honey, you're killing me here," he growled, turning the water on to rinse the plates. "I know you said you weren't ready for a life mate, and I'm trying to give you space, but I find you irresistible, and bringing this up has me hard as a bone. So, unless you want to be ravished on the kitchen table, I suggest you—" His words died abruptly when she clasped his arm and leaned up to press a kiss to the corner of his mouth.

Quinn knew she wasn't being fair. She really wasn't ready for a life mate, but she found him irresistible too, and he wasn't the only one who'd been excited by their discussion. She wanted him, and the idea of being ravished on the kitchen table excited the hell out of her. So she was relieved when Jet groaned in response and turned his head to claim her lips. Quinn opened her mouth at once to him, a moan sliding up her throat when his tongue delved in to fill her, and then he'd turned fully and his arms were around her, his hands clutching and squeezing the derriere he'd claimed fit into them perfectly.

When he lifted her by that hold, and pressed her tightly against his groin, Quinn gasped and wiggled against him, her legs wrapping around his hips and her arms snaking around his neck as she tried to get closer still.

Jet set her on a hard surface a moment later, but it was the counter, not the table, and suddenly his hands were everywhere. She didn't notice his undoing the zipper of the jacket, but felt him push it off her shoulders, and arched her back, offering her breasts to him. But he didn't caress and squeeze them right away as she'd hoped. Quinn didn't understand why until she felt his hands at the back of her bra, undoing the snaps. She shivered in anticipation as the lacy cloth loosened and fell away. When his warm, rough hands finally closed over her excited nipples, kneading the flesh of her small breasts, Quinn gasped into his mouth and shifted closer on the countertop until his groin pressed against hers again.

They both groaned then, the kiss briefly broken on the sounds as liquid heat poured through them at the move. Jet leaned his forehead on hers, his hands almost rough on her breasts, as he growled, "You're so fucking perfect. God, I love your body. I just want to—"

Quinn cried out and bucked on the countertop when

one of her breasts was released and that hand slid down and inside her pants to glide between her legs.

"Oh God, you're wet for me," he moaned with despair, and then kissed her violently as he began to caress her.

Quinn was kissing him back just as passionately when he tore his mouth away and rasped, "You have to tell me what you want, Quinn. I don't want to push you into—Ahhhh," he gasped when her hand found him through his dress slacks and closed over his erection.

"I want you," she muttered against his mouth, her hand rubbing over the length of his hardness and adding to the excitement a hundredfold. "Please, Jet," she moaned. "I want you inside me. I need—Oh God," she cried, her behind rising off the counter as one of his fingers slid inside of her and stayed there while his thumb ran circles around the nub of her enjoyment. "Yes, please. I—Oh God, just—"

Quinn clutched his shoulders and shook her head frantically. She wanted him to make love to her. She wanted to feel him inside of her, but knew that wasn't going to happen. There was already too much pleasure. They were too close, and then his finger slid out and thrust back in. Quinn couldn't hear his shout over her own cry as the pleasure exploded between them.

Eight

"Are you tired, or would you like to watch a movie or something?"

Quinn turned at that question from Mary Bonher Notte and watched as the blonde walked to a cooler plugged into the wall next to the first of the two double beds in the room. She wasn't surprised to see the neatly stacked bags of blood inside once it was open. Quinn also wasn't surprised when she felt the shifting taking place in her mouth as her fangs descended. She'd been experiencing cramps for the last hour and a half since she and Jet had boarded the helicopter to leave the fly-in fishing lodge.

"Movie or sleep?" Mary asked again, straightening with four bags of blood caught between her hands.

"Movie," Quinn decided as she watched Mary nudge the cooler lid closed with her knee. "Unless you're tired and just want to go to sleep?"

"No. I'm good," Mary assured her as she set three of the bags on the desk beside Quinn and then handed her the fourth. "You go ahead and get these down while I go to the bathroom, and then we'll see what's on the idiot box."

"Thank you." Quinn accepted the bag Mary was holding out, and then simply held it as she watched the blonde recross the room to slip into the bathroom by the entry door.

The moment the door closed, Quinn slapped the bag to her fangs and closed her eyes briefly as they started to draw in the blood her body needed. She stood like that until the first bag emptied. It wasn't until she'd replaced it with a second that Quinn bothered to look around at the motel room she was to share with Mary for however long they were in Cochrane.

Her gaze slid over the two double beds, the couch, and desk behind her that ran along the wall under a row of curtains hiding whatever view the wall of windows offered, and finally to the long built-in kitchenette opposite the beds. There were upper and lower cupboards, a fridge, sink, Keurig machine, and a selection of Keurig coffees as well as bowls holding packets of both sugar and creamer. The whole room was decorated in earth tones, from the rust-colored bedspreads to the dark brown leather couch.

Switching out the now empty second bag for another, Quinn sat down on the couch, her thoughts immediately going to Jet. He was in the room next door and she wondered what he was doing and how he felt about what had happened in the kitchen at the lodge.

They hadn't had a chance to talk after their little romp on the kitchen counter. Quinn had woken up on his chest on the kitchen floor sometime later at the sound of someone shouting their names. Alarmed as the voice drew closer, she'd leapt off of Jet, snatched up his jacket from where it lay on the floor, and just managed to pull it on and zip it up before Anders had appeared in the kitchen door.

"There you are," he'd said with exasperation. "Dante has searched every bedroom in this place for the two of you." His gaze had dropped then to Jet just stirring on the floor and the man had shaken his head before raising his gaze back to Quinn and lecturing, "Lesson number one for new life mates: always seek out soft surfaces before risking life mate sex. Especially if one of you is a mortal. Jet could have cracked his head open when you both fainted and you wouldn't want that."

Quinn was pretty sure she'd blushed like a schoolgirl at those words. She'd also immediately glanced to Jet to see what had given them away, but he was fully clothed.

She hadn't figured it out until Anders said, "Grab your bra off the floor, help your life mate up, and let's go. The helicopter is here."

Quinn could feel her blush deepening now at the memory, and reached into the pocket of Jet's jacket to tug out the scrap of white lace she'd shoved there after snatching it up off the floor. She hadn't had to help Jet up, though; by the time she'd grabbed the bra and moved to him, he'd been on his feet. He hadn't said a word, just bent to kiss her cheek, then took her arm and followed Anders outside to where the helicopter was waiting.

Talking on the helicopter had been impossible. Quinn had never been on one before, so had been rather amazed to find it so damned loud inside the thing. Even the noise-canceling headphones she'd been given to wear hadn't helped much, though she suspected that was because of her immortal hearing. Jet hadn't seemed bothered by the noise, but she'd been grateful to escape it when the helicopter had landed in Cochrane.

Cochrane was apparently a relatively small town of five thousand plus people and was one hundred and sixty miles from the fly-in fishing lodge.

Mary had told them that. The friendly blonde had been the one waiting to collect them from the airport and bring them to this motel. Mary Bonher Notte was married to Dante Notte, the twin brother of Abigail's husband, Tomasso. That family connection was part of the reason that she and Dante were up here in Northern Ontario, involved in the search and rescue operation. The couple had been visiting Marguerite when Mortimer had called with news of the missing plane.

Quinn had no idea why Marguerite had been contacted, unless the woman had been keeping tabs on her. But on hearing the news from Marguerite, Dante had immediately called his brother. He'd known that with Abigail's connection to Jet, she'd want to know. He'd spoken to both Tomasso and Abigail, and assured them he'd help with the search and rescue operation and would contact them as soon as Jet was found.

After explaining that, Mary had handed the phone to Jet and told him to call Abs. Dante had already called to let her know he was found and fine, she'd said, but she was sure Abigail wouldn't fully relax until she heard his voice.

While Jet was making his call, Mary then explained the other reason for the couple's presence here. Apparently, after calling his brother, Dante had followed that up by calling his cousin Santo, and spoken to him and

Quinn's sister, Pet, telling them what was happening. He'd then made the same promises to them as he had his brother: that he and Mary would head north at once and join the search party, and that they'd call when she was found.

Once Jet had finished reassuring Abs that he was fine and promised her he'd phone her again when he was home, he'd ended the call and passed the cell to Quinn so she could call her sister. Despite having already heard from Dante that she was fine, Pet had been relieved to hear her voice and had had Parker join the call on another line. But they'd only talked briefly before Mary had pulled into the motel. Quinn had told them both she loved them, asked them to give Santo her love, and promised to phone again once she was settled in Toronto and then ended the call to follow Mary out of the car.

Quinn didn't know which of them had been more surprised, she or Jet, when Mary had explained that they'd rented several of the motel rooms in a row and then handed Jet a key, saying, "This one is yours. You'll probably have it to yourself unless Dante gets back before you two leave. There's coffee, pop, food, and clean clothes in there. Go on in, take a shower, and relax. You probably have several hours before the plane gets here to take you to Toronto." As she'd turned to head toward the next room, she'd added, "Quinn and I will be just next door if you want company."

Quinn had hesitated briefly, but then managed a weak smile for Jet before following the other woman into this room. She hadn't known what else to do. It wasn't like she had a right to expect to stay with Jet. They weren't a couple or anything. Well, aside from that whole life mate business. But she'd admitted to Jet that she didn't think she was ready for a life mate, and one make-out session under a tree in the woods, and then something a little more than just making out in the kitchen of the lodge, did not make them a couple. Did it?

"Oh, dang. You probably want a shower or bath."

Quinn looked around at those words to see that Mary was out of the bathroom and eyeing her with a frown. Eyebrows rising at her expression, Quinn tugged the now empty fourth bag from her fangs and glanced down at herself. Jet's jacket was still in good shape, but her black dress slacks were a mess. They were wrinkled, torn in spots, and covered with dirt and even a couple of drops of blood. She supposed the blood was from when she'd hurt her stomach on the tree, and then noticed that her leather dress shoes were ruined and that her hands were just as dirty as her slacks. How long had she been running around looking like a kid who'd been making mud pies? she wondered.

"I ran out and bought both you and Jet clean clothes the minute I got here. It's just a T-shirt, jeans, cotton panties, and a bra, but I figured they'd do until you had your own clothes back," Mary said. Smiling wryly then, she added, "I wasn't even sure if you'd need fresh clothes. They hadn't located the plane yet when we arrived and we didn't know what to expect. We had no idea what was happening—if the plane had just been forced to land early at another airport, or on a highway, or—" She ended on a shrug, but Quinn suspected what she wasn't saying was that they hadn't been sure if the plane hadn't gone up in a ball of flames on crashing and she wouldn't need clothes at all because she'd have been ashes.

Standing, Quinn gathered the empty blood bags and deposited them in the garbage as she said, "A shower and clean clothes would be great. Thank you for thinking of them."

"My pleasure. I was happy to be able to do something useful while waiting for news," Mary admitted, moving to the desk under the curtained windows and scooping up a department store bag that she then handed to her. "There's a hairbrush, soap, shampoo, and cream rinse in there too, and a razor and blades."

"Thanks." Quinn smiled warmly as she took the bag, really appreciating her thoughtfulness. "I'll be quick."

"No, you take your time if you want. You might enjoy a soak after everything you've been through."

Nodding, Quinn turned and headed into the bathroom with the bag, but had no intention of a long soak. She rarely had time in her life for soaking in a tub. At least she didn't used to, she thought unhappily. Dr. Quinn Peters had always been too busy to waste time on a soak. She'd done nothing but shower for a good twenty years thanks to her schedule, first as an intern and then as a surgeon, and while she'd had more time these last four years, she hadn't changed her habits. A shower would do. At least that's what she thought until she'd got a look at her hairy legs. Quinn immediately squawked with alarm and dropped the stopper in the tub, then pushed in the button to switch the water from the showerhead to the tap to run a bath.

"Quinn? Is everything all right?" Mary called through the door. "You made a funny sound."

"I'm okay," Quinn called out, then grabbed one of the large towels hanging over the towel bar, wrapped it around herself, and opened the door to explain. "I just got a glimpse of my legs and realized a bath might be better so I can shave."

"Ah." Mary nodded wisely. "It's so much easier to shave sitting down than standing. I once had a friend who slipped in the shower while shaving and sliced out a chunk of her ankle. A real mess," she pronounced, wrinkling her nose. "I've shaved in the bath ever since."

"Hmm. Well, I don't normally bathe, but I haven't shaved my legs in four years, so sitting down for it seems like a good idea," Quinn said grimly, glancing down at her hairy legs. "God, a person could be forgiven for mistaking me for Sasquatch."

Mary's eyebrows rose. "I don't know whether to ask why you haven't shaved for so long, or why you're bothering to now."

"Oh . . . er . . ." Quinn flushed with embarrassment, but didn't know what to say, so just shook her head and started to close the door.

"Shout if you need anything," Mary said, turning away.

"Thanks," Quinn murmured as the door closed. She then leaned her forehead against it briefly, before moving to check on the tub.

Even with four years' worth of body hair to remove, Quinn was quick at her bath, but then she spent several more minutes rinsing out the tub before getting dressed and running the hairbrush through her wet tresses. There was no makeup in the bag, but Quinn didn't mind. She hadn't worn makeup since waking up after the turn, so once she'd finished brushing her hair, she dropped the brush in the bag with the other items and then glanced down at herself in the jeans and T-shirt.

Quinn hadn't worn jeans in a very long time. She

didn't even own a pair anymore and hadn't since med school. Her daily outfit was made up of dress pants and blouses and had been since graduating. Patients expected a certain professionalism from their doctors, even when they spotted them outside of the office. At least that was what Patrick had always said. Now she peered down at the jeans and tried to decide if she liked them or not. They seemed heavier to her in comparison to dress slacks, and they were definitely snugger, hugging her body almost lovingly. But then so did the white T-shirt, she acknowledged, wondering if her bra was visible through the white cotton. She didn't bother looking in the mirror to see. It didn't matter anyway. The bra was white like the T-shirt and she didn't have anything else to put on, so she grabbed the bag, stuffed her dirty dress slacks and panties into it, grabbed Jet's jacket, and headed out to join Mary for that movie she'd mentioned.

"Are you all right?"

Quinn pulled herself from her thoughts and glanced around at Mary at that question. Sitting up a little straighter where she sat on the double bed closer to the window, she nodded quickly. "I'm fine."

Mary nodded slowly, but then said. "You don't really appear to be interested in this movie. Should I find something else?"

"No, no," Quinn said quickly, and grimaced before admitting, "I was just thinking. This is fine." She focused on the screen where Indiana Jones was talking.

"Okay," Mary said slowly, and then asked, "Is there something troubling you? Did you want to talk about it?"

"No. I'm good," Quinn said at once, turning to offer her a smile.

Mary nodded, but said, "If you change your mind, just let me know and we can have a natter."

Quinn nodded, turned toward the TV briefly, and then swung her head back around to Mary and asked, "What do you know about life mates?"

Mary hit the mute button on the television and shifted on the bed to face her sitting cross-legged. She raised her eyebrows and asked, "What do you mean? Are you asking who I know are life mates, or—"

"No," Quinn interrupted, and explained, "I mean, what are they exactly?"

Mary seemed startled by the question and Quinn supposed she, like Jet, would have expected an immortal who had been turned more than four years ago to already know this, but Mary didn't ask about that. Instead, she said, "Well, life mates are what the name suggests. They are life partners for immortals." Mary paused briefly, a dissatisfied expression on her face, and then shook her head. "That doesn't really do it justice, I suppose. They are much more than life partners."

"How?" Quinn asked.

"Well, immortals, as you know, can control and hear the thoughts of mortals and even immortals who are younger than them."

"You mean read them," Quinn suggested. "They read our thoughts."

Mary's eyebrows rose. "You've been an immortal for more than four years, Quinn. Surely, you've noticed that you don't always have to read thoughts from people to hear them. At least with mortals."

"Really?" she asked with surprise.

Mary stared at her for a minute, and then frowned. "You haven't learned to read and control mortals yet."

When Quinn shrugged uncomfortably, and glanced down at her crossed legs to avoid her gaze. Mary sighed, and then said, "Okay. I've only been an immortal a year longer than you, but I've found while they call it reading thoughts, that isn't always what is happening."

Quinn's eyebrows rose at this news. She hadn't realized Mary hadn't been born immortal, but asked, "What *is* happening, then?"

"Well," Mary said, "sometimes, even when I'm not trying to read a person's mind, their thoughts come at me. They're usually disjointed, just fragments, but they still come without my trying to read them."

"Really?" Quinn asked with surprise.

"Yes. It seems to be thoughts with strong emotion behind them: anger, hatred, fear . . ." She shrugged. "I would guess it's their emotions spilling over. They are having trouble containing the emotion connected to the thought and so the thought spills out too." She tilted her head. "You haven't experienced that around mortals?"

Quinn shifted uncomfortably and admitted, "I haven't been around mortals since I was turned."

Mary's eyes widened. "Not even to practice and train in feeding and . . . ?" Her voice trailed off when Quinn shook her head stiffly.

"I see," Mary murmured. She was silent for a minute, and then sat up a little straighter and said, "Well, that can happen: thoughts coming at you free-flow without your attempting to read them," she explained, and then added, "It can be a bit distressing at first. Especially if you're in a public space where there is a large crowd of mortals. You'll have these thoughts and feelings coming at you from all directions—a word here, a fragment of a thought there accompanied by anger or pain or grief. It's like standing in a room with several radios on, each with a different station playing and not one of them properly tuned in. It's just squawking all around you," she explained. "It could drive you crazy if you didn't block it, but constantly having to block other people's thoughts and feelings can get exhausting pretty quickly."

"Something else to look forward to," Quinn muttered unhappily.

"Yes. Well, it can only be worse for older immortals. I'm sure they pick up more," Mary pointed out. "And then on top of that is the need to keep your own thoughts to yourself and try to block others from reading them, or yourself from broadcasting them to others."

"We can stop others from reading us?" Quinn asked with interest. She did find it annoying not to have a lick of privacy when everyone around her could read her thoughts.

"Yes. It takes practice, and it doesn't always work if the immortal near you is really old, but we can put up sort of a mental wall like a privacy fence between our thoughts and the world at large," Mary assured her. "Of course, having to do that for hours is exhausting too."

"Of course," Quinn said dryly. What about being an immortal wasn't hard? she thought grimly. Drinking blood was disgusting, losing everything you ever knew and loved was unbearably hard, and—

"That's why life mates are so important," Mary said now, distracting Quinn from her inner griping. "Life mates can't read or hear each other's thoughts and can't control each other. It gives an immortal someone they can be with without having to keep their guard up, and that's important," she assured her solemnly. "A lot of older immortals tend to withdraw from society to avoid all of that, and that can lead to their going rogue. But with a life mate, they don't have to be alone. They have someone they can be with and be relaxed and at peace with, and that person, their life mate, is more important to them than life itself."

"I see," she murmured, and kind of did. At least she understood what Mary was saying, but it didn't really have any relevance to her. She couldn't read minds, and hadn't noticed picking up on anyone's thoughts or feelings. Of course, every immortal she'd met since being turned was ages older than her, except for Pet and Parker, and she had avoided being around mortals since the turn. She didn't go shopping or . . . well, anywhere. She'd mostly stuck around Marguerite's home in Toronto, and then Santo and Pet's. When she'd moved out of their place to the small cottage she'd rented in Italy, she'd stayed there, avoiding people—both mortal and immortal alike—as much as she could. Really, until getting on the plane in Italy for Toronto, she hadn't seen anyone but Pet, Santo, and Parker for three and a half years. She'd become a shut-in, she realized unhappily.

Sighing, she asked, "How do you know if you've met your life mate?"

Surprise again flickered on Mary's face, but she cleared her throat and answered the question. "There are several signs with an older immortal. Apparently, after a century or two of life, most immortals tend to weary of the more sensual pursuits."

"You can't mean sex?" Quinn asked, sure she couldn't. While her interest in it had dropped off with Patrick by the end of their marriage, Quinn couldn't imagine ever getting tired of it with Jet. God, just thinking about it made goose bumps rise all over her body.

"Yes, sex is one of the things they tire of. Food is another," Mary told her. "I asked Dante's older sister, Bellela, about it once and she said, 'Imagine one thousand soulless one-night stands in a row that were just passable or all right, or imagine eating steak for the thousandth time as well. Everything becomes boring eventually, even living.'"

Quinn grunted at that. She used to like salad and such at one time, but after ten years of salads and seeds and little else, it all just tasted like dreck to her, so she supposed everything could get boring eventually. But— "What has that to do with life mates?"

"Well, while a single immortal can weary and start abstaining from such pleasures, on meeting a life mate an immortal's desires are reawakened, including their desire for, and enjoyment of, food and sex," she explained. "It's one of the symptoms of having met a life mate."

"Oh," Quinn sighed. While she'd grown bored with salad, she hadn't stopped enjoying muffins and yummy things like that. She just hadn't allowed herself to eat them. This symptom did not help her at all.

"Another symptom is that all immortals, even really old ones who no one can usually read, are suddenly easily read by everyone. Although, again, I would say that the reading part isn't really necessary. Their emotions are so new and raw and powerful that I think they are projecting big-time. That is another symptom."

Quinn just shook her head. Since she had no idea about how to block her thoughts from being read, and was such a new turn on top of that, basically every immortal she encountered could read her. So, again, this wasn't helpful for her.

"And then there's the shared pleasure."

Quinn glanced at her sharply. "Shared pleasure?"

"Hmm." Mary nodded. "You share each other's pleasure during sexual pursuits. Touching him brings pleasure to yourself as well and vice versa, but you also share the pleasure you're both experiencing. It merges and builds in mounting waves that grow bigger with each pass until it feels like you're drowning in it. That's why new life mates faint the first year or three after finding each other. Their minds have to adjust to such heightened passion and excitement."

Quinn bit her lip. She wasn't sure about the sharing pleasure part. She had touched Jet, but both times she'd only done it after he was already caressing her, so had just thought what she was experiencing was from what he was doing. They *had* fainted, though, after finding their release.

"And shared dreams are another."

Quinn sat up straight at that announcement. "Shared dreams are a symptom of life mates?"

"Yes. Only life mates can share dreams," Mary said, eyeing her with interest. "You and Jet have shared your dreams?"

"I—" Quinn hesitated briefly, and then admitted, "I think so. I mean, I know we did, but then it kind of spilled over into reality and I don't—" Sighing, Quinn simply described the dream to her, including the sexual parts and the ending. She did so in about as clinical a manner as possible, and ended with a plaintive, "But I don't know when the dream ended and reality started.

Or even how it happened for certain, though Jet seems to think I must have turned to him during the dream and because we were so close we just started acting it out in real life as we were dreaming."

"I suspect he's right," Mary said with a nod. "I've never heard of it happening before, but from what I understand, usually when life mates have shared dreams they aren't in the same bed or grassy knoll. But if he was spooning you when he fell asleep and you were face-to-face when you realized you were biting him, it would seem to me that you must have rolled toward him while dreaming and the two of you started acting out what you were doing in the dream."

Quinn nodded solemnly, and then released her breath on a dispirited puff and asked, "So he is my life mate?"

"Yes. That seems obvious," Mary assured her, and then smiled crookedly. When Quinn just slumped unhappily, she pointed out gently, "Most immortals would be grateful to have met their life mate. Especially so soon. Many have to wait centuries or even millennia before finding their life mate."

"Yes, well, most of them probably aren't as screwed up as me, and don't have a boatload of crap to sort out before they should even be considering taking on a life mate," Quinn said bitterly.

Mary actually grinned at that, but wiped the expression from her face when Quinn scowled at her. "Sorry," she murmured. "But I'm afraid you're wrong about that."

Quinn blinked at those words and then asked uncertainly, "About what?"

"Quinn, I haven't met a single solitary person in my life, mortal or immortal, who hasn't been just as screwed up as you feel you are," she assured her. "They may be screwed up differently, or they may already have sorted out their boatload of crap, but nobody gets through life without trauma and tragedy touching them and bending them one way or another. Everyone just hides their bent parts from others because they want to seem normal when the truth is there *is* no normal. Abnormal is really the normal."

Quinn shook her head. "I worked with a lot of people at the hospital who were perfectly normal without traumas and—"

"Do you really think so?" Mary asked with amusement. "And what do you think they thought of you?"

"What?" Quinn asked with confusion.

"Don't you think they saw you the same way? The beautiful and brilliant cardiothoracic surgeon with the equally brilliant son, and handsome oncologist husband. The happy nuclear family, supportive and loving, and you always presenting a put-together professional front. I'm sure they had no idea that your marriage was crumbling and your son was ignored by his father, or that you were struggling to hold it all together."

"You've read my mind," Quinn said stiffly with resentment.

"No," she assured her quietly. "You're projecting . . . and have been since I picked you up from the airport."

"I am?" Quinn asked with alarm.

"Oh, yes. Very loudly and very strongly," Mary assured her. "I'm not just being bombarded with a word here or there, or a fragment of thought or feelings. Your mind is shouting whole chapters out to the world and your emotions are all over the place."

"Oh God," Quinn moaned, wondering who all had

heard her shouting mind. The Russians? Lucian? Anders? Dante?

"Any immortal who has encountered you has probably heard it," Mary assured her.

"Even Pet and Parker?" she asked with alarm. "They were turned the same time as me."

"Perhaps they were, but I suspect they haven't been neglecting their training and practice as you obviously have," she said quietly. "So yes, I'm sure they have been bombarded by your thoughts and feelings whether they wanted to or not."

Quinn scowled at the suggestion. She hadn't neglected her training; she'd simply refused it outright. She hadn't asked to be turned into a damned vampire, and she didn't want to be one, so she'd refused to learn anything that had to do with immortals.

"That's a very dangerous attitude to take," Mary said solemnly. "Not just for you, but for any mortals you encounter and even for immortals, which includes your son and sister now. Being able to read mortals helps us know if they are a threat. If they mean us harm, but also if they've seen or heard something that might give away our existence. And being able to control them helps us prevent their doing or saying anything to harm us or give away our existence until their memories can be changed or wiped. These are abilities that protect all immortals from exposure and eradication, and very necessary." She shook her head. "I'm amazed that you've been allowed to mingle with mortals when you haven't had the proper training."

Quinn waved that away impatiently. "I told you, I don't mingle with mortals. I hadn't mingled with anyone but Pet, Parker, and Santo in three and a half years until the plane crashed," she told her, but was more concerned with the possibility that Parker might have been able to read and hear her thoughts. She'd never considered that and didn't like having to now, though it would explain why he'd avoided her as much as possible the last couple of years or better. Frowning over that, she said, "You don't really think Parker could hear or read my thoughts, do you? I mean, immortals aren't supposed to be able to read older immortals and I'm almost thirty years older than him."

"The older immortal bit isn't referencing biological age, Quinn, but how long a person has been immortal. A twenty-year-old born immortal would have no problem reading a newly turned fifty-, sixty-, or even eighty-year-old immortal. It's skill level, not really how old they are," Mary explained. "And you and Parker are the same age when it comes to when you were turned . . . only he has no doubt been training and practicing while you haven't. So yes, I'm sure Parker can read and hear your thoughts," Mary told her, and then added, "But I'm more concerned about you, Quinn. You're a walking bundle of pain and rage. You're furious and hurt by what you see as your husband's betrayal. And you're soaking in guilt over not being able to save your son from him. You're howling so loud inside that it would be impossible not to hear it, and I suspect you have been for the last four years."

She paused briefly to shake her head and then said, "I don't know how you bear it. Why haven't you arranged to talk to someone? You don't have to feel this way. You shouldn't *have* to feel this way."

Quinn felt tears sting her eyes and lowered her head to hide them, but her mind was repeating Mary's words in her head. A bundle of pain and rage? Damned right she was. Patrick had taken everything from her. Her home, her career, her friends, even her humanity, and then the bastard went and got himself killed, leaving her to deal with the fallout.

"Your humanity?"

Quinn lifted her head at Mary's words. "What?"

"Your husband stole your humanity?" Mary asked quietly.

Quinn's mouth tightened. It was damned annoying not even having your thoughts to yourself.

"Is that how you see yourself now? Inhuman? A monster?" Mary asked softly.

An image of Nika flashed through her mind—neck twisted, body emaciated, fingers almost locked in bird-like claws. Quinn could even hear her voice like grated glass in her ears. "Cooome, Jee-ot."

"Nika was sick," Mary said quietly.

"She was in the throes of blood lust," Quinn countered. "She was scary as hell and would have ripped Jet to shreds. She even looked like a monster, a cross between a zombie and—"

"Funny, because the image that flashed through your mind when you thought of her looked more like a picture I once saw of those poor victims of concentration camps like Auschwitz. Or maybe even like one or two cancer patients I've counseled who were at death's doorstep, emaciated and colorless," Mary said solemnly.

Quinn looked away, her mouth tightening, because Mary was right. Working in the hospital, she'd seen more than one cancer patient who had looked not unlike Nika. But—

Turning back, she said solemnly, "Cancer patients

don't have fangs. We do, and we feed off the blood of mortals."

"We need to take in bagged blood to survive, just like hemophiliacs occasionally need, or people with thrombocytopenia, anemia, kidney disease, liver disease, sickle cell disease, and countless other illnesses." She raised her eyebrows. "Are they monsters too?"

"They don't have fangs," Quinn said stubbornly.

"Okay, so you're a monster," Mary said with a shrug. "What about Pet and Parker?"

"What about them?" Quinn asked warily.

"Are they monsters too?"

"No!" Quinn gasped with horror.

"Why not? They're immortal. So, if your being immortal means you're a monster, so are they," Mary reasoned.

Quinn frowned at her logic and shook her head. "But—"

"But?"

"Parker isn't a monster. He's a victim," she said miserably.

"And you aren't?"

"I'm the idiot who married Patrick." Sighing, she closed her eyes briefly and then added, "I married him, and then rather than divorce him when I should have, I just let things go because it was easier than having to deal with it . . . and Parker paid the price."

"I see," Mary said quietly. "So, is that what the last four years have been about? Punishing yourself for what happened to Parker?"

Quinn blinked her eyes open with surprise. "I haven't been punishing myself."

"Haven't you?" she asked softly. "You certainly haven't

done anything to make yourself happy, or to help you move past this. You haven't even considered what you want to do professionally, or where you want to live permanently. You rented a house in Italy close to your sister and then shut yourself into it, stewing in your misery. You haven't done a thing for yourself. You haven't even shaved your legs in four years, Quinn," she pointed out, and then admitted, "I originally thought perhaps it was depression, but now I suspect you've been punishing yourself . . . or perhaps it's a combination of the two."

Quinn closed her eyes again, considering that. Had she been depressed? She'd felt so angry she hadn't considered that she might be depressed. She hadn't even realized that anger was a part of depression. She'd thought it was just sadness, hopelessness, and exhaustion. Although to be honest, she'd suffered all three of those the last four years too.

As for punishing herself . . . as much as her first instinct had been to deny it, she may have been doing that. If so, it was probably no less than she deserved. She'd failed Parker miserably. Sighing, she opened her eyes, sat up, and straightened her shoulders. "That's why I came back. To talk to Greg Hewitt and try to fix myself."

"There's nothing to fix, Quinn. You aren't broken. You just need to accept your new reality and embrace it. And you need to stop taking the blame for Patrick's actions. He turned Parker, and there was nothing you could have done about it. Patrick had already attacked and turned you when it happened. You were in the throes of the turn, completely unconscious and incapable of protecting your son."

"But it was my job," Quinn moaned, and then scrubbed her hands over her face, muttering, "I should have never married Patrick."

"Then there would be no Parker," Mary pointed out.

Quinn didn't even want to consider that outcome. She loved Parker dearly. So, she supposed she was glad she'd married Patrick, after all, but—"Then I should have divorced him when it first became apparent that he wasn't going to be a proper father to him."

"Coulda, shoulda, woulda," Mary said with exasperation, and then shook her head. "What if you had? What if it had just been you and Parker living there when the rogue who attacked your husband moved in next door? Maybe it would have been you who encountered the man and got turned. Or maybe he would have just drained you dry and killed you. Or maybe he would have just killed Parker," Mary pointed out, and then added, "Either way, you definitely would have lost Pet once Santo arrived to investigate the matter. She's his life mate, and as such couldn't have resisted him." Mary shrugged. "One way or another Pet would have been turned, and once she was, if you hadn't been turned, she'd have had to leave you behind."

Quinn was scowling over that, when Mary added, "Or maybe Parker and Pet both would have ended up turned and you'd have been mortal still and would have been fed some story that they died in a car accident." She arched her eyebrows. "Frankly, looking at the different permutations, it seems to me that this was the happiest of outcomes. The three of you were turned and still have each other."

When Quinn just frowned, Mary added, "And as a

mother who had to remove herself from the lives of her children and grandchildren after being turned, I cannot express how much I envy you that."

Quinn was just absorbing the shock from those words when a knock sounded at the door.

Nine

"I'll get it," Mary said quietly, and stood to walk to the door.

Quinn watched her go, her mind in an uproar of confusion as bits and pieces of their conversation looped through her mind. There were a lot of things she wanted to examine more closely, but right now, uppermost in her mind was Mary's revelation that she'd had to "remove herself" from her children's lives. Quinn couldn't imagine it. She had been away from Parker for several months directly after the turn, and was away from him right now, but this was just temporary. She loved her son and couldn't imagine having to give him up permanently.

Or Pet, she thought with a frown. Aside from being her twin sister, Pet was her best friend. She'd always been there to cheer her up, cheer her on, and to help out with Parker. God, she couldn't have survived without their girls' weekends when Patrick had been away at conferences or other work-related trips. The two of them would drink too much wine, get giggly, and then sing and dance around the living room with Parker to the latest dance music.

Actually, Quinn thought, she could do with one of those weekends now. They hadn't had one since this whole immortal business started four years ago, and she supposed they never would again. At least not with wine. Apparently, wine didn't have the same effect on immortals.

"What are we watching?"

Quinn glanced around with surprise at that question. She stared wide-eyed as Jet flopped onto the bed next to hers, arranged the pillows behind his back so he could lean against the headboard, and then crossed his legs at the ankles and clasped his hands over his stomach as he surveyed the muted TV.

"Where'd Mary go?" Quinn asked, her gaze sliding toward the entry even as she quickly dashed away any traces of tears on her face. God, she probably had a red nose and—

"She said she had to go out and get something. She'll be back as quickly as she can," Jet answered, picking up the remote and hitting a button to turn on the channel guide. *"The Shawshank Redemption,"* he said. "That's a hella good movie."

"Yeah," Quinn agreed quietly. "One of my favorites. But it must have just started. *Raiders of the Lost Ark* was on earlier. Not that we were watching it," she added wryly.

"Sacrilege!" Jet said with feigned horror. "How could you not watch *Raiders*? It's a classic."

Quinn smiled with amusement at his teasing and shrugged. "You know girls. We like to talk."

"Hmm. Loudly too," Jet said solemnly, and when she raised an eyebrow in question, he admitted, "The walls here must be paper-thin. I heard most of your conversation."

"Oh." Quinn felt her cheeks heat up, but was too busy going back over the conversation to see what he'd heard. Way too much, she decided with dismay, and then said unhappily, "So, now you know what a mess I am."

"You aren't a mess," he assured her, getting up and moving to sit on her bed so he could slide his arms around her. Pulling her against his chest, he rubbed her back soothingly and added, "At least no more than most people. I mean, come on, child of an alcoholic here, remember? And latchkey kid pretty much raised by the nice neighbor lady."

Quinn gave a surprised huff of laughter. "So you're saying we're both messed up?"

Jet shrugged. "Like Mary said, most people are."

"Good Lord, you *did* hear everything," Quinn muttered, burying her face against his chest in embarrassment.

"Yes. Sorry. I considered turning the television on to give you privacy, but didn't want to," he admitted.

That brought another laugh from her and she sat back to eye him dryly. "At least you're honest about it."

Jet's expression turned serious. "I'll always be honest with you, Quinn."

"Thank you," she whispered, suddenly aware of how close they were. How good he smelled, the heat from his body, his hand on her back.

She suspected Jet was suddenly aware of their closeness as well because he closed his eyes briefly on a groan and then opened them again and smiled wryly. "In the interest of honesty, I should probably tell you that while I thought you were hot in your dress pants and silk blouse, I find you really, really hot in a T-shirt and jeans."

"Oh," Quinn breathed, and was quite sure her nipples had just gone hard.

"I want to make love to you," he added. "But Mary will come back soon so I don't dare."

"No," she said with disappointment, and then cleared her throat and nodded. "No. We'd better not."

"But I really, really want to run my hand over you in that T-shirt," he announced.

"Run your hand over me?" she asked with bewilderment.

"Yes. I want to see if it feels as good as it looks," he said wryly, and then added, "I wouldn't take it off. I just want to run my hands over top of the cloth. If that's all right with you."

Quinn licked suddenly dry lips and nodded. "Yes," she whispered, and then leaned back a bit when he urged her to and watched his tanned hand move to her stomach and then glide across it briefly over the white cotton before sliding up over one breast and then to the other.

"Your nipples are already hard little pebbles," he groaned, closing his hand over one breast and kneading lightly.

Quinn bit her lip and watched with fascination as her body responded, her back arching into the caress, her legs shifting restlessly. When he then narrowed his attention on one breast, finding and rolling the nipple through the cloth with his thumb and finger, Quinn gasped and clutched at his shoulders, murmuring his name in a pleading tone.

"I know, love," he moaned, and kissed her hungrily as he continued to fondle her. But when his knee slid between her legs and rubbed against her through her jeans, Quinn pulled away with a groan and shook her head. "No. Wait. I want—"

"What do you want?" he asked when she hesitated.

She licked her lips again and met his gaze before telling him, "Mary explained about life mates to me. She told me about shared pleasure."

"Yeah," he murmured, running his thumb over her nipple and back through the bra and T-shirt. "It's good."

"But I haven't really—I mean, so far you've already been caressing me when I touched you and I've never really been able to tell what was my pleasure and what was yours. I'd kind of like to touch you without you touching me," she admitted, blushing and embarrassed but too curious not to ask.

Jet's thumb stopped moving and he pulled back slightly to peer at her. "Yeah?"

Quinn nodded.

He considered that briefly and then asked, "Can I kiss you?"

"Yes, of course," she said, a smile pulling at her mouth, and then stopped him when he started to lean down to do just that, and added, "Just not right away. Not till after I start touching you."

"Oh." He straightened again. "Okay. Go for it."

When he squeezed his eyes closed as if in preparation for a punch, Quinn almost laughed. But she restrained herself and then reached out tentatively to press her hand against his groin. She heard him suck in a gust of air and felt his arm stiffen slightly, but she also felt a shaft of pleasure shoot through her own groin as if in response to being caressed. Fascinated, she pressed more firmly, and began to run her hand up and down over the bulge of his erection, her mouth opening slightly in small pants as excitement, need, and pleasure began building inside her in response.

When Jet's mouth covered her open mouth, she kissed him back eagerly, and then released him to blindly unsnap his jeans and carefully ease the zipper down. She felt his stomach jump in tune with her own as she snaked her hand inside his jeans and boxers to find and clasp him, and then she began to caress him in earnest as her body demanded.

Quinn had barely got three strokes in when Jet broke their kiss to growl, "Oh God, I want to make love to you."

"Yes," she groaned, squeezing him a little harder.

"When we get to Toronto," he promised, pressing feverish kisses across her eyes and cheek.

"I rented a hotel room there," she panted.

"Then we'll go there," he gasped, his hands clutching at her shoulders, and hips bucking into her caress. "I'll strip every inch of clothing off of you and—" They both froze as a knock sounded at the door, and then Jet leaned his forehead on hers and groaned, "No."

"Toronto." She sighed the word like a promise and then released him and eased her hand out of his pants, her body aching in protest at the interruption.

"Toronto," he agreed on a sigh. "Or the plane if we're alone. We can join the mile-high club."

"Like you aren't a charter member?" she teased lightly, disentangling herself from him.

"How could I? I'm always the pilot," he pointed out.

Quinn chuckled at that and then looked toward the door and sighed when the knock sounded again. "I'll get that. You'd better . . ." She gestured to his open jeans and then slid off the bed and walked toward the door, taking her time to be sure he was able to get himself put back together before she opened the door. But he was quicker than she'd expected. When she reached the door and peered back, he was already back together and standing in front of the Keurig, making coffee.

Smiling crookedly when he glanced her way, she turned back to open the door and her eyes widened with surprise when she was confronted with Lucian Argeneau. Once Quinn got over the shock of seeing the man she'd thought was still at the lodge, her eyes immediately shifted to his shoulder. Quinn started to open her mouth, but before she could say anything, Lucian growled, "If you apologize one more time for shooting me, woman, I will be most irritated."

Quinn snapped her mouth closed, and then muttered, "I suspect that's a common state for you," as she turned to walk back to Jet. She'd planned to make herself a coffee, but Jet was already doing that for her.

"Where's Mary?"

Quinn turned back with surprise at that question to see that Dante had followed Lucian into the room. Several more people were on his heels. She eyed them with curiosity, recognizing Justin Bricker as an immortal she'd met while staying with Marguerite during the first several months after she was turned, and she'd met Anders and of course Dante at the lodge. But she didn't know the others.

"Mary said she had to go get something and she'd be

back in an hour," Jet explained as he mixed sugar and powdered creamer into both coffees.

"Probably food," Justin Bricker said happily, and when Quinn eyed him with curiosity, he explained, "Dante texted her we were on the way back, and he's always hungry. She probably went out to pick up something for everyone to eat."

Quinn nodded, but wished Mary had said something. She would have gone with her to help. She was distracted from that thought when Jet held a coffee out in front of her. Murmuring, "Thank you," she accepted the cup of steaming liquid and sipped at it cautiously as her gaze slid over the people now filling the room.

Dante, Justin Bricker, and the Enforcer named Anders, who had so enjoyed watching her harass Lucian about his wound. There was also a couple made up of an ice-blonde woman and a fair-haired man who she didn't know, but it was the last three people who really caught her attention. They were just such an odd trio. They were two women and a man Quinn had never met before. While one of the women was short and curvy, with long blond hair and conservative business clothes, the other had dark hair with fuchsia highlights and was dressed in a scoop-necked T-shirt, tight black jeans, and high-heeled boots. At five-foot-ten she was also at least six inches taller than the blonde, but the dark-haired man between them was even taller, and damned near as wide as he was tall. Most of the male immortals she'd met were big men, but this one was exceptionally large.

"You know Dante, Anders, and Bricker," Lucian said, and then gestured to the couple and added, "My niece Basha and her husband, Marcus Notte."

Quinn's eyes widened slightly at the name. The man

was obviously another relative of her brother-in-law, but the woman was all Argeneau. The two families seemed to be well interconnected, she thought. Marguerite had originally been an Argeneau but was now married to a Notte, and so was this woman, Basha.

"The other three that you don't know are Tiny and Mirabeau MacGraw, and Jackie Argeneau," Lucian announced. "Jackie is the wife of my nephew Vincent, and Tiny and Mirabeau are family."

"Who isn't?" Quinn muttered, bringing startled laughs from everyone but Lucian.

"Justin isn't," he announced dryly.

"Hey!" the Enforcer protested. "Why single me out? Anders isn't an Argeneau either."

"His wife saved the lives of my wife and children, that makes her—and by connection, him—family," Lucian said mildly.

Justin scowled at the proclamation and then dropped to sit on the end of the first bed, which acted as a cue for everyone to spread out around the room in search of seats. Several sat on the beds, a few took up positions on the couch, and Dante hefted himself up to sit on the kitchen counter until only Lucian, Quinn, and Jet still stood by the coffeemaker. Lucian Argeneau then positioned himself directly in front of Quinn and Jet and inspected them like they were butterflies pinned to a spreading board.

Quinn eyed him warily back and then her gaze dropped from his face to his chest again. Guilt immediately flickered through her and she opened her mouth.

"I did warn you about apologizing," Lucian reminded her.

Quinn grimaced at that. "Well, I'm sorry, but I'm sorry. I mean, I thought it was Nika or Marta. I wouldn't have shot you if I'd realized it was you," she assured him.

"How could you think Lucian was Nika or Marta?" Justin Bricker asked with disbelief, his amazed gaze moving over the large man.

"Her eyes were closed," Lucian said dryly.

"What?" Justin squawked with disbelief. "You shot without even looking to see who you were shooting? What if it had been Jet? He's mortal. He would have died."

"It couldn't have been Jet. I'd just finished locking him in the booze box behind me," Quinn snapped, but could feel the blush rising up her cheeks. It really hadn't been well done of her to shoot without at least looking first to be sure she was shooting at the right person.

"Well, it could have been another mortal who—Wait, you locked Jet in a booze box?" Justin asked with disbelief. "What the hell is a booze box? Man, I missed a lot while I was stuck at the crash site feeding blood to Annika."

Quinn scowled at him and then turned to arch an eyebrow at Lucian. "I'm guessing there's a reason you're here?"

Lucian was silent for a minute and then asked, "What do you remember about the crash?"

Quinn was surprised at the question, but answered readily enough. "I was sleeping and woke up to noise, chaos, and cold," she began, and quickly ran through what she recalled of the crash. But at the end, she hesitated and then admitted what she hadn't told Jet at the time because she hadn't wanted to upset him. "When I got to the cockpit, I saw that we'd hit a cliff face. But at an angle. Miller must have seen the rock face ahead and either tried to turn the plane away to avoid the rock wall, or he deliberately turned the plane so that Jet wouldn't be hurt. Whatever the case, Jet's side was clear and only Miller's side hit the rock wall. It pushed the front of the plane in, crushing him."

She had felt Jet go stiff beside her as soon as she'd started to talk about that, but she didn't look at him. She did let her hand drop down to clasp his, though. When she squeezed gently, he squeezed back.

"So, you didn't hear an explosion before the window was blown out?" Lucian asked abruptly.

"An explosion?" she asked with amazement.

"Kira and her guards all heard two explosions in quick succession just before the plane plummeted," he announced.

Quinn swallowed, but shook her head. "I was asleep. I suppose that could be what woke me up, but . . ." She shrugged helplessly.

When Lucian turned his gaze to Jet, the pilot said quietly, "I heard a popping sound. But only one before we lost the engines."

"But you are mortal and were in the cockpit," Lucian murmured. "The women were in the back by the engines and are immortal with immortal hearing."

Jet nodded agreement to that. "So, you think both engines blew?"

"We know both engines exploded," Lucian assured him. "Jackie and Tiny did a preliminary examination and found curled metal everywhere on both sides of the crash site."

"That's—" Jet shook his head. "Engines don't just explode, and two of them blowing at the same time—"

"They found evidence suggesting bombs had been placed in both engines," Lucian said quietly. "We'll know more after the special investigator arrives and does a more in-depth examination of the plane, but it would appear that one of the bombs was either placed wrong, or was defective and didn't do as much damage as the other. That is the only reason Miller was able to get that engine going again, and level out the plane. Otherwise, it would have been a straight plummet to earth and no doubt a fiery ending for you all."

"Christ," Jet breathed, paling at the thought, and then he frowned and asked, "But why blow up the plane?"

When Lucian's gaze slid back to her, Quinn straightened abruptly. "What?"

"Would anyone want you dead?"

The question surprised a startled laugh from her, and she pointed out, "Everyone I know already thinks I'm dead thanks to you and your people. Well, except Pet and my son," she added dryly. "Are you suggesting Pet hired someone to blow up the plane?"

Lucian shook his head and glanced at Jet. "What about you?"

He shook his head at once. "Not that I know of."

Lucian nodded as if that was what he'd expected, and then announced to the room at large, "Until we figure out which person on the plane was the target, everyone who was on it will have to be under a protective detail."

"Kira already has her own guard," Anders pointed out, and the comment made Quinn frown slightly as she wondered why the woman had bodyguards that traveled with her. She hadn't realized the women accompanying the blonde Russian were her guard at first. She'd just thought them a group of females traveling together.

Now she wondered why Kira would need protection. She was immortal, after all, and able to take care of herself.

She'd have to ask Jet later, Quinn thought as Bricker commented, "Yeah, she does, and I doubt she will be happy to have our people added to it."

"I am sure you are right, but I want a tail on her, watching for trouble, until this is over anyway," Lucian said grimly. "Mortimer can assign one of you to partner her until then too. An extra pair of eyes when she's working cannot hurt."

"And Jet and Quinn?" Anders asked.

Quinn scowled at the dark-skinned man sharply for dragging Lucian's attention back to them, and then shifted her gaze to Lucian as he said, "I want full-time protection on both of them. Keep them together. At the Enforcer house is probably best. It will take less manpower. I also want—"

"Wait a minute," Quinn protested. "I have a room booked at the Four Seasons."

"And I have flights that I'm scheduled to pilot," Jet pointed out.

Lucian scowled at Quinn for interrupting and said, "Then Mortimer will unbook your room." Turning to Jet, he added, "And Bastien shall reschedule your flights to someone else. You two are now under protection."

"Prisoners again, you mean," Quinn said resentfully, seeing the possibility of finally making love to Jet in Toronto crumbling before her eyes.

Ignoring her, Lucian turned to the others and said, "Dante and Mary will ride back to Toronto with Jet and Quinn. But I will need someone to fly to Italy to survey the security tapes. Whoever tampered with the plane may have been caught by the security cameras either inside the hangar or out."

"The bombs could have been placed on the plane in Russia," Jet pointed out. "That was our first stop before Italy and we were there awhile to refuel."

"Yes," Lucian agreed with a frown. "I'll contact Kira's father. He can have his people check the security footage there."

"He might refuse the suggestion purely because you made it," Anders pointed out.

Lucian shook his head at once. "Not when this might have something to do with an assassination attempt on Kira. The man is an asshole, but he does care for his daughter."

Anders nodded, and then all conversation paused and everyone glanced to the door when it opened and Mary bustled in carrying half a dozen bags with KFC on the side.

"Food!" Bricker said gleefully, bounding off the bed and rushing forward to help Mary.

But she turned sideways and scooted around him, saying, "There are pizzas out in the SUV. I couldn't carry everything."

"On it," Bricker said, heading for the door.

"Thank you for seeing to food for us, Mary," Lucian said, stepping aside so that she could set the bags on the kitchenette counter. "You'll have to take yours to go. The plane is here and I'd like you and Dante to escort Jet and Quinn back to Toronto. Immediately."

"Okeydokey," she said easily, starting to go through the bags and selecting various items from them to make a meal for the four of them.

"Where is your suitcase, *tresoro*?" Dante asked, stepping up behind his wife and clasping her hips as he bent to press a kiss to the top of her head. "I will put it in the SUV."

"It's already there," she assured him, and then turned to hand him the bag she'd packed with food. "So is yours. The only thing we need now are Jet, Quinn, and their things."

Quinn set her coffee cup on the counter and moved over to the head of the bed to collect the bag that held her dirty clothes and the items Mary had supplied for her. She'd set it on the floor next to the bed she'd been sitting on. When she straightened, Jet was there taking it from her, his jacket already in hand.

"I'll take this and go grab my bag and put them both in the SUV while you put your shoes on," he said, and then seemed to hesitate, as if he wanted to kiss her or something, but in the end he merely smiled and turned to hurry out of the room.

She watched him go, then bent to pick up her shoes and sat on the bed to put them on.

"Does she need blood before you go?" Lucian asked suddenly.

Quinn glanced up with annoyance over his asking Mary rather than her. She wasn't a child, and detested being treated like one.

"She should be fine," Mary told him. "I gave her four bags when she got here and there's blood on the plane."

Lucian grunted at that and turned to the food on the counter.

Shaking her head, Quinn stood and headed out of the room, more than happy to escape the bossy man who seemed to like to interfere in her life. She'd been furious when she'd come out of the turn and found out that he'd arranged it so that everyone thought she was dead. Now she was pissed at him again for this business of her and Jet having to stay at the Enforcer house indefinitely. Aside from disliking being treated like a child, his decision put a spanner in the plans she and Jet had had for getting together once they reached Toronto. On top of that, she'd had other plans for her stay in the Canadian city that she now couldn't pursue. Chief among them was seeing Dr. Gregory Hewitt so she could get her life back in order. Unless he made house calls, she would have to wait on that.

Originally, Quinn had only made the appointment and arranged to fly back to Toronto to please Pet. Distracted with "new life mate brain," her twin sister hadn't really seemed to notice the state Quinn was in the first two years. Pet had only started to pick up on it the last two years as she'd begun to regain a little control of her hormones and her brain cells. At least Quinn presumed that was the case, because that was when Pet had started trying to gently broach the subject of her state of mind, how she was living in isolation, and really pushing for her to attend family gatherings with her, Santo, and Parker. But Quinn hadn't been ready to go anywhere, and had ignored her fretful lectures until Pet had finally lost it on her and told her flat out that she was messed up and likely to mess up Parker if she didn't get her shit together and get help.

That had upset Quinn. She loved Parker, and while she didn't understand why her not wanting to go out would mess up her son, she had caved in under the fear of it happening. Basically, she'd made the appointment with Gregory Hewitt under duress at first, but she'd quickly come to realize that it was a good idea. Aside from not wanting to damage her son . . . well, quite frankly, Quinn didn't want to continue to live the way she was. But she knew she couldn't fix things alone. She needed counseling, and Lucian was putting a spanner in her efforts to get it.

The bastard, she thought resentfully as she crossed the parking lot to the SUV where Jet was loading their bags into the back. Well, she wasn't going to let that happen. She'd have to find some way to get the help she needed despite Lucian Argeneau's dictates.

Ten

"Mary sleeping?"

Quinn had been looking out the plane window, staring blindly at the clouds moving past, when Jet asked that question. Turning her head, she watched Dante settle into one of the seats across the table from them and nod.

"*Sì.* Mary has not slept since we heard about the crash," Dante said on a sigh. "I did on the plane on the way up, but I know she did not, and then neither of us has slept since arriving."

"And yet you're awake," Jet pointed out with amusement.

Dante shrugged, and rather than address that, said, "I am wondering if anyone took the precaution of checking this plane for bombs before we left?"

Quinn felt Jet stiffen beside her, and knew Dante's words were making her do the same.

"Syd Wheeler is the pilot. I know him. I'll go ask if a check was done," Jet said abruptly, getting up.

Dante nodded, and watched him go, then turned to smile at her crookedly. "I suppose it would have been better for me to think of that before we were in the air."

"At least you thought of it," she pointed out. "Considering what Jet and I went through during the last flight, it should have been on the top of our minds when Anders drove us to the airport."

Dante smiled faintly, and then turned to glance toward the front of the plane. When there was no sign of Jet yet, he settled back in his seat with a sigh.

They were both silent for a minute, and then Quinn cleared her throat and said, "Mary mentioned that she had to leave her children after she was turned."

Dante looked startled at the comment, and then sadness and regret crossed his face and he nodded. "*Sì*. They are grown, with children of their own, and she had to give them up as well as her grandbabies for me."

"And yet she still agreed to the turn?" Quinn asked with wonder, not sure if she was more surprised that the woman was old enough to be a grandmother, or that she had given up her children like that. Quinn didn't think she could have done it. In fact, she was quite sure she couldn't have.

"She was not given a choice," Dante admitted quietly. "I had to turn her to save her life after the RV we were in was forced off the road and rolled. Her children and grandchildren believe she died in that accident."

"Oh," Quinn breathed.

Dante considered her briefly, and then said, "I am surprised she would share that with you. She normally does not speak of it."

Quinn recalled the woman's words at the time. *"Frankly, looking at the different permutations, it seems to me that this was the happiest of outcomes. The three of you were turned and still have each other,"* she'd said, referring to her, Pet, and Parker. *"And as a mother who had to remove herself from the lives of her children and grandchildren after being turned, I cannot express how much I envy you that."*

Their conversation had been interrupted then, but Mary hadn't really spoken to her since. True, she'd gone for food and then there had been the rush to the airport, boarding, getting seated, and so on, and now the woman was sleeping, but Quinn couldn't help wondering if Mary also might not be avoiding her. That perhaps she resented Quinn for not appreciating how lucky she'd been. Because Quinn was beginning to see that she had indeed been very lucky in that respect. She still had her son and her sister—and Mary was right, it easily might not have turned out that way. Any one, or all of them, might have been killed by Dressler. Or Pet and Parker might have been turned alone, and she, still mortal, might have been left to think they were dead, the victims of a car accident or some other tragedy, as Mary's family and her own adoptive parents now believed about them. Quinn wasn't sure she could have survived that outcome.

"My *tresoro* has a generous heart," Dante said quietly. "She will not resent you, or begrudge you your good fortune. She is just tired."

Quinn managed a smile for the man's kindness in telling her that, and then glanced up with surprise when Jet appeared to reclaim his seat.

"According to Syd, Lucian has ordered that all the Argeneau planes be guarded when on the ground, and then are double-checked for any tampering before take-off too. Including this one," he informed them as he did up his seat belt. "We should be good."

"Good," Dante said, the tension leaving his body. "Then I think I will go get some sleep too." Standing, he nodded to them both and then moved up the aisle to the front of the plane and disappeared from sight when he settled back in the seat next to where Mary was sleeping.

"I guess joining the 'mile-high club' is out of the question with Dante and Mary on board," Jet murmured, reaching out to take her hand in his.

Quinn smiled wryly, her gaze moving to his hand encompassing hers. She watched his thumb move gently back and forth over the inside of her wrist, amazed to find even that small caress was affecting her. Shaking her head at that realization, she squeezed her legs together and murmured, "Toronto too."

"Yeah, it's gonna be hard to find any privacy with a houseful of Enforcers around," he agreed on a sigh, and then shook his head. "This life mate business is a bit crazy. I've never wanted anyone like I want you. Just holding your hand like this is—" He broke off and shook his head again, his fingers tightening around hers.

"I know," she assured him solemnly.

"We should probably talk about something else," he muttered, shifting uncomfortably in his seat. He grimaced and reached down to tug at the front of his jeans as if trying to make more room, and Quinn couldn't help looking. Her mouth went dry when she saw that he was sporting an erection inside the tight jeans that appeared to be trying to push its way out of the heavy cloth. It looked huge and made her realize that while she'd touched him she hadn't actually seen him naked. She wished she could now. She wished she could just unsnap and unzip his jeans and ease him out so that she could look at him. She also wished she was wearing a dress or skirt instead of the jeans Mary had got her. Then she could have crawled into his lap, straddled him, and found out what it was like to have him inside of her. The idea was ridiculously exciting to her as she considered that they'd have to be quiet so that Dante and Mary didn't hear, and—

"Jesus, Quinn, don't look at me like that," Jet growled. "All I want in the world is to tear your clothes off and make love to you right here and now, and you looking at me so hungrily isn't helping."

Quinn closed her eyes and took a couple of deep breaths, trying to stop thinking what she was thinking. It was hard, though, especially with his thumb moving over the pulse at her wrist, back and forth and back and forth.

Tugging her hand free, she sat up in her seat, relieved to find that made it easier. A couple of deep breaths later, her mind had cleared enough that she was able to come up with something they could talk about that was far away from anything to do with life mates, sex, or life mate sex.

"Who do you think the bombs were meant for?" she

asked, and risked glancing at Jet. She noticed he seemed to be regaining his composure too, now that they weren't touching. Apparently, refraining from hand-holding would be a good idea in future. Which just seemed ridiculous to her. Hand-holding had always seemed a relatively benign way to show affection before now, but they couldn't even manage that without wanting to tear each other's clothes off. Jet was right, this was madness.

"Kira," he said finally.

"Me too," she admitted, and then said, "I don't know why, though. She seems nice to me."

"Yeah," he agreed. "But who else could be the target? Like you said to Lucian, everyone already thinks you're dead. As for me, as far as I know I've never pissed off anyone at all, let alone enough to make them try to kill me."

"But you think Kira has?" Quinn asked with interest.

"I mean, she has a guard for a reason," he pointed out, and then frowned slightly and added, "Although, to be fair, it's because of who her father is, and any attempt on her life might be to get back at her father for something."

"Why? Who is her father?" Quinn asked with curiosity.

"Athanasios Sarka, and I can believe he's pissed off a lot of people," Jet told her, and then explained, "He's the head of the Russian Immortal Council. Like Lucian is here."

"So, he's probably as much of an ass as Lucian, then?"

"Worse, from what I hear," Jet said dryly.

"Not possible," Quinn assured him.

"Athanasios means 'immortal death' in Greek," he informed her. "His people named him that when he lived in Greece ages ago. I was told it's because he seemed immortal to them and brought a swift and brutal death to his enemies. I gather he's a bloodthirsty bastard."

"Well, to be fair, all immortals are bloodthirsty," Quinn pointed out dryly, referring to their need to drink blood.

A startled laugh slipped from Jet, and then he shook his head. "I love your mind. But the kind of bloodthirsty I'm talking about is dragging the man Kira loved from her bed and cutting his head off in front of her because he didn't approve of the relationship."

"What?" she gasped with dismay. "Really?"

Jet nodded solemnly. "She told me that herself. His name was Bogdan or something."

"She *told* you that?" Quinn asked with surprise.

"Yeah." Jet smiled faintly. "It was on a flight to British Columbia. She was going out to do some job for the Council. I guess her guards had all fallen asleep, she was lonely and bored, and came up to the cockpit for company."

"And she told you something like that?" she asked with obvious disbelief.

Jet shrugged. "Well, she'd just propositioned me and I guess she felt it was only fair that she let me know what I was risking if I took her up on the offer."

"What?" Quinn snapped, sitting up abruptly as jealousy roared through her like a tsunami. Glowering, she turned on him, snarling, "That bitch propositioned you?"

"No," he said quickly on a laugh, and caught her fisted hands in his. "I was just kidding. She never propositioned me. We just talked. For some reason females often like to talk to me like I'm a girlfriend and tell me all their troubles," he admitted. "I always figured it had something to do with my growing up with Abs and Mom-Marge as my main influences."

Quinn narrowed her eyes on him. "Kira really didn't proposition you?"

"No," he assured her solemnly, and then considered her briefly before saying, "But I find it interesting that you'd react so jealously when you aren't interested in having me as a life mate."

"I didn't say I wasn't interested. I said I wasn't ready," she pointed out sharply.

Jet stared at her silently for a moment, finding himself annoyed with those words. Quinn might be saying she wasn't ready, but he was hearing "I don't want you," and frankly it stung as much this time as it had the first. And she had the nerve to glare at him while she said it, like it was his fault. That stung too, and he found himself asking, "Ready for what exactly, Quinn? Because it certainly doesn't seem to be the sex."

Even as he released her hands and sat back in his seat, Jet was silently asking himself why he was acting like a teenage girl with a boyfriend who wouldn't agree to go steady.

They were both silent for a minute, and then Quinn muttered, "We haven't had sex."

"No. We haven't," he agreed. "And maybe it's good that we'll be at the Enforcer house and unable to do anything. It's probably better if we keep it that way until you're 'ready' for a life mate anyway," he said grimly, and then closed his eyes. "I'm going to take a nap now. Wake me up when we're about to land."

Jet knew she was looking at him. He could feel it. He could actually even feel her confusion and upset at his words and had no idea why he was acting the way he was. Except that he wanted her so damned bad he could taste it, and it burned that she claimed she "wasn't ready" for a life mate but was all over him like a dirty shirt every chance they got.

Not that he wasn't all over her too, he acknowledged. But his uncertainty as to whether he was willing to be a life mate had fled at some point since that conversation in the woods. He wanted her. But he also liked her, respected her, wanted to protect and pamper her . . . especially after hearing the conversation he'd overheard between her and Mary. He hated that she blamed herself for not being able to protect her son, and her shutting herself away from the world these last four years since being turned was just criminal. It was hard for him to align that knowledge in his mind with the self-possessed woman who had charged through the woods with him over her shoulder, and then had shown such courage at the lodge. Quinn had placed herself between them all and the Russian women in that basement without hesitation, ready to defend them to the death. And it really *could* have been her death if the women had come through the door rather than Lucian Argeneau. Kira's bodyguards certainly knew how to kill another immortal and—in their madness—might have twisted, or cut, her head off. If that had happened and help hadn't come soon enough to put her back together, she would have died.

The very idea shattered him. Quinn was beautiful, and smart, and he adored the way she mouthed off to Lucian. Just watching the tiny five-foot-nothing Quinn standing up to the huge and most powerful immortal around turned him on like crazy. It made him want to tear her clothes off and fuck her all day, every day, until the world ended. Which might be crude but was the truth. The woman had got under his skin. Worse yet, she had him by the balls. One squeeze and she could bring him to his knees. Hell, he thought, she already had him there. But she obviously didn't feel the same way.

Jet sighed and gave his head a shake. He was expecting too much too soon and he knew it. He'd been obsessing about her for four years—thinking of her, fantasizing about her, and listening for any whisper of news about her—but as far as she was concerned, they'd only just met. He should be more patient, give her the space and time to deal with the stuff she needed to.

Not that he really thought there was anything to deal with. He suspected Mary was right and Quinn felt guilty about not being able to protect her son and had been punishing herself for what she saw as her failure.

But what if punishing herself included *never* "being ready" for a life mate? That was what was scaring the hell out of him. His mother had been punishing herself for the argument that had led to his father joining the navy and dying for most of Jet's thirty-one years and showed no sign of stopping. If the saying was true that you married a woman like your mother, Quinn could punish herself that long or more and might never be ready for a life mate during his lifetime. What if that's what happened? Did he want to spend his life as her plaything, trailing her around like some modern-day Renfield to her Dracula? He pictured himself drooling after her and popping bugs into his mouth as he waited for her to pay him some attention, all the while hoping against hope that someday she'd "be ready." Is that what he wanted?

Did he have a choice? Jet thought grimly. For while he had said it was probably good they couldn't do anything at the Enforcer house, he was already trying to figure out a way for them to sneak away together. The woman was like a drug and he an addict, and he'd seen what his mother's alcohol addiction had done to her.

Sighing, he pushed these thoughts from his mind and really tried to sleep, thinking it might help to clear the confusion from his mind so he could figure out the best thing for him to do about Quinn.

"You ladies go on in, Sam's expecting you. I'm just going to run the guys down to the garage to see my new toy."

Quinn stopped walking and glanced around at that announcement, just as Mary turned to smile and wave the men off, calling, "All right."

They both watched Garrett Mortimer hit the gas and speed off with Jet and Dante in the Jeep, and then Mary turned to Quinn, her smile dropping like a pancake sliding off a plate. "Something's up."

"What?" Quinn blinked at the suggestion. "What do you mean?"

"I mean, something's up, and Mortimer's taking the boys out back to fill them in without us around."

Quinn peered after the vehicle as it disappeared around the house they'd been dropped in front of.

"What makes you think that? Maybe he got a new car or something he wants to show them."

"He did get a new vehicle," Mary assured her, and then added, "The Jeep he's driving them in. And he showed it to Dante while we waited for the plane to arrive to take us to Cochrane."

"Oh." Quinn frowned and then started to move when Mary urged her toward the house, but said, "Well, maybe he wanted to show it off to Jet, then."

"Jet's no autophile. He's a pilot. Now, if Mortimer wanted to show him a new plane, he'd be all over it, but cars?" She shook her head. "Nope. It's something else."

"What do you think it is?" Quinn asked, a little annoyed at the possibility that she'd been left out of a discussion about the plane accident. It affected her life too. She should have been included. If that's even what was happening.

"Well," Mary said thoughtfully, "it can't be anything new about the plane—the special investigator won't arrive until tomorrow."

That was news to Quinn. Lucian had mentioned a special investigator, but she hadn't realized they had one scheduled to show up so soon.

"So, it must be that they've found out something that gives them an idea of who the target was," Mary decided.

Quinn stiffened, and turned on her with amazement, but then shook her head. "Surely they would have included me if that was the case?"

"Probably," she allowed with a nod, and then added, "Unless you were the target and they were concerned about how you'd take it."

Quinn gaped at her. "I wasn't the target. I couldn't have been. Nobody knows I'm alive but Pet, Parker, and Santo."

"Pet, Parker, Santo, and every Notte who knows them, as well as most Argeneaus," she corrected, and then added, "Plus probably twenty other Enforcers and immortals who were involved in the operation in Albany. Then there are the immortals who helped to make it look like you, Pet, and Parker died in a car accident with your husband, as well as the ones who arranged new IDs for you all, and the other ones who arranged it so that your house, cars, and belongings were sold, and the proceeds from it, along with your savings and the money from insurance and whatnot, all made their way to you."

Quinn chewed on her bottom lip as she considered that. She hadn't really thought about how much work must have gone into erasing her old life and arranging her new one. Not to mention making sure she and Parker didn't lose the money she and Patrick had made over the years. She wasn't really sure how they'd managed that. Their wills left everything to one another in the event of one of them dying, and their son if they had both died. But Parker was supposedly dead too, so the money probably should have gone to her parents. But it hadn't. It had been put into an account for her. Obviously, Lucian had arranged that, and somehow made it okay with her parents and everyone else, probably through mind control and whatnot.

"Fine," she said now. "But why would any of those people want me dead?"

"I don't know," she admitted with a shrug. "People are weird."

That surprised a small puff of laughter from Quinn, and then she asked, "Okay, then, why would the men be concerned about how I'd take it?"

"Probably because you shut down and retreated from the world after waking up to find yourself turned and they see you as weak and fragile."

Quinn was stiffening at the suggestion when Mary added, "They aren't trained psychologists like me so don't see that you're actually quite strong and resilient with an incredibly robust self-defense system in that wickedly smart brain of yours."

Now she was blinking again with confusion. "Do you really see me as—Wait, you're a psychologist?"

Mary grinned. "I used to be. I retired not long before I was turned."

"Oh," Quinn murmured.

"But I've been considering putting out a shingle again now that Dante and I can manage an hour or two out of bed at a time." Smiling, she urged her to start walking again. "We smart girls need something to keep our minds busy or we get depressed. Or into trouble," she added wryly, and then left Quinn to think about that as they walked up the sidewalk to the front door of the large white house that was apparently the base for the Toronto branch of the North American Enforcers.

Mary reached it first, and opened it, but rather than enter, she gestured for Quinn to go in ahead of her.

Murmuring a polite, "Thank you," Quinn stepped past her into the house and immediately froze when a bark drew her gaze to a large German shepherd charging up the hall toward them.

"Bailey!" Mary squealed behind her, and then moved around Quinn to drop to one knee to greet the excited animal. "That's my girl. Did you miss your momma? Momma missed you. Yes, she did."

Quinn watched wide-eyed as the ferocious-looking dog did a good impression of a puppy, licking Mary's face excitedly, her tail wagging madly, and then sliding onto her back and wiggling ecstatically as Mary petted her belly and continued to coo at her happily.

"Bailey missed her."

Quinn turned to find Marguerite standing beside her and shifted uncomfortably. The auburn-haired beauty had been kindness itself to Quinn, seeing her through the turn, and then cutting short her RV trip with her husband, Julius, and taking her into her own home to try to help her adjust. Truly, Marguerite had done everything she could to try to help, but Quinn had refused her aid at every turn until the woman had given in and allowed her to fly to Italy to join her son and sister. Looking back at it now, Quinn supposed she would have been better served to let Marguerite help her. She'd certainly be further ahead now if she had.

"You were not ready," Marguerite said with gentle understanding, obviously reading her mind. "And you did not choose this. You are not the first new immortal to be turned without their permission who struggled with finding themselves changed, and you are not even close to the worst case of denial and rejection of the change that I have seen."

"Really?" Quinn asked solemnly.

"Really," Marguerite assured her, sliding an arm around her waist and giving her a quick hug. She then released her and smiled widely. "And you are here now, ready to get help to accept and embrace your new reality. That is wonderful."

Quinn flushed under her praise, feeling she didn't deserve it, and admitted wryly, "Only because Pet made me."

"That may have been the impetus at the beginning, dear. But I can see that you are ready now to make the change." She patted her arm and then glanced to Mary as the other woman gave her dog one last pet and then straightened. "So is our Mary, it seems."

"So is our Mary what?" Mary asked, giving Marguerite a hug in greeting.

"Ready for a change," Marguerite explained as they broke apart. "Are you really considering working in your field again, dear?"

"Oh." Mary smiled. "Yes. I think it's time."

"Well, then I'll call Bastien and put a bug in his ear about getting the paperwork together for you. Diplomas and licenses—or whatever psychologists need—in your new name will be necessary, I'm sure. In the meantime," she said, glancing from her to Quinn. "Since you're already stuck here helping to guard Quinn, you can practice on her. She wants counseling and I think the two of you would suit each other beautifully. Besides, it seems you've already made a good start of it with her."

Mary's eyebrows rose at the suggestion and she considered Quinn briefly, before saying, "I'd be willing. But only if Quinn is okay with that. She planned on contacting your son-in-law and may prefer that."

"I—No. I'd be glad to have you therapize me," Quinn said at once. She liked Mary, but more importantly, a lot of what Mary had said to her made sense. She also hadn't pulled any punches. Quinn suspected the woman was exactly what she needed.

"Good, then it's all settled," Marguerite said on a satisfied little sigh.

"Are you guys ever coming in here? The tea's getting cold."

They all smiled at the sound of Sam's voice from the kitchen and, with Bailey following, made their way into the large room where Mortimer's wife was setting chocolate chip cookies on the kitchen table. It was already set for tea for seven. Obviously, Sam had expected the men to join them.

Quinn found herself eyeing the woman with curiosity as the tall, slender Sam gave Mary a hug in greeting. She knew she'd met the woman when she was last in Toronto, but that had been three and a half years ago, when she was waiting for the plane that was to take her to Italy. As she recalled, the woman had been cheerful and chatty, but Quinn had not. She'd been tightly wrapped up in her anger and desperation to leave North America for Italy. So, she was a little surprised at the warm, sympathetic smile Sam Mortimer offered her now as she turned to her.

"Wow, look at you," Sam said, taking in her outfit. "Last time I saw you, you were all buttoned-up and businesslike. Now you're a raging hottie. Jeans look good on you, Quinn."

"I'm afraid I can't take credit," Quinn said self-consciously. "Mary bought this outfit for me."

"She and Jet lost their luggage in the crash," Mary explained.

Sam's eyes widened and she squealed with delight. *"Shopping trip!"*

"Oh, yes," Marguerite agreed with a wide smile. "I'm in for a shopping trip if I'm invited."

"Of course you are, Marguerite," Sam said as if there should never have been any doubt.

"Er . . ." Mary said, looking uncertain. "I'm not sure we'll be allowed to take Quinn shopping. Lucian wanted her and Jet under protective custody."

"Pffft," Sam said, waving an unconcerned hand. "That just means we'll have to take a couple of the boys with us to play babysitter. I'm thinking Francis should be one."

"Oh, definitely," Mary agreed, the concern slipping from her face to be replaced with glee. "And he'll love it."

"More importantly, he's good at it," Marguerite said with amusement, and patted Quinn's arm. "He'll have you looking so hot Jet won't be able to keep his hands off you."

"He already has that problem," Mary said with amusement.

Quinn felt herself flush with embarrassment, but shook her head. "He's mad at me and—" Halting abruptly, she turned on Marguerite. "How did you know Jet and I—"

"He's your life mate, dear. Of course you and he . . ." She waggled her eyebrows comically.

Quinn stared at her blankly, and then glanced around at the women. "Can everyone tell?"

"Well, our little conversation about life mates was pretty telling," Mary said. "But I would have realized it pretty quick anyway. The way you can't take your eyes off each other is a very big tell as well."

"Marguerite told me," Sam put in. "She didn't want me to be startled if I stumbled over the two of you after you'd passed out naked or half-naked in one room or another here as new life mates are wont to do."

Quinn covered her burning cheeks with her hands and shook her head.

"But now," Sam said, pulling out a chair, "sit down and let's have tea while you tell us why Jet is mad at you."

Eleven

"What is the Brass Circle?" Jet asked. "And what does it matter if a couple of their members were spotted in Italy?" His gaze slid from Dante to Mortimer as he waited for an answer, because the man hadn't dragged them out to the garage/jail cell at the back of the property to show them anything. He'd wanted to talk to them away from the women and tell them the latest developments that had come to light about the plane crash and the bombs that had caused it.

At least, that's what he'd told them he was going to do as they'd finished talking to the pilot, Syd, and headed to the Jeep where the women had been waiting. However, he'd started this conversation with the announcement that members of the Brass Circle had been spotted in Italy, and Jet had no idea who the hell they were or what it had to do with bombs on a plane.

"The Brass Circle are a group of rogues in China," Mortimer explained quietly.

"But they aren't like other rogues," Dante put in. "They're not insane and running around turning or killing mortals willy-nilly. They're in it for money and power, and they're organized and deadly. They operate like a mortal crime syndicate, but where a mortal syndicate might run an underground trade in sex slaves, they run something similar with mortals to be used as cattle to feed from. Things like that."

"And you guys haven't done anything about it?" Jet asked with amazement. "I thought you were Enforcers and that taking care of stuff like that was your job?" He addressed the question to Mortimer because Dante wasn't really an Enforcer. His official job was with the Notte Construction company, but he occasionally helped out if the Enforcers needed a hand. Mortimer, however, was supposed to be the head of the Immortal Enforcers in North America.

"Did you miss the part about it being a group in China?" Mortimer asked dryly. "We don't have any more right to go over and take care of the Brass Circle than the mortal police could send cops over to take care of the mob in Italy." He scowled at him briefly, and then admitted, "Lucian and a couple of the other Council heads from Europe have offered to help out to eradicate the Brass Circle, but the head of the Council in China refused their offer."

"Why?" Jet asked at once. He thought they'd want to be rid of a group like that by any means possible.

"They say because it would start a dangerous precedent. But we suspect it's really because members of the Council over there are paid off, or blackmailed into letting the Brass Circle do what they want."

"Hmm," Jet muttered, thinking, *Didn't that figure?* He supposed he shouldn't be surprised that there might be corruption among immortal governing officials just as there was with mortal ones. Immortals were just humans with long lives. They suffered under the same greed and flaws as mortals.

Sighing, he pushed those thoughts away and said, "Okay, so what does a couple of their members being spotted in Italy have to do with my plane crashing?"

Jet glanced at Dante first, but he shook his head, apparently having no idea.

When Jet then turned to Mortimer, the man hesitated, but finally said, "Well, Pet and Quinn's mother and stepfather were murdered by the Brass Circle when they were children."

"Shit, what?" Jet asked with amazement.

Mortimer nodded. "It's why they were sent to live with the Stones in America. Mrs. Stone was their mother's best friend since school, and was their godmother, but they still did have family in China on their mother's side who could have raised them. However, the Enforcers on their case thought it would be safer for them to disappear."

"Why?" Jet asked at once. "And why were their mother and stepfather killed?"

"Their stepfather was an Enforcer who was pursuing the Brass Circle and—"

"Wait, wait, wait," Jet interrupted. "Quinn and Pet were mortal until four years ago or so, weren't they?"

"Yes," Mortimer verified. "But their stepfather was immortal. And their mother was his life mate. So, while the children were still mortal, he had turned their mother and adopted the children."

"Oh," Jet said with surprise.

"Anyway, as I was saying, the stepfather was trying to uncover the higher-ups in the Brass Circle. Actually, he was part of a task force of Enforcers trying to unravel the group. But the story is someone was passing information about the task force to the Brass Circle. Members were being identified and killed off one after the other, and their families were killed along with them as brutally as possible as a warning to others to leave the organization alone. I gather the stepfather was taking steps to protect his family. His wife wouldn't leave him, but he convinced her to arrange for the children to go to America to stay with her dear friend, Mrs. Stone, for a while. The Stones flew over to collect the girls and take them back to America, but they arrived the morning after the murders. They were the ones to find the charred remains in the courtyard and Pet and Quinn hiding in a closet inside the house."

"Hell," Jet breathed, imagining a sweet-faced little Quinn cowering in a closet, listening to the screams of her parents being murdered. Taking a deep breath to clear the thought from his head, he asked, "So, the Enforcers were worried the Brass Circle might try to kill Quinn and Pet if they stayed in China? A couple of little girls? Why would they bother?"

"Because it would scare the hell out of the other Enforcers," Mortimer said simply.

Jet supposed that was true enough. Still—"Okay, but they'd hardly come after them now, all these years later, would they? And how would they even know who and where they were?"

"How did they know who the Enforcers were that were chasing them?" Mortimer asked with a shrug, and then answered the question himself. "By paying for the information, probably." He was silent for a minute and then added, "As for their coming after them now, after all these years . . ." He shrugged. "They're known to be vengeful and to have long memories."

"And they were spotted in Italy?" Jet asked with a frown.

Mortimer nodded.

"When?"

"Santo noticed some men watching Pet and Quinn at the airport and recognized that they were immortals. He couldn't read them, but he didn't like the way they were watching them. He said it was predatory."

"Santo's pretty old," Jet pointed out with concern.

"Very old," Dante agreed. "He was born in 965 B.C."

Jet took a second to absorb that and then said, "Well, hell, if he couldn't read these guys—"

"They must be older," Mortimer finished for him.

"Right," he breathed, and then shook his head. "Okay, so Santo sees some old immortals watching the girls . . . and?"

"And he was starting to get twitchy about it, but then the men left and he forgot about it. He didn't think of it when he heard about the plane being missing, but he did when he found out about the bombs on the plane," Mortimer explained. "He immediately went to the airport and got pictures of them from security footage and took it to the main Enforcer base in Italy. One of their people was able to identify them as Yun Xiang and Ziying Liang, although they'd say it the other way around in China: Xiang Yun and Liang Ziying. They say the last name first over there," he explained, and then went on. "Both men are apparently suspected of being members of the Brass Circle."

"Did the Council put protection on Pet?" Dante asked with concern.

Mortimer nodded. "Pet, Parker, and Santo were immediately taken into protection."

Jet had been listening silently, but now said, "I still don't understand how the Brass Circle tracked down Quinn and Pet after all this time. You don't have some kind of file on them listing their history or something, do you?"

"No," Mortimer assured him, and then grimaced and added, "I wish we had. Then we might have thought to have Quinn pick a different name for the new Canadian ID and bank accounts that were set up for her last week when she arranged to come here."

Jet glanced at him with surprise. "She changed her name?"

Mortimer nodded, and then said, "Finally. We've been trying to get her to pick a new name and birth date ever since she was turned, but she refused. Since she was going to be in Italy where no one was likely to know the name Quinn Peters, we didn't push it. But Lucian insisted she had to if she wished to come back to 'this side of the pond,' as he put it."

"Why?" Jet asked.

Mortimer shrugged. "I suspect it was just his way to make her finally choose a new name and birth date. Greg thinks doing that often helps a person adjust to their new circumstances."

"Greg Hewitt? Marguerite's son-in-law, the psychologist?" Jet asked, and when Mortimer nodded, he asked, "So what is her new name?"

"She's Quinn Feiyan Meng now on her paperwork, and Parker is Parker Meng."

Jet liked it. He thought Feiyan was a beautiful name. But he didn't understand why it would have made her a target.

Mortimer seemed to realize that because he said, "Quinn and Pet's mother was Feiyan Meng after she married Tian Meng, her life mate. Quinn probably took her mother's name to honor her, but—"

"But it's brought the Brass Circle down on them," Jet breathed with realization.

"She probably didn't think it would matter this long after her parents' deaths," Dante murmured, but Mortimer shook his head.

"She doesn't know it would matter anyway. According to Pet, Quinn doesn't remember anything from their past in China. As far as she's concerned, their mother and stepfather died in a car accident and the Stones adopted them."

"How is that possible?" Jet asked with disbelief. "You said they were found hiding in a closet? I assumed they witnessed the murders, or at least heard them. Otherwise, why were they hiding?"

"They witnessed them," Mortimer assured him. "Pet remembers it all, but I guess Quinn blocked it from her memory. She came away not remembering any of it, and when she asked where their mother was, Mrs. Stone said she'd been in a car accident, and Quinn believed her and has believed it ever since." He shrugged. "Pet apparently tried to tell her the truth when they were still kids, but Quinn didn't believe her and got angry at her for trying to scare her with what she called monster stories. Pet never tried again."

"Which is why you're telling us all of this out here," Jet realized.

"Lucian doesn't want her told," Mortimer admitted solemnly. "At least not by us. He wants it left to whoever counsels her to handle it. To get her to remember on her own to avoid any more damage being done to her psyche."

Jet's eyebrows rose slightly. Lucian Argeneau had always been square with him. He was the one who actually gave him his job as a pilot with Argeneau Enterprises. But he knew the man had a rep as a total hard-ass among the immortals, so was somewhat surprised by his handling this so sensitively.

"Don't be too impressed," Dante said with amusement. "Lucian just doesn't like having to put down lame immortals and is hoping to avoid it."

Jet glanced at him sharply. "Put down? He wouldn't kill Quinn?"

Dante hesitated, and then said, "It won't be an issue. We won't tell her, and risk her going crazy. She'll dig it up naturally in counseling and be fine."

"We don't even know yet if the Brass Circle planted the bombs," Mortimer pointed out before Jet could pursue the matter of Quinn's possibly being put down. "The two men Santo saw might have just been looking at the girls because they're attractive."

Dante scowled. "I'm surprised Santo didn't get the security footage of the plane while he was getting the pictures of—"

"He did," Mortimer interrupted. "Apparently, they're

being viewed now. But there are hours of tape from several different cameras to look at. They'll contact us if they find anything."

Dante nodded and then commented, "Well, at least Basha and Marcus won't have to make a trip to Italy to get them."

"Yes, and Bastien won't have to scramble to find a pilot to take them," he pointed out unhappily, and told Jet, "Bastien is going to be very happy if it turns out that the Brass Circle are behind this and you can be released from protective custody. He's going crazy trying to cover all the flights out there right now. He's down two pilots with Jeff dead and you in lockdown."

"Yeah, well, if it turns out that the Brass Circle is behind this and they're gunning for Quinn, he can forget about my going back to work until it's resolved. I'm not leaving her side until this is over and she's safe."

"Hmm. Sounds to me like Jet's feeling hurt and ultimately rejected," Marguerite decided when Quinn finished telling them about what had happened on the plane.

"I haven't rejected him," Quinn protested at once.

"Dear girl, you've told him you are not ready for a life mate," Marguerite pointed out.

"Yes, but we could still have sex and—"

"Make him a booty call?" Marguerite suggested.

Quinn flushed at the gentle accusation. Marguerite made it sound so tawdry. What was wrong with taking him as a lover rather than this life mate business?

"Maybe he's hoping she'll decide she's ready for a life

mate, after all, if it's the only way she can have sex with him," Sam suggested into the silence that followed.

"That's possible," Marguerite agreed, and then glanced at Mary. "What do you think? You are the psychologist. Hurt feelings, or blackmailing her into accepting him in exchange for sex?"

"My diagnosis would be extreme sexual frustration, and feeling out of control, combined with a fear of losing her," Mary said slowly.

"Feeling out of control?" Quinn asked with surprise.

Mary raised one eyebrow. "Do you feel like you have any control over your desires or body when he's around? Because I know I didn't with Dante . . . and good Lord, it was awful," she admitted without embarrassment. "I was a retired old widow, and Dante looked like he was younger than my own children. I felt like a dirty old woman lusting after a baby, and lectured myself repeatedly to behave, but all he had to do was touch me and I went up in flames and tried to climb him like some young hotsy-totsy. Still do," she admitted with a grin.

As the women chuckled softly, she continued. "The desire spurred between life mates is irresistible and leaves the couple feeling out of control. It can be most alarming. And for Jet, that's compounded by the fact that for him it started four years ago."

"What?" Quinn asked with amazement. She had a vague recollection of Jet mentioning that he'd been attracted to her since first meeting her, but that had been in the dream. Besides, being attracted to her was far away from the madness that overcame them every time they touched one another.

"He's felt this uncontrollable attraction for you since welcoming you to his plane the night he flew you, Marguerite, and Julius back to Toronto from Albany four years ago," Mary explained. "Every woman he's dated and had relations with since then has worn your face when he closed his eyes, and he's sought out information about you at every turn, feeling like a stalker even as he did it, but unable to stop himself. He was starting to worry that there was something wrong with him psychologically and he should seek help."

"But if we're life mates, why didn't I feel that way?" Quinn asked with concern. "I don't even remember him . . . or the flight even, really."

"You were not in a good place then," Marguerite said solemnly. "You weren't aware of much of anything. Your mind was having trouble accepting what had happened and kind of shut down for a bit to allow you to adjust. That's why we didn't drive back in the RV as we'd planned, but flew you back to Toronto."

There was silence for a minute and then Sam muttered, "Poor bastard. It must be hell for him right now. I mean, if he thought he was going crazy before even touching you, now that he knows what he'd be missing, the possibility of losing you must make him bonkers."

"He's afraid that if Quinn refuses him as a life mate as part of her self-punishment, he'd turn into a crazy Renfield, eating bugs and following her around like a lapdog," Mary told them.

"What?" Quinn turned on her with horror.

"That's the fear uppermost in his mind," Mary assured her.

"But that wouldn't happen, would it?" she asked with concern.

"Why?" Mary asked, arching one eyebrow. "*Are* you planning on using him as part of your self-flagellation as he fears? Having sex with him when the urge strikes you, but never claiming him and allowing a proper relationship?"

Quinn scowled. "What's wrong with that? It's not like this is the nineteenth century. People take lovers all the time. Why do I have to *claim* him? What does that even mean? Marriage?" She shook her head. "Marriage is an antiquated institution, and I don't plan to have any more children, so why can't we just be lovers and enjoy each other?"

"How thoroughly modern of you, Quinn," Marguerite said with amusement, and then explained, "Claiming him has nothing to do with marriage. It means turning him, and accepting him into your life as a partner. It's a lifetime commitment. There is no divorce with immortals. Once you fully bond, it is for life."

Quinn winced at those words, her mouth tightening at the thought of doing to Jet what her husband had done to her. She hated Patrick for turning her. How could she then do that to someone else? And how would Jet feel if she turned him into a monster like she had become?

"Wow, now I think my feelings are hurt," Sam said wryly, and when Quinn glanced at her in question, explained, "Well, it's never nice to know someone sees you as a monster."

"I don't think you're a monster," Quinn said wearily, and then scowled. "Besides, it's your own fault for reading my mind."

"Fascinating," Marguerite murmured.

Mary nodded. "Her reasoning mind doesn't think we are monsters just because we are immortals, but her subconscious, what Freud called the id, does. That suggests a phobia. Perhaps her subconscious is reacting to a past experience." She narrowed her eyes on Quinn and asked, "Have you encountered immortals before, Quinn?"

"What?" she asked with a start, and automatically shook her head, though a flicker of memory tried to rise up in her that she almost habitually pushed back down.

Mary's eyes narrowed further and she asked, "Are you sure? You'd never even heard of immortals before Patrick attacked and turned you?"

Quinn hesitated, recalling Pet trying to tell her some story about their parents at one time. But the memory was a whisper she couldn't quite hear, and finally, she shook her head again. "No."

"Couldn't Patrick's attack be at fault?" Sam asked. "I mean, that must have been traumatic. I hear he was crazy-looking and his clothing was filthy, torn, and covered with blood. And then he ripped his wrist open and nearly drowned her making her swallow his blood. That could give anyone a phobia. Heck, the turn was traumatic for me and I knew what to expect. Quinn didn't."

"Hmm," Mary murmured, but she was looking at Quinn in a way that made her terribly uncomfortable.

"Well," Marguerite sighed. "You'll have to work on that with her, Mary."

"But what if she can't help Quinn get past her phobia?" Sam asked with a frown. "We just leave poor Jet to be her Renfield?"

Quinn scowled at the suggestion. Jet wouldn't be her Renfield. They could be lovers and friends and—

"No, of course not," Marguerite said. "He deserves a chance at a life with a partner who can love him as he deserves. If Quinn can't move past this phobia of hers, we will wipe his memory and let him go find a mortal woman who can give him love and children and a happy mortal life," she announced.

Quinn stared at her with dismay at this news, and then the woman added, "Or perhaps I can find him another immortal who he might be a life mate to."

While Quinn gasped over that, Sam asked dubiously, "Is that likely? Life mates are pretty rare."

"It's happened before that a mortal was a possible life mate for more than one immortal," Marguerite said with a shrug, and then grimaced and added, "It might mean Julius and I having to travel around quite a bit to find one, but he wants to travel more anyway. We haven't got out much since our RV trip was derailed."

"But he—I—You can't—" Quinn stammered, unable to get her protests out.

"We cannot stop you from punishing yourself, Quinn," Marguerite said gently. "Only you can decide to move past this self-destructive urge. But we cannot allow you to punish Jet along with yourself. He deserves to be happy." She let her think about that for a moment, and then added, "But this probably isn't a worry anyway. You're going to be working with Mary to clear up your issues. I'm sure everything will turn out fine."

Apparently done with the conversation then, Marguerite turned to Sam and asked, "How are your sisters, dear? I haven't seen Jo and Alex in a while. Everyone is always so busy with their lives nowadays."

Quinn didn't hear the other woman's answer. She was caught up in her thoughts and a sense of resentment at what she was being threatened with. Basically, unless she "accepted" Jet, which apparently translated to her turning him, and making a lifetime commitment to him, they would take him away from her.

Aside from the whole turning him into a monster issue she had, commitment was anathema to Quinn at the moment as well. She'd been married once, and that was enough. She'd watched it fall apart and suffered the ultimate betrayal when Patrick had basically killed her by turning her. Oh, sure, she was still alive physically, but she wasn't human anymore and Quinn Peters was dead. She was the immortal Quinn Feiyan Meng now and had to start a new life. She'd lost everything that mattered to her.

Well, not everything, she acknowledged. She still had Parker and Pet and she *was* grateful for that, but Quinn had gone to school and trained for sixteen years to be a cardiothoracic surgeon. Closer to thirty years of her life, really, if you included kindergarten to grade twelve. The majority of her life had been put toward her career, and then in one moment of selfish cruelty, Patrick, the man who had vowed before God and man to love and cherish her, had ripped it all away. Only a fool would risk trusting another man enough to let him into her life after something like that. Taking Jet as a lover was one thing, but committing to him? And turning him? She'd rather go back to her dull, empty existence in her cottage in Italy, avoiding people both mortal and immortal, and just let time sweep by until she was fortunate enough to die.

Quinn winced at the thought. Even she knew it wasn't a healthy one. And what about Parker? What kind of mother could she be to him like that? Sure, Pet would step in and help, but it was the equivalent of Jet's mother crawling into a bottle and leaving him to be raised by Abigail's mom, only in Parker's case it would be his aunt taking up the slack rather than just some neighbor lady.

So, what should she do?

Obviously, she needed the counseling she'd come here for, but she wasn't looking forward to it. Quinn knew it would take a while—many sessions and hard work and all that crap. She wished there was just a pill they could give her. Or that they could erase her memories of Patrick, and being turned and whatnot. Maybe they could make her think she'd always been immortal and that she was content to be one. That would be nice, but nothing was ever that easy and she suspected that would be the case here.

Quinn scrubbed her face with frustration. She was so tired of being angry and confused. The only time she didn't feel like that was when Jet was with her. Then she felt alive and excited and like there was some hope in the world. But when he wasn't nearby, all these worries and fears crowded in and exhaustion settled over her like a smothering blanket. She wished she could just go to bed and forget everything for a while, but she had no idea where she was supposed to sleep, so she stood abruptly and muttered, "I'm going out to get some air."

When no one protested, she moved away from the table and headed out of the kitchen. Quinn wasn't aware that Bailey had followed until she got to the front door and the dog bumped against her side. She glanced at her briefly, and then called, "Mary, is it okay if Bailey comes out with me?"

"Sure. She probably needs to go potty anyway," Mary answered.

"Potty, huh?" Quinn asked the dog, and smiled crookedly when the German shepherd wagged her tail wildly and barked.

"Potty, it is," she said wryly, and opened the door.

Twelve

"You're awfully quiet this morning."

Quinn glanced up at that comment from Jet and managed a smile. "Sorry. I was just thinking."

"About what?"

Quinn looked out over the yard they were walking, her thoughts swooping and diving in her head. She'd been thinking about a lot of things. One of which was what he was thinking. They hadn't spoken since the plane. He and the other men had just been coming in the back door as she'd entered through the front with Bailey after her walk.

Unsure how he would greet her after their disagreement on the plane, Quinn had found herself eager to avoid him. So, she'd popped her head into the kitchen and announced that she thought she might like to lie down. Sam had immediately jumped up to show her which room she was to have while at the Enforcer house, and Quinn had said good night to Marguerite and Mary and followed Sam quickly upstairs just as the men had reached the front hall. She'd been able to feel Jet's eyes following her, but hadn't turned to offer him a good night.

Once alone, Quinn had immediately got ready for bed, brushing her teeth, washing her face, and changing into the white cotton nightgown Sam had already set in the room for her to use. But she hadn't slept well. Her mind had been busy spinning out copies of the conversation she'd had with Marguerite, Mary, and Sam downstairs earlier, followed by her different interactions with Jet. It had almost been a relief when morning had come and she could give up trying to sleep and get up. But there had been no one around when she'd made her way downstairs. It was only then that she'd realized that the other immortals probably kept night hours, as opposed to her day hours. That was one thing Quinn had insisted on since being turned. She'd refused to sleep during the day and be up all night like some hormone-driven teenager . . . or a vampire.

She'd made Parker keep normal hours too, waking him in the morning to have a healthy breakfast and then start on his schoolwork. She'd homeschooled him these last four years. There hadn't really been a choice. He hadn't been allowed to attend a mortal school for fear of it somehow being discovered that he was an immortal. Besides, apparently the only place they had a school that immortal children could attend was in some small town called Port Henry, which she'd been told was three or four hours southwest of Toronto, in Canada, with traffic. Since they'd been in Italy, commuting hadn't been a possibility.

Quinn hadn't minded. Homeschooling Parker had helped fill the time. Although it had also been harder than she'd expected. It hadn't been the schoolwork itself; that had been fine. But she imagined homeschooling one's child was like teaching them to drive. It took a lot of patience and discipline to keep him on track. Fortunately, they'd finished out that year's lessons before she'd left for Canada.

Thoughts of him had made her call her son to check in and see how he was doing. Parker was spending his summer break with his aunt Pet and uncle Santo. She'd called his personal cell phone and they'd chatted briefly, but she'd noticed that his voice had the rough quality it often had when he'd just woken up. It was six hours later in the day in Italy, though, well past noon, and she suspected he was probably sleeping all day and up all night while she was gone.

Quinn had been fretting about that while she made coffee when Jet had entered the kitchen. She supposed now that she shouldn't have been surprised to see him up so early. He was mortal, after all. But she *had* been surprised, and a little flustered. However, he'd apparently got over his irritation with her and acted like everything was fine, and they'd worked together to make breakfast. Well, she'd acted more as the supporting cast, setting the table and making him coffee while he'd made them a breakfast of French toast and sausages, assuring her as he did that Sam had said to have whatever they wanted for breakfast if they were up before the others.

The French toast was as good as the omelet he'd cooked for her had been, and they'd chatted about what life was like for him as a pilot, and about her homeschooling

Parker, while they'd eaten and sat over coffee afterward. It had been nice, easy . . . so when he'd suggested a walk after, she'd agreed. They were just heading out the door when Bailey had come running down the stairs, barking excitedly to ensure they didn't leave her behind. Spotting Dante just starting down the stairs behind the pup, his long hair a tangled mess around his sleepy face, Jet had chuckled and suggested he go back to bed and have a sleep-in, saying he'd look after Bailey and feed her for them.

But when they'd come back inside with Bailey fifteen minutes later, it was to find Mary up, Bailey's food ready, and Mary with two cups of coffee in hand and determination on her face.

"Time for your first official counseling session," she'd announced, and Quinn had found herself following the woman into a small office up the hall that Sam apparently used for work but had said they could take over for her counseling.

What had followed was some of the most exhausting work Quinn had ever experienced. Who knew that delving into your life and past could be so wearing? Emotionally, she'd been put through the wringer. Anger, pain, resentment, grief, and countless other emotions had kept her on a roller coaster ride for the next three hours. Quinn had once performed surgery on a patient with poor cardiac function who had needed two valves replaced but had complications that included needing several arteries bypassed as well as an aneurysm in the aortic arch. She'd come out of that ten-hour operation feeling less exhausted than her meeting with Mary had left her.

"Quinn?"

"Oh, sorry." She offered Jet a smile, and shrugged, admitting, "Mostly I was thinking about my session with Mary."

"You two were in there a long time. I was expecting an hour, but you were at it for three," he pointed out. "Did it go well?"

"I think so," she said slowly, debating what she was willing to share with him. In the end, she shared it all. "Actually, we got a lot more done than I expected."

"Oh?" He sounded hopeful.

"Mostly it was about my marriage," she admitted. "Mary made me see that I was viewing it through a myopic lens."

Jet raised an eyebrow, but didn't comment and merely waited.

"I've been blaming Patrick for a lot of stuff that maybe wasn't all his fault," she explained.

"Like what?" Jet asked softly.

"Well, we kind of fell into a pattern where he made decisions and I was either fine with it or resented him for it, but never said anything."

"Hmm," Jet murmured.

"The worst part is I realize now that I kind of set it up that way," she muttered with a little irritation.

"How's that?" Jet asked.

"Well, we kind of split chores and decisions between us at first after we were married, but then when Parker was born . . ." She shook her head. "Hours for an intern are often crazy. The most hours I booked in a week was one hundred and thirty-six, but eighty hours was the usual. So, I'd come home from a twelve- or sixteen-hour shift, pump breast milk for the nanny to feed Parker the next day, spend what time I could cuddling him and listening to Patrick talk, then stumble to bed only to pop up at four the next morning to start over. Unfortunately, oftentimes what Patrick was talking about were things that he felt needed doing, or wanted us to do, and frankly, most of the time I was too tired to even listen. I can't tell you the number of things I agreed to without even realizing it because I was half-asleep and just mumbling 'uh-huh' or 'yes, dear' so that he would stop making me think, or distracting me from sleeping."

"Ah," Jet said with understanding. "And eventually that turned into his just making the decision rather than pestering you when you were obviously exhausted."

"Yes," she breathed, glad he understood. "But how did you guess?"

"Because I probably would have done the same thing to try to take some of the burden off you," he admitted. "I think most men would."

"Oh," she muttered. "Well, hell."

"What?" Jet asked with concern.

"Well, you're not an arrogant asshat oncologist who thinks his shit doesn't stink, so if you'd do it too . . ."

Jet chuckled at her disgruntlement and then asked, "Wouldn't you have done the same for him if the roles had been reversed? I presume he had finished his interning and was an actual oncologist with better hours by then?"

Quinn nodded. "We waited until he'd finished and found a position before having Parker."

"Well, there you are. He had more time, and probably more energy, so was able to do more."

"Yeah," she agreed on a sigh. "And I maybe appreciated it at the time, but after my internships were over and my hours weren't so crazy, he continued to make the decisions."

"It had become a habit," Jet suggested quietly.

Quinn nodded. "And rather than say anything, I just resented him for it."

"Ah," Jet said again.

"I guess I wasn't very good at communication, or speaking up for myself," she confessed unhappily. "And then to compound it, I blamed him for continuing to do what he'd done for years."

"Hmm," Jet murmured.

They were both silent for a minute and then Quinn said, "Mary thinks Patrick turned me and Parker because he loved us."

Jet hesitated and then asked, "What do you think?"

Quinn sighed, and then told him, "She said that she had been told that Dressler turned Patrick and wanted him to leave with him when he realized that the Enforcers were next door. But Patrick refused to go without Parker and me."

"That's the story I heard too," Jet told her quietly.

"Where did you hear it?" she asked, turning to glance at him with surprise.

"I don't recall for sure—one of the Enforcers who was in Albany, though," he said, and when she continued to stare at him, he reminded her, "I told you, people like to talk to me for some reason."

"Oh. Right," she murmured, turning to glance over the yard again as Bailey chased after a squirrel with the Enforcer guard dogs on her tail. Quinn had been nervous about bringing Bailey out with them when they'd come out to go for a walk once she'd realized that the guard dogs were out, but Mary had assured her the Enforcer dogs and Bailey were old friends. That was obviously true, she decided as she watched the beasts romp about.

"So, I guess Patrick is looking less like the bad guy to you?" he asked.

Quinn grimaced. "Yeah. I guess. I mean, he still had his faults. He wasn't a very good father to Parker, but who gets it right the first time? I probably wouldn't have got good grades on my mothering either while I was interning." She shrugged. "But he isn't the bad guy in our marriage. We both made mistakes."

"And his turning you?" Jet asked.

Quinn felt the sting of her nails biting into her palms as she clenched her hands into fists, and forced herself to ease the hold. "I wish he hadn't," she said quietly. "And I wish he'd talked to me and asked before doing it, but . . ."

"But that wasn't the pattern. He made decisions for both of you as a rule, rather than the exception, by that point," Jet said quietly.

Quinn nodded. "I think he was probably a little off his rocker by then too. I mean, I was a little off my rocker when I woke up after the turn, and I had Marguerite and the others explaining everything in the gentlest most patient way possible. I doubt Dressler was gentle or patient."

"Probably not," Jet agreed.

"I'm not as angry at him anymore," she admitted quietly.

"No?" Jet asked.

"No," Quinn assured him, but then grimaced and added, "Don't get me wrong, I'm still mad at him for turning Parker and me," she assured him, and then shrugged. "But it's not the same. A lot of the rage is gone . . . "I haven't forgiven him yet, but I think I will someday and that's something I never expected to say."

"I'm glad for you," Jet said seriously, and when she glanced at him in question, he pointed out, "Well, your being angry at him doesn't really affect him anymore, does it?"

"No," she acknowledged. "Just me."

"And Parker," he pointed out. "Patrick is his father, and while what happened must be confusing for him too, I'm sure it will be better for him if you aren't loathing the man who contributed half his DNA."

She was frowning over that when he asked, "How is Parker handling all of this? It must have been traumatizing for him too."

Quinn snorted at the suggestion. "That was my main concern the whole time I was away from him in Canada. But when I got to Italy, I found he was just fine. Pet says Santo's mother spent a lot of time with both of them, helping them adjust and deal with things and teaching them what they needed to know. She says the woman is ancient, older even than Santo. Well, I suppose that's obvious," she added dryly, giving her head a shake. "But anyway, I guess she's a pretty daunting lady. She's been a warrior, a countess, a businesswoman, and all sorts of stuff. But Pet says she's surprisingly sensitive too, and went out of her way to help Parker accept his new life."

"Did you like her?" Jet asked.

"I haven't met her," she admitted. "Pet wanted me to meet her, but I . . ." She shrugged. "I was playing possum, as Mary put it."

"Playing possum?" he asked with amusement.

Quinn nodded. "Her description for my retreating to the little cottage I'd rented and refusing to see anyone."

"Ah," Jet murmured again.

She could hear the laughter in his voice and feigned a scowl that died when the back door opened and Mary called, "Marguerite's here to go shopping. Are you ready, Quinn?"

"Oh. Yes. I'm coming," she called out, and started across the yard.

"Shopping?" Jet asked with concern, following her.

"For clothes. Last night while we were talking, Mary mentioned that we lost our luggage in the crash and the ladies decided we had to go shopping for a new wardrobe. Which is good. This is the second day wearing the T-shirt and jeans I have on. I don't relish another before they're washed." She stopped to call Bailey to them, and then glanced to Jet as she started walking again. "Maybe you should come with us. You'll need more clothes too, and I'm sure the women won't mind. I guess we're having some bodyguards along as well. They can babysit both of us."

"Oh . . . my . . . God! You are a goddess!"

Quinn flushed with embarrassment at that pronouncement from Francis and shook her head. "Goddesses are tall leggy blondes. I'm a short Chinese chick with black hair. Well, hair so dark a brown it often looks black anyway," she added, turning to peer at herself in the mirror and noticing that the light overhead made her hair look more brown than black.

"Then you're a pocket-sized goddess with gorgeous

dark hair," Francis said with a shrug. "That dress is perfection on you."

Quinn let her gaze drop over the royal blue gown she wore and stared at herself with fascination. It was a long satin gown with a sweetheart boat neck, fitted waist, and a slit in the flowing skirt that only showed when she walked. It was stunning, and it made her look and feel beautiful, but it wasn't something she was likely to need, so she shook her head with regret. "It's nice, Francis. But I don't see myself going anywhere I'd need a dress like this. It's kind of fancy."

"It's an elegant evening dress, my dear," Francis corrected her as he walked around, tugging her skirt out so that it made more of a bell shape that emphasized her tiny waist. "And I'm sure Jet would love to take you somewhere you could wear it. Wouldn't you, Jet?" Pausing in front of the pilot, he pushed the other man's mouth closed and grinned before repeating, "Wouldn't you, Jet?"

"Huh?" Jet muttered, his eyes sliding hungrily over Quinn.

"Well, if he won't, I will," Tybo, another one of the four Enforcers accompanying them on this trip, offered with a grin.

Valerian, also an Enforcer, gave his opinion in a more solemn tone. "It would be a shame for you not to buy that dress, Quinn. It's stunning on you."

"It is," Marguerite, Mary, and Sam agreed in stereo. Russell, the fourth Enforcer, merely grunted in the affirmative.

Biting her lip, Quinn turned to peer at herself in the mirror. She was sure it was a foolish purchase. It would probably be years before she had an opportunity to wear it if at all, but in the end, she couldn't resist and nodded at Francis.

"Oh, goodie!" Francis clapped happily. "Then my work here is done. We have absolutely everything you could possibly need for a proper wardrobe. Except the frilly feminine bits," he added. "But I shall leave that up to you ladies and take Jet to be properly outfitted. First, though, Quinn, go slip out of that gown and we'll pay for it and your other selections while you get dressed. Then Valerian and Tybo can take them to the SUV while Jet and I go to a men's store and Russell escorts you ladies to one of those expensive intimate apparel stores."

"No," Valerian said at once. "We're supposed to guard Quinn . . . and Jet," he added when Francis elbowed him in the side.

"And you will as soon as you finish moving the clothes to the vehicle," Francis responded soothingly. "But that's why Russell and I are here too, and I will guard Jet, while Russell guards Quinn. On top of that, Sam, Mary, and Marguerite will be with Russell and our sweet Quinn until you return. I'm sure the four of them can keep her safe for a few minutes."

Valerian didn't look pleased, but didn't argue further. Instead, everyone turned to look at Quinn, who was frowning at Francis and not heading into the dressing room as instructed.

"I just realized I don't have my purse or . . . anything," she ended weakly. "The plane—"

"Yes, dear, we know," Marguerite said reassuringly, ushering her into the changing room. "That's why Francis said we would pay. It is going on the Council credit card."

"But—"

"Your luggage was lost in the plane crash. Insurance will pay to replace them and reimburse the Council. It's fine," Marguerite assured her, closing the dressing room door, and quickly unzipping the dress.

"Are you sure?" Quinn asked with a frown. It hadn't even occurred to her that insurance might pay to replace her clothes, although she supposed if it had been a commercial flight she would have expected it.

"Of course I'm sure. Here, step out of the dress, dear," she instructed, drawing the gown off her shoulders and down for her to step out of. "There we are. Now I'll leave you to dress and take this out to the men so they can take everything to the register."

Marguerite was gone before Quinn even realized that she was standing there in nothing but a pair of panties. Shaking her head, she picked up the bra she'd had to remove when trying on the blue gown. She quickly put it on and did it up, but her mind was on that elbow Francis had thrown at Valerian before the other Enforcer had added Jet's name. There had been several little incidences like that on this outing. Tybo's teasing comment that he was there to guard her body . . . and Jet's too, of course, he'd added after Valerian had nudged him. The way Tybo, Valerian, Francis, and Russell had ranged themselves around her as they'd walked from the car into the shopping center, leaving Jet and the other women to follow. Why hadn't Jet been in the center of the men with her?

Those were just a couple of examples. There had been more and Quinn fretted over them as she pulled her jeans and T-shirt back on. She was doing up her running shoes when she recalled Mary saying she suspected Mortimer had taken the men to the garage because they had some news about who the target of the bomb might be. She'd then speculated that the two of them hadn't been included in the talk because the target was Quinn, and they were concerned that she was too fragile to take the news well.

Call her paranoid, but she was beginning to be convinced Mary had been right. The question was whether the other women had been let in on it or not by now. She suspected Dante would have told Mary, but surely, if that were the case, Mary would have shared the information with her? Quinn thought, and immediately frowned at the possibility that the other woman did know and hadn't told her, because that meant she too believed Quinn might not handle it well. Had her comment that the others didn't know how strong she was just been something to build up her self-esteem?

Or, Quinn worried, after learning who might be behind the attacks, had Mary agreed that she might not be able to handle it? That was a distressing possibility, especially when she considered that everyone in her previous life already thought her dead . . . except Pet and Parker. And they were the only ones in her new life aside from Pet's husband, Santo. But Quinn didn't for a minute think one of them could be behind these attempts to kill her. Although, she acknowledged, she'd definitely have trouble accepting that either of them might want her dead. Shaking her head at the ridiculous direction her mind was going, Quinn decided that rather than let her mind run off in crazy directions, she would wait and question Mary on the subject in their next session, which would apparently be in a couple of hours.

The thought made her sigh. She was not looking forward to another grueling three-hour emotional roller coaster ride, and had been taken by surprise when Marguerite had mentioned perhaps going to dinner and a movie after shopping, only to have Mary nix the idea, saying she planned on another session with Quinn that night. She hadn't known a second session was planned for that day and was a little dismayed to learn there was. Quinn wanted to clear up her issues and move on with life, but hadn't expected to try to do it all in a week.

Now that she was thinking about that incident, she recalled Sam catching Marguerite's arm and urging her away from where Francis was holding up a blouse in front of Quinn to see if the color would suit her. She'd watched with curiosity as Sam had whispered in the older immortal's ear, and now recalled the surprise and concern on the woman's face, and then her murmured, "Oh, I see. Another time, then, of course."

Pondering that little incident, Quinn left the dressing room to join the women and Russell, who immediately positioned himself at her side and took her elbow to escort her from the store.

Tybo and Valerian were just finishing up at the till as they passed them, and Russell stopped to get the Council credit card from him. He then urged the men to be quick at taking the bags of shopping to the vehicles, before urging Quinn and the other women out of the store.

The lingerie shop was at the opposite end of the mall, and the women talked and laughed excitedly as they made their way there. It soon became apparent to Quinn, from their chatter, that she would not be the only one leaving the shop with purchases, and she wasn't surprised to hear Russell's resigned sigh as he escorted them into the store. The man followed her around like a guard dog, positioning himself a few feet away with his arms crossed and a forbidding expression on his face each time she stopped to look at panties and bras. That expression was enough to keep two of the four salesgirls from bothering him, but she suspected he used mind control on the other two when they approached to bat their eyes and ask if he "needed help."

"Oh, this would look lovely on you, dear," Marguerite said, grasping her wrist and tugging her to the next display table where a red lace bra and panty set was on a model of a female torso.

Quinn eyed the set dubiously. The bra was pretty, but the panties—"It's a thong, Marguerite."

"Yes, dear." She picked up a pair off the table and held them up in front of Quinn's hips. "Aren't they sexy?"

Quinn peered down at the scrap of red lace, pursed her lips, and grimaced. "Maybe, but wearing thongs for any length of time can irritate your vajayjay. At least they do on me. And this one is synthetic," she added, taking the thong from Marguerite and examining the material. "That's just an invitation for bacteria to camp out down there. The last thing I want is to have to take in more blood because my body is fighting bacterial vaginosis due to a thong that isn't even comfortable."

"Oh," Marguerite said, nonplussed. Snatching the thong back, she dropped it on the table. "We'll find something else, then."

"What about this?" Sam asked, holding up a pretty white lace bra and panty set. Turning it inside out, she indicated the strip of cloth at the crotch and said, "I think this little strip is cotton."

Quinn walked around the table she was at to reach

Sam and took the set from her. It was pretty, probably sexy on, and the lace was along the top of the panties, leaving only cotton where her skin needed to breathe to avoid infections. She nodded. "This is nice."

"Oh, good, they have them in several colors," she pointed out. "I'll go see what else I can find while you pick out the color and size you want."

"Thank you," Quinn murmured, and quickly selected sets in white, pink, and baby blue. She raised her head to glance around the store then, hoping something else would catch her eye, but froze when her gaze landed on a man standing outside the store, staring at her through the window.

He was tall for an Asian, and extremely good-looking, but for some reason Quinn felt fear explode inside of her like Fourth of July fireworks. Every corner and crevice of her body was suddenly filled with a terror she didn't understand . . . and she wasn't the only one. Someone was screaming beside her, the sound loud and panicked, but there were other screams too, these ones just as full of fear but tinged with agony. She began to tremble as a chill started to slide over her body, like a will-o'-the-wisp, following the terror coursing through her.

"Quinn?"

She was surprised to be able to hear Marguerite call her name over the panicked shrieking, but couldn't look away from the monster. She didn't dare, and then a shopper stopped at a table between her and the man and he was briefly blocked from view. When the shopper moved on a heartbeat later, he was gone.

"Quinn?" Marguerite was starting to sound alarmed, she noted in some separate compartment of her mind, and wondered how long the woman had been trying to get her attention. And who was that screaming? Why wouldn't they stop?

"Quinn!"

Turning toward the woman now approaching her with concern on her face, Quinn took a step toward her and then suddenly dropped as every muscle in her body went limp. She felt the crack of her head slamming into the floor before the lights went out.

"Are you sure you don't want to try anything on?"

Jet smiled and shook his head as they set the clothes Francis had helped him pick out on the counter. "I'm good, Francis. We got everything in my size. Thanks for your help. It went faster with the two of us working."

"My goodness, yes, it did. But that's only because you didn't balk at some of my selections like Russell and the other he-men immortals would. It's their age, of course," he added with a little shake of the head. "Every one of them thinks black is the height of fashion."

Jet grinned at the claim, but didn't counter the man's words. He saw a hell of a lot of black on his plane at times. It often looked like he was flying a funeral procession around, but he said, "After years of wearing mostly green or the brown desert flight suits in the navy, I like color."

"And it looks good on you," Francis assured him, and then smiled at the woman who rushed up to start checking them out. She was quick and efficient and nearly done when Francis's phone began to ring.

Jet raised an eyebrow when Francis pulled out his phone and frowned at the display.

"It's Russell. Here, pay for this while I take the call," Francis said, handing over a Council credit card.

Nodding, Jet accepted the card and watched the man move toward the door of the store as he answered the phone and pressed it to his ear. Shrugging, he turned back to the woman as she announced the amount owed and smiled at her as he handed over the credit card.

"Does he have to sign, or can you?" the woman asked a moment later.

"I will," Francis announced, suddenly appearing beside him.

"What's happened?" Jet asked at once. The man's usual good humor was noticeably missing, his expression one of grim concern.

"I'm sure it's nothing," Francis murmured, forcing a smile for the cashier as he finished with her and began to gather up the bags. "Let's go."

Jet helped with the bags and followed the man out of the store before asking again, "What's happened? What did Russell say?"

"It was Sam using his phone. Hers is apparently home, plugged into the charger. She forgot it," Francis told him. Moving more quickly now that they were out of the store, he added, "Quinn fainted in the lingerie shop. Russell gave Sam his phone and told her to call us."

Jet felt concern slide through him at this news, and asked, "Was she low on blood or something?"

"Sam didn't think so. She said she wasn't sure what happened. She heard Marguerite call out Quinn's name and glanced up to see her rushing across the store toward her and then Quinn turned, took one step, and just collapsed," he explained, and then added grimly, "Apparently, she hit her head when she fell. She must have hit hard, because Sam said she lost quite a bit of blood before the nanos stopped the bleeding. They're taking her back to the SUV, and hope she will be awake by the time they get there so they can give her blood."

"Why would she faint?" Jet asked, trying to understand something that seemed incomprehensible to him. "I've never heard of an immortal just fainting suddenly like that. I didn't even think it was something that could happen to you guys."

"Neither did I," Francis admitted. "Short of post–life mate sex or being shot with a dart, immortals don't faint."

"You don't think she was shot with a dart?" he asked with alarm.

Francis shook his head at once. "Russell would have made sure Sam mentioned that."

"Unless he didn't notice the dart," Jet pointed out.

Francis considered that briefly, and then cursed and pulled his phone back out. A moment later he was talking to Sam again, asking if they'd checked for a dart.

"They're going to check once they get her to the SUV," he told him as he put the phone away a moment later.

Jet nodded, but didn't comment as they began to walk a little more swiftly, moving at just short of a run.

"There they are," Francis said a few moments later as they rushed into the parking garage under the mall.

Jet grunted. He could see the small group gathered at the back of one of the two SUVs they'd used to transport everyone here. All of them were there, even Valerian and Tybo. Either the two men had still been at the vehicle when the others had reached it, or they'd encountered the group on the way back inside and had returned to the SUVs with them.

"How is she?" Jet asked sharply, pushing his way through the group, desperate to see for himself that Quinn was all right.

"She's still unconscious," Marguerite told him as he reached the woman who sat sideways on the back bumper, brushing hair away from Quinn's face as she lay in the back of the SUV. Marguerite's voice was filled with concern as she added, "I think we should get her back to the house and give her blood using an IV."

Nodding, Jet leaned past her, tossed his bags on the other side of Quinn, and then scooped the petite woman into his arms. By the time he walked quickly around to the back door on the driver's side, Valerian was there holding it open for him. Jet immediately slid in and settled Quinn in his lap.

"Do you want me to do up your seat belt for you?" Sam asked as she got into the back next to him, with Marguerite following.

Jet started to nod and then said, "Wait." His gaze slid to Valerian and Tybo as they got into the front. "Did you guys check the vehicles?"

"Check them?" Tybo asked blankly.

"Well, they blew up my plane," he pointed out grimly. "I wouldn't put it past them to . . ." He didn't bother finishing; both men had cursed after his comment about them blowing up his plane, and were already out of the car.

"You don't really think . . . ?" Sam began with concern, and then jerked around with surprise as Marguerite suddenly opened her door.

It was only then Jet heard Valerian barking, "Get out, get out, get out!"

Cursing, he turned toward his own door, relieved

when Tybo opened it and he was able to scramble out of the vehicle with Quinn.

"Away from the car," Tybo muttered, grabbing his upper arm and urging him quickly back toward the elevators they'd taken down to the parking garage. Clasping Quinn tight to his chest, Jet glanced over his shoulder to see Valerian, Francis, and Russell hustling the women after them.

Thirteen

"Which part of full-time protection at the Enforcer house did you people not understand?"

Quinn closed her eyes as that bellow increased the pain crashing around inside her head. She'd only woken up moments ago, and had immediately been confused by both the fact that her head hurt and that she was cradled in Jet's arms as he carried her into the Enforcer house. She hadn't noticed that the rest of the members of the shopping party were following them until Jet had stopped abruptly in the entry and the others had slid past and fanned out around them. Now she turned her head to scowl at the man who was the reason Jet had stopped and the source of the bellowing that had such a detrimental effect on the pain hammering inside her skull at the moment.

Lucian Argeneau. He'd obviously returned from up north while they were shopping. Pity, she thought, laying her head wearily back on Jet's shoulder. It was pounding like crazy, almost enough that she could ignore the aches and pains that seemed to be plaguing her entire body. God, she felt like she'd been hit by a bus, Quinn thought, her nose twitching as she noticed that Jet smelled good. Which wasn't new. He always smelled good to her, but at the moment he smelled especially yummy, she thought, inhaling deeply.

"This is my fault, Lucian," Marguerite said solemnly, drawing Quinn's attention from how nice Jet smelled. "Mary mentioned that Quinn and Jet had lost their luggage in the crash and had nothing but the clothes on their backs, so I thought we should take them out to get more and—"

"That's not true," Sam said at once. "Thank you, Marguerite, but—" She turned to Lucian. "I'm actually the one who suggested shopping was in order when Mary mentioned they'd lost their luggage. I—"

"But I thought it would be fine," Marguerite interrupted, and told Lucian, "We took four Enforcers with us, and there were eight of us altogether to protect Quinn: the four Enforcers, Jet, Mary, Sam, and me. I thought surely that would be enough to dissuade anyone from trying anything."

"And you thought wrong!" Lucian roared. "I nearly lost all nine of you!"

"If you're going to yell at anyone, yell at me," Mortimer growled, coming up the hall from his office and slipping an arm around Sam when she moved to his side. "I approved the trip. I'm ultimately responsible for our nearly losing everyone, including my own life mate," he added grimly, and then assured him, "It won't happen again."

Quinn watched Sam lean up to press a kiss to Mortimer's cheek, and then she rested her head back on Jet's shoulder with a sigh, envying the easy show of affection. She wished she could just kiss Jet on the cheek like that. Or the neck, she thought, unconsciously easing her nose a little closer to his throat and inhaling deeply again. God, he smelled so good. She wanted to kiss and lick and—

A gasp of shock slid from Quinn's lips when her head was suddenly yanked back by what she thought was a handful of her hair. Surprisingly enough, it didn't hurt. It was the only thing that didn't hurt at the moment, she thought as she heard several gasps around them, and then her attention refocused on Lucian as he snapped, "Get her a bag of blood before she makes a meal of Jet."

Quinn was aware of movement around them as someone rushed to do his bidding, but she was busy staring at Lucian with mounting dismay as she realized she very well might have been about to do just that. Dear God, her fangs were out and she hadn't even felt them descend. Realizing that Lucian was no longer scowling at her, but instead seemed to be looking at her hair—or at least something on her head—with surprise and what might even be concern, she asked, "What happened?"

Rather than answer, he took the bag of blood Tybo was suddenly there offering, and popped it on her fangs.

"Living room. Now," he ordered, releasing the hold he had on Quinn and turning to walk into the large living room across from the kitchen.

Placing a hand to the base of the bag to prevent it slipping off her fangs, Quinn leaned her head against Jet's shoulder again as he followed the others into the living room. By the time he had settled her on the couch and seated himself next to her, the bag at Quinn's mouth was empty.

The moment she pulled it from her fangs, Tybo was in front of her, taking the empty bag with one hand and offering her a fresh one with the other.

"Thank you," Quinn murmured, and popped this bag to her fangs, then glanced around at the people situated around the room. They were all seated now; even Bailey was sitting between Mary and Dante. The dumb dog was staring adoringly at Lucian, she noticed with disgust, but everyone else seemed to be looking from her to Lucian and back. It made her shift uncomfortably and glance down at the bag at her mouth.

"Report," Lucian said abruptly, and several people started to speak at once. He immediately raised one hand for silence and then pointed at Valerian.

The blond man sighed with resignation and said, "Everything was fine at the beginning. We went to the mall, and guarded Quinn while Francis helped her pick clothes." He paused briefly, and then grimaced as if not pleased to have to admit it, but said, "And then Tybo and I took the shopping bags back to the SUV while Russell escorted the women to the lingerie shop and Francis and Jet went to get his clothes. We were as quick as we could be," he added solemnly. "But when we were a couple of storefronts from the lingerie store where we were supposed to meet them, Russell came rushing out carrying Quinn."

"At first we thought they'd been attacked." His gaze slid to Quinn briefly and then back to Lucian. "But they explained she'd fainted and hit her head when she fell, so we went back down to the parking garage. They tried to revive her, but when they hadn't been able to by the time Jet and Francis caught up with us, we decided to head back here."

There was another pause where he ran a hand through his hair, again seeming reluctant to admit whatever was coming, but then he continued. "We were all in the car, about to leave, when Jet suggested checking the vehicles for bombs."

"Jet did?" Lucian growled. "The mortal pilot thought of checking for bombs, not the immortal Enforcers who were supposed to be the protectors?"

"Yes," Valerian admitted unhappily.

Lucian glowered at him briefly, and then gestured for him to continue.

Valerian cleared his throat, and said, "Tybo and I got out to look under the car and spotted a bomb under each vehicle. We immediately got everyone out of the SUVs and moved them back into the mall. We had no idea if or when the bombs would go off, so Tybo stayed by the elevators to prevent any mortals from going into the parking garage, and I ushered the others to the opposite end of the mall in case the cars exploded. Once I had them what I considered to be a safe distance from the danger zone, I called Mortimer. He sent out several Enforcers. Two immediately brought us back in the SUVs they arrived in, and the other men stayed to handle the bombs."

Lucian eyed the man narrowly and then, his voice dangerously soft, asked, "You left your assigned post of guarding Quinn to take the shopping bags to the car?"

"That's my fault," Francis said before Valerian could respond. "Valerian didn't want to leave Quinn, but I insisted he and Tybo take the bags back to the SUV. It seemed the sensible thing to do. Russell would be with

Quinn, as would all the women, and it would only be a few minutes and they'd be back with her. They wouldn't have been much good at protecting her with their arms full of bags anyway," he pointed out, and then added quickly, "Not that she needed protecting. She wasn't attacked. She apparently fainted."

"Immortals do not faint except after life mate sex," Lucian said dryly.

"That's what I thought too, but that's apparently what happened," Francis assured him. "Ask Russell."

Lucian shifted his gaze to Russell expectantly.

"I do not understand it myself, Lucian, but that's what it looked like to me," Russell assured him, and then hesitated before admitting, "I did not see anything that might have caused it. I was keeping an eye on the people in the store, watching for trouble, when I heard Marguerite calling Quinn. I shifted my attention to the two women; Marguerite was rushing toward her with concern and Quinn . . ." He glanced at her and frowned slightly. "She was looking toward the front of the store with her hands on her head, and then she lowered her hands, turned, took a step, and just collapsed."

Lucian gave a short nod and then shifted his attention to Marguerite. "Why were you concerned? What did you see?"

"Not much. It was just . . ." Marguerite shrugged slightly. "I called Quinn to come and see a pretty little white lace panty and bra set with garters and matching stockings that I spotted, but she didn't seem to hear me. I called again, louder, but she . . ." Marguerite frowned slightly. "She suddenly covered her ears and just stood there stiff and frozen, staring out the front window of the shop. I knew something was wrong, so I tried to read her mind as I rushed toward her, calling her name again. This time she seemed to hear me. Her hands fell away from her ears and she turned toward me, took one step, and then . . . I'm not sure if she fainted, but she did drop. And I do mean drop," Marguerite assured him. "She didn't fall, didn't stumble or trip; she just . . . dropped," she finished helplessly, and then closed her eyes and shuddered as if seeing the moment again in her mind. "Her head hit the floor with a crack and she was unconscious with blood pouring from the wound when I got to her, and then everybody was surrounding us. It took several moments for Russell and the other women to control the shopgirls and other shoppers and send them away, and then we wrapped Quinn's head in that cotton nightgown. It used to be white," she added dryly.

Eyes widening, Quinn raised a hand to her head and felt the wet cloth there. When she pulled her hand away it was covered with the blood that must be soaking the nightgown around her head. Apparently, Lucian hadn't grabbed her by the hair, he'd grabbed the wrapping around her head, she realized.

Marguerite continued. "Russell handed Sam his phone and told her to call Francis and Jet to tell them to meet us at the SUV, and then Russell scooped up Quinn and we headed out of the store." She shrugged. "Valerian told you the rest."

Lucian nodded agreement, but asked, "What did you find when you read her mind?"

Face solemn, Marguerite said, "All I could hear was screaming."

Quinn pulled the now empty bag from her fangs as Marguerite's words reminded her of what had happened. She'd seen that man, and she'd heard screaming. It had seemed to come from all around her, but had been loudest from right next to her and that had sounded like—"Pet."

"What about Pet?" Mary asked, drawing her attention to where the woman sat in a chair positioned next to the couch.

"Pet was screaming," she explained, and looked around expectantly. "Where is she?"

"Pet isn't here, Quinn," Mary said quietly. "She's in Italy."

"But I heard her," she protested.

"Why was Pet screaming, Quinn?" Mary asked, rather than address what she'd heard.

"I—" She paused, confusion filling her mind. "I don't know. I saw the monster at the window and everyone was screaming, but I'm sure Pet was the one screaming beside me. It sounded like Pet."

"What window, love?" Jet asked, rubbing her back soothingly.

"The shop window," she explained.

"Can you describe him to us?" Mary asked.

Quinn opened her mouth, and then hesitated; all she could remember was—"A mean smile and black eyes with brass flecks."

She heard Lucian murmur something and glanced over to see Tybo rushing from the room.

"Quinn," Mary said softly, drawing her gaze back to her. "Can you tell us what happened? What you saw? Start a couple minutes before you saw the monster," she instructed.

Quinn peered at her with confusion, wondering why Mary was calling the man a monster, but then made herself think back, and placed herself in the store again. Just before she'd seen the man she'd been—"I had selected three pairs of the bra and panty set that Sam had shown me. I looked around to see if there was anything else I wanted," she recalled. "But then I saw the man at the window, and everyone started screaming. I heard Marguerite call my name, but I didn't dare look away from the monster. I didn't know what to do, but then a woman stepped in front of me briefly and when she moved he was gone."

"The monster had gone?" Mary asked.

"Yes." Quinn nodded. "So, I turned to see what Marguerite wanted, and tried to go to her, but—" She shifted her gaze down to her body, remembering how it had betrayed her. It was as if every muscle inside of her had just abandoned ship, leaving her to flop to the ground like a puppet with its strings cut.

A rustle of sound drew her head up to see that Tybo had returned and was handing a file to Lucian. He immediately stood and crossed the room as he opened the file. Pulling out a large photo, he held it in front of her. "Was one of these men the one you saw outside the store window?"

Quinn stared at the two figures in the photo. It was obviously some kind of security shot. The men were in what could have been a bus station or airport; there were people moving past with luggage. She scanned the two men who had been circled with a red marker, her gaze moving quickly over the first man, but then stopping abruptly on the second as someone started screaming again, increasing the pain in her head that had already been building as she consumed blood and the nanos started to repair the injury her blood loss had prevented.

Feeling suddenly sick, Quinn pushed the picture away and stood up, intending to rush to the bathroom, but she didn't get that far. Lucian was blocking her way, and her legs decided to give out on her just as her stomach rebelled. She was already dropping when she began to spew, and she watched as if from a distance as she splattered vomit from Lucian's waist to his shoes before passing out.

"Quinn!" Leaping to his feet, Jet caught her by the upper arms just before she landed on the floor, but she was limp, her body sagging in his hold. Ignoring a cursing Lucian, he scooped her into his arms and carried her around the man now staring down at his vomit-covered clothes with disgust.

As he left the room, Jet heard Tybo say, "Well, I'm thinking that's a 'Yes, it's the guy she saw.'"

If he weren't so worried about Quinn, Jet would have laughed at the words. But he *was* worried about her. So much so that he didn't realize anyone had followed him until he was nearly to the door to Quinn's room and Marguerite rushed ahead to open it for him.

"Thank you," he murmured, carrying her inside.

"Wait. Don't put her in the bed until we clean her up," Marguerite said, hurrying toward the door to the bathroom.

"There's nothing to clean up, Marguerite. She didn't get any vomit on herself," he assured her as he reached the side of the bed and set Quinn gently down on it. Sitting on the edge of the mattress, he brushed her hair back from her face, and when Marguerite came to stand next to him, he asked, "What the hell's going on? Immortals don't faint except for new life mates during sex, and I have definitely never heard of one vomiting. I didn't even know it was possible," he said with amazement.

"I suspect both were emotional responses rather than physical."

Jet glanced around at that comment to see Mary and Sam entering the room. His gaze settled on Dante's wife. "An emotional response to whoever she saw outside the store?"

Mary hesitated and then said, "Perhaps, but I suspect it's bigger than that. I think seeing this man has sparked her memories and they're trying to come back."

"Can that happen?" Jet asked with uncertainty. "You said they were blocked or something."

"Blocked, not erased," Mary told him quietly. "They're still there. Her brain blocked them as a defense mechanism to protect her young mind from the trauma she endured when her mother and stepfather were murdered."

"Why would they come back after all this time?" Jet asked.

Mary shrugged. "It could be because her brain has decided that she's ready, but more likely because it realizes that her not remembering is now a threat to her well-being."

"I'm surprised the nanos wouldn't have fixed it so she had the memories again when she was turned," Sam murmured.

"That's because you think that her repressing the memories is a sign of some kind of fault with her mind. I believe just the opposite is true," Mary said thoughtfully. "I think she has a very strong mind, and well-developed defenses."

"But Pet went through the same thing and didn't have

to block memories to handle it," Sam pointed out. "So, doesn't she have the stronger mind and defenses?"

"Do not assume that just because they were both in the same room they had the same experience," Marguerite said quietly.

Jet noted the exchange of glances Mary and Marguerite shared and narrowed his eyes. "You two know something we don't, don't you?"

There was another exchange of glances and then Mary admitted, "We've known you and Quinn were life mates pretty much from the start."

"What do you mean from the start?" Jet asked uncertainly.

"From the moment four years ago when we brought her onto your plane," Marguerite said softly.

"What?" He stared at her with amazement. "I didn't even know then. How could you?"

"Marguerite has a certain skill at recognizing possible life mates," Mary said softly. "She's put a lot of couples together, and saw that you two had the same energy about you, or whatever it is." She glanced at Marguerite, who nodded that she'd got it right. Mary then continued. "She told Pet and Abigail, and they put their heads together to try to figure out a way to get the two of you together. But Quinn made it impossible. You went to every Notte family shindig Abigail invited you to, but Quinn refused to go. Worse yet, she became a shut-in."

Mary paused briefly and then said, "Of course, as twins, Tomasso and Dante are close, and we eventually got pulled into the scheming too. When Pet found out I used to be a psychologist she started talking to me about Quinn in the hopes that I could come up with an idea that might work. She started telling me about Quinn's marriage, how she was always the dutiful daughter, and so on. She even told me about their parents' deaths and that Quinn didn't remember it and believed they'd been in a car accident. Of course, I immediately suspected the deaths had something to do with why she was reacting so poorly to being turned."

"That still doesn't make sense to me," Sam complained. "Pet went through the same thing and actually remembers it, yet she had no problem accepting the turn and becoming an immortal."

Mary turned an amused eye her way and suggested, "Okay, let's look at it, then."

Sam nodded at once, apparently happy to.

Mary opened her mouth, but then closed it again and narrowed her eyes before asking, "What exactly do you know about the death of Quinn and Pet's parents?"

"All of it, I think. Mortimer told me that their stepfather was an immortal Enforcer chasing some organization of rogues called the Brass Circle. The Brass Circle got wind that he was hunting them, and murdered him and their mother and an older sister too." She frowned and then said, "Or it might have been a cousin." She pursed her lips and then asked, "A cousin raised as their sister?"

Mary nodded.

"Right," she said with relief. "So anyway, Mortimer also said that while Pet remembers everything, Quinn doesn't."

"He didn't mention how they survived?" Marguerite asked.

"Oh, yes, sorry—they were hiding in the closet. Their mother had put them in there."

"Well, you got the gist of the story," Mary said wryly. "But the Brass Circle didn't just murder the rest of the family; they tortured them first, and the girls witnessed it all. But I think the most important part of the story is that, after finishing off the rest of the family, the head guy sent the other men off to search for Quinn and Pet and then he apparently decided to search that room and found the girls hiding in the closet."

Jet stiffened at this news, imagining the tortures and torment that must have been visited on the twins for Quinn to block it from memory.

"Pet said he had a mean smile and black eyes with brass flecks."

"That's how Quinn described the man she saw at the mall," Jet said at once.

Mary nodded. "Yes."

Jet lowered his head to peer at Quinn and asked sadly, "What did he do to them?"

"Nothing."

"What?" Jet's head whipped around with disbelief.

Mary nodded again. "Well, not much anyway. Pet said she could feel the ruffling of his reading her mind, and then he grabbed her by the hair and turned to Quinn and his gaze narrowed, but then widened and he looked shocked. She said they stayed like that for a while, him staring at Quinn and the girls staring back, terrified, and then one of the men returned and he quickly released Pet's hair, stood, and closed the doors on the closet." She paused and arched her eyebrows as if to suggest they should sort something out from that. "And then, not only did he not reveal their presence in the closet to his men, but while they had planned to set the bodies on fire right there in the room where they had killed them, which surely would have seen the girls dead, he ordered the men to take the bodies outside and burn them in the courtyard."

"Quinn was obviously a possible life mate to this Brass Circle man."

Jet glanced to the door, his eyebrows rising when he recognized the tall, blonde woman now entering Quinn's room.

"Basha." Sam stood, and walked forward to hug her in greeting. "I didn't know you were here too."

The blonde hugged her back, explaining, "Marcus and I laid down to sleep on arriving. Well, he slept; I was lying there unable to sleep and then heard you talking in here and decided to join you. I apologize for listening in," she added solemnly.

Marguerite smiled with amusement at the apology as she took Sam's place to hug the woman. "With immortal hearing it's impossible not to hear conversations in this house . . . or any other. Hello, Basha, dear. Do you know Mary?"

"Mary and I met briefly in Cochrane," she assured her, and greeted the woman. "Hello again, Mary."

"Hi," Mary said easily.

"And you know Jet," Marguerite added, turning toward him.

"Yes. Jet has piloted for Marcus and me many times," Basha said, offering a warm smile to him.

Jet didn't return the smile; his mind was still on what she'd said as she'd entered. "Quinn can't be that guy's life mate, Basha. *We're* life mates."

There was a moment of silence as the women exchanged glances and then Marguerite walked over and squeezed his shoulder. "There have been occasions, many more than one would expect, where an immortal or mortal has been a possible life mate to more than one individual."

Fear shot down the back of his neck as the possibility of losing Quinn increased a hundredfold in his mind. Desperate not to believe it, Jet instinctively opened his mouth to protest again, but before he could say anything, Marguerite continued. "We don't know for sure that she is a possible life mate to him, but it would explain why he let the girls live. In fact, it seems the only explanation."

"It would also explain why she blocked the memory where Pet didn't," Mary said quietly.

"It would?" Sam asked, and then shook her head. "How? He didn't tell Quinn that they were possible life mates. Or did he, and you left that part out?"

"No, he didn't say that," Mary assured her.

"But," Basha said solemnly, "if he touched Quinn, she may have felt an awareness or attraction to him. Imagine how shattering that would have been when he was the monster who had moments earlier tortured and murdered her family."

"She was only six," Jet snapped with disgust. "You can't think she experienced life mate passion for this bastard at six."

"I did not say it would be passion or desire," Basha said quietly. "Or that she would even understand what his touch evoked in her. But any kind of benevolent feeling it caused in her for him would have been anathema to a child who had just watched him torture and murder the people she loved most in the world."

"Did Pet say he touched Quinn?" Sam asked with a frown.

"No," Mary answered. "She doesn't recall his doing so, but she was a terrified six-year-old in a traumatic situation, and she admitted she was staring at his face, not his other hand," Mary told them. "He may have reached for Quinn's arm or wrist without her seeing. In fact, it's more than likely that he did."

Jet shook his head. He didn't want to hear any of this. He didn't know what scared him more: that Quinn had another possible life mate, or that the bastard was a murdering sicko who had found her again.

"She would not choose him over you," Marguerite said soothingly.

Jet frowned, and then asked, "Do you believe this crap?"

He was hoping she didn't, and silently begging her not to, and he supposed she read that in his mind, because her expression was apologetic when she said, "I'm afraid I do. I believe that she did feel something when he touched her. Something she didn't understand, but didn't like feeling, and that has shaped her life."

Mary nodded. "I think whatever she felt that day is the reason she blocked the memories. Because she couldn't bear to remember whatever kind thoughts or feelings he inspired in her. I think that's also why she's always been the dutiful daughter without a hint of the usual teenage rebellion. Ashamed or terrified that she could have a benevolent thought or feeling for a monster, she was as good as she possibly could be to try to make up for it, and prove—if only to herself—that she wasn't a monster like him."

"And speaking of monsters," Marguerite said. "That is probably why she also sees herself as a monster now that she too has been turned."

"She called him that when you asked her to tell us what happened," Jet recalled wearily.

"Yes, she called him a monster several times and yet didn't even seem to realize she had," Mary told him. "When we called him a monster back to her, she was confused as to why we would."

"Mary also believes this is why Quinn has locked herself away for the four years since she was turned," Marguerite said. "Because she is afraid if she doesn't, she could become a monster, which she fears she may already be because as a possible life mate he inspired something in her."

"Shit," Jet breathed. Everything the women had said made sense. Quinn's reactions were perfectly reasonable when explained like this. As much as he didn't want to, he also now believed that she was a possible life mate to this bastard as well as himself. It fit everything perfectly. Except—

"Then why is he trying to kill me?"

Jet swung around, his mouth dropping when he saw that Quinn's eyes were open and she'd obviously heard most, if not all, of their conversation. She'd also asked the very question that he'd been about to ask. If this monster was her life mate, why was he trying to kill her?

Fourteen

Quinn noted the shocked expressions on the faces of the people in the room and felt her mouth compress. She didn't know how long she'd been unconscious, but she'd woken up to find herself being carried into her bedroom. Humiliated that she'd basically puked all over Lucian Argeneau in front of everyone, she'd kept her eyes closed and feigned that she was still unconscious, fully expecting that she'd be put in her bed, and left to rest and heal. She hadn't expected Jet and the women to have a powwow in her room that would tear away the blinders she'd worn since she was six. But the moment Jet had asked what was going on and how she could faint and vomit—both of which were things she too hadn't expected or even imagined were possible for an immortal—she'd had to listen.

It had been hard not revealing she was awake. She'd

had to bite her tongue to keep from gasping at several points, and a couple of revelations had been horrifying enough to cause nausea in her again. A possible life mate to the bastard who had murdered her beautiful mother and cousin, as well as her stepfather, the kindest man she had ever known? The very thought made her shudder with dismay.

But they were right; the scenario they painted explained her life perfectly. She'd been manipulated by fears she hadn't even known she'd had her whole life. And a self-loathing she hadn't understood the source of, Quinn acknowledged. Because it had been self-loathing that had made her the dutiful daughter and submissive wife, afraid to think for herself or even consider doing something her adopted parents or Patrick might not have agreed with. Yes, when she thought about it, this did explain her life. But that explanation didn't at all match with the monster's actions.

"Well?" she said now, shifting to sit up in bed and lean against the headboard. "Why would this leader of the Brass Circle try to kill me if I'm a possible life mate? Shouldn't he be desperate to claim me?"

"Well, hell," Mary muttered. "You weren't supposed to hear any of that."

"No, of course not. Why should I know my own history?" she asked dryly.

"Because you are supposed to discover it in therapy, gradually, as you are mentally ready to learn it. Not have the veil ripped away and your past forced on you when you might not be prepared to hear it," she said on a sigh, and then eyed her briefly before asking, "How do you feel?"

"Pretty goddamned pissed, Mary," Quinn said grimly. "I've been manipulated my whole life by my own mind and I don't think I enjoyed the ride."

"Oh, now, Quinn, that's . . . well, actually, a pretty apt description," she acknowledged.

"Having to always be the good girl, the dutiful daughter, anything to please Mom and Dad, and then Patrick, lest they figure out I'm—"

"Tainted?" Basha suggested quietly. "Somehow wrong inside? Unredeemable for feeling anything benevolent for a monster?"

Quinn let her breath out on a puff and nodded unhappily. "Although I didn't know about the benevolent feelings for a monster part," she said wearily. "I just always thought there was something wrong with me, and if I didn't behave everyone would figure it out and . . ." She shrugged.

Quinn sat up straighter and waved those feelings away. They could wait. Raising her eyebrows, she peered around at the women in her room, and said, "Well? Why would a possible life mate try to kill me?"

"Unfortunately, that is the one thing we have not worked out yet," Marguerite admitted solemnly, and then turned to Mary. "Unless you have?"

Mary shook her head. "It's a new and unexpected development."

"Maybe he's jealous that Jet is your life mate and you appear to be choosing him," Sam suggested.

"Except that Jet hadn't even spoken to Quinn before the plane crash caused by the bombs," Mary pointed out. "In fact, if anything, the crash did more for getting those two together than any of our scheming to get him on that plane when Pet finally convinced Quinn to come to Canada for counseling."

Quinn turned to Jet with surprise to find him eyeing Mary and Marguerite narrowly. But then he seemed to sense her attention on him and offered her a crooked smile. "It was supposed to be my day off, but then Bastien called and asked if I could copilot for Jeff Miller on a long-haul flight: Russia to Italy to Toronto." He shrugged. "I didn't have any plans, and Miller was a friend, so I agreed and caught a red-eye to Russia."

"Yes," Marguerite sighed. "When Pet called to tell me she'd convinced Quinn to come to Canada for counseling, I asked Bastien to arrange for you to copilot her flight. The intention was to throw you two together naturally. But what we had not considered was that as the copilot you would not meet and greet the passengers as you do when you are the pilot. Jeff greeted them while you stayed in the cockpit doing preflight checks. If not for the crash, you may not even have known she was on board unless one of the Russian girls got bored and came to talk to you in the cockpit and mentioned it," she said with a frown.

Jet shook his head. "That wouldn't have happened. Jeff was old-school. He didn't like anyone in the cockpit but the pilot and copilot, and discouraged anyone from thinking they should come up."

"Just so," Marguerite said on a sigh. "I cannot call the crash lucky, because I liked Jeff Miller and he lost his life in it. But the two of you would not have met and found you were life mates on that flight without it."

"Right," Sam muttered, drawing everyone's gaze back to her. "So, the Brass Circle monster who may be Quinn's life mate isn't trying to kill her out of jealousy." She pursed her lips briefly, her face scrunching up in thought, and then her eyes suddenly widened and she suggested, "Maybe it's not him that's trying to kill Quinn. Maybe it's the Brass Circle trying to kill her. Maybe they're worried that he might abandon the group to be her life mate, and even join the good side and spill all their secrets. Maybe he's here because he's trying to save her from them."

Well, that definitely had everyone thinking, Quinn thought wryly as she peered around at the reactions on the faces of the others. Jet and every woman there was looking wide-eyed at the suggestion. Because it was possible, and definitely made more sense than that the monster was trying to kill her if she was his life mate.

"Then why hasn't he tried to contact her?" Jet asked, and turned uncertainly to Quinn. "He hasn't, has he?"

"No," she assured him solemnly, and didn't miss the relief on his face.

"How was he supposed to contact her?" Sam asked. "Call the Enforcer house and ask to speak to her? What would he say when Mortimer or I asked who was calling?" Taking on a deeper voice Quinn supposed was meant to be male, she said, "Uh, well, she may not remember me, but I'm the guy who killed her parents so horribly, and I'm sorry for that now because it turns out we're life mates." She raised her eyebrows at the end as if to say, *Ridiculous.*

They were all silent for a minute, and then Basha pointed out, "His being here to try to save her from the Brass Circle would explain things nicely."

"Yes," Marguerite agreed thoughtfully, and then

frowned. "I wish the Enforcers in Italy would hurry and get through those tapes. It would help if we knew if he was the one who planted the bombs or not."

"They have finished and we do know," Basha told them. "The second man in the picture is the only one caught on film around the plane. It seems he was interrupted as he set the second bomb and had to hide, then slip out of the hangar. We believe that is the only reason the second bomb merely damaged the engine it was placed in and did not destroy it completely like the first bomb did to the other engine. It is the only reason Captain Miller was able to get that second engine going again. The special investigator Lucian called in says the engine was damaged enough that it could only have worked at half capacity, but that was enough for him to get the nose up, even if it was too late to avoid a crash altogether."

"Then it is possible that he is not involved in trying to kill her," Mary murmured.

"But he was at the airport with the one who did," Jet pointed out.

"He could have been sent to help kill her, but is pretending to go along with it and trying to warn her at the same time," Sam suggested.

"But he hasn't warned me," Quinn reminded her.

"Well, he did show himself to you outside the store," Sam said slowly. "Maybe that was him trying to warn you. It's not like he could have walked in and talked to you with Russell and the rest of us there."

Quinn was considering that when Marguerite said, "You need more blood, dear. You're pale and your head doesn't seem to be paining you as it did after you downed the first two bags. The nanos must have stopped repairs until you get more blood for them to work with."

"Maybe they're done," Quinn said hopefully, and immediately had Mary at her side unwinding the cloth from around her head.

"Not done," she assured her solemnly, but didn't re-wrap her head. "The wound is closed, but your head is still dented. You need more blood."

"Here." Sam walked to the bedside table, and opened the door, revealing the interior of a refrigerator stocked with bags of blood. Retrieving three of them, she handed them to Jet and then closed the door. Straightening then, she noticed the other women eyeing the bedside table with interest, and said, "Custom-made. You each have one in your room. Except maybe for you, Basha," she added apologetically. "I had no warning you and Marcus were coming. I'll go down and fetch some blood for you now so you can put it in the refrigerator next to your bed."

"I will come help you," Basha said, following her out of the room.

"I guess we should leave you to feed and rest," Marguerite said now. "We can talk about this more later." Her mouth firmed before she added, "After we talk to the men and find out if they have any kind of plan to end these attacks on your life before the Brass Circle crashes through the gates in a van rigged out as a car bomb and blows us all up."

"Or they take control of a pilot's mind and make him crash his plane into the house," Mary added dryly, moving around the bed to follow Marguerite to the door. Once there she paused and glanced back to offer, "If you feel the need to talk about anything, I'll be downstairs. Otherwise, I guess we can have another session tomorrow, same time as we did today."

Quinn managed to hold back a grimace and whispered a polite, "Thank you," as the woman left.

"You seem less than eager for more counseling," Jet said with amusement once the door had closed behind the women.

Quinn shrugged, and accepted the bag of blood he held out to her. "I kind of just want a little time to absorb what I've learned so far."

"It has been a lot," he said solemnly.

"Yeah," she sighed, and then smiled crookedly and said, "Lucky you, getting stuck with the most screwed-up immortal possible for a life mate."

Jet was silent as she popped the bag of blood to her fangs, and then took a minute to rearrange their pillows so that they could both lean back against the headboard. Once they were settled comfortably, he said, "I think I mentioned that people like to talk to me on the flights I pilot."

Quinn nodded, and eyed him with curiosity over the bag of blood at her mouth.

"Well, it's because of that I can tell you that you are not the most screwed-up immortal out there," he assured her. "Heck, Mary, Marguerite, and Basha can all probably give you a run for your money on that count."

Quinn's eyes widened and she pulled the bag from her mouth as it finished emptying. "No way," she said with certainty as he took the bag and replaced it with a fresh one.

"Way," he said, urging the hand holding the bag toward her mouth until she popped it in place. "Marguerite apparently had a monster of her own who she thought was her life mate, but wasn't. The bastard spent a couple of centuries doing some horrible things to her," he announced, and then added, "And Basha?" He grimaced. "She probably wins the award for most screwed-up life thanks to a monster named Leonius Livius. She spent more than twenty-seven hundred years in a sort of hell thanks to him." He was silent for a minute and then said, "It's not just the female immortals who have their demons either. Santo has one hell of a history. You should ask Pet about it sometime. It'll make you grateful you only had thirty years or so of what was basically mental conflict to deal with."

Quinn frowned. His words made her troubles sound somehow trivial, and she was torn between being offended and wanting to believe they were and therefore might be easier to get over. Which is why she almost laughed around the bag at her mouth when he said, "Not that I'm trivializing what you've been through."

Pulling the now empty bag from her mouth, she arched one eyebrow and asked, "No?"

"No," he assured her, taking the empty bag to drop in the garbage bin on his side of the bed. He picked up the last full bag from his lap, but didn't hand it to her right away. Instead, he shifted it from hand to hand, and said, "I can't imagine what it must have been like to watch those men from the Brass Circle torture and murder the rest of your family. And then to feel whatever you did when the murderer touched your hand or arm afterward and you felt whatever you felt." He shook his head. "I'm staggered that you came away from it as well as you did. I mean, that has to seriously screw up a kid. But you packed those memories away where they couldn't hurt you and got on with life."

"But they did hurt me," Quinn said with a frown. "I was always struggling to be good for fear I might be as bad as him."

"Is that so bad?" he asked solemnly. "I mean, I know it wasn't good for you emotionally to never feel secure in love, but you didn't get into drugs, didn't end up a statistic of teenage pregnancy, you didn't even flunk out of school and become an alcoholic or something. Instead, you became an overachiever. You're a cardiothoracic surgeon, Quinn. You yourself told me there are less than four thousand of those in America. And you even had a son while you were at it, and a brilliant son, who you did a hell of a job with."

"Do you think so?" she asked with concern.

"Oh, hell, yeah," he assured her. "I really like Parker. He's smart, he's funny, and he's not afraid of anything as far as I can tell from the couple of dozen times I've talked to him."

"That many?" she asked with surprise.

Jet shrugged. "I didn't just talk to him on the plane when they flew places. Pet and Santo were always bringing him to the Notte family shindigs, and for some reason the boy usually ended up coming to talk to me. He's a good kid."

"He did talk about you a lot after the family functions he went to with Pet," Quinn admitted. "I had no idea who you were, but he seemed to like you a great deal."

"I'm glad, but right now I'm more interested in his mother, and I have to tell you, I think you really rocked your mortal life. I suspect you'll do the same with your immortal life too. But more importantly, I think you're a good person. I like you, Quinn. When we're together, whether we're talking or whatever, I feel like we're on the same wavelength."

"I do too," she acknowledged softly.

They stared at each other silently for a minute, and then Jet cleared his throat and held up the last bag of blood. "Here. You'd better get to work on this before I'm tempted to kiss you."

Quinn accepted the bag and popped it to her fangs, but really would have rather he'd kissed her. Because she liked him too, and she was really starting to think she might not have as much stuff to work out as she'd thought. She supposed finding out the motivation behind her actions helped. She suspected Mary and Marguerite were right about what had happened after her mother and stepfather had been murdered. As they'd speculated on what may have happened, she'd had a flash of her wrist being grabbed, and a sudden rush of confusing feelings. She still wasn't sure what they would be called. Her adult mind hadn't recognized it as desire when she'd experienced those sensations again in her memory. Quinn could only say it had been an odd awareness, and a tingling that had pushed her terror and grief away and left a yearning for the safety she sensed she would find from the man touching her.

Which hadn't made any sense at all, especially when she had watched his brutal abuses of her mother, stepfather, and cousin just moments before. So Quinn had immediately been ashamed of herself and tried to distance herself from the feelings. Apparently, she'd found a way, by blocking the memory of it from her mind.

But it had meant blocking the memories of most of her childhood as well, which had made it impossible for her to understand her own motivations most of the time.

A shaft of pain slid through her head and Quinn's fangs nearly tore through the bag at her mouth before she forced her jaws to relax.

"What is it?" Jet asked, turning toward her. "Are you in pain?"

She started to nod her head, but that just exacerbated her pain, and she closed her eyes on a moan.

"Oh, yeah, you are," Jet breathed, sounding dismayed, and she opened her eyes to see him staring at her forehead with fascinated horror.

Quinn reached for the bag at her mouth, wanting to ask what was wrong, but Jet caught her hand.

"No. Leave it. You'll get blood everywhere. Besides, it's almost empty," he told her, and then added, "And you'll need it."

Quinn grunted impatiently and raised her eyebrows when he shifted his gaze down to her face, the best she could do to ask why he'd said that.

Apparently, he got the gist. After a moment to grimace at whatever he was seeing, Jet explained, "You really hurt yourself when you fainted. You had an open wound on the side of your forehead that was bleeding, but it was also . . . well, it looked like your skull was all broken and caved in where it hit."

Quinn winced at the description. That explained her pounding head.

"When Mary removed the bloody nightgown from your head and checked your injury up here, the wound was closed, but you still had a great dent in your head," he continued. "But I'm pretty sure the nanos are repairing your skull now. The dent is kind of pushing its way back out."

Quinn heard the end of that through a terrible, rending pain. It felt like someone was sawing the top of her head off rather than repairing it. She knew the brain didn't have any pain receptors, but the meninges—a membranous covering of the brain—and periosteum—a membrane covering on the bones—as well as the scalp itself did have pain receptors and every one of those receptors appeared to her to be screaming in agony. It was unbearable, and she couldn't stop a whimper from slipping out.

"Okay. Okay," Jet said soothingly, wrapping his arms around her and drawing her against his chest. He held her like that for a minute, rubbing her back, and then stopped to tug the finally empty blood bag from her mouth.

"What can I do? How can I help?" he asked as he tossed the bag onto the bedside table. When she hadn't answered by the time he turned back, he eased her to lie down on the bed, and started to slide away. "I'll go see if there's some kind of drug they can give you. I know immortals are drug resistant, but there must be something they can—" His words died abruptly when she grabbed his hand to stop him, and tugged, although not as hard as she could have. She didn't want to force him back into bed against his will; she just wanted to stop him.

Quinn had been given drugs to help her through the turn four years earlier and hadn't cared for the hungover feeling she'd had on awakening. Besides, she suspected she wasn't going to be conscious long anyway. The pain in her head was building to a crescendo that kept her fully occupied as Jet settled back on the bed, eased down to lie next to her, and drew her onto his chest.

He started to rub her back again, and she could hear him murmuring soothingly through her pain, but couldn't understand what he was saying. Still, it was comforting and she appreciated it, right up until the pain suddenly intensified and her screaming shut out his voice.

Fifteen

"Wow. I didn't expect this."

Quinn lifted the paint roller off the wall and turned to blink at Jet when she saw him standing in the open door of her house, staring at the brown wall of the entry that she was painting a pale blue-green color. Looking at Jet now, she realized that it was a paler version of his eye color. Wondering what that meant, if anything, she tilted her head and asked, "What didn't you expect?"

"This." He gestured around the room. "To find you painting, of all things."

"Oh." Quinn smiled faintly, and turned to dip the roller in the paint tray, ran it back and forth on the washboard section to remove the excess, and then turned back to the wall to continue painting as she said, "I always hated this color, so I just decided to get rid of it."

"Okay," he said with amusement, moving into the entry. "I'm guessing you didn't pick it, then?"

Quinn shook her head. "Patrick. He liked dark colors."

"I wonder what it indicates that in your dreams you're making changes to a house you no longer own."

Quinn blinked and then spun around to look at him again. "This is a dream?"

Jet nodded. "Pretty sure. I mean, it's not like Patrick could have picked colors for your house in Italy. He was dead before you moved there. So, this must be your house in Albany, which someone else now owns. So, I hope it's a dream, or we might both get arrested for trespassing soon."

Quinn stared at him, and then back at the wall with a small sigh. She was painting someone else's wall in her dream. Or painting her own wall from the past. Whichever way you looked at it, it was a waste to paint a wall that wasn't hers anymore. She dropped the roller brush in the paint tray and wiped her hands on the jean shorts she'd never owned in real life, and led him out of the house. But she stopped on the porch to peer around at the houses on the street.

"Your old stomping ground?" Jet asked, looking around as well.

"Yes." She sighed the word, sadness filling her.

"Seems perfect," Jet announced, taking it all in. The quiet houses, lush lawns, beautiful full-grown trees everywhere.

"It was a good place to live. Good neighbors, good neighborhood . . . But when I came out of the turn it was already sold and gone and I was told I'd have to live somewhere else."

"Something else you lost, then," he said quietly.

"Well, yeah," she admitted. "But—" She broke off as a yippy little French bulldog came running up onto the porch, barking and snapping at their ankles.

"Oh, dear, no, Rufus. Behave," an older woman with short, dyed red hair called ineffectually as she hurried up the walk. "Bad boy," the woman crooned, scooping the dog up and cuddling it as she reprimanded in a singsong voice, "You're such a naughty boy. Yes, you are. Kiss, kiss, kiss, kiss, kiss." She suited action to words, plastering little kisses all over the squirming dog's head.

"Morning, Mrs. Lawson," Quinn said with resignation.

"Oh, good morning, Quinn dear. Isn't it a nice day? Where's Patrick? And who is this? My, my aren't you a strapping fellow?" she added, petting Jet's arm with excited eyes. "My goodness, a woman could be forgiven for adultery with a tempting man like you around."

Jet gave Quinn a *What the hell?* look and she grinned with amusement, her irritation with Mrs. Lawson slipping away. This might be a dream, but Mrs. Lawson had been an annoying busybody of a neighbor with a little mutt that liked to terrorize everyone in real life too. This was some part of Quinn's mind that had decided to remind her of that and brought the woman to her porch to do so.

Mrs. Lawson hadn't been the only irritant here. There were neighbors a couple of houses down who had thrown parties nearly every night in the summer, playing raucous music all afternoon and evening. That had driven her crazy when she went to bed early and tried to get extra sleep for a big operation the next day.

"Turns out the neighborhood maybe wasn't so perfect," she told Jet. "Let's go somewhere else."

"Where?" he asked at once.

"I don't know," she said slowly, searching her mind, and then suggested, "Take me to your favorite place."

"My favorite place," Jet murmured, and then he suddenly grinned.

Quinn supposed that grin should have warned her. The next thing she knew they were in—"Six Flags?" she asked with disbelief.

Jet shrugged, but he also blushed a little. "I always wanted to go here as a kid, but of course with my mother that was out of the question. But Abs and I came here our last year of high school. And we had a blast," he said, smiling widely as he looked around at the food stalls, the rides, and the people milling about. Then his gaze returned to her. "Do you like roller coasters?"

"I don't know. I've never been to a theme park before," she admitted self-consciously.

"What?" He looked amazed, and then said solemnly, "Oh, Quinn, you're a theme park virgin, and I'm so going to enjoy popping your cherry. Come on."

Grabbing her hand, he rushed her through the crowds of people to something he called the Iron Rattler. Dreams were a lovely thing and they didn't have to wait in line for the ride, but instead rushed up and just hopped in. She screamed and laughed her way through that ride and several more before he dragged her off to an ice cream cart, and then they wandered along, contentedly licking their cold treats.

"I can't believe you've never been to an amusement park," Jet commented after a moment. "Didn't Parker ever want to go?"

"He never asked to go. Although Pet did take him to Disneyland once and he apparently had a great time," Quinn said, frowning as she recalled that. She should have taken him to Disneyland, she thought now.

"We should take him somewhere when this is all over. He'll probably be shocked that his staid, very professional mother is a closet coaster junkie," he teased.

"I am not," she laughed, bumping him with her hip.

"You are," he said with amusement. "Tell me you aren't having a blast."

"All right, fine. I'm having fun," she admitted. "But man, is it always this hot here?" she asked, plucking at the neckline of her T-shirt and lifting and lowering it to allow some air inside.

"Yeah. It is hot," he murmured, glancing around. "It was blistering the day Abs and I went, so I suppose my mind just gave us the same kind of day. But I wonder if I can—Oh, look! The Texas Tumble. That'll cool us off."

"What's the Texas Tumble?" Quinn asked when he grabbed her hand and started hustling her through the crowds.

"A water ride," he told her with a mischievous grin. "You'll love it."

Despite the misgivings his expression gave her, Quinn did love the raft ride, and it definitely cooled them off. She was completely soaked by the end, and much cooler than when they'd started.

They were stumbling away from the ride, laughing and telling each other their favorite parts, when Jet suddenly said, "Oh, my, it's a good thing this is a dream."

"Why?" Quinn asked with amusement.

"Because you'd be arrested for indecent exposure otherwise," he teased, his gaze dropping to her chest.

Quinn immediately glanced down to see that her T-shirt was soaked and now see-through, and she wasn't wearing a bra. She stared blankly for a minute, pretty sure she hadn't set out to paint her house braless in a T-shirt so thin it turned opaque when wet. Jet must have done it, of course, she thought, and lifted her head to look at him with raised eyebrows. "Another one of your contributions to the dream?"

"It is supposed to be shared sex dreams," he pointed out with a small smile, raising one hand to brush his knuckles lightly over the nipple of her breast once, and then again.

Quinn swallowed as she watched her nipple grow hard and erect under the attention.

"And," he continued, brushing her nipple again, "what guy doesn't fantasize about his girlfriend getting all wet so that her T-shirt is plastered to her body and see-through?"

"I don't know," she mumbled, clasping his arm to steady herself as she swayed toward him.

"Of course, in the perfect dream, that's followed by her finding him irresistible and throwing herself at him," he added in a near whisper, and she lifted her face to his again. When she saw that he'd lowered his head, she slipped up on her tiptoes and kissed him. That was as much throwing as she knew how to do. It was enough. Jet's arms were immediately around her, pulling her close and lifting her as he straightened.

Quinn immediately wrapped her legs around his hips, her hands clutching at his shoulders as his tongue thrust into her mouth. She felt his hands clasp her bottom and squeeze and knead even as he urged her closer, and she allowed her own hands to roam, sliding them over his muscled shoulders, and down what she could reach of his back as he devoured her mouth with his.

She had no idea how they ended up lying down, but when he broke the kiss and lifted his head, she was staring up at him, the sun behind him, shining in her eyes and blinding her briefly as he began to tug her T-shirt up. Quinn closed her eyes and helped, yanking the wet cloth out of her jean shorts and up over her breasts. She would have happily removed it altogether, but he didn't give her the chance. Greedy, he covered her breasts with his hands and kneaded briefly, then shifted one hand to cup it around one breast so that he could take the nipple into his mouth and swirl his tongue over it.

Gasping, Quinn arched into the caress, a long "Ahhhh" of sound slipping from her mouth, and then she was tugging at his hair, urging him back to kissing her. Once he was, she took him by surprise and rolled him onto his back, wanting to play with him now. But instead they both cried out as something crashed down on top of them.

Blinking her eyes open, Quinn glanced around at her room in the Enforcer house, and the IV stand lying across them. It was attached via a tube to her wrist, and when they'd rolled, she'd dragged it with her until it hit the side of the bed and fell over.

"Damn," Jet breathed.

Quinn turned back to him, noting the disappointment on his face. He obviously thought she'd want to stop now. But she was straddling his hips, her T-shirt and bra caught about her breasts, and his erection nudging insistently against her through the jeans she wore.

The last thing she remembered before the dream was him holding her as pain had rocked through her body. Obviously, he'd gone for help when she passed out and somebody had hooked her up to an IV to make sure she got the blood she needed to repair her injury without her having to regain consciousness to consume it. He then must have fallen asleep next to her and joined her in the dream they'd then shared. But in bed, side by side, they'd started to live out their shared dream in reality again . . . and she didn't want it to stop.

Reaching out, she pushed the IV away, uncaring when the catheter was dragged out of the back of her hand and taken with it as it fell to the floor. When she turned back to Jet, his eyes were open and he was watching her with a question on his face. Smiling, she shifted against his erection, and their eyes widened at the pleasure that it sent through them both. Then she bent her head to kiss him.

Jet groaned into her mouth with appreciation, and then his hands were on her breasts, kneading the small mounds as he kissed her. The sensation that stirred up in both of them was a thousand times more erotic and frantic than the dream pleasure had been, and Quinn rubbed herself over him again, grunting into his mouth when sharp pleasure shot through her.

She didn't complain when his hands left her breasts, because they had dropped to the button of the jeans she'd fallen asleep in. He made quick work of undoing it, and then the zipper. Once those two tasks were done, he began to push the heavy material off of her hips. But it had nowhere to go. She was straddling him on her knees.

Growling into her mouth with frustration, he broke

the kiss and sat up abruptly, taking her with him. He caught her by the waist and lifted her. Quinn immediately shifted her legs and pushed up into a standing position, then shifted to stand between his legs and finished pushing the jeans down. She tugged them off one foot, and kicked them off the other so that they hit the floor, and then gasped in surprise when he took advantage of the position and began to kiss the inside of one knee.

Turning back, Quinn caught his hair in her fingers to steady herself, and laughed a little breathlessly. "Jet, let me—" The words ended on a gasp as one of his hands slid up the inside of her thigh and found her moist heat. Moaning now, she closed her eyes and clutched his head with both hands, holding on almost desperately as his mouth trailed up her leg and his fingers caressed her. Her legs were trembling madly, her body tight as a bow, pleasure just coming into reach when he suddenly withdrew his wonderful, magical fingers.

Quinn opened her eyes, and then gasped in surprise when he caught her by the waist and tugged her down with him as he dropped back on the bed. Only her immortal-fast reflexes kept her from landing directly on the man's groin and had her straddling him instead . . . with his erection hard and hot beneath her.

Smiling, she leaned forward to kiss him, her hair a dark curtain around their faces, and then she sat up, lifted herself until he sprang free beneath her, and then lowered herself onto his hot hard length.

Quinn was vaguely aware of his groan as she lowered herself, but it had been a very long time for her, and most of her concentration was focused on the feel of him slowly filling her, and her body expanding to take him. But when Jet reached between them and began to caress her, pleasure rolled through her, doubled, and rolled through her again.

Quinn began to move. She raised and lowered herself on him, vaguely aware of his encouraging words, gasps, and moans, even as those same sounds left her. But mostly her attention was on the pleasure rolling over her in increasing waves, and pulling tight inside of her at the same time until it exploded over them in a shower of darkness.

Quinn woke up on Jet's chest and lay still for a moment, just enjoying his scent, his heat, and being close to him. But after a minute, she sighed and started to move, only to gasp in surprise when he suddenly rolled her onto her back and came down half on top of her.

"Hi," he whispered with a grin.

"Hi," she whispered back. "I thought you were still sleeping."

He shook his head, his gaze sliding down over the bra and T-shirt tangled over her chest, and then dropping to her breasts when his hand pushed the cloth back up almost under her chin. "I've been awake forever. Just holding you and thinking of all the things I want to do with you."

"What's that?" she asked a little breathlessly as he caught one nipple between thumb and finger and began to roll and tweak it.

"Disneyland for real. Fishing. Camping. Oh, and a big barbecue with the Notte family there so I can show you off."

When his words surprised a chuckle from her, Jet's fingers stilled and he eyed her in question.

"Sorry, I was just kind of expecting a list of sexual positions or something," she admitted with a self-deprecating smile.

"Oh, that would take centuries to list, and easily a millennium to act out," he assured her, and then bent to flick her neglected nipple with his tongue while his finger and thumb returned to toying with the other.

Quinn closed her eyes as his lips closed over the nipple he'd been flicking, and when he began to draw on it, she groaned, "We have time."

Jet froze and lifted his head. "We do?" he asked carefully..

Quinn nodded and pointed out, "We're life mates."

"I thought you weren't ready for a life mate?" he said uncertainly.

"And I thought I was a monster," she said solemnly.

Jet's eyebrows rose at that. "You don't anymore? Just because you know what happened with your parents?"

Quinn hesitated. "Let's say, my eyes are open and I'm willing to consider that maybe this world isn't black and white but shades of gray." Reaching up she caressed his cheek gently. "You don't look at me like I'm a monster. Or even a she-pire," she added dryly.

Jet grimaced at the word. "I don't really think of female immortals as she-pires," he assured her. "How could I? Abs is one, and she's still the same, wonderful gal I've always known," he pointed out, and then explained, "She-pires is just a kind of defensive nickname."

"Defensive?" she asked with surprise.

Jet nodded and turned his head to kiss her palm. "Immortals have some powerful mojo. I suspect it's some kind of pheromone that the nanos send out to make you more attractive to us mere mortals. It probably makes us easier prey," he added thoughtfully, and then shrugged. "Anyway, Jeff and a couple of other pilots warned me that it was easy to act a complete idiot around the immortals because of it. They said thinking of them as she-pires makes it easier to remember that what we're feeling isn't real. So I started using it too."

"Oh," she murmured with a small frown. "You don't think that's what's happening now? For you?"

"No," he said firmly. "Sweetheart, I've been mooning after you for four years without even seeing you and experiencing the benefits of immortal pheromones. I'm pretty sure this is life mate business."

Quinn relaxed, but said, "I guess I should ask if you're willing to be my life mate."

Jet jerked his head up, his eyes going wide with exaggerated shock. "Why, Quinn Feiyan Meng, are you proposing to me?" he asked, and while she flushed bright pink, he said in wonder, "My stars, proposing to me. How thoroughly modern of you."

"Have you been talking to Marguerite?" she asked suspiciously.

"About what?" he asked with confusion.

"She called me thoroughly modern too," she explained.

"Ah. Then you must be. That or she's also seen *Thoroughly Modern Millie*," he added wryly.

"What's that?" Quinn asked at once.

"What's that?" he echoed with more feigned shock, and then smiled and said, "A really old movie that Mom-Marge loved. She used to make Abs and I watch it with her every time it was on the local classic movie channel . . . which must have been six times a year. I think the host had a thing for Mary Tyler Moore. She was one of the actresses in it," he told her.

Quinn nodded, but said, "You never answered my question, Jet. Are you willing to be my life mate?"

Jet's expression turned serious. "Yes, Quinn. I'd like that very much."

Quinn sighed out a breath of relief, and then frowned slightly as uncertainty claimed her. Had she done the right thing? Was she really ready? Was he? Did he want to be turned, or was he just agreeing to be her lover? And could she bring herself to turn him if he did want to be turned? Oh, wait! What if he thought she had been proposing marriage? He had asked if she was proposing to him. Dear God, what if that's what he'd thought? Not that she was completely opposed to the idea of marrying him someday . . . ten or twenty years from now, maybe. Or fifty. What was the rush? They had loads of time and—

Thoughts dying abruptly, Quinn turned her head slightly, a frown claiming her lips as she listened.

"What is it?" Jet asked, watching her.

"I'm not sure. I hear . . ." She paused as the murmur of voices and the sound of soft footfalls distracted her, and then her eyes widened incredulously. Covering her ears, she gasped, "Oh my God!"

"What?" Jet asked with concern.

"I can hear Basha and Marcus," she said with embarrassment.

"Okay," he said slowly. "But why are you blushing. Are they having sex or something?"

"No," she moaned. "They're talking softly and dressing. Almost whispering," she added with dismay.

"Umm . . ." Jet shook his head. "I'm not sure why that's upsetting you."

"Because they're whispering and I can hear them well enough to catch every word," she explained, and when he still looked uncomprehending, she added, "We have not been whispering or even trying to be quiet when talking . . . or other things," she added pointedly.

"Oh," he said with understanding, and then, "Ohhh."

Groaning, Quinn slid out from under him and grabbed her jeans off the floor.

"What are you doing?" Jet asked with surprise.

"We left our clothes in the SUV at the mall," she said with realization. As she noted that her jeans were inside out, and tried to right them, she muttered, "I hope they didn't blow them up."

"Quinn, honey, come back to bed," Jet suggested, patting the mattress beside him.

Quinn opened her mouth to say no, but paused as her gaze landed on him in the bed. He had his clothes on and for a moment she was flummoxed. When had he put his clothes back on, she wondered, but then recalled that he'd never taken them off. The only thing they'd actually removed was her panties and jeans; her bra and T-shirt were still tangled and caught under her chin, and all they'd done with him was undo his pants and slip his cock out. Cripes.

"Quinn." His voice was soft and sexy and she instinctively started toward the bed, but paused as she heard a laugh from the next room.

Giving her head a shake, she started to untangle her panties from her jeans and turn them both right-side out.

"Quinn, honey, so what if they hear us? We're all

grown-ups here, and you're a medical doctor, for heaven's sake. You know it's natural and even healthy to—"

"I'm hungry," she said, rather than explain that the good girl inside of her, or the side of her that had always tried to be the perfect daughter and wife, still held sway. She knew she'd get past that eventually, but eventually wasn't now, and it was impossible for her to climb back into that bed and do all the things she wanted to with Jet when she knew every immortal in the house would probably hear.

"You go ahead and rest, and I'll just go down and grab something to eat and see whether they brought our clothes back," she said, stepping into her panties and pulling them up. Fresh clothes would really be nice. But this was all she had to wear right now.

"No. I'll come with you," Jet said, sliding his legs off the bed to stand. As he tucked himself away and did up his pants, he admitted, "I'm hungry too, now that you've mentioned it."

Quinn didn't say anything. She just concentrated on pulling her jeans on and doing them up. She ducked into the bathroom once she was done, to run a brush quickly through her hair and brush her teeth, and then returned to the room and smiled at Jet. "Ready?"

Nodding, he walked to the door and opened it, then waited for her to pass him and step out into the hall before following. Quinn paused to wait for him as he closed the door, and then glanced up the hall as the door next to hers opened and Basha led a tall good-looking man out of their room. The couple smiled when they saw them and waited for them to reach them before saying, "Congratulations," as they turned to lead the way to the stairs.

"For what?" Jet asked with surprise, sliding one arm around Quinn as they followed.

"For becoming life mates," Marcus explained with a smile over his shoulder. "I'm glad everything has worked out."

Quinn felt Jet stiffen with surprise but didn't look at him. She knew she was blushing like crazy. She could feel the heat in her cheeks as she took the words as proof that they had heard everything that had gone on in her bedroom. It was so embarrassing! And it made her decide that they should abstain from any more anything until they sorted out this issue with someone trying to kill her, so she could check into the Four Seasons and hopefully gain some privacy . . . unless they had immortals staying there or on staff. It was a decision she was sure Jet would not be happy with. But she couldn't help that.

Sixteen

"Absolutely not," Jet growled.

"Jet," Quinn reasoned. "We need to find out what is happening. And we need to capture the members of the Brass Circle who are trying to kill me. Or," she added quickly when he shook his head and opened his mouth again, "I'll be stuck living in the Enforcer house for eternity."

Jet snapped his mouth closed. She wasn't terribly surprised. It was a bit inhibiting living in the Enforcer house. Aside from the fact that every single immortal in this place could read their thoughts, there was the problem that while the walls weren't paper-thin, as Basha had suggested, they didn't muffle sound enough for an immortal not to hear what they got up to. Something that Quinn found terribly upsetting. She shouldn't. As Jet had said, they were all grown-ups, and she was even a doctor. Sex was a perfectly natural function and she knew that, but that didn't mean she wanted everyone hearing her moaning, groaning, panting, and screaming as she and Jet fulfilled that perfectly natural function. Unfortunately, she couldn't be quiet about it.

She had tried.

After coming downstairs the night before, heating up the leftover Greek chicken Sam had made for supper, eating it, and then asking about the clothes they'd bought and finding out that they had indeed been returned to the house, she and Jet had dragged the clothes upstairs to put away. Quinn had far more bags than Jet, and he had carried some of hers up for her. When she'd given him a kiss to thank him, it had quickly gotten out of control. They had been rolling around on her bedroom floor, ripping each other's clothes off while trying to touch every part of one another, when she'd heard Marcus and Basha's door open as they came up to retire.

Quinn had frozen for a minute, but Jet, not having immortal hearing, hadn't and didn't even notice her hesitation. Moments later she found herself trying to continue, but attempting to be quiet about it. Unfortunately, that was just impossible for her. Life mate sex was so feverish and frenetic that she'd quickly been huffing and puffing like the big bad wolf. And short of taping her mouth shut, she didn't know how to stop the moans, groans, and mewls of pleasure that kept slipping out. She hadn't had the discipline or control to stop it that time, but she'd woken up first afterward and had taken her pillow into the bathroom attached to her room and slept on the cold tile floor in there to be sure Jet didn't wake up and tempt her to go for another round.

Of course he'd noticed her absence and come knocking

to be sure she was all right. Afraid Marcus and Basha would hear, she'd quickly opened the door and slipped out, then dragged him onto her balcony to whisper what her issue was. Much to her relief, he hadn't given her a hard time about it. She was sure he thought she was being silly, but he'd said he'd sleep in his own room so she could have her bed, kissed her forehead, dressed, and left her alone.

Quinn had missed him. She knew that was completely ridiculous; she'd slept alone for four years, and had only slept with him for several hours that day, but it was true nonetheless. It was as if asking him to be her life mate had changed something fundamental inside her that she didn't understand . . . and for all she knew it had.

Whatever the case, she'd been eager to see him on waking, and had been happy to find him in the kitchen, eating toast. But Quinn had barely poured herself a coffee and sat down to join him when Mary had arrived and announced it was time for another session. Sighing, she'd reluctantly stood and followed the woman to Sam's office for another three-hour gruel-fest. But they had worked through a lot of her issues. They weren't gone or anything, but she was starting to see things more clearly and accept the changes in her life. She was also quite sure that they *would* be gone soon.

Quinn had left the session, hoping to find Jet and slip away for a walk or something with him, but instead she'd found everyone gathered in the kitchen, waiting for her. Including Marguerite, who wasn't even staying there, but had gone home and returned. She'd soon learned why. After leaving her room last night, the women had gone downstairs and discussed everything with the men, and they'd come up with something of a plan to resolve this problem of the Brass Circle trying to kill her. Lucian wanted to capture both men in the picture he'd shown her, and ransom them back to the Brass Circle for the promise to leave her alone. The problem was, Lucian wanted to use her as bait to capture them, and that was what Jet was balking at.

"Fine," Jet said finally, his voice grim, and then staring Lucian defiantly in the eye, he added, "But whatever the plan is, it better allow for me to go with her, because I'm not letting her be bait alone."

Quinn scowled at him for even suggesting it, and said, "No. You are not immortal. They could kill you."

"They could kill you too," he pointed out shortly.

"Yes, but it's much harder to kill me. As a mortal, you are much easier to kill."

"Then turn me," he said with a shrug.

"Good idea," Lucian announced abruptly. "She can turn you and you can take her to dinner at a restaurant where either Yun Xiang will approach to tell her he's a possible life mate and that the Brass Circle is out to kill her and why and we can capture him. Or Ziying Liang can make an attempt on her life that we will thwart before capturing him." He nodded with satisfaction. "Either way we catch at least one of the bastards and have a bargaining chip to use with the Brass Circle."

Quinn scowled at the ice-blond man briefly, and then turned back to Jet. "Are you sure? You don't have to do this. I promise I'll be fine. The men will be watching and—"

"I'm sure," Jet said firmly, and then asked quietly, "Aren't you?"

"If you mean am I sure I want you for a life mate, then yes, of course. But this is—"

"It has to be done eventually, Quinn," he said gently. "Better to get it done now so I can be on hand while you play bait. Besides, delaying it will just give me more time to worry about how painful it might be."

"Oh," she said softly, and then heaved a sigh and nodded. "All right, then."

"Good." Lucian stood at once. "Let us get to it, then."

Quinn and Jet turned shocked gazes on the man, but it was Jet who asked, "What? Now?"

"Yes, now. When did you expect it would be done? Next week? We need to clear up this issue with the Brass Circle."

"I know we do," Jet said at once. "And I wasn't thinking next week, but I thought I'd at least have an hour or two for my last—I mean, favorite meal or something before it happened."

"Last meals are for prisoners about to be executed," Lucian said with exasperation. "You are being turned into an immortal. Your favorite meal will taste better *after* you are turned. Your taste buds will be more sensitive."

"Yes, but—" Jet began, only to have Lucian interrupt him.

"The sooner we get it done, the sooner we can move forward with our plans, and the sooner we can end the threat to Quinn and Pet, and possibly everyone else."

When Jet blinked in surprise at that, he pointed out. "Every minute that we delay raises the risk of an attack being launched on this house."

"Right," Jet breathed. "We do it now, then."

Lucian nodded and turned to Quinn. "Can you insert a peripheral venous catheter?"

She blinked in surprise. "Yes, of course."

"Good." He turned to Tybo and Valerian. "Fetch what we will need and meet us up in Jet's room."

Quinn watched worriedly as the men hurried to do his bidding, and then joined Jet to follow Lucian from the room when he headed out of the kitchen. She was aware that everyone else was following. Marguerite was directly behind them, but Mary and Dante, Basha and Marcus, and Sam and Mortimer were on her heels, and Quinn wondered a little dazedly if it was because there was some kind of ritual that had to take place first, or if they would be needed. She had no idea what to expect, really. Patrick had just grabbed her, ripped his arm open, and covered her open mouth with his bleeding arm, then pinched her nose so that she was forced to swallow the blood to get it out of her mouth and find air. But he had been half-mad and rogue, so she doubted a proper turn would go anything like that.

"Get on the bed."

Jet blinked and took in his surroundings at Lucian's order, saw that they'd entered the room he'd been given during his stay at the Enforcer house, and wondered how they'd got here so quickly. The walk from the kitchen to here had passed in something of a blur for him as his brain had run around inside his head freaking out and squawking, *Oh my God, I'm going to be turned. Oh my God, what am I doing? Oh my God, do I really want this? What have I agreed to here? And how painful is it going to be?*

Very, was the answer in his head, because several immortals had gleefully told him it was a painful process full of nightmares and agony since he'd started piloting them around. But maybe they'd just been joking around, he thought suddenly. Maybe it wasn't bad at all.

"Do you want this?" Lucian asked, echoing one of the questions presently occupying his mind.

Jet hesitated and then shifted his gaze to Quinn. The moment his eyes landed on her concerned expression a stone-cold calm slid over him. Yes, he wanted this. Quinn was his life mate. He wanted that. He wanted her. Turning back to Lucian, he nodded firmly.

"Then get on the bed," Lucian ordered.

Nodding again, Jet straightened his shoulders and walked to the bed to stretch out on it, but then paused and sat up. "On top of or under the covers?"

"Actually," Sam said, hurrying around the people following them into the room, "we need to strip the bed first. There's a protective cover on all the mattresses in the house, but there's no sense ruining the sheets."

"Oh," Jet said, nonplussed, and scooted quickly off the bed. He tried to help when Sam began to strip the blankets and sheets from the bed, but the other women shooed him away and helped in his stead.

"Are we good?" Lucian asked when the bed was bare but for a white mattress cover.

"Good to go," Sam assured him, dropping the sheets and pillows on a chair in the corner of the room.

Lucian turned to him, but Jet was already moving back to the bed. It was much less comfortable without the pillows, but he stretched out flat on the bed and then glanced nervously toward Quinn. Finding her looking at Lucian uncertainly, he shifted his gaze to the man who was simply standing there in a waiting attitude.

"What happens now?" Quinn asked.

"We wait for Tybo and Valerian to arrive with the drugs and other items."

Quinn nodded, and then hesitated briefly before moving to the bed, and sitting on it sideways with her feet on the floor. "Are you all right?"

"I am," he assured her solemnly. She seemed upset and anxious, so he reached for her hand and squeezed it gently.

Managing a smile, Quinn squeezed back and then held on while they waited, but a moment later Valerian and Tybo arrived with the items they'd gone to fetch and Quinn stood up. Jet's gaze skated over the cooler of blood, the small black bag, and the IV stand Valerian carried and then moved on to Tybo and froze on the chains he had.

"Why does Tybo have chains?" Quinn asked before he could.

"They are to ensure Jet does not hurt himself during the turn," Marguerite said soothingly.

"Hurt himself? How could he hurt himself?" she asked weakly.

"They are just a precaution, dear," Marguerite assured her.

Jet had no idea if Quinn was reassured, but *he* wasn't. Still, he didn't protest or fight when the men began to chain him to the bed spread-eagle. But watching Tybo chain one of his wrists down, he commented nervously, "I've been told this is pretty painful?"

"Oh, yeah, big-time. It's agony. And the nightmares are apparently bad too. The whole process is just nasty," Tybo assured him cheerfully as he worked. "But on the bright side, you might not remember any of it afterward."

"I *might* not?" he asked with a frown.

"Some do. Some don't," he said with a shrug.

"Great," Jet muttered. "With my luck I'll remember everything."

"Come on, man. Don't say that," Tybo chided. "You have to think positive."

"All right," Jet muttered. "Then I'm positive I'll remember."

Tybo shook his head and chuckled as he fastened the chains to the bed.

Quinn watched the men chaining Jet down to the bed with a small frown, unsure why it was necessary. She was also fretting about what she was expected to do. She knew she was supposed to turn him; he was her one turn. But she wasn't sure how. Her gaze slid to the black bag Valerian had set on the bedside table and then she glanced at Marguerite and asked, "Should I be preparing the shot?"

"He won't need a shot. The drugs are administered through the IV," Marguerite explained. "Actually, it might be a good idea to insert the catheter into his vein now while he's quiet. But leave actually hooking it up to the IV for now. The drug we use is too strong for a mortal and could kill him. Do not actually start infusing the fluid until he's well into the turn."

Quinn frowned, but nodded and moved to the black bag. As she expected she found needles, catheters, and tubing inside. She quickly gathered what she needed, settled the items on the bedside table, and then waited for Tybo to finish and get out of the way before going to work. It was a relatively quick procedure, but she was relieved when it was done and murmured, “Sorry,” for any pain she’d caused.

“Didn’t feel a thing,” Jet assured her.

Quinn smiled as she taped the catheter in place, but knew he was lying. She used to be pretty good at it, but surgeons didn’t usually perform the procedure, so she was out of practice. On top of that, she was anxious for him and her hand had trembled a bit. She was positive he was just being kind, and bent down to kiss the corner of his mouth for it.

“I’ll be right back,” she whispered as she straightened, and then stood and moved back to Marguerite and whispered, “You said he won’t need a shot?”

“No, dear, the saline bags are specially prepared. The drugs are already in it. You just hook him up once he’s in the turn, and then switch out the bags as they empty.”

“Oh, good, but I’m more concerned about how we get my blood from me to him? I assumed we’d draw blood from me and—No?” She stopped with a frown when Marguerite started to shake her head, and then asked, “Not how Patrick did it?”

When Marguerite nodded silently, she squawked, “What?”

“What what?” Jet asked nervously from the bed.

“Nothing, honey,” Quinn said quickly, and then flushed at using the automatic endearment, a little uncomfortable until she saw his surprised pleasure. Relaxing, she turned back to Marguerite and hissed, “That’s barbaric.”

“It’s the only way to do it,” Marguerite assured her, and quickly explained, “The job of the nanos is to heal and repair any damage their host incurs. To do that, they have to stay in the body, so avoid leaving it. You might get one or two nanos by withdrawing blood, but that isn't enough to start a turn. Only catching them by surprise and incurring a large, fast wound can get enough out to turn him."

"Well." She scowled and shook her head. "Then I'll slice my wrist open."

"Not large enough. You have to bite hard, deep, and fast and tear the flesh away, then immediately put your wrist to his mouth to get enough nanos into him."

"Oh God," Quinn breathed, not sure she could do that.

"Yes, you can do it," Marguerite said soothingly, obviously reading her mind. That or she was projecting.

"What's happening?" she heard Jet ask behind her.

"Marguerite's just explaining to Quinn what she has to do," Valerian said soothingly.

"She didn't know?"

"Apparently not," Valerian answered, and then asked, "You did?"

"A couple of immortals have mentioned the procedure to me. At least that part and the why of it. No one mentioned being chained down, though."

"You can do this," Marguerite repeated, rubbing her shoulder.

"Time's a-wasting, people," Lucian growled. "Let's get to it."

"How bad is this going to hurt?" Quinn asked with a frown. Maybe the nanos would ease the pain of it for her. She hoped. She was not a big fan of pain. In fact, if she were to be honest, she'd have to say she was a big wussy when it came to pain.

"It will hurt some. But it's only a moment."

"A moment?" she asked.

Marguerite nodded, and then urged her to the bedside. "Now. Remember, bite deep and then press the wound quickly to his mouth," she told her as Quinn sat on the side of the bed. Turning to Jet, she added, "Open your mouth and be ready, Jet, and the second she presses her wrist to your mouth, start sucking."

"Suck on her wound?" he asked with a grimace.

"It will help get more nanos before they stop the bleeding," she explained, and then added, "If you do not get enough the first time, she will have to make a second wound."

"Suck hard," Quinn growled, because she was not doing this twice.

"Right," he sighed, and muttered, "Suck," to himself as if he might forget the instruction when it was the only thing he had to do.

"Okay." Marguerite turned to her and offered an encouraging smile. "Go on. Remember to bite deep, tear away fast, then press it over his mouth. You do not want to have to wound yourself twice."

Sighing, Quinn nodded and raised her wrist to her mouth. Telling herself it was like tearing off a bandage—"a little ouchy, and done" as she used to tell Parker—she then let her fangs slide down and just did it. She ripped into her wrist so deeply her fangs scraped bone, and then she snapped her mouth shut and jerked her head away, tearing out a large chunk of skin and meat with it, which she immediately spat out on a howl as the pain hit her brain. Quinn was so shocked at the extent of it and what she'd done that she didn't then slap her wrist to Jet's mouth but grabbed it with her other hand and howled like a baby. Fortunately, Marguerite then tore her hand away and shoved the gushing wrist over Jet's mouth.

"Suck," she barked at Jet, and Quinn's eyes opened on another howl as he did. God, it hurt! Every nerve in her wrist was screaming, and the pain was making her stomach roil violently. Afraid she was going to vomit on him, she snapped her mouth closed, cutting off her own howling, and turned her head away from him. She then squeezed her eyes tightly closed and clenched her teeth as he sucked, and sucked and sucked.

Quinn sagged with relief when he stopped and pulled his mouth away to mutter, "No more blood is coming out."

Not having him suck on the wound lessened the pain. Not by much, but enough she hoped she wouldn't vomit, after all, as she instinctively covered her injured wrist with her other hand again.

"Was it enough?" Jet asked with concern, and she heard the chains clank as if he was trying to reach for her. "She doesn't have to do that again, does she?"

"I am not sure," Marguerite admitted on a sigh, and when Quinn blinked her eyes open and turned on her with horror, she pointed out, "You did not place it over his mouth right away."

"Gee, I'm sorry. This was my first time," she muttered sarcastically, and then scowled at her. "And you said it would only hurt for a moment, but it's been longer than that and still hurts like a son of a bitch."

"I was not being literal," Marguerite explained. "I meant it would just be a moment out of your life, a memory once done."

"Well, next time be literal," Quinn growled, closing

her hand tighter around her wound in the hopes of easing the pain a bit. It didn't help.

A bag of blood appeared before her mouth, and Quinn glanced up to see Sam smiling at her sympathetically.

"Thank you," she murmured, taking the blood, but rather than pop it to her fangs, she finally turned to look at Jet. He was watching her with concern, and she managed a smile for him, but then frowned as she realized he looked normal. As she recalled, she'd dropped to the floor and started to convulse almost the moment Patrick had finished forcing his blood on her and released her. But Jet was just watching her with concern, looking perfectly normal except for the blood around his mouth and on his chin.

"How do you feel? Does anything seem different?" she asked worriedly. God, she so didn't want to have to do that again.

He shook his head apologetically. "I thought I got a lot of blood. It seemed like a lot," he added with a grimace. "But nothing is—"

Quinn jerked in surprise when he suddenly went stiff as a board, his back arching so hard and so high that only his head and feet touched the mattress. She stared wide-eyed as he stayed like that for a moment and then he began convulsing and thrashing, and he crashed into her, sending her flying off the bed. She landed on the floor next to it with a thud, and then swung her head around to look at Jet, but she couldn't see him past the people suddenly surrounding the bed, trying to hold him down as if the chains wouldn't be enough on their own.

"Here." Sam was suddenly beside her, taking her arm to help her up. Once she had her on her feet, the woman bent to pick up the bag of blood from where it had landed on the floor and gave it to her, then steered her a little away from the noise and activity around the bed. "You need blood, Quinn. You need your wound to heal before you can do anything for Jet. I'll hook the IV to the catheter and turn it on to start the drugs going while you down this."

"Thank you." Quinn finally popped the bag to her mouth as she turned to watch the activity around the bed. She couldn't see Jet other than small, short glimpses of one part of his body or another as people moved, leaving brief cracks in the wall of humans around him, but it seemed pretty obvious he'd got enough nanos and she wouldn't have to bite herself again. Thank God, she thought, and then Jet began to roar in agony.

Seventeen

Jet woke up slowly, grimacing at a serious case of dry mouth. Moving his tongue around to try to work up some saliva, he opened his eyes and stared blankly at the pale blue room he was in. It took him a moment to recall where he was and what had happened. Glancing around sharply, he spotted Quinn asleep, slouched in a chair next to the bed, and relaxed with a sigh.

His gaze slid over her slowly, drinking her in, and then he looked down at himself. He was no longer chained to the bed, which was a relief. And the pain had finally ended. At least the worst of it. He wasn't one hundred percent, though; he felt achy and dried out, as if recovering from a flu. He needed water, and peered hopefully toward the bedside table, relieved when he spotted the glass of water there. Easing up onto one elbow, he leaned over and grabbed the glass, then brought it to his mouth to drink. The liquid was room temperature, but it did the trick, or at least half of it. It wet his mouth and throat as he gulped it quickly down, but it didn't do much for the rest of his body. His skin felt like it was crying out for moisture too, he thought grimly as he set the glass back on the bedside table.

"You're awake."

Jet turned to see Quinn getting up from the chair, blinking sleep from her eyes. "How do you feel?"

"Dry and achy," he admitted.

"You need blood," she said, and moved around to retrieve a bag from the small refrigerator in the bedside table. She pulled out three, then paused briefly before pulling out three more.

Settling on the bed next to him, she smiled faintly. "We have to get your fangs to drop."

"Right, fangs," he murmured, and ran his tongue over his top teeth curiously. They didn't feel any different, he thought, and then gave a start when something appeared in front of his face.

"What—?" he began, glancing down his nose to see what it was just as her finger came into focus with a spot of blood on the tip. The moment he got a whiff of the blood, Jet felt a strange shifting take place in his upper jaw and something poked him in the tongue.

Fangs, he realized, running his tongue gingerly over his teeth again.

"Open up."

Jet shifted his gaze to Quinn, and then reluctantly opened his mouth.

"Wider," she instructed, and when he widened his jaws farther, she placed a bag of blood in his hand and thrust it up into his open mouth. He wasn't sure if she'd actually impaled the bag on his fangs until he felt a strange cool sensation in his canines. Then he realized that was the blood being drawn into his system. But he didn't taste it, so it wasn't actually in his mouth as it had been when he'd had to suck at Quinn's wrist. The memory made him grimace around the bag. Blood was not tasty to him. Or it hadn't been; maybe that would be different now. He didn't know, but it had been repulsive to him as he'd sucked at her wound. Only determination had kept him from tearing his mouth away and spitting it out.

"Hold that."

His gaze shifted to Quinn as she removed her hand from his bag and slapped one of the remaining bags she'd collected to her own mouth. Jet stared at her silently as they waited for the bags to empty, and had to think feeding was kind of annoying. He had questions, but couldn't ask them. At least while eating real food you could stop between bites to ask questions, and speak. Although it was a surprisingly swift procedure, all things considered, he decided a moment later when Quinn ripped her own bag off her fangs and he glanced down to see that his bag was empty too.

Quinn took the empty bag from him when he tugged it off his fangs, and gave him a full one. "You try. Just pop it up firmly and hold it in place. But don't be too firm or the bag might rip," she warned.

Nodding, Jet popped the bag up and onto his fangs, relieved and pleased with himself when he managed it without making a mess. It wasn't until this bag was empty that he was able to ask, "How long?"

Quinn didn't need him to clarify the question and said, "You've been unconscious for a little more than twenty-four hours. But when the others left they said even though you would probably wake up soon, the actual turn wouldn't be over for a while and you can expect to need a lot of blood for the next few weeks while the nanos complete their work. So." She gestured to the bag of blood in his hand, and urged, "Get it down. You have three more bags after that one, then you can shower and change and we'll go find you some food. You must be starved."

He was actually, Jet thought as he popped the bag to his mouth. And he would definitely enjoy a shower and change of clothes, he decided as her words made him aware of the fact that his clothes appeared to be soaked with the same shiny slime that was coating his skin. It was pretty gross.

"Do you remember anything?" Quinn asked with concern as she took that bag when it emptied and handed him another.

Jet popped the new bag to his mouth and merely shook his head rather than lie outright. He remembered everything. At least he thought he remembered everything. If not, he remembered a hell of a lot. Mostly it had been just flat-out agony. It had felt like someone had dropped napalm on him, or injected him with it. He remembered screaming and struggling, trying to grab and claw at his skin, but unable to because of both the chains and the people half lying on him trying to keep him from breaking the chains. That had seemed to go on forever before he'd finally passed out, but the pain and burning had followed him into unconsciousness and he'd had nightmares full of blood and flames. He wasn't telling Quinn that. He suspected she'd feel responsible and he already felt bad for her having to rip her arm open to turn him.

That must have hurt like a bitch too, he thought grimly.

Certainly, Quinn's reaction had suggested it did. Actually, her reaction had surprised him. He supposed he'd expected that her being a doctor would make her more stoic when it came to pain. And to be fair, she certainly hadn't cried and carried on when she'd hurt herself on the log she'd broken in half. Not that she'd cried after ripping her wrist open, but man, had she howled, and he wondered if it was something to do with shock.

"Next."

The word made him realize that the bag at his fangs was empty and she was holding out another. He switched them automatically, finding it easier each time as he gained confidence. Once he was on the last bag, Quinn stood and disappeared into the bathroom. He was just ripping the last bag off when she returned.

"I started the shower for you so it would warm up. Can you walk?"

Jet sat up and swung his legs off the bed, then stood, surprised when the room swayed a bit. Quinn was immediately at his side, slipping her arm around him for support. She helped him to the bathroom and even helped him strip and step into the shower. When she started to slip away then, he caught her arm.

"You might as well join me. You got whatever this gunk on me is all down your side helping me in here. Besides, you wouldn't want me to slip and fall." Jet was pretty sure he wasn't going to slip and fall. The first shakiness when he'd got up had passed quickly and he was feeling fine. Better than fine actually, he thought as his gaze roved down her body.

Quinn hesitated briefly, but when she nodded, and then began to strip her clothes off, Jet grabbed the bar of soap from the shelf and quickly began to clean himself off. He felt like he'd been dipped in a vat of bacon grease or something, and he smelled too.

He was rinsing off when Quinn stepped into the shower, and Jet immediately caught her hand and pulled her under the spray with him. He caught her gasp of surprise with his mouth as he kissed her, and then he began running the soap down her body as he pressed her up against the wall and ground himself against her.

"Feeling better?" she gasped with amusement when he broke their kiss a minute later to step back and begin running the soap over and around her breasts, leaving a trail of lather.

"Oh, yeah," he muttered, setting the soap aside and using his hands to spread the lather around, before simply stopping to knead her small, perfect breasts.

When Quinn moaned, her head tipping back against the wall, he bent his head and kissed her again, and then nipped at her lower lip when her hand found his erection and squeezed encouragingly.

"Witch," he muttered into her mouth, unable to keep his hips from bucking to thrust him into the caress.

Quinn laughed breathlessly, and then groaned when one of his hands slid down across her stomach and between her legs. She kissed him almost desperately as he caressed her, and then broke away to gasp, "We should rinse off and move to the bed. If we pass out in here—" She stopped on an excited cry as he thrust one finger into her, but she didn't have to finish what she'd said. He understood, and knew she was right. But goddamn, this felt so good he almost couldn't stop. But finally, he covered her mouth with his and spun them both under the shower to let the water rinse them. Then he caught her at the waist and carried her out of the shower.

Quinn wrapped her legs around his hips rather than dangle in front of him, and Jet stopped with a groan as they rubbed against each other. Then he raised her a little higher until his cock wasn't trapped between them anymore and he could lower her onto it.

They both cried out as he filled her and for a minute Jet thought he was going to blow his load right then she was so hot and tight around him, but Quinn dug her nails into his shoulders and broke their kiss to gasp, "Bed."

Grunting, he started walking again, but the movement just increased the friction and the accompanying excitement. They didn't make it to the bed, but at least the bedroom carpet offered a softer landing than the shower would have.

"Would you care for drinks while you peruse the menu? Wine, perhaps?"

Quinn glanced up from the menu she'd been pretending to read, and managed a nervous smile for the waiter, but shook her head. "Water for me, please."

Nodding, he turned to Jet. "And you, sir?"

"What do you have that's cold but nonalcoholic?" Jet asked.

Quinn turned to glance around the restaurant as the waiter began listing beverages. She couldn't see any immortals around that she knew, but there was supposed to be a couple there who were police officers from Port Henry, and her gaze slid quickly over the other diners, trying to spot them. The officers were a couple and had driven up today to Toronto to help with this situation, driving straight to the restaurant rather than risk anyone seeing them entering the Enforcer house. The hope was they wouldn't be recognized as connected to the Enforcers. Lucian had apparently given them the particulars over the phone, and texted a photo of Yun Xiang and Ziying Liang. But this couple, Teddy and Kat, as Marguerite had called them, were only one of the precautions Lucian had taken. The restaurant itself was owned by an immortal couple related to both Marguerite and Sam. The wife, Alex, was the chef and Sam's sister. The husband, Cale, was a nephew of Marguerite's. He helped run his wife's restaurants, but also had his own businesses. They were apparently on the alert and ready to help as well if anything happened in the restaurant. But there was a lot more help out on the streets. Lucian had Enforcers situated all over the place from what she'd been told, some in other restaurants, cafés, or bars, seated where they could watch for her and Jet to leave this restaurant. Others were in vehicles in the parking lot, as well as on this road, and others nearby where they could be called in.

She had to hand it to the guy, Lucian Argeneau sure knew how to organize people, Quinn thought as she turned back to the table. Jet had only woken up six hours ago. Well, the first time. It had apparently been half an hour after they passed out on the bedroom floor that knocking at the door had woken them up. While Quinn had hid in the bathroom, Jet had wrapped a towel around his waist and answered the door. It had been Sam. Lucian had sent her to tell them to come downstairs now that Jet was through the worst of the turn. He had a plan, and wanted to put it in motion that night.

While Jet had showered again and dressed, Quinn had scampered back to her room in a borrowed towel, and quickly showered and then dressed herself. They'd met in the hall and made their way downstairs, both wondering aloud what Lucian's plan was.

This was it. The premise was that Jet had brought her out for a romantic dinner at a fine restaurant. Lucian expected that either Yun would approach her to tell her he was her life mate, or Ziying would try to kill her. Either way, Lucian hoped to catch one of them.

"You look beautiful."

Quinn glanced up from the menu, and smiled weakly at Jet's compliment. "Thank you. You look very handsome."

Jet smiled crookedly at her return compliment. "Even with red and watery eyes?"

"They aren't—" Her words stopped as her gaze shifted to his pedestrian brown eyes rather than the gorgeous silver and teal they now were, or even the stunning teal they had been when he was mortal. The color was the result of colored contacts meant to hide the silver that would give away that he was no longer mortal. Lucian was positive that the men trying to kill her must have realized Jet was mortal after tracking them at the mall as they had. He thought hiding the fact that Jet had been turned would be a good ace in the hole, so had insisted on his wearing the contacts. But immortals didn't wear contacts well. The nanos saw them as a foreign body and tried to force them out of the eye, just as they were trying to do with Jet. He kept having to push them more firmly back into his eyes, and between that and the nanos, his eyes were painfully bloodshot.

"Does it hurt much?" she asked with concern as he pushed on his eyes again.

"Not as much as the turn," he muttered. "I'll live."

Quinn stiffened, concern claiming her at once. "I thought you didn't remember the turn?"

Jet stilled, and then grimaced and waved away her concern. "It's coming back—just bits and pieces, though. It's fine. It's all done. I survived and it's all good."

Quinn was silent for a minute, watching him, and then suggested, "Maybe you should go to the men's room and splash some water in your eyes. It might help."

"Yeah," he agreed, starting to rise, and then stopped abruptly and settled back in his seat. "I'm not leaving you alone till this is over."

Quinn frowned, but then stood herself. "Well, I have to go to the bathroom. So, you can either come along and stand outside the door, or take the opportunity to slip into the men's room and take care of your eyes."

She didn't wait for his answer, but heard his soft curse and the scrape of his chair sliding back from the table as he followed her. Quinn didn't look back until they'd entered the small hall where the restrooms were. Stopping at the ladies' room door, she glanced back and said, "Go splash water on your eyes. I promise not to leave the ladies' room until you knock on the door to let me know you're out of the men's room."

When he sighed and nodded, Quinn smiled and then slid into the ladies' room. She didn't really have to go, so she took a moment to check herself in the mirror. Her hair was up in a loose chignon, her only makeup was a deep red lipstick Sam had insisted on putting on her, and she was wearing one of the new dresses Francis had picked for her, a short, black mini cocktail dress with a V-neck. It hugged her upper body, but flared out around her hips. It was fun and flirty and yet sexy too, she thought.

Jet had certainly seemed to appreciate it if his expression as he'd watched her walk down the stairs at the Enforcer house was anything to go by. She suspected if everyone else hadn't been standing around the entry waiting to leave, he might have grabbed her hand and dragged her back up to his room.

Smiling faintly at the thought, she peered at herself, trying to see what he saw. It had been a long time since she'd really looked at herself. She hadn't done so since right after the turn when she'd examined all the changes to her body and face. Quinn had been thirty-six when she was turned, a young professional. Well, relatively young. So okay, she'd had crow's-feet at her eyes, and those indentations around her mouth, as well as a few gray hairs on her head. Just a few, though. Still, she'd looked her age, or maybe a little older thanks to the stress of her job.

After the turn she'd been like a shiny new penny. Like she was now. She didn't have crow's-feet anymore or indentations. Her skin was flawless and dewy, and there wasn't a gray hair on her head. She didn't look a day over twenty-five, and rather than appreciate that at the time, she'd been furious. Because it was the reason they'd made it look like she was dead and forced her to leave behind her job, her home, her parents, her town even.

But now she recalled the look on Jet's face as his gaze had skated over her body—the desire and fire, and the way the silver had flared to fill his beautiful teal eyes—and she didn't mind looking the way she did. And if what Marguerite and the others said about life mates was true, he would always look at her the way he had, and would always want her.

Maybe Patrick's turning her hadn't been such a bad thing. Maybe she'd just been looking at it wrong. Sure, she'd had to give up her career and home, but she'd read somewhere that the average human changed their career three times in their life. Besides, it wasn't like she couldn't work in her field at all. She could be a general surgeon, or even train to be a neurosurgeon or something else if she wanted.

Or maybe she'd get out of the medical field for a while. Her career had eaten into her family time more than it should have. In fact, she'd enjoyed that aspect of the last four years, getting to spend more time with Parker. But now, with Jet in her life too, she was definitely thinking she wanted a career that was a little less taxing. Or maybe she should even hold off on a career until they got past the new life mate stage where they couldn't keep their hands off each other. She and Patrick had made and saved a lot of money between them, and investments had only increased that. She could afford to take a little more time off to get to know Jet better, and spend time with her son before he got too old to want to spend time with her. Her options were really pretty much wide open. She apparently had a lot of time ahead of her if she wasn't murdered by the Brass Circle.

A tap sounded at the door. Quinn winked at her reflection, and then walked over to open it. She smiled when she saw Jet on the other side, but her smile faded when she saw his expression. When he started to fall on her, she caught him around the upper chest just under the arms as hc crashed to his knees; and then she stared at the Asian man behind him with a dart gun in his hand. Ziying Liang, the second man in the photos.

The one who had set the bombs in the plane and was apparently trying to kill her.

"Pick him up."

Concentrating on keeping her thoughts blank, Quinn shifted Jet and hefted him over her shoulder. Once she'd turned to Ziying, he gestured with the dart gun for her to step out of the restroom, and then nodded down the hall toward the emergency exit sign above a door there.

Quinn hesitated, but didn't see much choice here. Not wanting Ziying to read the thoughts in her mind, she tried not to think of the Enforcers stationed in the parking lot, and the road. But couldn't help the brief thought that she hoped to God they were paying attention, and that one of them saw the situation as she carried Jet to the back of the building and then out through the emergency door.

"The van."

Quinn glanced around until she spotted the van almost in the corner of the parking lot. It was white, its side door already open and waiting. She walked silently to it, and started to climb in with Jet, but paused with one foot in and one out when she saw that there was a side door on the other side of the vehicle. It was wide open too, as was the side door of what looked like a black van parked next to this one.

"On your knees and get moving," the man behind her ordered, pressing the dart gun against her back.

Quinn's arms tightened around Jet, but she retrieved her foot and shifted one knee inside, then her other, and crossed the width of the van on her knees as Ziying got in and closed the door.

"Keep going," her kidnapper said when she hesitated at the second door, and then he snapped, "Quickly."

Quinn crossed from one van to the next on her knees, and then gasped when she was suddenly pushed and sent sprawling with Jet still over her shoulder. Releasing him, she rolled onto her side and watched warily as Ziying followed her inside and quickly closed the side door of the white van. He then slid the door of the van they were in shut too, before turning to look out the window into the next van with concentration.

Quinn heard an engine start, and then Ziying crouched down until he was almost out of view as the sound of the engine began to move away. The white van was leaving. At least that's what she thought was happening. She couldn't actually see the van, not even the top of it; the windows of this van were as black as the outside had been. In fact, Quinn wasn't sure why Ziying was bothering to stay out of sight. She was sure no one could see him from outside, unless he was concerned that the metallic flecks in his eyes might be seen through the covering on the windows. She supposed that was possible. They did tend to glow in the dark and it was dark in the back of this van.

Ziying turned to her suddenly, and Quinn's speculation died as she waited warily and acknowledged she might be in a fix here. The two-van thing was really quite clever and she was a bit worried that Lucian's men may have fallen for it and would now follow the white van, completely unaware that she and Jet were in the black van that had been parked next to it.

"They *are* following the white van," Ziying announced with a tight little smile. "Ma Yuan will be surprised to find Lucian Argeneau is so easily tricked and will praise us for this venture."

"Who is she?" Quinn asked, starting to ease up into

a sitting position, but freezing half upright when rage poured over the man's face.

"*He* is our leader and the head of the Brass Circle," Ziying said coldly.

"I meant no offense," she murmured warily. "I thought Ma was a nickname like Ma Kettle or something."

"You have been too long away from China," he growled with disgust. "Ma is his family name. It means horse. Yuan means silver."

"So, he's Silver Horse." She nodded, thinking that Yuan Ma probably had silver in his eyes like the Argeneaus.

"He does," Ziying said, proving he was monitoring her thoughts. "But it is Ma Yuan, not Yuan Ma. Do not dishonor him by turning his name around."

"I didn't mean to dishonor him. In America the given name comes first while the family name is second. It is just natural for me to put them in that order."

"Then do not even think his name," he snapped.

Quinn shrugged, not really caring one way or another. She was more concerned about Jet right then, and her gaze slid to him now.

"Do not worry for your mortal lover. He is as good as dead already. The strength of the drugs needed to incapacitate an immortal are deadly to a mortal. I am surprised his heart has not already stopped."

Lover, lover, lover, Quinn thought over and over in an attempt not to think about the fact that Jet wasn't mortal anymore. That ace in the hole might very well save them, after all . . . if he woke up from the effects of the drug in time. But that was something she was trying not to think about, and really struggling with it. She turned an anxious gaze to Ziying, only to see that he had moved up between the two front seats and was talking to someone in the driver's seat. Even as she noted that, the two men switched places, the driver slipping out of the seat and taking the dart gun as Ziying slid past him to take the driver's seat.

Quinn inhaled sharply when she recognized the man now moving toward her as Yun Xiang. She tensed, waiting for the screaming to start in her head, because her last session with Mary had made her realize the screaming she'd heard when she'd first seen him had been a scrap of memory from the night her family had been slaughtered, not reality. But this time it didn't come. Thinking that must be a good sign, she let her breath out slowly and watched with conflicting emotions as he approached. Part of her was furious and full of loathing for the monster who had led the gang that had tortured and killed her stepfather, mother, and cousin. But the other part was relieved. He was a possible life mate to her, so presumably wouldn't be able to stand by and watch her be murdered. At least not if what Marguerite and the others said was true.

She'd barely had that thought when he raised the dart gun and shot her. Quinn blinked in surprise, and then lowered her head to stare at the dart now sticking out of her chest as she slowly just sank back toward the floor. She was unconscious before she landed on it.

It seemed to Jet he woke up by increments. His mind was the first thing working and he became aware of smells, sounds, and movement around him, but couldn't open his eyes or move anything. With no other choice, he lay still, trying to sort out where he was and what was happening. The last thing he recalled was leaving the men's room and knocking on the ladies' room door to let Quinn know he was ready to return to the table when she was. He'd been about to move to the wall next to the door and lean there while he waited for her when someone had punched him in the back. At least that's what it had felt like.

Jet had tried to turn to see what had happened, but he couldn't; his muscles wouldn't listen to him. In fact, he'd started to sway on suddenly shaky legs when the ladies' room door had opened and Quinn appeared. The last thing he recalled was her smiling at him before he'd fallen forward toward her. Now he was lying on a hard surface, his body bent almost in half and his ear and cheek against cold metal that felt almost like it was vibrating a bit. The only sound he could hear was the drone of an engine.

He tried to open his eyes again, and was relieved when this time they flickered, opening just a little and then closing again. It wasn't much, but it was better than not being able to open them at all. It also gave him hope that whatever had caused his paralysis, or whatever this was, was fading. He waited another moment, just listening, and then tried again to open his eyes. Instinct had him only trying to open them to slits. He managed the feat and took in what he could of his surroundings.

He was lying in the back of what looked to him to be a van, and Quinn was lying next to him, a dart in her chest. Mouth tightening, he tried to look toward the front of the vehicle to see whether it was Ziying Liang or Yun Xiang who had them, but his head wouldn't move.

Yet, he told himself, and then stopped thinking and

concentrated on listening as the van slowed. His body slid toward one wall a bit as they turned a corner and then they were bumping over some extremely uneven ground, or a pothole-ridden driveway. A long driveway, he thought after a couple of moments, or maybe a really bad country road. And then the van stopped and he heard doors open. Jet closed his eyes just before he heard the side door slide open and someone say, "Grab the mortal and bring him inside."

"Why? He's dead, or soon will be."

"Because I want her to see him. His loss will add to her pain as we torture her," the first man said. "And she should suffer for what she did to Qing."

Jet wasn't sure if his face could make expressions yet, but concentrated on ensuring it didn't as someone grabbed his arm and dragged him across the ribbed floor of the van, then hefted him over their shoulder with a grunt.

Eighteen

Quinn woke up abruptly to pain. Someone was slapping her face, she realized, and moaned as she opened her eyes.

"That's it. Wake up!" Another slap swung her head to the side, and she raised a hand to press to her cheek as she turned back to face the man in front of her.

Yun Xiang, she realized, and then he turned and started talking to Ziying. It had been more than thirty years since Quinn had spoken Chinese, but she did catch most of what he said. At least she thought she did, and that he was telling the man to go out and start a bonfire.

Listening to them talk, she cast a quick glance down at herself, surprised to see that she wasn't tied up or anything. She was sitting in a rickety old chair, set on a dirt floor with patches of old, rotting straw here and there, Quinn noted, and looked swiftly around the interior of the large building until she spotted Jet. He was slumped against a wall some six or so feet from her, and appeared to still be unconscious, which made her frown. He'd been shot before her, and should have come around first.

Unless his being newly turned affected his recovery somehow. He should wake up soon, though, she reassured herself, and then wiped all thoughts of him from her mind, lest one of the men read it. The last thing she needed was for these men to learn Jet had been turned and wasn't dying, and she knew it, so shifted her attention to their surroundings. There wasn't much to see. They were in what appeared to be an ancient abandoned barn, but it was empty of anything but a few rusty old tools on the wall, and scattered patches of nasty, rotten straw on the floor.

With nothing else to see, she turned back to their kidnappers. Just as she did, they finished talking and Ziying stomped out through the open barn doors. Yun watched him go with a grim expression, and then turned and strode toward her.

Quinn eyed him warily. If his shooting her with the dart gun hadn't told her their analysis of the situation had been all wrong, the look of loathing on his face as he approached would have. She suspected life mates did not look on each other that way. They'd definitely got it all wrong, she decided. But if she wasn't a possible life mate for him, then why had he let her live as a child?

"I didn't."

Quinn blinked, slow to realize he was responding to her thoughts. Narrowing her eyes, she said, "Yes, you did. You found us in the closet, but left us there and didn't tell the others. That is the only reason Pet and I are still alive."

"No. Not me," he assured her.

Quinn shook her head with confusion. "I saw you."

He gave a short laugh at the suggestion. "I would have drank you dry and thrown you on the pyre with the rest of your puling family. Not let you live like Xiang Qing did."

"Xiang Qing?" she echoed slowly, her confusion finally clearing. "Were you twins?" Yun looked almost exactly the same as her memory of this Qing he claimed had saved her and Pet.

"He was my father," Yun spat. "And he dishonored our family by disobeying Ma Yuan and letting you live." He scowled at her as if it were her fault before adding, "A mistake he paid for with his life."

Quinn didn't miss the grief that flickered over the man's face. He might be speaking with disgust and rage at what he saw as his father's betrayal, but he still grieved his loss. Clearing her throat, she said quietly, "I'm sorry. But from what I understand it would have been impossible for him to kill me if we were life mates."

"Life mates," he growled with rage. "What good is a life mate if you are dead? He should have just killed you quickly and hoped to meet another. But no, he let you live and then paid for it with his life. But not before suffering the tortures of the damned," he told her grimly. "Do you want to know what they did to your life mate?"

Quinn shook her head slowly. She really didn't. Her feelings about this Qing were already confusing and conflicted. The man had killed her family. But he'd also let her and Pet live. However, that had only been because they were possible life mates . . . and what did that say about her? How could she possibly have been a life mate to someone like that? The very thought disgusted her and she decided she was definitely going to need more counseling to come to terms with it.

"Disgust?" Yun roared with fury and backhanded her, then grabbed her by the hair and forced her face up to look at him. "You didn't deserve him. You should thank God every day for what he did for you. He died for you, and most horribly," he spat, and then released her and paced away, his voice cold as he informed her, "Ma Yuan was very angry with my father and used him as an example. He called in all of our people for the execution so they could witness what happened to those who disobeyed him. And all of us were made to stand witness to his punishment."

Turning back, he eyed her coldly. "First came disemboweling. It was followed by death by a thousand cuts, and countless more cruel and painful tortures. But he saved the best for last. The Iron Maiden."

Quinn bit her lip, unable to keep from thinking that the Iron Maiden sounded almost anticlimactic after disemboweling. Although she supposed it could be bad if he was left in the upright iron coffin for any amount of time. The nanos would probably try to heal him around the metal spikes piercing his body, and would have to mine his organs for blood to do it, since he would have lost a lot of blood from his wounds.

"Oh, no, I am not talking about your puling English Iron Maiden," Yun said bitterly, reading her thoughts. "In China, the Iron Maiden is worse. Sometimes they have spikes, and sometimes they do not. Ma Yuan's does have spikes. But that is only the beginning of the torture. The Chinese Iron Maiden has a platform at the bottom of the upright iron coffin with a metal grate on top, rather than just wood. Once the prisoner is closed inside, and bleeding from the spikes piercing their body, hot coals are placed in the platform under the iron grate and then water is poured over those coals, so that boiling steam rushes up through the Iron Maiden, steaming the prisoner alive."

Quinn swallowed the sudden bile in her throat, and lowered her head.

"Most prisoners scream until their throats rupture, but not my father. He bore every torture stoically, never making a sound . . . until they finally set him on a pyre and burned him alive. Then he screamed and screamed and screamed." Yun swallowed. "I should have beheaded him when he asked."

Quinn lifted her head abruptly and Yun scowled at her.

"I read it in his mind on the way back to our meeting with Ma Yuan to make our report. I had never been able to read him before that, but I read the memory as clear as glass. He had found you and your sister, and he had *let you live.* A betrayal of our leader. I confronted him, and realizing that if I could read him, Ma Yuan certainly would, he asked me to behead him." His shoulders slumped. "But I could not do it. He was my father. How could I kill him?"

Quinn didn't think he was talking to her anymore. She wasn't even sure he was aware of her presence at that point. He almost seemed to be arguing with himself, or perhaps his conscience.

"So, I told him that doing so would dishonor our family further, and he should confess all to Ma Yuan," Yun continued after a moment. "But had I known what he would do to him . . ." He closed his eyes and shook his head with regret.

Quinn felt pity stir in her for him. She couldn't imagine putting Parker in that position. She just couldn't have asked it of him, no matter if it would have saved her the tortures Qing had gone through.

"He should have killed you," Yun snapped, suddenly furious again. "Sparing you killed him. I wanted vengeance but you and your sister had disappeared. And then, two weeks ago, Yin Jiangnu, one of the spies Ma Yuan has in the Argeneau offices, reported that she had found a name on a requisition for ID for a Quinn Peters. The name that was being changed to was Quinn Feiyan Meng and I knew it was you, returning to your original name."

Quinn blinked at that, realizing only then that she had indeed taken back her original name. Or at least the name she'd borne after her stepfather had adopted her. Though she hadn't had a middle name then and now had her mother's first name for a middle name.

"I thought finally I would have my vengeance," Yun went on. "I asked Ma Yuan for permission to lead the team that would kill you. But Ma Yuan said no," he told her with disbelief. "He said you were under the protection of the North American and European Councils and he wanted no trouble with them. I was to do nothing that would bring their anger down on our organization. You were to be left alone."

"And yet here we are," Quinn said quietly.

"Because my father's soul calls out for vengeance. I cannot ignore it. I will see your broken body on a pyre or die trying."

"So, this is suicide by murder."

That comment in a gruff voice drew Quinn's shocked gaze around to see Jet standing where he'd been slumped moments ago. He looked relaxed, his stance loose, and his expression was mildly inquisitive as he waited for Yun's answer.

"You should be dead," Yun said with amazement. "Mortals cannot survive our drugged darts."

"Yeah. But I'm not mortal," Jet said with a shrug, and then pointed out, "You haven't answered my question. Is this your way of committing suicide? Because this leader of yours, Ma Yuan, surely won't be any more pleased that you went against his wishes than he was with your father. So, if you kill her, he'll do the same to you, won't he? Disemboweling, the Iron Maiden, and so on."

When Yun merely glowered at him, Jet added, "Or perhaps you aren't as honorable as your father and don't plan to face the music. Maybe you plan to dishonor your family and run and hide from the Brass Circle for the rest of your life like the coward you proved yourself to be when you could not end your father's life."

Quinn's eyes widened in alarm when Yun immediately spun around and grabbed a dart gun lying on the table next to him. But by the time he turned back and raised it, Jet had crossed the distance between them and was kicking out at the arm holding the gun. Much to her relief, the blow knocked the gun from Yun's hand, but in the next moment the two men were in a full-on battle.

At first, Quinn was so taken aback by this turn of events that all she could do was watch with her heart in her throat as the men began to kick, punch, and perform all sorts of fancy footwork as they threw each other around the barn. But then she realized that she was just sitting there watching Jet fight for their lives, and gave her head a shake.

Standing up, she turned to the wall where she had noted the farm tools earlier and quickly rushed to them. The one she wanted was an old hand sickle with a wicked-looking curved blade. It was dark with age, and probably dull as well, but should still be able to take off Yun's head, she thought grimly as she reached up for it. A curse slid from her lips when she found it was a couple inches too high for her to grab. Who the hell had lived here? she thought with disgust. Giants?

Grinding her teeth, she jumped for it, managing to knock it off the spike it hung from. Only her immortal reflexes kept her from being impaled by the damned thing as it fell to the floor. Muttering under her breath with irritation, she bent to snatch it up and then turned, raising it over her head as she charged toward Jet and Yun.

Quinn hadn't taken two steps when the scythe was snatched out of her hand. Whirling, expecting to find Ziying there, she blinked in surprise when she found herself staring at Lucian Argeneau. Shock was followed by relief and she turned to gesture toward Jet, her mouth opening, only to close as she saw that there were several Enforcers now spread around the interior of the barn. However, they weren't interfering but simply watching Jet and Yun fight.

Spinning back to Lucian, she gasped, "What are they doing? Why aren't they helping him?"

"He does not need help," Lucian said, hanging the scythe back on the wall without taking his eyes off the fight.

"But . . ." She turned back and watched worriedly as the two men continued to battle.

"Jet can fight his own battles. On top of being trained in combat while in the navy, he took martial arts as a young man," Lucian informed her, crossing his arms as he watched.

"He did?" Quinn asked weakly, but supposed she should have realized it. The man was performing all sorts of fancy moves that she recognized from Pet's competitions when she was taking martial arts when they were young: roundhouse kicks, flying side kicks, jumping back kicks, and then blasting him with power punches in between. Jet was really quite good.

"Yes, he did," Lucian responded finally, drawing her back to the conversation, and then he informed her, "Like you, our Jet is an overachiever. I suppose that is why the nanos made you life mates."

"An overachiever?" she asked uncertainly, never taking her eyes off Jet.

"Aside from his fighting skills, Jet also had his pilot's license by the age of seventeen, has a bachelor of science in engineering, was awarded the Flying Cross for valor in battle, and was the second youngest lieutenant commander the navy has ever given the title to."

Sensing her shocked look, he turned to peer at her and nodded to assure her that everything he'd said was true. "As I said, an overachiever like you."

Lucian's words played through Quinn's troubled mind, clear and strong, as she watched Jet. His body moved with incredible fluidity; his movements were economical and controlled. She was suddenly quite sure he could end this fight anytime he liked, and yet he wasn't.

"Yun bears great guilt over his father," Lucian informed her. "Not only for not beheading him, but for insisting he confess to Yuan Ma to restore the family honor, which his father did out of love for him. The memories of what his father went through haunt him. He wants to die. As Jet guessed, these attempts on your life were suicide by murder. Jet knows that. He also mistakenly thinks we need information from Yun, though, so is trying to wear him down so that he can apprehend him without having to tear his head off."

"Mistakenly?" she asked sharply, never taking her eyes off Jet. "Don't you need information from Yun?"

"I had completed reading Yun's mind before you had managed to get the sickle off the wall," Lucian said with a shrug. "There is nothing else he can tell me."

"Well, then, why don't you tell Jet that so he can stop trying to wear the guy out?" she asked with exasperation.

"Because I am enjoying watching him fight. He is quite good. He would be a good Enforcer."

"He's a pilot," Quinn snapped. "He is not going to become one of your Enforcers."

Lucian scowled down at her. "My God, you are truculent. What happened to the well-behaved good girl who did what she was told and did not cause waves that they claim you used to be?"

"She got turned into an immortal and didn't feel she had to behave anymore," Quinn growled, glaring back at him, and then frowned and asked, "Did you at least take care of Ziying before coming in here?"

"He is taken care of," Lucian muttered, and then a scream of pain had them both turning to see that Jet had apparently wearied of the battle and ended it. Yun was on the ground, his neck broken. He wouldn't die, but he was definitely incapacitated. For now.

"There," Lucian said with exasperation. "You made me miss the ending."

Ignoring him, Quinn rushed to Jet, gasping in surprise when he caught her up in his arms and hugged her tightly.

"Are you all right?" he asked, pulling back to look at her face.

"Me?" she asked with disbelief. "You were the one fighting."

"But he hit you," he said with a frown, setting her down to run his fingers gently over the cheek Yun had struck.

Quinn flinched in surprise. The spot was tender. Yun must have hit her harder than she'd realized in the moment.

"She is fine," Lucian answered for her, irritation in his voice as he added, "Annoying as usual, but fine."

When Jet looked to him with surprise, he waved away the question in his eyes, and said, "Take her back to the Enforcer house. The SUV you drove to the restaurant is outside. I had Tybo drive it here when we followed the van."

Nodding, Jet slid an arm around her and ushered her quickly out of the barn.

Jet steered the car down the dark country roads, following the GPS directions, and glancing worriedly at Quinn every couple of minutes. She was being awfully quiet. She hadn't said a word since they'd left the barn. Something was obviously wrong, but he wasn't sure what. As far as he could tell, this evening had actually gone pretty much to plan. He didn't like that Yun had hit her, but otherwise they'd done what they'd intended. More even. Instead of capturing one of the men, they'd got both of them, and now they didn't have to stay at the Enforcer house for eternity.

That thought gave him an idea, and he punched up the GPS on the SUV and gave it new directions. Once finished, he glanced at Quinn again. She was sitting in her seat, her arms folded over her chest and a worried expression on her face.

"You're quiet," he said finally.

Quinn glanced around with a look of surprise, as if she'd forgotten she wasn't alone, and then murmured, "Oh, I was just thinking."

She then turned to look out the window, her facial expression hidden from him.

"What about?" he asked.

Quinn was silent for a moment, and then sighed and faced him. "You took martial arts when you were young and combat training in the navy. You had your pilot's license by the time you were seventeen, have a bachelor's in engineering, earned a Flying Cross, and you're a freaking lieutenant commander," she listed off, and then added dryly, "The second youngest lieutenant commander given the title."

Jet shifted his attention back to the road, muttering, "Wow, someone's been gossiping big-time."

"Lucian told me that," she informed him, and his head swiveled sharply her way.

"Really?" he asked with surprise.

"Yes."

"Oh." Jet frowned slightly, then shifted his attention back to the road again. He hadn't even realized Lucian knew all of that about him. But he supposed Argeneau

Enterprises would have checked him out before hiring him. Or he guessed Lucian had probably read his mind before offering him the job.

"You're an overachiever," Quinn said suddenly.

That surprised a laugh out of him. "This from the cardiothoracic surgeon."

"Yeah, but I'm a mess!" she cried unhappily. "I'm even in therapy, for heaven's sake. While you're . . . perfect," she ended miserably.

Cursing, Jet pulled over onto the side of the road, turned off the engine, and shifted in his seat to face her. "First of all, honey, you are not a mess. You're a beautiful, successful woman who was struggling with a past you didn't even remember. That's like boxing the Invisible Man. Impossible. And when you realized it was getting the better of you, you sought out help. That, in my book, is the opposite of messed up. Messed up would have been continuing on the way you were, or going rogue, or something. You are not messed up," he said firmly.

"As for me," he added after taking a breath, "I hate to disillusion you, but I am far from perfect. What you call overachieving in me was actually me desperately trying to earn my mother's love."

Her head came up, her eyes wide.

Jet nodded. "I was a straight-A student in school, purely in the hopes that it would please my mother, and get her attention."

"Did it?"

"Hell, no, but it got the attention of the jocks who thought that was a good reason to bully me," he said dryly. "So I got into martial arts to be able to defend myself, half hoping maybe that would impress her."

"No?" she asked softly.

"No, but that impressed the jocks, and the next thing I knew I was playing sports as well. My mom didn't even notice. So, I got my pilot's license, thinking she'd loved my dad, and he was a pilot . . ." He shook his head. "The degree in engineering followed, and then the navy, and I worked my butt off to make my way up to lieutenant commander. She didn't even come to the 'pinning on' ceremony."

"Oh, Jet," Quinn whispered, reaching for his hands.

He squeezed hers briefly, and then just held her hands gently as he continued. "Mom-Marge and Abs were there, though," he told her quietly. "Mom-Marge did the pinning, and then she hugged me and said she loved me and was proud of me. And that felt good," he assured her. "Part of me was happy as hell, but another part was thinking I wished my mother was there."

He shook his head with self-disgust at the memory, and then said, "Quinn, you may have spent your life trying to prove you were good, and not a monster like Qing, but most of my life has been one long attempt to be good enough to gain the love of the woman who was supposed to love me no matter what. And that's pretty screwed up."

"She still hasn't . . . ?"

Jet smiled crookedly and shook his head. "And I no longer expect her to. I visit once a month to be sure she hasn't drank herself to death yet, but I stopped trying to gain her love when Mom-Marge died and I realized I'd had that love my whole life from her.

"So," he said, reaching out to brush her hair away from her face, "I'm not perfect. No one is. We're all just doing the best we can. However," he added solemnly, "I think you're brilliant, beautiful, a wonderful mother, and perfect for me."

"Oh, Jet," she whispered.

He smiled, and pressed a kiss to her nose and then added, "I don't know how the nanos know this stuff, but I'm pretty sure they got it right with us. I love you, Quinn."

Jet had hoped for a declaration in return, but what he got was Quinn crying out and launching herself at him over the center console. Smiling, he caught her against his chest and kissed her back when her mouth covered his.

As usual, that's all it took to set them both aflame. Thrusting his tongue into her mouth, he ran his hands down her back, pressing her upper body tight to him. Then he reached down to work the electronic lever to ease his seat back as far as he could and caught her by the waist to lift her over the console and into his lap so she straddled him on the driver's seat.

Breaking their kiss then, he nuzzled his way across her cheek to her ear and nipped it lightly before muttering, "God, I've wanted to do this all night," as he slid his hands up the outside of her legs, under the skirt. "You look so damned sexy in that dress."

He kissed her again, only to break it on a startled sound a moment later when his hands reached her ass. Pulling back, he pointed out, "You aren't wearing panties."

Thanks to his new immortal eyes, Jet could see the blush that rose to her cheeks in the dark car interior as she explained, "We didn't end up buying any after I fainted. They just left everything I'd selected and rushed out of the store. And the one pair I did have got ripped the last time we—Oh," she gasped as he began cupping and squeezing her sweet cheeks, his fingers dipping between and brushing against her core as he did.

A little hum of pleasure slipped from his lips as a shaft of pleasure slid through him as he caressed her, and Jet did it again.

"Ohhh," she moaned, and then kissed him hungrily.

Jet was so caught up in the pleasure he was giving both of them as he continued to caress her that he didn't notice she'd reached down to undo his pants until he felt her hand close over his cock. Groaning into her mouth as that sharp pleasure was added to what he was doing, he broke their kiss and released her behind to grab her shoulders as he shook his head.

"No, babe, we—ahhh," he gasped as she suddenly lowered herself onto his aching shaft. Damn, she was so tight and hot and wet, he just wanted to—No. The Four Seasons, he reminded himself, and tried to regain control of the situation. "Quinn, love," he growled. "I want—" The rest of what he'd been going to say was lost on a groan as she raised and lowered herself again.

"I want you too," Quinn gasped, and then covered his mouth with hers before he could explain he'd been going to say he wanted to take her to the Four Seasons and do this right.

Next time, he told himself, and gave it up to kiss her as she rode him off a cliff into darkness.

It was something tickling his nose that woke him up sometime later. Blinking his eyes open with confusion,

Jet jerked his gaze around until it landed on Tybo. The Enforcer was sitting in the passenger seat next to him with a mini car duster in hand. That was what had been tickling his nose, he surmised, and scowled at the man.

"What the hell, Tybo?" he growled.

"Shh. You'll wake Quinn," the man admonished.

Jet glanced down when the man gestured to his chest, and blinked at the woman slumped in his lap.

"We spotted your SUV off the road on the way back to the house," Tybo explained. "Thought you'd had an accident or something, but realized that wasn't the case when we found you unconscious inside like this." He grinned. "I'd have just left you two to your own devices, but Lucian insisted we should tow you back to the house. He didn't want some mortal cop finding the two of you and calling an ambulance when he couldn't wake you up. Too much work to clean up if that happened. Minds to wipe, reports to change . . . A real pain in the ass," he assured him. "So, we got the chains out, hooked this SUV to ours, and dragged you back here."

Jet glanced around at that news to see that the SUV was now parked in front of the garage behind the Enforcer house.

"I had to sit hunched over on the center console to steer and work the brakes," Tybo added. "Most uncomfortable hour of my life."

"Sorry," Jet murmured, knowing that really had to have been uncomfortable for a man Tybo's height.

"All in a day's work," Tybo assured him, and then announced, "Which I thought was done when we got here, but when I got out, Lucian sent me back to wake you up and tell you to try to restrict your sexual congress to private arenas in future. His words, not mine," he added with amusement when Jet grimaced.

"He also said to tell you to forget your plan to take Quinn to the Four Seasons. He wants to keep her here until he deals with Jiangnu Yin and Yuan Ma. He thinks everything should be fine now, but wants to be sure before he 'releases her to the wild.' Also his words."

Jet sighed unhappily at this news, but supposed it was better to be safe than sorry.

"Well, my work here is done," he announced, opening the passenger side door. "I'll leave you two to it. Night, Quinn," he added with amusement as he slid out and closed the door.

Jet peered down swiftly to see Quinn open her eyes with chagrin.

"How long have you been awake?" he asked as she sat up and glanced out the window to watch Tybo walking away toward the house.

"Since you barked, 'What the hell, Tybo,'" she admitted, turning back to him and pushing the hair from her face. Tilting her head, she asked, "Were you really going to take me to the Four Seasons?"

"Yeah." He smiled crookedly. "I thought with Yun and Ziying being caught it would be fine. But I suppose it's better to wait and see how their boss reacts to losing them and the spy he had at Argeneau Enterprises."

Quinn wrinkled her nose, but nodded and then said, "Thank you."

"What for? I couldn't control myself long enough to get you to the Four Seasons," he pointed out with a wry smile. "If I had we might have at least enjoyed one night away from the house before Lucian located us and dragged us back."

"Nah," Quinn said dryly. "The man's a control freak. He probably has locators on the SUVs or something and would have been pounding on the hotel room door an hour after we got there."

"Maybe," he agreed with a faint smile.

"But I wasn't just thanking you for that," Quinn said now, her expression going solemn. "Thank you for thinking of it. Thank you for saving me back in the barn, and thank you for loving me with all my flaws, Jet." Reaching out, she caressed his cheek, and whispered, "I'm pretty sure I love you too."

Jet stilled. "Say that again," he rasped.

Instead, she said, "I love you, Jethro Lassiter. You're smart, funny, strong, and caring and so damned supportive I think you should get a medal for it. You're an amazing man, and I think God made you just for me."

Jet closed his eyes briefly, her words branding themselves on his heart. She loved him. Opening his eyes again, he said solemnly, "I love you too, Quinn." Leaning forward, he kissed her nose. "Let's go inside so I can show you how much," he suggested.

Quinn glanced toward the house, bit her lip, and then turned back and said, "I have a better idea. Show me here."

"Here?" he asked with surprise.

"No one in the house will hear us from here," she pointed out, sliding her hands up his chest and shifting in his lap.

"Damn," Jet breathed as her movement woke up Mr. Happy and he realized he was still inside of her. "Here," he agreed, kissing her.

Epilogue

"Jet's here!"

Quinn smiled at that excited shout from her son and the clatter of his feet as he rushed downstairs and out the front door.

"Man, Parker doesn't get that excited when I come over," Pet said dryly, placing glasses onto the tray already holding a pitcher of iced tea.

"Eh. You're old news," Quinn teased.

"Hey!" Pet protested.

"Oh, you know I was joking, sis. Parker loves you to bits," Quinn said with a chuckle, stopping to hug her briefly before continuing on to the window to look out at her son and Jet as they met on the walkway. Parker would be thirteen soon and had shot up the last couple of years. He was five-foot-four now, four inches taller than her, but still more than a foot shorter than Jet. She had to look up at them both, Quinn thought as she watched Parker chattering away. Jet was grinning, his arm around the boy's shoulders as he listened to whatever her son was telling him and steered him up the walkway toward the house.

"Jet is really good to him," Pet commented, stepping up next to her to watch as well.

"He's good to both of us," Quinn assured her.

"Yeah, but he gives Parker a lot of attention and affection," Pet said quietly. "Which is pretty impressive for a new life mate with his brain in his pants."

"Pet!" Quinn protested on a laugh.

"Well, it's true," she insisted. "Trust me, Santo and I have been there and done that, and the way you guys manage to control yourselves to make sure Parker doesn't feel like a third wheel is impressive."

Quinn smiled crookedly and admitted, "It's hard sometimes. New life mate brain is no joke, but Jet wants to be sure Parker feels loved and secure. He's a good man." She was silent for a minute as Jet stopped indulgently to look at something Parker was showing him on his iPad, and then said, "He'll be a good dad."

"Are you two thinking of having a baby?" Pet asked with surprise.

Quinn shook her head. "Jet doesn't think we should do that until Parker is older and on his own. He says we have all the time in the world and he doesn't want him to feel like an outsider in his own family."

"Wow," Pet said solemnly. "He really does care for Parker."

Quinn glanced at her in question.

"Abs says he's always wanted kids, so for him to put it off for Parker's sake . . . Again. Impressive."

Quinn nodded, and then blurted, "He wants to adopt Parker after the wedding."

"Oh? And how do you feel about that?" Pet asked.

"I think it would be wonderful. He's already more of a father to Parker than Patrick was. He takes him fishing and to games. He's even let him ride with him on a couple of his shorter flights. Jet calls it 'take your kid to work' day," Quinn said with a smile, and then grimaced and added, "I suspect he's been giving him flying lessons and letting him take the helm or whatever it is in a plane, but they both deny it," she added dryly.

Pet nodded, but asked, "Have you asked Parker if he would like Jet to adopt him?"

Quinn shook her head. "No. Jet wants to broach the subject with Parker himself. He plans to do it tomorrow when they go to that soccer game with Santo and Tomasso."

"Football," Pet corrected her. "It's called football here in Italy."

"Whatever." Quinn waved that away. It was all the same to her. Football, soccer, baseball . . . Hell, they all had grown men chasing balls around a field of some description. She watched Jet finish with whatever he'd been looking at on the iPad and turn a serious look on Parker. Clasping his shoulder, he said something, and then Parker threw his arms around the tall man and gave him a hug.

"God, I love those two," Quinn breathed.

"And they love you," Pet said, wrapping an arm around her and hugging her tight to her side before adding, "And so do I."

"I love you too," Quinn assured her, leaning her head to the side until it rested against Pet's. But then she straightened and shook her head. "If you'd told me five years ago that I'd give up the career I worked so hard for and end up a widowed vampire with a flower shop and a younger pilot for a life mate—" She shook her head.

"I know, right?" Pet asked. "Who would have imagined you a flower shop owner?"

"Yeah, *that's* the shocking part," Quinn said dryly, bumping her with her hip.

"Well, come on, Quinn. Sixteen years of med school and internships and you toss it all aside to arrange flowers?" Pet said with amusement.

"I find it soothing," Quinn said with a shrug. "And flowers make people smile. I like that." She paused briefly, and then said, "I'm not saying I won't go back to surgery someday, but right now I'm happy with my little flower shop."

"And I'm happy you're happy," Pet assured her.

"Thank you. I'm happy you're happy too," she responded with a grin, and then peered out at Parker and Jet. They were starting toward the house again. She stared at them, a well of love bubbling up within her, and marveled, "I'm so lucky. I mean, I hated Patrick for so long for turning me, but in the end, it was the best thing that ever happened to me."

"Yeah," Pet agreed. "It almost makes me like the asshat. But then, it's always easier to like assholes when they're dead and can't insult you anymore."

"Pet! You're awful," Quinn laughed, and pushed her away. "Go on, take the iced tea outside before everyone comes looking for us."

"Yes, ma'am. Are you coming?" Pet asked as she collected the tray.

"In a minute. I'll just greet Jet first."

Pet nodded and headed for the door leading out onto the back patio, saying cheerfully, "I'll come wake you two up if you aren't out in half an hour."

"Thank you," Quinn called with amusement, and headed for the door to the hall just as Parker rushed in.

"I told Jet about the barbecue and everyone being here. See you outside, Mom. Love you," he called out as he hurried through the kitchen to the back door.

"Love you too," she called as the door closed behind him, and then continued on out into the front hall. Her smile widened when she saw Jet toeing his shoes off and tugging at his tie. He looked so handsome in his pilot's uniform, she thought as she moved into his arms and reached up on tiptoe to kiss the corner of his mouth.

"Mmm, there's my beautiful lady," Jet breathed, his arms sliding around her. Hugging her close, he said, "Guess what Parker was showing me just now?"

"I give. What was he showing you?"

"An article on adoption," he announced with a grin.

Quinn pulled back slightly, her eyes widening. "What?"

"Yeah. He wanted me to know it was all right with him if I wanted to adopt him after we marry," he said, almost beaming.

"Oh, honey." Quinn hugged him tightly, and then pulled back to ask, "What did you say?"

"I told him that was something that I had planned to talk to him about, and I'd be proud to call him son," he said solemnly.

"Oh," Quinn breathed, and hugged him tightly. "I love you so much."

"I love you too," he murmured, kissing the top of her head. They were silent for a minute, and then he said, "I hear we have a houseful of guests."

"I'm afraid so," she admitted, pulling back to offer an apologetic expression as she explained, "Pet said that Santo wanted to try your barbecue to see if he wants to get one, and I said anytime. The next thing I knew, tonight was the night and Abs, Tomasso, Mary, and Dante were invited. Sorry."

"Don't be," he admonished. "We always have fun when the group of us gets together."

"I know, but I'm sure you're tired after two long-haul flights in a row, and you know they'll stay late and really I just want to drag you upstairs and—" She kissed him hungrily rather than say what she wanted. Jet moaned and started to kiss her back, but then stopped and pulled away.

"We have company," he reminded her on a groan.

"Pet said she'd wake us up in half an hour if we weren't outside by then," she told him huskily.

"Oh, well, then." Breaking into a wide grin, he scooped her up and started up the stairs to the bedrooms on the upper floor, asking, "Have I mentioned that I think your sister is awesome?"

"No, but I'm pleased you think so," she said on a laugh, and truly was.

"Damn, I'm a lucky man," Jet breathed as he reached thc uppcr floor and started up the hall.

"Not as lucky as me," she assured him, leaning her head on his shoulder.

Can't get enough of Lynsay Sands?
Turn the page for a sneak peek
of the historical romance

HIGHLAND WOLF

Available January 2022!

One

Claray was standing at the window, debating the merits of leaping to her death rather than marry Maldouen MacNaughton when knocking at the door made her stiffen. The loud banging sounded like a death knell. It meant her time was up. They'd come to take her to the chapel.

Claray's fingers tightened briefly on the stone edging of the window, her body tensing in preparation of climbing up and casting herself out. But she could not do it. Father Cameron said that self-killing was a sin certain to land you in hell, and she was quite sure that ten or twenty years of hell on earth as MacNaughton's wife were better than an eternity in the true hell as one of Satan's handmaidens.

Shoulders sagging, Claray pressed her cheek to the cold stone and closed her eyes, silently sending up one last prayer. "Please God, if you can no' see yer way clear to saving me from this . . . at least make me death quick."

Another knock sounded, this one a much louder, more insistent pounding. Claray forced herself to straighten and walk to the door, brushing down the skirt of the pretty, pale blue gown she wore as she went. She wasn't surprised when she opened it to see her uncle Gilchrist framed by the two men he'd had guarding her door for the last three days since her arrival. She *was* a little surprised by the guilt that briefly flashed on his face, though. It gave her a moment's hope, but even as she opened her mouth to plea that he not do this, Gilchrist Kerr raised a hand to silence her.

"'Tis sorry I am, niece. But I'm tired o' being looked down on as a lowlander and MacNaughton has promised MacFarlane to me do I see this through. Ye're marrying him and that's that."

Claray closed her mouth and gave a resigned nod, but couldn't resist saying, "Let us hope then that ye live a long time to enjoy it, uncle. For I fear yer decision will surely see ye in hell for eternity afterward."

Fear crossed his face at her words. It was closely followed by anger, and his hand clamped on her arm in a bruising grip. Dragging her out into the hall, he snapped, "Ye'll want to be watchin' that tongue o' yers with the MacNaughton, girl. Else ye'll be in hell ere me."

Claray raised her chin, staring straight ahead as he urged her up the hall toward the stairs. "Not I. Me conscience is clear. I may die first, but 'tis heaven where I'll land. Unlike you."

She'd known her words would anger him further, and wasn't surprised when his fingers tightened around her arm to the point she feared her bone would snap. But words were her only weapon now, and if what she'd said gave him more than a sleepless night or two between now and when he met his maker, it was something at least.

Claray tried to concentrate on that rather than the trials ahead as her uncle forced her down the stairs and out of the keep. The man was taller than her, his legs longer, but her uncle didn't make allowances for that as he pulled her across the bailey. He was moving at a fast clip that had her running to keep pace with him. Claray was concentrating so hard on keeping up that when he suddenly halted halfway to the church, she stumbled and would have fallen if not for that punishing grip on her arm.

For one moment, hope rose within her that his conscience had pricked him and he'd had a change of heart. But when she glanced to his face, she saw that he was frowning toward the gate where a clatter and commotion had apparently caught his attention.

Hope dying in her chest, Claray turned her disinterested gaze that way to see three men on horseback crossing the drawbridge. Guests arriving late to the wedding, she supposed unhappily, and shifted her attention toward the chapel where a large crowd of people awaited them. The witnesses to her doom were made up mostly of MacNaughton soldiers and a very few members of the Kerr clan. It seemed most did not wish to be a part of their laird's betrayal of his own niece.

"The Wolf," her uncle muttered with what sounded like confusion.

Claray glanced sharply back at her uncle to see the

perplexed expression on his face and then surveyed the three men again. They were in the bailey now and riding straight for them at a canter rather than a walk, she noted, some of her disinterest falling away. They were all large, muscular warriors with long hair. But while the man in the lead had black hair, the one behind him had dark brown, and the last was fair. All three were good looking, if not outright handsome, she decided as they drew nearer.

Claray didn't have to ask who the Wolf was, or even which of the three men he might be. The warrior who went by the moniker "the Wolf" was a favorite subject of the troubadours of late. Every other song they sang was about him, praising his courage and prowess in battle as well as his handsome face and hair that was "black as sin." According to those songs, the Wolf was a warrior considered as intelligent and deadly as the wolf he was named for. But he was actually a lone wolf in those songs, because he spoke little and aligned himself with no particular clan, instead offering his sword arm for a price. He was a mercenary, but an honorable one. It was said he served only those with a just cause.

"What the devil is the Wolf doing here?" her uncle muttered now.

Claray suspected it was a rhetorical question so didn't bother to respond. Besides, she had no idea why the man was here, but she was grateful for it. Any delay to this forced wedding was appreciated, so she simply stood at her uncle's side, waiting for the men to reach them.

"Laird Kerr," the Wolf said in greeting as he reined in before them. He then reached into his plaid to retrieve a scroll. Holding it in hand with the seal covered, he let his gaze slide briefly over Claray before turning his attention back to her uncle. "I understand your niece, Claray MacFarlane, is visiting. Is this her?"

"Aye," her uncle muttered distractedly, his gaze on the scroll.

Nodding, the Wolf leaned down, offering him the sealed message. Claray resisted the urge to rub the spot where her uncle's hand had gripped her so tightly when he released her to take the missive. Her upper arm was throbbing, but pride made her ignore it as she watched him break the seal and start to unroll the scroll.

Claray was actually holding her breath as she waited. Hope had reared in her again, this time that the missive might be from her cousin, Aulay Buchanan. Perhaps this was his response to her cousin Mairin's plea for help on her behalf. She might yet be saved from the fate the MacNaughton would force on her. Distracted as she was, Claray was completely caught off guard when the Wolf suddenly scooped her up off her feet as he straightened in the saddle.

She heard her uncle's shout of protest over her own startled gasp, and then she was in the man's lap and he was turning his mount sharply and urging it into a run toward the gates.

Claray was so stunned by this turn of events, she didn't even think to struggle. She did look back as she was carried out of the bailey though. She saw the two men who had arrived with the Wolf following hard on their heels, and beyond that, her uncle's red face as he began to bellow orders for the gate to be closed and the drawbridge raised. A quick look forward showed the men on the wall scrambling to follow his orders, but the gate was released one moment too late. The spiked bottom slammed into the ground behind the last horse rather than before them, and while the bridge started to rise as they rode across it, it was a slow process and had only risen perhaps two or three feet off the ground by the time they'd crossed it.

The Wolf's horse leapt off the tip without hesitation, and Claray instinctively closed her mouth to keep from biting her tongue off on landing. She was glad she had when they hit the hardpacked dirt with a bone-jarring jolt she felt in every inch of her body. Teeth grinding against the pain that shuddered through her on impact, Claray glanced back again to watch the other two men follow them off the bridge. She was more than a little surprised when the fair-haired warrior caught her eye and gave her a reassuring grin followed by a wink.

Flushing, Claray turned forward once more and tried to sort out what was happening and how she should feel about it. However, her thought processes weren't very clear just now. She'd had little to eat these last three days but what Mairin had managed to sneak to her that morning, and she hadn't slept at all. Instead, she'd spent that time alternately pacing as she tried to come up with a solution to her situation, or on her knees, praying to God for his intervention. She was exhausted, bewildered, and frankly, all her mind seemed capable of grasping at that moment was that this did seem to be an answer to her prayer. She would not be marrying Maldouen MacNaughton today.

Relief oozing through her, Claray let out the breath she'd been holding and allowed herself to relax in her captor's arms.

"She's sleeping."

Conall lifted his gaze from the lass cuddled against his chest and glanced to Roderick Sinclair who had urged his horse up on his right. The man looked both surprised and amused at the woman's reaction to the situation she found herself in. Conall merely nodded and shifted his gaze back to the lass, but he was a little surprised himself.

Lady Claray MacFarlane had been asleep before they'd got a hundred feet from the drawbridge of Kerr's castle. Conall had been a bit befuddled by that at the time, and still was. He'd basically just kidnapped her. She had no idea who he was, yet hadn't struggled or even protested. Instead, the lass had curled up like a kitten in his lap and gone to sleep. He wasn't quite sure what to make of that and had fretted over it as they'd met up with his men and then galloped through the morning and afternoon, riding north at a hard pace that he'd only just slowed to a trot because the sun was starting to set.

Aside from the fact that the horses couldn't keep up that speed indefinitely, Conall wouldn't risk one of their mounts or men being injured by traveling at such a pace in the dark. They'd have to travel more slowly and with a great deal of care through the night. But they wouldn't stop. Despite the information in the scroll he'd given her uncle, Conall had no doubt Kerr would have sent men after them. Even if he didn't, certainly MacNaughton would. From all accounts the man was determined to marry the lass no matter that her father wouldn't agree to the match.

Conall didn't really understand the man's tenacity on this issue. The lass was bonnie enough, he acknowledged as his gaze slid over the waves of strawberry blonde hair that framed her heart-shaped face. But she wasn't so bonnie it was worth going to war with your neighbors over.

"So ye told her who ye are while we were riding?" Payton asked with a surprise that Conall knew was born of the fact that it was hard to talk at the speed they'd been moving. The pounding hooves of so many horses and the rush of wind would have meant having to yell, not to mention taking the risk of biting your own tongue while you did it.

Conall hesitated, but then admitted, "I've told her naught."

A moment of silence followed his announcement as both men turned stunned gazes to Claray sleeping peacefully in his lap.

"But—" Payton began, and then paused and simply shook his head, apparently not having the words to express his amazement.

"She's slept quite a while," Roderick said suddenly, a touch of concern in his voice. "Is she ailing?"

Conall stiffened at the suggestion, his gaze moving over her face. She looked pale to him, with dark bruising under her eyes that suggested exhaustion. Concern now slithering through him, he shifted his mount's reins to the hand he'd wrapped around her to keep her on his horse, then used the back of his now free hand to feel her forehead. Much to his relief, she didn't feel overly warm. But his touch apparently stirred her from sleep. Her lids lifted slowly, long lashes sweeping upward to reveal eyes the blue of a spring morning and then she blinked at him before abruptly sitting up to glance around.

"Are we stopping?" Her voice was soft and still husky with sleep as she took in their surroundings.

Conall opened his mouth, intending to say, "Nay" but what came out was, "Do ye need to, lass?" as he realized she might wish to relieve herself after so long in the saddle. Actually, he could do with a stop for the same reason.

Claray turned a shy smile to him, and nodded with obvious embarrassment. "'Tis the truth, Laird Wolf, I do."

Conall blinked at the name he'd battled under for the last twelve years, surprised that she knew even that much about who he was, but then shifted his gaze to survey the landscape around them. He'd come this way often and knew exactly where he was and what lay ahead. Lowering his eyes to her once more, he said, "There's a river no' far ahead if ye can wait just a few moments. But if yer need is urgent, we can just stop here."

Claray considered the trees bordering either side of the path they were on, and then peered over his shoulder and stiffened, her eyes widening.

It made Conall glance over his shoulder as well. He had no idea what had startled her so. The only thing behind them were his men. But then perhaps that was what had overset her. There had only been the three of them and her when they'd ridden out of Kerr. She'd been asleep by the time they'd met up with his warriors who had been waiting in the woods around Kerr while he, Payton, and Roderick had ridden in to get a lay of the situation. In the end, they hadn't needed the men, so it was good he'd left them behind. He suspected an entire army riding up to the keep would have got an entirely different welcome than just he and his two friends had received.

Turning back to Claray, he raised his eyebrows in question. "Here or the river?"

"I can wait 'til we reach the river," she assured him quickly, and then managed a smile. "I'd like to splash some water on me face to help wake meself up ere I tend to other business."

Nodding, Conall tightened his arm around her and urged his horse to a gallop, leaving the others behind. Moments later he was reining in next to a river that was really just one step up from a babbling brook. Claray seemed pleased, however, and flashed him a smile before sliding under his arm to drop from his mount. She did it so quickly that Conall didn't get the chance to even attempt to help her down, and then he dismounted himself and headed into the woods on the other side of the clearing to water the dragon.

When he returned a couple moments later it was to find that the others had caught up. Roderick, Payton, and Conall's first, Hamish, were waiting in the small clearing by his mount, while the rest of the men were gathering on the path beside it, some dismounting to wander into the woods on the opposite side of the trail to take care of their own business, others watching the horses.

"Where's Lady Claray?" Payton asked as Conall walked to his horse.

Conall nodded toward the trees she'd disappeared into as he mounted.

Payton's eyebrows rose slightly. "Ye let her go off into the woods by herself?"

Settling in the saddle, Conall glanced to him with surprise. "O' course I did. She's tending personal needs and would no' want an escort for that. Besides, 'tis no' as if she's like to get lost."

"Aye, but . . ." Payton grimaced, and then asked, "What if she tries to escape?"

The suggestion amazed him. "Why would she try to escape? We came to save her."

It was Roderick who said, "Mayhap. But ye said ye'd had no chance to explain, so she does no' ken that. She may flee out o' fear o' what ye plan to do with her."

Conall frowned at those words in Roderick's deep rumble. The man was not much for talking. Which was why when he did speak, Conall and anyone else who knew him, listened.

"She did no' seem afraid," Conall muttered, his eyes scouring the woods Claray had disappeared into. He was now worrying over the fact that she hadn't yet returned, and fretting over whether she hadn't burst into a run the moment she'd got out of sight and was even now trying to fight her way through the forest.

"Nay, she did no' seem afraid," Payton agreed, but sounded more troubled by the knowledge than relieved before asking worriedly, "Does that seem right to ye? I mean, ye did just scoop her up away from her uncle and ride off with her moments ere she was to marry another."

"She was to marry Maldouen MacNaughton," Conall reminded him grimly, still disgusted by the very idea. "The man's a lying, conniving, murdering bastard."

"But does she ken that?" Roderick asked.

"Probably no'," Payton answered for him. "All she probably kens is that he's handsome, wealthy, and would marry her. And no doubt he's taken the trouble to be charming to her in the wooing." The warrior shook his head. "Meanwhile, ye carried her off with no explanation at all. Even were she no' taken in by his good looks and sweet lies, surely she must still be concerned about being kidnapped?"

"I did no' kidnap her," Conall growled. "Her own father sent me to rescue her."

"But she does no' ken that," Roderick reminded him.

A knot forming in his chest now, Conall turned to peer toward the woods again. He debated the issue in his head, and then cursed and dismounted. He had no desire to embarrass the lass by intruding on her privacy while she was relieving herself, but now he was concerned she might just be making a run for it. He wouldn't have explained that he was her betrothed, that had to remain a secret, but he could have explained that her father had sent him to fetch her back. That should have soothed her, he knew, and berated himself for not doing so. Especially before letting her rush off.

Silently calling himself an idiot, he strode into the woods.

MORE IN THE ARGENEAU VAMPIRE SERIES
FROM *NEW YORK TIMES* BESTSELLING AUTHOR

VAMPIRE MOST WANTED

978-0-06-207817-9

When sexy immortal Marcus Notte shows up and is determined to bring Basha Argeneau back to her estranged family, she'll do anything to keep far, far away from the past she can't outrun.

THE IMMORTAL WHO LOVED ME

978-0-06-231600-4

Whatever Basileios Argeneau expected in a life mate, funny, outspoken Sherry Carne isn't it. But mind-blowing chemistry and instinct don't lie. And Sherry's connection to the immortal world goes deeper than she knows.

ABOUT A VAMPIRE

978-0-06-231602-8

Mortally wounded, Holly Bosley wakes up with a bump on her head, a craving for blood, and a sexy stranger who insists they belong together. She needs Justin Bricker's help to control her new abilities, even as she tries to resist his relentless seduction.

RUNAWAY VAMPIRE

978-0-06-231604-2

Dante Notte has heard it said that love hurts. He just wasn't expecting it to run him over in an RV. Still, a punctured lung and broken ribs are nothing compared to the full-body shock he feels whenever he's near the vehicle's driver, Mary Winslow.

LYS9 0518

NEW YORK TIMES BESTSELLING AUTHOR

LYNSAY SANDS

The Highlander Takes a Bride

978-0-06-227359-8

Raised among seven boisterous brothers, comely Saidh Buchanan has a warrior's temper and little interest in saddling herself with a husband . . . until she glimpses the new Laird MacDonnell bathing naked in the loch. Though she's far from a proper lady, the brawny Highlander makes Saidh feel every inch a woman.

Always

978-0-06-201956-1

Bastard daughter to the king, Rosamunde was raised in a convent and wholly prepared to take the veil . . . until King Henry declared she would wed Aric, one of his most valiant knights. While Rosamunde's spirited nature often put her at odds with her new husband, his mastery in seduction was quickly melting her resolve—and capturing her heart.

Lady Pirate

978-0-06-201973-8

Valoree has been named heir to Ainsley Castle. But no executor would ever hand over the estate to an unmarried pirate wench and her infamous crew. Upon learning that the will states that in order to inherit, Valoree must be married to a nobleman—and pregnant—she's ready to return to the seas. But her crew has other ideas . . .